Charming. Irreverent. Haunted.
Alastor Vega is the sole challenger in a brutal battle for succession. Against all odds, he must stop his power-mad brother, Tycho, before he destroys the Numina. Though he never wanted to rule, he must claim the throne and liberate his people, or the consequences will be calamitous. Yet only the surprising support of a beautiful Animari doctor gives him the fortitude to fight.

Focused. Analytical. Solitary.
Dr. Sheyla Halek has always been more interested in research than personal contact, but family ties—and the needs of her pride—keep her in Ash Valley, deferring her dreams. Brusque and abrasive at the best of times, she never expected to bond with anyone, let alone Golgoth royalty. Strangely, Alastor seems to need her as no one has before, and not only for her medical skills.

Their attraction is forbidden, likely doomed beyond the wildness of wartime, but these fires burn too hot and sweet to be contained...

THE DEMON PRINCE

Ann Aguirre

Copyright Information
THE DEMON PRINCE
Copyright © 2017 by Ann Aguirre
Print Edition

Edited by Victoria West
Cover art by Kanaxa

This is a work of fiction. Names, characters, businesses, places, events, and incidents are either the products of the author's imagination or used in a fictitious manner and are not to be construed as real. Any resemblance to actual persons, living or dead, or actual events is purely coincidental.

All Rights Reserved. No part of this book may be reproduced, scanned, or distributed in any form whatsoever, without written permission from the author except for brief quotations embodied in critical reviews or articles.

For Señora Dennesy,
Her skill and dedication
make it possible for me to write.
Thanks for everything.

—

Para la Señora Dennesy,
Su habilidad y dedicación
Hacen posible que siga escribiendo.
Gracias por todo.

Acknowledgments

First, thanks to the readers who have been so eager but so patient while I wrote this story. Alastor and Sheyla are a special couple and hope their romance moves you as much as it did me.

As always, thanks to Karen Alderman, Fedora Chen and Pamela Webb-Elliot for their motivation. Without them, there would be no book. I'm also grateful to Bree Bridges, Courtney Milan, Rachel Caine, Melissa Blue, Kate Elliott, Suleikha Snyder, and Kristen Callihan for the emotional support during some rocky times. I live in fear of omitting someone, so let this line encompass anyone who's ever spared me a moment or a kind word.

Much appreciation to Kanaxa who continues to create beautiful art for this series. Thanks also to my editor, Victoria West, who's almost as excited about this project as I am. I can't forget to thank Lillie, who proofs these stories. Her diligence is vital to creating clean, beautiful books.

Finally, I thank my family for their patience. They gladly work around my schedule and never hesitate when I ask strange, theoretical questions. I'm giving special mention to my son, Alek, who helped with one of the action scenes in this book (and it's pretty kick-ass. Look for our robot / alien SF collaboration in 2018).

I hope you enjoy the Ars Numina series as much as I do. The story will get bigger and more epic as we go! (Look for a hint in this book about who the next couple will be.) Thanks for supporting my work, and as always, read on.

The Story So Far...

In *The Leopard King*, Latent shifter Pru Bristow went after the pride leader, Dominic Asher, who had holed up at the seer's retreat after the death of his wife, also Pru's best friend. With the conclave approaching, Ash Valley couldn't afford to let Dom's second, Slay, run the show. It was rocky going, and they were attacked by Eldritch assassins. In the furious fight that followed, Pru finally shifted and saved Dom's life.

In time, she convinced Dom to come back to Ash Valley because the fate of the pride rested on completing the conclave and renewing the Pax Protocols (a peace treaty between supernatural communities). Her success didn't come without a cost, however. She agreed to become Dom's mate and lead the pride alongside him.

Their return startled a lot of people, Slay most of all, because he'd always thought that Pru would wait for him forever. Since he didn't want her when she couldn't shift, she didn't want him once she could, and Pru devoted herself to working with Dom to make the conclave go smoothly.

That wasn't in the cards. Though the attendants all arrived safely, the Pine Ridge wolf pack and the Burnt Amber bear clan hated Lord Talfayen of the Eldritch, and nobody knew what to make of Prince Alastor of the Golgoth. Everything that could go wrong, did, including the murder of an Eldritch envoy. Talks broke down, culminating in treachery, but the Eldritch Lord's plot went awry, as the bombs he'd set detonated too soon, catching his own people in the trap. King Tycho of the Golgoth attacked thereafter and it was all Ash Valley could do to hold.

Meanwhile, Dom and Pru tried to keep things together while falling in love. They did battle with their enemies and each other, before eventually admitting their true feelings. Slay vanished mysteriously and the leading couple finally had a wedding party, once Ash Valley was safe. Soon after, the visiting dignitaries departed and the Numina prepared for war.

1.

THE DEMON PRINCE wasn't a model patient, but he *was* killing Sheyla's patience.

"I told you not to drink while I'm assessing your response to the new serum." Keeping her voice level required some effort.

From the sound of it, the party was still winding down outside. The hospital still didn't have four solid walls, and she had been fielding complaints from people in pain all night. For some, sleep offered the only respite and tonight it had been impossible. Now she had Alastor Vega, the Golgoth prince, in her office, reeking of hard liquor.

"Dr. Halek." Somehow his tone came across as both mocking and reproachful. "It seemed churlish to refuse to toast my host's happiness."

"Per the breath analysis, you've had considerably more than one."

That wasn't the point anyway. Tonight, she couldn't get the accurate test results his life depended on, and that inefficiency made her want to bite through a durasteel column. By the time he showed symptoms, it might be too late for her to correct course in his treatment. Add in the fact that she hadn't even studied Golgoth physiology, and this felt like malpractice already.

"Consider me chided," Prince Alastor said.

"Do you even *want* to live?"

"Not always." That quiet honesty silenced her.

Sheyla didn't like people at the best of times, which these weren't. Occasionally pride mates asked why she'd decided to study medicine, but she did love the research side and the logic of how body systems cooperated. Through a microscope, the world made sense and samples behaved in predictable ways. While she wasn't equipped for counseling, it seemed callous to refer him for mental health assessment without another word.

"The pride seer is still awake. I can get Arran—"

"Why? Will he tell my fortune? I suspect I can make a relatively accurate prediction without the use of cards or bones."

"He doesn't—" Aggravated, Sheyla bit off the rest of her explanation. The prince was clearly baiting her as a means of declining a counselor's ear, so he didn't care how Arran's abilities functioned.

The smile didn't reach the prince's eyes. "Thank you for the offer."

"I need you to abstain from all recreational chemicals and alcohol for the next twenty-four hours."

"Does that mean mood-altering mushrooms are fine? All natural."

Doctors are not allowed to punch patients. Ever.

"Drink plenty of water. Eat healthy meals. That's all I want in your bloodstream when I run the full battery of tests."

"If you tell me where you last saw your sense of humor,

I'll help you look for it."

She wouldn't let him bait her into snarling, no matter how tempted she might be. With effort, she completed the exam by taking his vitals, checking reflexes, and generally evaluating his condition. He watched her with amused jade eyes, demonstrating exaggerated patience. Her jaw hurt from clenching it, and maybe she wasn't as gentle as she could've been in assessing his joint mobility.

When the prince flinched, she made a note. "How long has this been hurting?"

"As long as I can remember."

For once, he didn't seem to be joking. Leaning in, she spotted a bruise forming. She didn't have nearly enough data on his illness, but sending away to his brother for a complete medical file was impossible. Saving Alastor might provide the key to weakening the Golgoth enough to turn the tide in the war. While Sheyla wouldn't follow the prince into a pub, his men seemed devoted, so he probably had hidden capabilities.

"Yes, it hurts more if you press it," he said mildly.

"That's not what I'm checking for." Side effects from the new serum might be causing a fresh blood disorder, too soon to diagnose. "That does it for now. You're dismissed."

"But your bedside manner is so charming and the environs, beyond inviting."

The office that doubled as an exam room was many things, but inviting would never be one of them. Cracks spread up the wall from the explosion that had taken out of the west wall, so what used to be internal medicine had been converted as a makeshift morgue. Her equipment had been damaged too, but getting replacements from Burnt Amber would be a difficult proposition.

"I'm immune to sarcasm."

Unfortunately, she wasn't immune to exhaustion. Since the bombs went off, she hadn't slept more than two hours in twenty, and while this asshole played word games, her pride mates were suffering. If the new matron hadn't begged, she would've balked at taking on such a difficult patient when she could least afford the distraction. In terms of pure research, she welcomed the challenge, but Sheyla could easily spend ten hours *just* working on Prince Alastor's illness, and that wasn't fair to everyone else.

"A useful quality, if many of your patients are like me."

"They're aren't. I'm going on rounds now. Feel free to rest on the cot or peruse one of my medical journals."

She didn't wait for his response, merely hurried to check on her critical patients. Two Latents, she suspected wouldn't last the night, and their families were gathered for the death watch. In their tired eyes, she saw her own helplessness reflected. Awkwardly, she lingered and wished she could offer more than silent support. She ended her rounds at Jase's bedside; he was the new pride matron's nephew, and while he hadn't woken yet, Sheyla entertained a cautiously positive prognosis.

His aunt was dozing in the chair nearby, so she kept her voice to a whisper. "Hang in there. Jilly's waiting for you."

The boy's finger twitched. She knew better than to ascribe too much meaning to a reflex, but that was a good sign. Wearily she straightened and crept out before she could wake Glynnis. Another hour went in conferring with nurses and volunteers. The Animari tended to recover quickly, even from grievous wounds, so patients were leaving the hospital almost hourly. In another two days, she'd have only a handful left, including Prince Alastor.

I'll have more time to devote to his condition, too.

To her surprise, she found him asleep on the cot when she got back. She hadn't expected him to take her invitation seriously when he had an apartment in the residential annex. The music had finally stopped a while ago—about time, as it was damn near dawn. But there went her plan to crash here for a few hours. Sheyla resisted the impulse to shake him awake and evict him. He must've remained here for a reason.

Sheyla eased into the chair behind her desk, but instead of tackling the files that disheartened her—there were deaths to certify and bodies she couldn't identify without more advanced testing—she leaned back, almost to the point that the chair must look like it was about to tip. Closing her eyes, she sought that elusive inner quiet, but she couldn't eliminate the nagging voice that insisted she should've done more, better, or faster. Sleep wouldn't come either, not with the demon prince breathing all over her office.

That wasn't a kind nickname for the Golgoth exile; she'd never seen his shifted form, which might *not* be monstrous. Like most in Ash Valley, she'd only heard stories about his people before the conclave. Sheyla was too tired to be fair.

Silent counting didn't relax her much, so she put her head on the desk. If sleep was impossible, rest might help. Before she could start the next round of *Please shut up, brain,* Prince Alastor stirred. From beneath her lashes, she watched him over the curve of her arm. With any luck, he would guess she was asleep and leave without additional conversation.

At first, he only rolled over and stared at the ceiling.

Long moments later, he pulled himself upright like an old man hauling a heavy load. His shoulders rounded, and he struggled for a few seconds to breathe. If he'd shown continued distress, she would've had no choice but to respond. That fact that he controlled it gave her the option to stay still and not engage further with someone she still felt was probably an enemy.

As he stood, he whispered numbers, and she realized he appeared to be counting backward. Why? She didn't know.

Until he said in a soft, hopeless tone, "Minutes left."

THOSE MOMENTS ALONE felt like freedom. All too soon, the taste of it faded like early morning mist. Alastor left swiftly, for his bodyguard would be searching for him. For once Tycho's schemes had backfired. When his brother assigned Dedrick as Alastor's keeper, he never anticipated that eventually, he would command his loyalty. Far from being his warden, the man served as both his closest friend and fiercest protector.

Unsurprisingly, he encountered Dedrick prowling the hospital hallway. "How are you?"

If he had a coin for every time he'd heard that question, he could buy and sell the Golgoth empire ten times over. "Fine," he said.

Lying had become second-nature. Most people didn't want an honest answer. Ded was an exception to that rule, but he would fret if Alastor detailed his current condition. He wasn't stoic by nature, and he'd learned to cover it with a certain insouciance. So he strolled toward his friend, lifting a hand in lazy salute.

"The bears have withdrawn, along with the wolves,"

Ded reported.

"Leaving us with the feline contingent and the new Eldritch order. What do you make of the princess?"

As they walked, Ded gave the question due consideration. "She's ruthless, certainly."

"My thoughts as well. Do you suppose I have a shot at seducing her?"

He got a gloomy look in response. "Did you actually want me to estimate your chances?"

"By your expression... I suppose not. But it would be helpful if I could, no? She has a host of warriors ready to die on her command. If I could secure a marital alliance and unleash them, it would minimize our casualties."

"I think your reach exceeds your grasp."

"Pity. But I appreciate your honesty."

Still, he wasn't ready to relinquish the idea. Politically, it would be the best move he could make, but competition would likely be fierce, and he had little to offer other than potential. Dedrick had spoken passionately in his defense, part of the reason that the Ash Valley matron had assigned a doctor to his care yet he couldn't envision leading forces against Tycho. The slaughter required for either side to claim victory churned his stomach, but if he didn't stop his brother's march to conquer, the cost would be catastrophic for all Numina.

All roads lead to damnation.

With determination, he set out for the back corner of the hold, where the men he privately dubbed the Exiles had been toiling on reconstruction. At this hour, they had just finished their breakfast and were prepared for another day of hard work. Not a single soldier complained though they were trained for the battlefield, not in masonry. Quietly, he pitched in beside them—to show solidarity and because manual labor gave him time to think. Before he approached the Eldritch princess, he needed to know more about her. Charm would only take him so far, and he was none too confident how his brand of it would translate.

Heavy lifting also strained his already-throbbing joints. With an impatient growl, Ded snatched the stones from his arms and pointed toward the flaming barrel, where a few of the men had set up a makeshift camp. The reality of his situation washed over him anew. *This,* what he could offer those who followed him: a crackling fire in enemy territory, broken cement slabs arranged for seating, and a gray sky spitting snow. Fat white flakes dusted his skin and lingered only a second before melting. There was a good chance he was running a fever, courtesy of the alcohol he shouldn't have had last night and the new medicine that was as likely to kill him as let him survive the week.

Because Ded was insisting, he sat near the fire and stared at the crackling flames for a few, hypnotic moments. The next thing he knew, someone was pressing a thermos into his hands. Alastor glanced up to find Rowena hovering.

"Have you eaten?" she asked.

She was half-caste, reviled in Golgerra as a 'stain', born from a union between a guard and one of the prisoners. Based on her silvery hair and fey features, her mother had probably been Eldritch. Early on, it'd seemed as if she would never learn to shift, but once she finally did, she was beautiful and ferocious in a way utterly unlike the other Golgoth, for she had wings.

"Not yet. Thank you, lovely." It was fun to make her blush, though he shouldn't.

She perched beside him, watching with anxious eyes as

he downed the soup. It was the same stuff they'd been given for days on end, but from what he'd seen, the cats weren't hoarding better provisions. When he finished it, she traded the empty thermos for one full of herbal-smelling tea. Alastor wanted that as much as a kick in the face, but when she poured some, he drank all of it.

"How long are we staying?"

Sometimes, their faith humbled him. No matter how often he denied it, no Exile ever accepted that he didn't have a master plan—that he wasn't biding his time. He'd come on this assignment because direct rebellion was impossible. At least this way, he got out of Golgerra and he'd brought a good number of his people to safety as well. When Tycho heard of his defection—that the cats had offered sanctuary—the followers who had remained in the city would likely be put to death.

"It depends," he said at length.

Rowena didn't ask; her eyes said she wanted to. In the end, she got up and returned to work. Not before he noticed that her knuckles were chapped and cracking, blood seeping from the broken skin. Her fingertips were scraped raw as well. When he looked closer, he noticed that his entire honor guard was visibly thinner. They all looked as if they'd gone to war, and that was what decided him.

If they're willing to work like this for me, I can't do less.

For the rest of the day, he mixed the mortar and wheeled it around. By sunset, his men had completely rebuilt the north wall. Everyone was tired and sore when they retreated to the apartments they had been allotted. Still no hot water, but a cold shower was better than nothing. Alastor shivered as he stepped out of the stall, silently relieved not to find Ded or Rowena waiting for him. If they appeared, he would need to keep up the pretense that he was holding together just fine.

With a muffled groan, he collapsed near the bed, shivers wracking him from head to toe. His chest tightened and he tried not to panic because that only made things worse. The constriction climbed to his throat, choking his air so that he went lightheaded. Sweat beaded on his brow, and he curled onto his side clinging to consciousness by a thread. Whispers of oxygen came in through his nose, not enough to keep him from familiar, visceral terror. In time, the episode passed. It had been years since it hit him so hard, proof that the medicine from the cat doctor wasn't working as it should.

That's why Tycho let me live. He figured time would take care of me.

Alastor was struggling to his feet when somebody knocked. Briefly, he contemplated ignoring the caller in hopes he went away, but a louder thump followed, definite impatience, there. Exhausted beyond bearing, he got to door, opened it with his best off-putting expression.

To his astonishment, Dr. Halek pushed past him into the apartment. "You lied to me. About a number of things. How am I supposed to treat you this way?"

"How do you know?" He stared in utter bemusement, as she looked... odd, outside of her usual setting, dark hair spangled with snow like a diadem of stars.

"I left a sensor to monitor your condition." In an efficient motion, she plucked a tiny, transparent patch from the back of his neck, a cunning gadget immune to hard labor and bathing. "And it's given me some fascinating insights."

Probably, he should be angry about this invasion of his privacy. "Now you know my secrets," he said lightly, though he wasn't sure what the device had revealed. "How thrilling. You don't know *how* long I've waited for someone who insists on absolute truth."

2.

"THAT ISN'T FUNNY," Sheyla snapped. "*You* might take your life as a joke, but if I fail, I need to know I did my level best to save your ass."

"Your failure means my death. Yet you're the one who's angry?"

Ignoring the question, she kicked the door shut behind her and surveyed the apartment for signs that his retainers might be lurking. They'd probably take offense to her chewing out the crown prince of derision. But he seemed to be alone.

"Damn right I am. You didn't even tell me you suffer from bronchial distress."

With a faint sigh, Prince Alastor stumbled to the sofa and collapsed on it. "I suppose there's no point in asking you to come back tomorrow?"

"None. You can sleep after you answer my questions."

"I collect you want the full description of my symptoms?"

Sheyla nodded and sat down on the chair opposite him, her notebook ready. While the monitor had given her some good data, his candor would be priceless, second only to consulting with his primary physician in Golgerra. In the artificial light, he was wan with exhaustion, green eyes glittering with a fevered light. Long black hair arranged in intricate braids only made him seem more delicate, like a strong word could break him. Yet appearances were deceptive, because surviving with a condition like the prince's was no easy task.

"Go on," she prompted.

"Intermittent—shortness of breath, chest pain, dizziness. Constant—joint pain, fatigue, body aches, an overall miasma of misery. Is that helpful?"

"Somewhat. Tell me about your condition. Tell me everything." Sheyla had the sense that the amused irony of his tone hid a much greater pain than he routinely displayed.

"I was born with a genetic anomaly, normally found in females. There is no cure. My mother begged the doctors to find some treatment to extend my life."

"Obviously, they did," she said. "And you know damn well that isn't what I'm asking."

"To put it simply, tumors grow inside me, particularly in my lungs, kidneys, and lymph nodes. Not just tumors, though, but also smooth muscle tissue that shouldn't be present. To deter that growth, the best physicians in Golgerra devised the serum."

"It would help if you had the formula they used," she said.

He laughed, but there was no humor in the sound. "Tycho would never permit it. My mother is dead, and the doctors work for my brother now. It was only a matter of time until they poisoned me."

Sheyla suspected her expression must be speaking of her

horror. "They would do that?" No matter how she felt about this Golgoth prince, if the pride leader came with a kill order, she'd boot him so fast, his head would spin. She might not believe in much, but she'd sworn her healing oath with complete sincerity.

"Of course. Following Tycho's commands is the only way to survive in Golgerra."

"We need to depose him," she said through clenched teeth.

The wave of ire startled her. Sheyla wasn't political. Her participation in the patrol roster was minimal, no more than what she had to do to maintain good status in the pride. Sometimes she went days without leaving the hospital, without talking about anything but medical issues and procedures. It was best when she could retreat to the lab and not talk to anyone at all.

That conviction felt foreign—but not wrong. If the would-be Golgoth King was ordering doctors to kill people, he had to go. No matter how bloody the battle became.

His smile was gentle; it didn't reach his eyes. They were green and hard, like the statue of a dragon handed down in Sheyla's family for five generations. "That's why I must survive."

"I'll help you," she promised.

This time it was more than a favor to the pride matron, more than reluctant acquiescence. She'd heard about the issue—Prince Alastor needed more medicine to manage his condition, but he didn't have the prescription, so she needed to analyze what he was taking and manufacture it. Otherwise, the war effort—and therefore all Animari—would suffer. A tall, damn order, considering her ruined equipment, and she'd synthesized an imperfect facsimile, but his welfare hadn't truly felt like her responsibility before.

I'll need more blood and tissue samples. I wonder if he'd permit a biopsy. While she'd lectured him earlier about the full complement of tests, her heart hadn't been in the work. It was now. To ensure she did no harm, she also needed a full body scan, so she could chart and study the physiological differences between the Golgoth and the Animari.

"You are unexpectedly kind."

Sheyla waved that away with a half-frown. "I'm sure you have more to say on your condition. Please, continue."

"If you insist. There's nothing I like better than expounding on my ailments. It makes me feel geriatric in the best possible way."

She bit her lip to keep from smiling. *He's not funny, dammit.* "The serum...?"

"There are side effects. My lungs are weak, as is my heart. Transplantation would lead to the new organs being damaged, so that's not a solution. In addition to controlling tumor and cyst growth, the medicine also suppresses my immune system, which means I'm prone to viral illnesses and quick fevers. My stamina is..." Here, he paused. One heartbeat. Two. "Not good. Otherwise, I can't think of anything more that would be helpful."

"Do you take anything for the pain?" she asked.

"I did for a while. But it interfered with the serum and I required surgery to remove tumors from my lungs and kidneys."

"Benign?"

"They don't seem so to me, but apparently yes. This is like cancer, but *not* cancer."

"That, I could cure," she muttered.

"Truly?"

"Certain types, provided they haven't progressed too far." She doubted he wanted to talk about the point when cancer cells metastasized. "But this isn't something we've seen here."

"It's apparently rare, even among females, and almost unknown in males." Something in the way he said those words, so carefully, as if sipping from the rim of a broken glass, told her that some great wound accompanied this truth.

"I suppose your brother made much of that," she said, studying his face.

The urge to comfort surprised her, almost as much as her words startled him. He sat forward as if he'd grab her and shake some answers loose, but he retreated at the last second without making contact. She was almost sorry about that—and she shouldn't be. As his doctor, she could only care so much about his emotional state, only insofar as it affected his prognosis.

He tried to play it off. "I have no idea what you mean."

"That you're weak, not a man, dying by millimeters of a lady disease. Does that about cover it?" Probably she shouldn't have spoken; it was past honesty, on toward cruelty.

A little tremor shook through him, along with a hiccup of a breath. "How odd. You sound just like him. I didn't realize you were acquainted."

She ignored the faltering attempt at humor. "You know that isn't true, right? Illness isn't a fault and certainly doesn't make you less of a man. It's just part of who you are, like green eyes or black hair."

"So, you did learn some comforting words in medical school."

"That was not meant as consolation," she said. "It is merely the truth."

"You cannot stop me if I take solace in it regardless."

"True. Well... I think that's it for now. Come to the hospital in the morning, first thing. We have a lot to do."

"Would you stay a little longer?"

Since Sheyla was already halfway to the door, the question tripped her up, both physically and mentally. She stumbled on a wrinkle in the rug and turned to face him, cocking her head. "Why? I don't have any other questions."

The prince didn't smile. For a few seconds, it seemed as if he wouldn't even answer. And then he said, "I want to listen to you breathe."

Um, what?

"That... is really strange."

"Not so much. I thought I wanted to be alone, but what I actually want is not to be with anyone who needs me. Do you need me, Dr. Halek?"

"No," she said.

At last, his eyes lit from within and they were luminous. "Search the cupboards. I think there's tea. Make a cup and review your notes or take a fifteen-minute nap. Please."

No matter what he claimed, it was such an odd request that she didn't have the heart to deny it. In an emergency, her phone would already be ringing, so she followed his instructions, only she brewed two cups and sat with him while he drank it in pensive silence. The quiet between two strangers should have been tense and awkward.

It wasn't.

THE PRICKLY DOCTOR would doubtless be mortified when

she realized she had drifted off in Alastor's apartment. For the moment, he enjoyed exactly what he'd requested—listening to her breathe. But there was also a certain clandestine pleasure in learning the lines of her face as well. She had lovely cheekbones, prominent beneath tawny gold skin. Her mouth was wide, fuller than he'd realized, because she normally compressed her lips in disapproval. Delicate jaw, pointed chin, and defiantly arched brows. Her hair was thick and curly, likely longer than anyone suspected, but she wore it pinned up in a style that wanted to be prim and efficient but wasn't because it revealed her lovely jaw and the sensual curve of her bare neck.

Dispassionately, he decided she was beautiful and would become more so with time. The fifteen minutes he'd asked for had been up for a while, and he no longer felt quite as shaky. Alastor rose, covered her with the couch throw and then retreated to the bedroom. With the door ajar, he could still hear her even breathing in the other room, and it was more comforting than he'd imagined. In time, he slept.

Dr. Halek was gone when he woke, of course. But she had left him a sternly worded note, in case he was likely to disregard her words. COME TO THE HOSPITAL AS SOON AS YOU READ THIS. He cheated a bit by showering first, delaying by drying his hair and redoing the braids that spoke of his status, not that he expected anyone here to understand. In truth, the prospect of a "full battery of tests" left him queasy. He'd spent much of his childhood being prodded while his mother stood guard, ready to change and disembowel anyone who threatened him. Of his father and his other siblings, he'd seen little, apart from his sister, Caia, the closest to him in age, and the one whose loss he grieved most.

When he finally emerged from seclusion, he heard it so often: *You don't look ill.* As if his medical history ought to be etched in his skin. He developed the sharp smile and a smooth retort, perfect defense against encroaching questions. It was one thing to pretend to be impervious; the effort left him tired. And the prospect of starting this battle all over again… Alastor let out a breath and let the soft pain dissipate. There was always some tightness in his chest, so he'd learned to compensate. His expression in the misty bathroom mirror looked none too hopeful, so he touched the names inked on his inner arm for fortitude.

Caia.
Efren.
Leander.

Those were the two brothers and one sister who died, causalities of Tycho's drive to power. In their memory and for those who followed him, he would climb this mountain all over again, submit to tests and experiments. If he succeeded in deposing his brother, even if he only led the Golgoth for a year or two after, that would be enough. He would put safeguards in place to ensure that whoever followed him to the throne could not continue the devastation.

He dressed simply and then followed Dr. Halek's orders. Dedrick showed up as he stepped out of the residential building but Alastor waved him away. "I don't require an escort. I'll head to the work site when I'm finished."

"Are you sure?"

"Assuredly sure. This will take quite a while."

"Understood." Ded didn't salute but there was an unnerving focus about him, the sort of single-minded devotion that would get him killed, sooner rather than later.

This morning, the hospital was quiet and fifteen rooms had cleared out. Alastor counted as he went to Dr. Halek's office. His people lacked the Animari's rapid-healing ability, compensating with greater strength and skin that became incredibly dense after transformation. Thus, he'd lost four men during the initial blast and two more succumbed to their injuries before rescue teams reached them.

Not an auspicious start.

"Good, you're here."

She led him past her office to the lab, which had taken some damage in the bombing. A couple of machines were broken entirely, likely making her life difficult. There was no sign of the woman who had dozed off in his flat the night before. No, today, she was all brusque business as she handed him a gown to change into, then a small cup with a capsule in it.

"What's this?"

"Biodegradable medibots. They'll help me with the biopsies I need and chart your systems for me. I have some studying to do."

"Your workload is less now?"

Pausing, she looked as if the question surprised her. "Why?"

"Because you seem less infuriated by dealing with my needs."

"That… well. Sorry. And yes, Dr. Bohalian is taking over the rest of my patients for the time being. I can devote myself to you, guilt-free."

"The past weeks have been difficult. It's understandable

that you would resent an outsider for stealing care your people need as well."

She turned. When her gaze met his, the impact of her full attention rocked him a little. Her eyes weren't merely brown, he decided. Sunlight would distill them to a fine liqueur that required a fanciful name, something like honeyed amber. Idly he wondered how a warm smile might shift the lines of her face.

"You're more generous than I would be," she said. "Let's begin."

Each time he thought he was about to divert her and make her act more as a person and less as a doctor, she reverted to type. If he wasn't careful, this could become quite an entertaining hobby. With remarkable obedience, he downed the capsule and lay back on the exam table. She was explaining the procedures, but he stopped listening. Alastor had lost interest long ago in what doctors did to keep him alive. He closed his eyes and didn't react when the needle sank in.

That would be my kidney.

This pain was sharper than the ones he lived with daily, but it went quicker, leaving a sore spot behind. She did his lung next. If she didn't work carefully, it might collapse in a day or two. The first time that happened, he was playing with Caia. He hadn't left the hospital for weeks after that. Memories of his sister carried him through the procedures, the blood drawing, and into the most bearable part of the examination. Light filtered through his closed lids, different than the normal brightness of the room. Cautiously, he opened his eyes and found the overheads off, allowing for projection. This was different than the clinical process at home. Intrigued, he shifted for a better look.

"Try to stay still," she said.

"Sorry."

"It's boring, I know. But invaluable for us, going forward."

From the corner of his eye, he watched the shape of his body take form in 3-D light, as if it were being shaped out of stars. Each system came together slowly, probably from data the medibots were acquiring. The complete picture took almost an hour to form, but once it did, the accuracy was minute and exquisite, unique to him in every detail.

"We don't have this technology."

"The medibots? Right now, they're purely a diagnostic aid. Imagine if we had the ability to send micro-surgical units in that would perform a correction and then dissolve. No need for invasive surgery at all."

"Imagine," he said, with only faint irony.

His tone apparently escaped her. "From your appearance, I can't tell how many procedures you've undergone. I would like to know. For your records."

"Seventeen. Our scar erasure is top-notch." His mother had insisted on it. She didn't want him to be a patchwork of seams and lines, but it was worse, somehow, for there to be no trace of his experiences. Not to mention how much the removal process hurt.

"I'll make a note. You can sit up now."

When he moved to comply, the room swam. Possibly skipping breakfast hadn't been his best move. She rushed to his side to steady him, touching his clammy brow with cool fingers. In confusion, he stared up at her, wondering what it would be like if she wasn't a doctor, if she wasn't assigned to his care and she simply... cared.

"You disregarded what I said about healthy meals?"

That was, apparently, a rhetorical question, because she hurried for the door and hailed someone in the hallway. Within minutes, she had a dish of that damned soup and hot cup of medicinal crap on a tray.

It took all of his self-control not to slap the rations out of her hands. To his surprise, she set them down and touched his shoulder briefly. "You don't want this. I wouldn't either. So just think of who and what you're fighting for, then choke it down."

"Such sweet, sage advice."

"I'm not known for that," she said. "I'm known for straight talk. We need you, Prince Alastor. Alive, and as strong as you can be. I'll get you there, but you *have* to work with me."

When she put the spoon in his hand, he took it, and for the first time, he felt as if the trials ahead might be mountains he could climb.

3.

Sheyla studied the anatomical model as Alastor downed the food with dogged determination. When he finished, she cleared the tray and checked the bruises she'd noted before. Until the test results came back, she wouldn't know if they signified a deeper problem, but she could treat them. Quietly she rolled up his sleeves and applied a salve to expedite healing, developed for their small latent population.

"That's not necessary," the prince said.

"Do I tell you how to do *your* job?"

He laughed softly. "No, but it would be helpful. Please, feel free."

His skin was pale, blue veins visible at his wrists. She smoothed the ointment over the contusions with care, watching his face to gauge his pain. From his reaction, it didn't seem as if he suffered from neuralgia. Instead, he gazed at her fingers with more interest than she felt the process warranted, leaving her self-conscious. Sheyla cleared her throat.

"It's impossible to piss you off, huh?" She capped the jar, more curious than she wished about his reply.

"Anger requires energy, so I prioritize what truly merits the time and effort. I have been enraged a time or two, but no, it's not easily accomplished."

Although she didn't ask the obvious question in response, she wanted to. "I sent your samples to the lab. We're short staffed but I'll notify you as soon as I hear back. I'll be studying your body systems in the meantime."

His gaze held hers for a beat too long. "You have me quivering with excitement."

Her heart fluttered at that look, a surprising and unwelcome reaction. "Whatever you're trying to do, stop. You must flirt in reflex, but I'm not receptive to that behavior."

"All business, hmm?"

"That would be ideal."

"Then you should share your credentials. I have little choice about accepting your treatment, but it's your role to reassure me of your capabilities."

"That's fair." After turning off the holo-model, she switched the overhead lights on and beckoned. "You can see my degrees in the office and I'll answer any questions you may have."

"Am I allowed to put my pants on first?" With a wry look, he indicated the patterned pajamas she had given him before the exams began.

"Certainly. I'll be waiting when you're ready."

Before leaving, Sheyla downloaded some preliminary data acquired by the medibots and carried it with her to read. The information only raised more questions, however, as he didn't track with a satisfactory baseline for an Animari patient. *That can't be right.* Frowning, she pulled a chart for comparison and was deep into analysis mode when the prince rapped lightly on her open door.

"Did you already forget you asked me to come?"

"Definitely not." But she *was* startled by his appearance, no concealing that, so she went with a rueful smile. "Come around behind the desk, my degrees are framed."

"You went to school in Hallowell?"

Sheyla could understand his surprise. That was the only mixed settlement, where Numina of all kinds resided—a neutral city that was a haven of education and industry with embassies from all factions. She had graduated from Wickford College with a degree in Biology and then studied medicine at St. Casimir, a university hospital run by the monastic order of war bears. She was qualified to treat all types of Animari, but she hadn't learned much about the Eldritch or the Golgoth, hence her disadvantage now. She had come home after years away to complete her residency in Ash Valley.

"I did. It was... eye-opening. In many ways."

He tapped the ornate lettering on her framed certificate. "If I'm not mistaken, this means you graduated with the highest honors."

"Your translation is correct."

"The monk-physicians at St. Casimir are infamous for tolerating no nonsense. That explains your bedside manner at least." His laughter rang out then, so genuine that Sheyla smiled reluctantly in response.

"Indeed."

She expected that to end their discussion, but he went around the desk to take a seat across from her, and for the next quarter hour, he asked about her philosophy, her ethics, for anecdotal evidence of her diagnostic style. Awkward at first but before she knew it, she had been telling patient stories for almost an hour.

"Thank you," he said at last.

"For what?"

"Being yourself. It is an inexpressible joy to be with someone who has no agenda."

"But I *do* have one." That was a poor attempt at humor.

Because he froze, long fingers curling into the arms of his chair as if bracing for a blow. "How you strive to wound and disappoint me. Alas, let's hear it."

"I want to make you well. Or as close as you can be."

His expression eased into a smile that shimmered into the sun-kissed pond of his eyes. "That's what all doctors want. I can live with that."

"Bad ones covet power over life and death. Sometimes they want…" She trailed off, wondering why she was saying any of this.

"That sounds like a story you want to tell me, Dr. Halek."

"Maybe someday," she said. "If you follow my instructions well."

"Ah, so you prefer the carrot to the stick."

"The stick is pointless, my prince. If you don't fear death, no pain I could inflict would make you comply." Afterward, she didn't know why she'd titled him so, when he was neither hers nor did her pride acknowledge royalty per se.

His gaze glittered in response. "That… is true. And what I fear is not death, precisely, but failing to accomplish what I must before my guttering candle burns down."

It took her a few seconds to process. "So, you think you matter more as a symbol of rebellion than as a person who has the right to live his best, most-fulfilling life."

Inexplicably, she ached over the memory of him counting. He knew very well how long he had without a fully-functional serum. She might be able to extend his life through other means, endless surgical intervention, but that would take a toll in other ways. He probably wouldn't have the strength to fight his brother.

And he must.

"I am not a person," he said softly. "I am a scarecrow, stuffed full of other people's yearnings. My mother's desperation, my sister's charity, my people's hope. Or perhaps it is more that I'm a cracked vessel and no matter how much others pour in, I cannot hold it."

For a moment, she wasn't sure if this was another game he was playing, but then she compared the half-smile to the lines around his eyes. She had to respond as if he meant precisely what he said, for he did. If she reacted otherwise, he would pretend it was a quip or a game. Already she could unravel him enough to know that was his practice—to say true things and then disclaim them with a careless chuckle.

"Bullshit. You *are* a person. One who carries a heavy burden, to be sure, but you can't let the needs of many erode who you are."

"Riddle me that."

"What?"

"Who I am."

Sheyla raised a brow. "Are you asking *me* who you are?"

"I was hoping you'd know. I haven't for a while."

Sighing, she made a shooing motion with her hands. "We're done here."

"But I wasn't. I had more absurdity saved up."

"Prince Alastor." She spoke in her best, *learned from monks,* warning tone.

"I liked it better when you called me your prince. So

deliciously territorial."

"Seriously, do I have to evict you forcibly from my office?" She stood up, ready to make good on what was more a promise than a threat.

"It would probably be fun. I like contact sports, even if I suffer for them afterward."

Only sheer willpower and years of training kept her from laughing. *So inappropriate.* "All right, that's—"

"I do have one more question."

Skeptical, she eyed him, but he was all innocence, so she finally said, "Go ahead."

"What kind of cat are you?"

For the love of—

It was like he thought she had nothing but time while his clock was ticking. She swallowed the mixture of amusement and annoyance. "I'm a cheetah."

His smirk was a thing of beauty. "Don't be so hard on yourself. From our short acquaintance, you seem like an honest person."

When she snarled and lunged at him, he ran.

ALASTOR FOUND PRINCESS Thalia deep in conversation with Pru, the pride matron. The conference room was warm, so someone must have fixed the corresponding generator; full power would take longer to restore. With most of the dust swept up, the room was reasonably clean, russet couches and stained carpet that would need more thorough treatment later. The table at which they sat had a crack at the far end, though most of the chairs looked sound enough.

He would rather circle back to aggravate the pretty doctor, but there were only so many hours in the day.

Despite Ded's unenthusiastic evaluation of his chances, he had to try. He watched them for a few seconds, trying to decide between approaching Thalia with an official alliance or coming in on a romantic cloud. Something about the set of her jaw advised against the latter. This was no damsel waiting for rescue.

When they reached a pause point, he made his presence known. "Am I interrupting?"

The pride matron stood automatically, her expression locking into a smile he'd privately dubbed Friendly Discomfort. Something about him bothered her, clearly, but he had no intention of putting her fully at ease. The effort would probably make her mate open his jugular. Princess Thalia showed no response, her face as cool and inscrutable as ever. A white-haired guard took a step forward from the far wall; her upraised hand forestalled the protective gesture.

"Not at all," Thalia said.

Her features truly were exquisite. Such symmetry rarely presented in nature, so he did wonder if her perfection had been tailored. Not that it mattered. At their invitation, he joined them at the table and declined an offer of hot tea. The silence swelled, making him think he had, in fact, stalled some important discussion.

He was ready to call this a dreadful failure when Pru said, "We were about to go over some preliminary scouting reports."

"Tycho's forces?" he guessed.

Thalia nodded. "Shall we begin?"

In response to the pride matron's signal, the lights dimmed and images appeared on the blank wall opposite. The intel seemed to be coming from wolf drones, along with pertinent data regarding troop movements. Compared to what he knew of the standing military in Golgerra, the number Tycho had fielded was staggering. But based on current camp locations, it was difficult to predict his next target. With the conclave disrupted and the leaders scattered, he probably wouldn't strike Ash Valley again right away.

"What do you think?" the pride matron asked, once she'd completed the report.

"He's fully committed to the offensive." That was a judgment they could make on their own, unnecessary to have personal experience with his brother.

Both women stared at him, expectant, waiting for more. There were so many stories he could tell that would shed light on the monster that was coming. But one incident stuck in his mind, haunting him fifteen years later. *This is what they must hear.*

"When I was young, my father threw a grand gala to honor my brother, his eldest son. It was ostensibly a birthday party, but we all knew it for what it was, a mark of the king's favor."

"Doesn't the eldest generally become the heir?" Thalia asked.

"Birth order plays less of a role in our culture. The strongest prevails." That was a teacup truth, sufficient for the story he was about to relate. "The latter portion of the evening was private, strictly for the nobility. But such was my father's delight in Tycho that he wanted to display his strength and valor for the whole city to admire. So, we held a festival in the palace courtyard, open to all."

Alastor remembered with perfect, awful clarity how the breeze carried so many scents that day: crushed apple blossoms and dried herbs, smoke and roasting meat, the hot spatter of grease and fried dough. It had been loud too, wild with cheering, laughter, shouts of excitement, and the thunder of roving feet. The doctors only let him out for a little while, and for a little while, it was magical.

"Why do I have such a bad feeling?" the pride matron whispered.

"Because you're perceptive, I suspect."

"Tycho held court, waving to the citizens from the top of the steps. Make no mistake, my brother is handsome. He is both admired and feared."

The pause was necessary for his composure, not dramatic. "A little girl broke free from her parents. She had a facial deformity… and a flower. Before the guards could get to her, she reached my brother." Saying it aloud might make him sick. But he had to. They needed to understand what they faced. "He kicked her down the stairs. Her head…"

Alastor let out a shuddering breath, recalling the pool of blood, but even worse, the indifference after. How the palace staff *mopped her up* and Tycho never stopped smiling. The festival went on. He'd nearly died of the horror, suffering a bronchial attack that left him bedridden for two days. In those days, he'd read endlessly: political treatises, war stratagems, and he'd imagined how it would be if he ever had the power to stop his brother.

Thalia cursed in high Eldritch, an archaic form reserved for their nobility. Though Alastor's syntax was rusty, the gist of it made his ears burn. "Your brother is a devil."

"I know," he said. "He culls the 'weak'. My people are known for it, and Tycho is merciless. If he conquers the Numina, he will not be kind. He will purge your populations and we will all eke out a miserable existence on our knees."

"That can't happen," Pru said. She was calmer than he'd expected, visibly troubled but pensive. "Anything you can predict about his strategy could help, anything at all."

He'd been asking himself that for days. The failure at Ash Valley would have infuriated Tycho, who had been known to flip tables over losing at board games. *What's his next move?* Unfortunately, Alastor had spent years avoiding his older brother—for obvious reasons—but an idea developed in flickers and flutters, like a light snow.

"I don't think he'll go after any fortified strongholds. He needs a victory to reassure the troops and keep morale strong. My people were born for battle."

At that, he noted Thalia's flinch. *Hmm. I meant it figuratively. Surely she doesn't believe the old stories?* Ancient legends suggested that long ago, the Eldritch had bred his people as war beasts and eventually lost control of their creations.

"What does that leave?" Pru asked.

With no military strength and few resources, small settlements were pointless. All at once, his head tingled with the force of the epiphany. "Can I see the map again?"

Five camps, arrayed like that...

Suddenly Alastor knew; he had no doubts at all.

"He's marching on Hallowell."

The city had no standing defense, and if Tycho took it, he could exert a dangerous level of control over shipping and industry. Plus, locking down the universities and diplomatic structure would put civilization in his cupped palm. His first move would be executing the weak along with any males strong enough to resist. Diplomats would die next. Before his brother was through, he would 'cleanse' the city and stamp it into the mold of New Golgerra.

"It won't even be a fight," Thalia breathed.

Pru was nodding. "A massacre. We have to warn them."

"What good will that do?" Alastor lurched out of his seat and strode over to the far wall, tapping the army camps with too much force. "With the numbers he's fielding, he can take the city and occupy it—with plenty of troops left for the next offensive."

"He'll convert the factories," Thalia said then.

While her cleverness probably wouldn't save them, he agreed with her assessment. "Any that can be swapped out to weapons or armaments, will be. The economic impact will be devastating. There will be shortages. He'll force us to ration if he can."

"We're already doing it," Pru muttered.

Thalia drummed her fingers, staring at the map while Alastor mastered the urge to put his fist through the wall. "They've disrupted supply lines already."

The situation was grim to the point that he hated thinking about it. Even worse that this was his responsibility.

"There's only one thing for it," he said with patently false cheer.

Pru cocked her head. "What's that?"

"I have to defend Hallowell."

4.

THE NEWS REACHED Sheyla the next day.

By then, she had the prince's test results and had been studying his physiology for almost eighteen hours. At first, she couldn't believe he was packing, but when she located the Golgoth cohort, they were clearing out of the apartments. It was the worst idea she'd ever heard—leaving the sanctuary of Ash Valley to do… what, exactly? In Hallowell.

"Are you out of your mind?" she demanded.

Alastor turned. "Possibly."

He clearly hadn't slept much the night before; his pale skin gave it all away, just as this ridiculous mission would eat up his strength and waste the time he did have. She could have made all those arguments aloud, but his expression made it clear it would be futile. So she changed gears to fact-finding.

"What's your goal?"

"To prevent my brother from taking the city."

"You have thirty men and no war machines," she pointed out.

Burnt Amber war machines were coveted and the bears

didn't part with them easily. Exceptional mobility, heavy artillery, missiles, laser weapons, all packed into a convenient metal frame suitable for one soldier. With a couple of those in the air, any infantry unit could feel better about its chances. The prince didn't even have a Rover to his name.

"History is full of great battles where a minuscule defense force faced a monstrous invading army."

Sheyla spoke through clenched teeth. "And the one thing those stories have in common? Crushing defeat."

"I'm glad I got to see you before our departure. Your pep talks are so bracing."

"There's no way I can talk you out of this?" Mentally, she was already cursing the juggling this would require.

The prince tilted his head and she instinctively mistrusted that look. "Careful. If you beg, I'll suspect you've grown attached to me."

"If you won't stay, I must go with you. In Hallowell, the equipment should be substantially better and will allow me to provide you with better care."

Alastor stilled. "I can't take you from your people. Not now. There may be another attack and without you—"

"They'll survive. Dr. Bohalian and the nursing staff may curse me, but if the pride master agrees, I'll go. Tell me when."

He searched her face for a long moment, and whatever he found, made him smile slightly. "Tomorrow, just before dawn. I'm still figuring out how we'll get there."

That was a good question. Vehicles left outside the hold had been destroyed by the enemy or blown up as weaponry, leaving few transportation options. The pride probably had a few Rovers stashed for emergency use, but it was doubtful that Dominic would turn them over to the Golgoth prince.

She'd love to know what Alastor planned to do in Hallowell with nothing more than an honor guard, but she wasn't signing on as a tactical advisor.

"Good luck," she said. "I have some arrangements of my own to square away."

With a wave, the prince dismissed her, and Sheyla hurried to what was left of the ops center. Normally Slay and Magda would be here with Dom, but Magda had gone with the wolves, and Slay... nobody had seen him in long enough to be worrisome. There was talk of Dom choosing a new second, but he was resisting. Dom must be trying to repair some of the surveillance equipment, get some perimeter security back online, but from his expression, it wasn't going well.

"Something up?" he asked.

Nodding, Sheyla summarized the situation as concisely as possible. "That said, I'm formally asking for permission to take leave at the hospital."

"This is a shitty time," Dom muttered. "But I'm not telling you anything you don't know. Did you talk to Pru?"

"Not yet." She liked that his first question was whether she'd looped in his mate. "I'll get her input next."

"Unless she objects, you've got my approval. Just... be careful."

That warning could've gone without saying, but she took his concern in the spirit in which it was intended. "Then I'm off to find Pru."

The pride matron had a few more questions, but in the end, she gave her blessing as well. But her conflicted mien made Sheyla ask, "Was there something else?"

"Getting drawn into the Golgoth succession battle..." Though Pru trailed off, Sheyla could guess at her concerns.

"Certain risks are unavoidable," she said. "I won't be fighting on the front lines, but somebody has to make sure that Prince Alastor can."

"Thank you for stepping up... if I have the right to say that. Something Arran said last night makes me think Alastor's role may be pivotal."

Science was her purview, but she'd never scoff at one of the seer's predictions. "Can you be more specific?"

Pru hesitated, seeming torn. Finally, she said, "He told me he saw a great darkness, like storm clouds, only they produced no thunder, no lightning, and it swallowed everything it touched. Standing in the path of that great tempest, he glimpsed a dragon from the old legends with a cheetah perched on its tale."

It didn't take a sign-reader to guess that Tycho must be the oncoming storm, and Sheyla's role was obvious, so that left Alastor as the dragon. *Together, the two of us can stop all of this?* That seemed unlikely. Still, she appreciated the intelligence.

"I'll bear that in mind. If anything, this only strengthens my resolve."

"Suspected as much," Pru said.

Sheyla nodded, heading for the door. "If you'll excuse me, I need to see my family."

She didn't expect they'd be thrilled with the news. Her parents were easy to find, but she had three younger brothers helping with relief efforts and/or rebuilding. There was no reason to chase them down when she could enjoy a rare moment of peace with her parents while she waited for the boys to come home.

The flat had visible damage, cracks in walls and ceiling, but her parents had done their best to make the place not only habitable, but inviting. Family pictures had been shifted around and an afghan her grandmother had knitted was hung over the worst patch. By candlelight, the living room was charming, and her mother glanced up in surprise when Sheyla stepped in.

"This is a pleasant surprise," Mum said.

She looked tired, but she was healthy and that made Sheyla grab onto her, hugging tighter than she normally would. *I don't know how long it will be until I see you again.* She heard her father's footsteps as he came down the hall and into the kitchen. The floor creaked as if he was shifting his weight, nervous or trying to get a look at her expression, so she schooled her features and let go. They were used to her composure, not her fervent affection.

"Is everything all right?"

"You'd think I never came home for dinner," she muttered.

"Not *never.*" Mum patted her arm as she stepped back. The soft touch said 'sorry for teasing', so Sheyla smiled. "I'm sorry I don't have more to cook…"

She waved away the typical concern. "We can't be feasting when everyone's on rations. Having everyone together is enough."

"Well said." Pap wrapped an arm about her shoulders, hugging gently.

She spent an hour checking on their health none too subtly, and as her folks got irritated with the questions, her youngest brother, Avi, trundled in, followed by Zaran, and finally, Darvid. At one point, she'd hated the noise that came with a family of this size, but as they took turns pouncing, squeezing her sides, and ruffling her hair, she decided they had been worth the effort of raising them. Still, it didn't mean she'd tolerate nonsense. When Avi went after her cheek, she bit him and growled deep in her throat.

"That's enough," Mum said in a reproving tone.

"Your sister has news, I think. We should hear her out."

"After dinner." That would be soon enough.

It was tough to know when they'd eat together again. She tried to keep her expression even, difficult to judge how well she succeeded. For the next hour, they talked and laughed while Sheyla luxuriated in the fact that her family was alive and well.

Which made it even harder to say, "I'm leaving."

Only she did it, as she did everything, with quiet efficiency. Avi stopped laughing, one hand on Zaran's shoulder. "What? Why?"

This time, it was complicated to explain because her family didn't care that much about external demands and cross-cultural politics. Four voices rose in dismay, everyone speaking at once, and then Pap slammed his fist into the table. A weighted silence fell.

"Are they forcing you to go?" Mum demanded.

Unclear if she meant the pride leaders or the Golgoth royal. Either way, the answer would be the same. "It's my choice to help the prince."

"You're *choosing* danger," Pap repeated, incredulous. "That makes no sense. They should get someone else, a doctor who specializes in demonkin."

Mum hit him, but he didn't look sorry. He folded his arms, intractable as ever, and Sheyla had to admit she got that from him. She locked eyes with her father, willing him to yield. Even if he didn't give his blessing, she'd still go. It would just hurt more.

One by one, her brothers stood and Zaran spoke for all

of them. "I'll kill that bastard for talking you into this."

IT HAD BEEN a long time since Alastor worked through the night. In truth, substituting 'never' for 'long' encapsulated the situation, and he hadn't worked so much as pleaded, but there were no resources to spare. While the cats appreciated his determination, they had nothing left to give. Sanctuary had offered some breathing room, but anything else had to come from his own efforts. That meant the Exiles must follow him to Hallowell on foot, carrying their own provisions. His eyes burned, tightness in his chest signified an impending reaction, but there was no time for him to retreat and ride it out in private.

Not now. This can't happen now.

Ded took a step closer, but Alastor waved him off. Rowena was watching his face with uncanny attention too, so he must look unsteady. Then three males shouldered to the front of the group, each dark-haired and handsome, bearing a strong enough resemblance to Dr. Halek that he collected he was about to meet her family. The tallest aimed a punch at his face, and he might've dodged it, if Ded hadn't caught the man's wrist first.

"Don't." The snarl came from deep in the guard's chest.

Alastor raised a hand, signaling Ded to stand down. "I surmise that you're unhappy with your sister's decision."

"She wouldn't be leaving if it wasn't for you," the boy accused.

Odd, but the tightness in his chest eased when Dr. Halek stepped closer, if as his body had already learned that she could alleviate his ills. "That is true."

"Stop this." Her tone made it clear this wasn't a request

but a command.

"If anything happens to her, anything at all, I'll kill you myself."

Alastor inclined his head. "I'll take responsibility for her."

"Zaran," she snapped.

But her sibling ignored the doctor and marched off. After a brief hesitation, the others went after him. It seemed that Zaran was the one they followed; they were all near enough in age that Alastor couldn't tell the birth order. That seemed to matter more in feline hierarchies whereas, in Golgerra, strength counted for everything.

"Looks as if I won't receive a beating just yet. But I wonder, will Zaran be greatly disappointed if my own sibling does me in instead?"

"That depends on what happens to *me*," Dr. Halek said.

"I'll do my best." Alastor wondered if she could feel his sincerity; he'd seldom meant anything more.

"That's why I'm going. So you can."

The pressure eased a little more. "You should sleep."

"There's no point. Besides, I'm used to going without."

He'd heard about the way doctors suffered for their credentials, so he supposed that was true. "Then I'll see you at the gate in a couple of hours."

Turning, Alastor startled when her hand closed on his forearm. "Wait."

"Is there something more?"

"What, exactly, should I pack?"

Alastor heard the unspoken follow-up question 'how bad will it get' and he wished he had an answer. But before he had to unveil the unvarnished truth, an angry-looking white-haired Eldritch shoved a path toward him. He recognized the male from his brief meeting with the pride matron and Princess Thalia. Dr. Halek stepped back, releasing her hold to make space.

"I'm sorry, I don't recall your name," Alastor said.

"Gavriel. We haven't been introduced." The terse reply told him volumes about how little the Eldritch liked his mission, whatever it was. "I've been assigned to your command by Princess Thalia. I lead twenty of her best, including all our surviving Noxblades. We are commissioned to ensure your safe arrival in Hallowell."

That was the first bit of bright news he'd had all night. Yet it looked as if Gavriel would rather cut off his own arm than comply. "Are you sure? You seem as if you'd prefer to stab me."

With effort, the Noxblade lowered his blood-red gaze. *Unnerving, those eyes, like staring into the heart of murder.* "My apologies, sire."

"It's fine. I'd be irate if I had to follow me into battle, too." The crooked smile came easily, but Alastor knew all too well that humor could only carry him so far. Gavriel didn't respond to the joke, so Alastor peered past him at the Eldritch mingling uneasily with his Exiles.

"You don't exactly inspire confidence. This is my lieutenant, Zandronicus."

"Nice to meet you." This Noxblade differed from his colleagues in three significant ways: ginger hair, gray eyes, and a friendly smile.

"Likewise," Alastor said.

Dr. Halek seemed torn between impatience and aggravation at being interrupted. Best to answer before she lost her temper.

He turned to her. "Warm clothes, any gear you'll need

for living rough. We'll be marching to Hallowell."

At first, her mouth opened, but no sound came out. "What?" she managed eventually.

"You heard me."

Gavriel cut in by stepping between them, and Alastor greeted him with a scowl. It took a surprising amount of restraint to keep the spines from piercing through his skin. A shudder ran through him, as it was the first time since he learned how to transform that he'd nearly gone bestial without volition. There was no time to ponder what that portended, however, as he locked his gaze on the Noxblade.

"I thought we were finished," he got out.

"Not quite. I bear some further news."

"Then deliver it."

I sound like my brother. And that was almost enough to force out an apology, but Gavriel was already speaking. "If we can make it to the rally point, Pine Ridge means to send both soldiers and supplies. There, we will rendezvous with Burnt Amber as well. The Order of Saint Casimir is donating a quarter of their operational war machines to defend Hallowell."

"Holy shit," Dr. Halek said.

He didn't think he'd ever heard the doctor swear before, but it encompassed his own reaction so well that he flashed her a smile. "To say the least."

"That means you need to step up—in a big way." The Noxblade didn't have to add the last comment. "All these people are putting their hope in your hands, understand? It's not just a family feud anymore. If you fail—"

"Do you know what insubordination means?" Dr. Halek snarled. "If you're under his command, then you shouldn't be saying these things. Return to your unit. Now."

She punctuated her words with an aggressive step forward and a snap of her teeth.

To his surprise, the Noxblade stood down, just as she had ordered. By Ded's tension, he hadn't expected that to work either. They swapped looks over the good doctor's head and Alastor shrugged. He had no idea how exactly dominance played out, especially between Animari and Eldritch. Back in Golgerra, that wouldn't have ended without a blood battle, but possibly since Gavriel was used to taking orders from a female, he was more likely to accept direction from an unranked woman.

Ded stepped up beside him to whisper, "She is... impressive."

"She's not involved in this."

That, he had to make crystal clear. As his personal physician, Dr. Halek was not a combatant, not part of the force he was assembling. He didn't want her getting pulled in, and whatever he could do to protect her from what was to come—well, it likely wouldn't be much. But at least he could establish that she was answerable only to him.

He was about to say something when she touched him. Again. The heat from her palm warmed his arm, a pleasurable shock that soothed raw nerves. "Don't."

"Excuse me?"

"Don't make a big deal of my role. I don't know what you're planning to say, but just keep quiet. It's nobody's business."

For a few seconds, he studied her and realized that *she* was trying to protect him. She must suspect that it would compromise his capacity to lead, if his infirmity became common knowledge among the Eldritch. "Then... they may think you've signed on as the company medic."

Dr. Halek shrugged. "That's fine. It's not like I'd refuse to treat a patient anyway."

Despite a slow-percolating warmth due to her unexpected loyalty, he tried one last time to make her see reason. "I'm concerned for your reputation. In this scenario, there's no excuse for the time we'll spend sequestered together. They may draw… certain conclusions."

"I don't give a rat's ass if the world assumes I'm your woman. Knowing the truth is enough for me when I have a job to do."

5.

IT WAS SNOWING when Sheyla left the hold, a fine dusting that would accumulate over time. While it was miserable for a march, the weather might cover their tracks. A group this size was vulnerable, too large to vanish into the wilderness, too small to prevail if Tycho's forces found them, so she'd be lying if she claimed no measure of fear. Yet nobody hesitated over following Prince Alastor into the swirling white, carrying their worlds on their backs.

I probably should have asked more questions.

She picked up the pace and tried not to focus on the fact that she was the lone Animari among Eldritch and Golgoth. Prince Alastor was flanked by his immense bodyguard and the ethereal woman who sometimes stared at Sheyla too long. As she approached, the female yielded her spot first, and then the soldier did.

She ignored that in favoring of inquiring, "How far is it to the rendezvous?"

"Five days if the weather doesn't worsen."

"You discussed the pros and cons of traveling like this?" She knew transformation took longer for the Golgoth and it seemed to be painful.

He lowered his voice to the point that it would be impossible for anyone to overhear. Even with her sharp senses, Sheyla had to tilt her head toward him. "The Eldritch couldn't keep up otherwise, and we need their aid. This is the start of an alliance and likely a test."

"Of whether you've truly committed to killing your brother?" No point in seeking gentler words, but for the first time, she realized that pain must accompany the prince's resolve.

If Zaran turned for the worst, it would be difficult to hate him entirely, and *if* she could because of all the evil he'd done, there was no changing that they were flesh and blood, connected down to the bone. As Alastor met her gaze, a little shock ran through her. This had nothing to do with his physical health, so she shouldn't want to comfort him. With effort, she curled her hands onto the straps supporting her pack.

"Likely, yes."

"And are you?"

His sigh puffed out in a smoky cloud, carried off by the wind. "Committed? Yes. I can't guarantee I'll succeed, mind you. I only know that I must try."

"You are so brave." She didn't mean to compliment him. Yet the words slipped out, and even the *tone* embarrassed her. Part of her feared he might take the words wrong, assuming she meant his illness, but she was referring to the war effort.

"No." Already shaking his head, he wore a rueful smile, the one that let him pretend he was simply a clown. "I'm not. I never have been. But you make me want to be."

Before Sheyla could ask what he meant, the Noxblade stepped up on his other side. "My scouts are reporting enemy movements, less than a klick out. To avoid them, we must reroute."

"That will delay our arrival at the rally point, yes?"

"Probable," Gavriel agreed.

"How big is the group?"

"Twenty-five or so. I think they're keeping tabs on the hold from a safe distance."

It was fascinating to watch the prince weigh all the factors; she could even read the tenor of his thoughts as they raced. "Do they have any resources we could use?"

"Other than food and basic camp supplies, they've got a communications array and a fully functional RVAC."

Radial Vector Auto Cannon—that was a killing machine, capable of laying waste to an entire town. The idea that there was a group of Golgoth brutes so close, ready to lay waste to the hold, made her want to run back the way they'd come and warn her family.

Alastor's attention sharpened. "Platform or shoulder mounted?"

"Platform, though I suspect we could field mod it, if one of your men is strong enough to tote the thing."

"That won't be an issue," the prince said. "We just need to take it."

A little shiver ran down Sheyla's back, nothing to do with the weather. People said that the Golgoth were brutal to the core, but she'd never glimpsed it in Prince Alastor before. He gazed at her askance, seeming to gauge something of her thoughts, but he didn't respond. She tried to back away from that reflexive fear since it didn't seem rational. The Eldritch and Golgoth likely had prejudices that the Animari were mindless animals.

"Then you wish to engage?" the Noxblade confirmed.

"Circumnavigating will take too long and we can't leave that RVAC. Two birds, one stone. Is an ambush viable?"

"Definitely."

The details came together fast; the Eldritch would lure the enemy in—small numbers, good bait—and the Golgoth would strike from behind. While Sheyla didn't want to fight, she also snarled over being instructed to hide, tucked away like part of the provisions. Fortunately, her ego wasn't large enough to impede progress with pointless protest and she well-understood that her skills would come in handy *after* the battle.

"I'll keep watch over our gear," she promised, as the prince seemed inclined to linger.

His scowl was instantaneous. "I'm concerned about *you*. At the first glimpse of trouble, shift and run. It'll be easier to hide as a cat."

While that was true, it wasn't his place to concern himself with her survival. "I think you've forgotten—"

He silenced her with a gloved fingertip across her mouth. "Yes, you're in charge of my care. But *I'm* responsible for everyone here. Stay safe, Dr. Halek."

As he rushed away, she thought, *I should have bitten him.*

That thought lost most of its rancor as the Golgoth stripped in the winter chill. It wasn't that she'd never seen an emergency transformation before, but there was a gravity in how the prince and his Exiles approached it, none of the casual joy present in the Animari. She guessed that the Golgoth were less comfortable in their skin; perhaps they had even been taught this was something that should be hidden, like a monster rising from the depths. And that simply wasn't true. For that reason alone, she didn't look away as Alastor skimmed out of his trousers.

Like he'd said in her office, he bore no scars from those seventeen surgeries. He was snowy pale, so fair that he could be an alabaster statue. Sheyla had rarely found beauty framed so, as pallor often presaged illness. From time to time, when she took someone to her bed, they were usually bronze or darker—not a rule, just a preference. Still, she didn't turn aside even when the prince's gaze met hers. This felt like a moment where he needed her to bear witness. She couldn't have said why, but she had faith in her instincts.

Usually, she paired intuition with the scientific method, but today, there was nothing to investigate except the brightening green of his eyes. They were like magic lanterns that blazed in the chill austerity of his etched features. Others might see his face and think such things as 'handsome' or 'sculpted'; Sheyla saw the compression of lips starting to turn blue, the vague imprint of pain discernable to someone who knew how to find its traces.

Then he shifted. It was a violence, all twisting, lurching, broken skin, and actual blood. She had seen live creatures being born that looked gentler than this. A fine crimson mist dotted the snow at his feet, the smell of copper permeating the crisp air. Inhaling, she drew him in, essence of Alastor and new-minted coins. The others took their cue from him, though they must be more practiced, as there was less blood, less pain. That struggle might result from his illness, she supposed, though it wasn't the time to inquire.

Some of the Golgoth were beautiful and terrible, like demonic angels. Her gaze lingered on Rowena, hovering above the rest on black-webbed wings. With maroon leathery skin and a barbed tail, she resembled an old depiction of a succubus, a devil woman who feasted on the life energies of those she took to her bed.

Yet Sheyla's gaze returned to Alastor as if drawn by a lure. Transformed, he was still silver-pale, scaled like a lizard, and massive as she could never have imagined. The reptilian face, elongated jaw, razor-sharp teeth, and claws took her attention first, and Sheyla noted the dorsal spikes and ventral plating later. This creature was a walking weapon. Only his eyes gave any hint who he was, still green and luminous, but they were changed too, more like a serpent. She wondered if they could speak during transformation—as the Animari could not—and this curiosity was answered when he uttered a series of clicks and hisses, intelligible to his people, apparently, but nobody else.

Alastor came to her on arched, clawed feet, and placed his clothes in her arms, a gesture that felt symbolic, somehow. She didn't understand the words when he spoke, even less when he pressed his thumb against her bare wrist and left a red imprint on her skin. The Eldritch and Golgoth rolled out, one group in silence and the others in a deafening horde, leaving her with inexplicably breathless dread and her heart thundering in her ears.

"WAS THAT WISE?" Ded asked.

Alastor didn't care, and let that show with a snarl that took the place of a shrug. The Animari wouldn't know what that mark meant; it was enough that his people did. As a result, they would afford her all courtesy and she'd said she didn't mind what stories circulated about them. Time would tell whether that was true. Or hell, Ded might be talking about something else—the battle, him leading the troops personally... the guard tended to worry.

No time for that.

Snow crunched underfoot as he ran. The world came at him, no color, sharper lines, and the smells that danced on the wind. He opened his mouth to savor them. Even at this remove, he could taste Dr. Halek in the air, crisp, and apple-sweet. There would be a reckoning for this transformation; there always was. But in this form, he couldn't feel it, only strength, sufficient to flip Rovers and uproot trees. The longer he stayed like this, the more he wanted to inflict that damage... and maybe that explained everything about Tycho. Instead of taking those impulses as a warning, he embraced them soul-deep, so he carried them in either skin.

With Rowena scouting, they reached their coordinates without running into trouble. Now they just had to wait for the Eldritch to do their part. If his skin wasn't so thick, he'd be feeling the cold, but thanks to natural body armor, it was no more than a vague discomfort. He crouched, encouraging the others to do the same. Most couldn't blend into the landscape, but staying low was better than nothing. If they had more time, he'd suggest digging in.

No more than half an hour had passed when he heard the first signs of pursuit. It wouldn't be the Eldritch; *should* be the Golgoth chasing them. Alastor pointed and hissed orders, and his troops obeyed so fast, it shamed him. That shame was a multi-tentacle beast, born of their unswerving devotion and his regret at killing his own people. Ignoring it, he rose and struck the nearest Golgoth from behind.

They didn't even shift.

Tycho must not have warned them how dangerous the Eldritch could be, about the broken alliance, or Alastor's defection, so they left the RVAC and tried to run the Noxblades down. But the Eldritch were shadows in the wood, and now the blood was everywhere: his face, his claws, black against the snow through these eyes, though he knew it was red. Some tried to transform, but they were too slow.

Rowena almost decapitated one, his head flopping backwards of a flap of skin. Ded snarled a warning and Alastor spun just in time to block a glancing blow. This wasn't a fight so much as butchery. Despite his roiling stomach, he fought on. No need to drag things out. The sound of a ballistic weapon startled him, more when the bullet bit into his arm. He lunged at the idiot who had shot him. By his third kill, he didn't mind the blood or the smell. Violence sang in him like some celestial choir. Each slash, push, pull, thrust, impalement felt good, righteous, even. A few more fights like this and he might be worthy of—

What?

Ruling the Golgoth.

The desire felt so wrong, so alien, that he came back to his proper mind and saw the corpses piled. A few were still twitching, and his men were putting them down with more enjoyment than he trusted. Even Rowena was crouched over her last victim, claws sunk in to feel the last trickle of blood from a desperate and dying heart. He clicked a warning so sharp that they all straightened.

"We bury them and then we move."

They got to work without looking at him, a sign of shame at getting lost in the bloodlust, but he could scarcely blame them for it. Not when it took him as well. He shoveled his share of snow, mounding it until it hid the worst of the carnage. Afterward, he took them past the half-frozen river, a detour, but he couldn't bring his group back to camp like this.

"We bathe. We wash it away."

The soldiers understood the order. They didn't whine. This was penance for losing control, and they all deserved it. That bastard Gavriel already didn't approve of this alliance. If he saw how brutal even the rebel Golgoth could be—well, Alastor couldn't have him running back to Princess Thalia with a reason to back out. No, this had to work; the peace *had* to hold and they must reach the rendezvous point to join forces with Pine Ridge and Burnt Amber. He felt like he was building a bridge out of fir needles, but that didn't mean he'd stop.

Alastor ran, ignoring the chill, the pain in his left arm. At this point, he only knew that Dr. Halek was waiting in the cold. Not shifted in protective feline form, either. She must be frozen... and furious. That drive kept him from the tide of mayhem, the yearning to ride the destructive wave all the way out to sea. But the hiding spot where he'd left his doctor held nothing at all. Their things were gone as well, a fact that made no sense, but his brain wasn't functioning well, neurons filling with rage and a need to see something—anything—burn.

As he fought to get a breath through the tightness in his chest, not sickness, but pure, visceral fear, the Eldritch leader stepped out of the shadows. "She's gone with my men. We have the RVAC and we're setting up camp, ten kilometers away."

It was just as well this asshole didn't speak base Gol, what they called their shifted tongue. Because he spat choice curses before indicating that he understood with the universal gesture of 'lead on'. The Eldritch set the pace, and it was brutal, a full-on sprint as the sun went down. Even through his natural armor, it was devastatingly cold. His feet burned with it, ice encrusted on his toe claws. At least the raw discomfort kept him from further violence.

Half an hour later, thanks to Gavriel's good navigation and Golgoth stamina, they reached the campsite. Tents had already been erected, including one that the Eldritch indicated. "That's yours. Up to you if you want to share."

Then the asshole flicked a look at Rowena, who had suffered a little on foot. She wasn't used to running hard, but it had been impossible for her to keep them in sight beneath the tight tangle of branches. She must be hurting now, though she didn't show it. The only sign came from her elevated breathing and her hate-filled eyes.

Alastor ignored the provocation. There were larger bivouacs where his men could bunk down. More importantly, he had to get out of sight before he shifted back. He could already tell he'd burned too much energy, and it would likely get ugly. Before he'd hardly looked for her, Dr. Halek was at his side, swearing over his wounded arm.

"You got shot?" she snapped.

"*Not for fun,*" he tried to say.

"Seriously? I don't speak that. Come with me. Now."

It was no hardship to let her wrap him in a blanket or a cloak, or whatever the hell, it was large and warm, and his head was swimming. But he couldn't let on to his men—or to the Eldritch—that he'd blazed through his allotment of brute strength—so he shoved his feet forward. One step, another, until they got inside the tent. Dr. Halek had promised to keep his secrets and to make him as well as he could be. Alastor clung to that promise like it was a rope, and he'd fallen off his fir-needle bridge.

He didn't even have the power to hold to his form. As he fell, he shifted back, naked and weak and bleeding. Everything hurt now, and he still couldn't breathe well. The air in his lungs felt like steel thread, as if someone had been sewing his flesh together. That feeling was intimately familiar, a sign that bad things were growing. The doctor had to perfect the serum or she'd have to perform surgery on him within a month.

After that...

"Stop," she ordered.

Her hands wrapped around his, and he could smell himself on her skin, soft and warm and fading, like yesterday's sex. Alastor stopped, his thoughts, his tremors. He held on to her.

"I have you."

She did. She just didn't know it yet.

6.

SHEYLA COULD ALREADY tell that the prince's condition wasn't good.

For a full minute, she held his hands, taking his pulse with a discreet fingertip. She needed to do like ten things at once, but training made assessment easier. The cold, combined with his weakness, was probably the greatest threat since the wound had coagulated—or maybe frozen shut. Either way, he wasn't bleeding, so she wrapped the blanket around him tightly and fired up the heater. Checking his fingers and toes didn't reveal signs of frostbite.

"D-don't let anyone in." It was clearly hard for him to speak, words scraped out through clench of his teeth.

"Quiet, you. Lean forward."

Because she'd witnessed the other attack via sensor, she saw this one coming on. Sheyla had exactly two inhalers, but she shouldn't use them unless it was a life-threatening attack. Otherwise, there wasn't much she could do in the field except coach his breathing and rub his back. His hand locked onto her again, her leg this time, and she didn't protest when his fingers dug in. He doubled all the way over, probably to hide his face, so Sheyla pulled him upright and spoke to cover what must be excruciating embarrassment.

"Try not to think. Open your mouth if it helps, push out a deep breath. Slow down if you can." When his respiration sounded less desperate, she said, "That's good. Sounds like the worst has passed."

"Easy for you to say," he mumbled.

"I know. Do you feel up to having that gunshot wound treated?" In an Animari, she'd be worried about his flesh sealing around the bullet, but the Golgoth didn't mend that fast.

"Let's get it over with." He pulled the blanket down to reveal his bloodied arm.

A brief inspection revealed no exit wound, and the increased density of his transformed skin meant it wasn't deep in his biceps either. *This will be easy.* Quickly, she popped open a sterile pack and got to work. Though his knuckles tightened, he didn't utter a sound as she extracted the misshapen metal. The injury didn't need to be stitched, so she cleaned and bandaged it well, and then studied his averted face.

"Nothing for the pain, right?" If she recalled correctly, he didn't take such meds because they interfered with the serum.

"It's not that bad," he said in an odd, husky tone.

"Is your throat sore?"

"You didn't wash it off." At first, those words made no sense. When he angled her hand to study the thumbprint he'd left, she understood.

"There was no chance." That wasn't exactly true. She'd hadn't found any running water, but she could've scraped the imprint off with snow.

"It would be better if you had."

"Maybe you should explain…" Sheyla trailed off, riveted by the look the prince was giving her. She felt a phantom caress each spot his gaze brushed—lips, throat, wrist—and she wet her lips.

"Keeping the blood mark means you accept me… that I have the right to protect you, plus certain other privileges." His voice raised actual goosebumps, so deep and… intimate.

"A mating ritual then." She swallowed, aware of how warm the tent seemed, steamy, almost. "But you must have done that for show?"

He's not my lover. He's a patient.

"I should say yes… but my head's not on right just now."

"What does that mean?" Alarmed, she leaned in to see if he had uneven pupils, maybe from cranial trauma she hadn't noticed.

"Oh," he said faintly. "I do wish you hadn't done that."

The blanket dropped and suddenly, she was in his arms. His body was lean and so icy that she yelped. Alastor smothered the sound with a kiss that was all kinds of inappropriate. The fevered contrast between his mouth and his chilly skin sent shivers through her. Sheyla set her hands on his shoulders to shove him back with full strength, but she ended up digging her nails into him instead. He made a sound against her lips that made her instantly want to hear it again, only louder and more plaintive. He tasted like winter and summer combined, a wildness echoed in the heat of his demanding tongue.

Clever hands roved her back, urging her closer. Her nipples tightened as he drew her down on top of him, lifting his hips in short, urgent motions. Each thrust jolted her with pleasure, so that her mind fogged. The sweetness of his mouth swelled, amplifying so that it emanated in delicious waves. Breathing him in, she softened more, her body slick and aching. She broke the kiss and knocked him backward; he landed on his elbows with her looming above. Sex lent his skin a rosy blush, and she didn't know where to look first because everything was a visual feast.

"Why... are you letting me..." It was hardly a whisper as he threaded his hand beneath her hair, cupping her nape.

Sheyla shuddered and tipped her head back, unable to frame a response. Something about that seemed wrong, but when his teeth found the side of her throat, she moaned. *More. Just a little more.* Rubbing her mouth against his shoulder, she breathed him in and then bit him. He was sprawled beneath her, completely naked and ferociously aroused. She moved on him with no further urging, her breath coming in gasps and groans.

A hard shudder ran through him and he rolled her away, scrambling back like she had the plague. Reflexively she crawled toward him; Alastor threw up a hand, still trembling.

"This isn't what you want," he got out. "I'm sorry."

At first that didn't sound right because she'd never wanted to fuck so much in her life, but as her pulse slowed and the golden haze faded, Sheyla curled her hands into fists. A snarl escaped her as she retreated to the far end of the tent. "What the hell did you do to me?"

"It wasn't on purpose."

"Explain, before I rip your guts out."

"Give me a moment. I need to dress. And you... go outside. Please. Walk around camp, come back later. I'll tell you. Just..." Alastor crouched with his back to her, head lowered like he was in excruciating pain. She could've counted the knobs of his spine, all abject abasement.

Only one decision made sense. "I'm gone."

Shakily, Sheyla stumbled out of the flap and rambled around the perimeter, trying to make sense of the exchange. Cold air shocked her back to her senses somewhat, but the sexual energy didn't dissipate, which only made things worse.

When the Noxblade leader stepped into her path, she stared blankly. "Something wrong?"

"I was wondering the same," Gavriel said.

She shrugged. "Just giving him some privacy."

"If you're certain." That was sheer skepticism, but it was none of his damn business.

The camp was quiet with watches set and the rest retired for a well-earned rest. She paced and counted—probably ten minutes went by—until she couldn't wait any longer and went back to Alastor's tent. What he had to say better be good. Otherwise, she might kill him.

"Get one thing clear, I'm not your fuck toy," she snapped.

From his stricken expression, he felt worse about what had happened than she did. Some of her anger evaporated.

"I should have warned you," he said softly.

"About *what*?"

"My people are prone to strong passions," he said. "We get lost easily. In sex. In violence. There is no delicate way to put it, so I won't even try. Right now, most of my men are probably fucking furiously, roused by the battle."

Sheyla tilted her head, puzzled. "That's not so different from the Animari."

"The issue," he said gently. "Is consent. We thrive on

conquest... and the deeper our desire, the more irresistible it becomes to the object of them."

"Are you talking about pheromones or something?" At his shamed nod, she swore. "Yes, you *should* have told me. If I'd known you'd be coming back from battle hot and fuck-hungry, I would've taken precautions."

The smell... there had been an insidious aspect to how fast she went from baffled to eager. This was a terrible ability, focused on undermining resistance and obviating free will. Golgoth captives who begged for more must hate themselves when the buzz wore off, and that explained a lot about the emotional scars that Eamon still bore.

"I wasn't certain how much it would affect me. I've never fought, never killed, and I've heard that I'm not a proper Golgoth my whole life. Consider me enlightened—at your cost. It won't happen again. Even if I'm dying, I won't let you touch me right after a fight."

Sheyla waved that away. It was impossible to nurse a grudge against someone who felt this guilty on his own. "Don't be dramatic. You shook it off enough to realize I wasn't on board. No permanent harm done."

"But there was," he said then.

She raised a brow. "Such as?"

"Now I know how you feel, how you taste... and how you sound. There's no unringing that bell, Dr. Halek."

ALASTOR HALF-EXPECTED THE doctor to punch him in the face. When she laughed, he took a second look. "Is that amusing in some fashion?"

"Slightly. Since you've had your tongue in my mouth, you may as well call me Sheyla."

Suddenly he wanted to smile, but he was afraid she'd take it to mean he wasn't sorry, so he schooled his features and spoke in a cautious tone. "Alastor. No need for formality then."

"Agreed. I'd still sort of like to hit you, but that would raise questions we can't afford and we're too tired to fight in place of fucking. Which might lead to fucking anyway."

Now that his hormone levels had dropped, his head was swimming, and he couldn't get a grip on the conversation, currently flopping at his feet like a fish out of a water. "Are you saying that combat could sub for foreplay?"

"In some cases," she said, her eyes amber and smoky and—

This isn't helping. Now he couldn't stop thinking about her skin glistening with sweat as she prowled toward him, mock-furious, teeth snapping. She would bite and claw. Most probably, he would love it, even if it hurt. Possibly—Alastor made a muffled sound that seemed to recall her to the original slant of the conversation.

"Why are we talking about this anyway? That wasn't my point at all."

"What was it?"

"That sometimes you *have* to laugh, because there's nothing else for it. Doesn't always solve things, but it's a... release." Awareness sparked in her eyes after she said it.

Alastor let the silence build, mostly because he had no idea how to break it. He still wanted her to the point of physical distress, but he had no intention of pulling her into a chemical haze. This didn't matter among the troops. If everyone had the same ability, everyone was desperate to get off, then it just turned into a hot and sweaty fuck pile. Imagining the Eldritch reaction to the noises they'd hear tonight distracted him—for all of ten seconds.

"So it is."

If possible, the tension thickened to the point that he heard her breathing along with the quickening pump of her heart. Her mouth was no longer flattened into a disapproving line. Alastor could see the traces of his kisses in faint swelling, in the deepening bruises where her throat met her jaw. *Rougher than I meant to be.* But there was no denying a certain satisfaction in admiring those marks.

"I see no point in prevaricating," she said, and for a glorious moment, he hoped she was about to suggest something delightfully wicked. "You see, I'm having the same problem, and it's even more inappropriate on my end. It's not uncommon for patients to develop an infatuation with their doctors. The reverse is both deeply unprofessional and profoundly dangerous."

Of course.

"Somehow you're not dissuading me, if that's your intent. We could consider this a war-time exception. You know, adrenaline, high-risk situations, who knows if this is the last time we'll see each other alive—"

"Nice try. Instead, how about I accept your apology and we call it even?"

Alastor nodded. "I had intended for you to sleep here, as this affords the most privacy and comfort, given our circumstances. But if you wish to make other arrangements..."

"It's fine. You didn't do that on purpose."

Her forgiveness felt better than he'd expected. With a faint sigh, he let go the last of his regret and focused on unearthing the provisions that Ded had set aside. The soup wouldn't last more than a day or two; it was already lukewarm, despite being well-insulated. After that, they would need to hunt.

"I appreciate your faith."

Quietly, he poured two servings from the thermos, and it had been long enough since he'd eaten that even the meat and barley porridge didn't look so bad. Alastor downed it without pausing to reflect on the taste, and then he turned off the heater. They needed to conserve energy, as they could only gather so much solar power on the move. With the tent flap closed, their bodies would create sufficient heat to let them sleep in relative comfort.

When he glanced over at her, she was finishing up her share of the rations. She lifted her cup in a mock toast. "Cheers. Don't think you're getting away without tea."

"Perish the thought."

The strained atmosphere between them eased as they passed the thermos back and forth. Once it was empty, he set it aside and dimmed the lamp. Amenities were basic: thermal tent and bedrolls, one solar light, one heating unit. Further luxuries had to come from their personal packs; on his part, he had a bottle of expensive liquor stashed in anticipation of a night much colder and darker than this. Alastor reckoned he would crack it open only if he was staring at sure defeat, or perhaps awaiting execution.

"You look grim," she observed.

"It's that sort of mission. We should get some sleep… do you prefer the right or the left?" By which he meant the side of the tent, nothing suggestive.

Her smile said she understood as much. "Left, though it doesn't much matter."

"If only everything could be so easily settled."

The interior was all shadows as he unspooled his bedroll, slippery fabric that was cold until he climbed into it, but it warmed in contact with his skin. It was beyond intimate listening to her settle in, close enough to touch... but he wouldn't. Alastor rolled away, offering Sheyla the scant privacy of his back.

Weary as he was, sleep should have claimed him straightaway. Instead, he listened to her breathe and thought of the night she had drifted off in his apartment. Wonder crept over him when he grasped how fully she'd committed to his cause. In that moment, Alastor realized how much he trusted her. There was no comparison between Sheyla Halek and the physician who had treated him for years, none at all.

Her voice in the dark startled him. "I've never slept in a tent before."

"It's a first for me too. Are you warm enough?"

She hesitated. "Not quite."

The sounds he'd thought would surprise the Eldritch started, rumbled grunts and groans that made their origins unmistakable. He tried to modulate his pulse and not remember how good she tasted, how sweet she felt. "Try to ignore it."

"You did tell me your people are aroused after a battle. Would it…"

"What?" Listening to this, there were so *many* interesting things she might ask him to do.

"Would it bother you if I shifted?"

You deserve to be disappointed, he told himself. "Not at all."

With resolute discipline, he didn't look as fabric rustled—presumably Sheyla stripping out of her clothes—and then he heard the scrape of claws on the bedroll. She growled a little, nudged her sleeping bag toward his, so he dragged them together fully, and then she tried to burrow in. Her claws made that difficult, so he ended up tucking her in.

So very strange, truly.

Alastor wanted her in his arms, tangled around him until his skin shimmered with her scent, but when she curled against his back, solid weight and incredible heat, his entire body relaxed. The effect was almost narcotic in terms of relief. His chest eased, and Alastor closed his eyes. No need for an alarm, Ded would wake him at first light...

It wasn't dawn when he stirred, and he wasn't even sure *why* he was awake. Delicious warmth and softness made this the best awakening in recent memory, then he realized. He'd gone to sleep with a great cat at his back and roused with a naked woman in his arms. Alastor had no idea *how* this had happened, though at least his cohorts had apparently spent their passions and left the camp peaceful.

Her bedroll was layered on his, and one gorgeous thigh had been flung across his leg, so close to his cock that a minute shift would feel exquisite. *No. I'm not doing that.* Seconds passed as he reveled in her closeness, hardly daring to breathe. Sleeping, she had no inhibitions and her hands stirred on his back. Acute pleasure robbed him of the ability to think, then he wrangled his wayward impulses into submission.

Do the right thing. Now.

He was trying to move her when her eyes snapped open. "Care to explain?"

7.

IT WAS ENTERTAINING to watch Alastor struggle, but he wasn't responsible for her nocturnal shift. In fact, she had a muzzy recollection of getting overheated in cat form, and everything unfolded from there. One of the dangers of being sleep-deprived was operating on automatic.

This... is not one of my better outcomes.

"Relax, it's not your fault."

Some of the tension left him, likely because he wasn't worried she was about to twist his dick off. "Indisputably. Yet I'm mystified as to why you went to such lengths to sleep with me. Whatever you may have heard, I'm not at all averse to naked people."

Sheyla shifted away slightly, but his arms didn't loosen. It had been long enough since she shared a bed that his heat was comforting, seductive, even, so she ran through all the reasons this was a terrible idea. She still didn't move—and not because it was tough to break his hold.

Since she was perilously close to making a bad decision, she decided to screw with him instead. She rested her chin on his shoulder, close enough that she could just make out his features in the gloom, and spoke in a breathless tone.

"I've never slept with a man before."

His entire body jolted. "There are several possibilities: you're a virgin, you prefer females, or you're a liar. Which is it?"

"One of those options is, indeed, correct," she said solemnly.

Under these circumstances, she shouldn't be having this much fun; odd, she hadn't once wished she was back in the lab. He levered up on an elbow, putting his face next to hers.

"You're messing with me."

"Excellent deduction. Ergo, answer C, I'm a liar."

"No, there's a difference between lying and teasing. I've had my fill of the former, not nearly enough of the latter."

In the dark, his honesty flowered between them with irresistible allure. She could dismiss flirtation, much harder to defend against sheer candor. "You must have friends—"

"I have followers," he cut in. "Who hope I can accomplish the impossible, and yes, they would die for me. Does that fit your definition of friendship?"

"Not really."

"When Caia was alive, I could talk to her. A little less with Efren, and Leander, not at all. He was too busy diverting Tycho's wrath from the rest of us. He... died first."

That was the most specific and personal thing she could recall Alastor saying, and maybe she should shut this down. Yet it seemed to Sheyla that he *wanted* to tell her.

"I'm listening," she said.

"You're naked."

"Does that mean you can't concentrate?"

His low chuckled rumbled against her ear. "Would you think less of me if I said yes?"

"Yes and no. Nudity isn't a huge issue among the Animari, so it's a little strange to hear. But it's a bit... flattering as well, I think."

I definitely shouldn't have said that. The longer she lay like this, the less he seemed off-limits and the more she wanted to get to know him. Even imagining the reprimand she'd receive from her advisor at the Order of St. Casimir didn't offer much of a deterrent.

"Doubtless you expect me to stroke your ego now. I refuse," Alastor said. "Too much praise will render you insufferable."

"According to my brothers, I am already."

"Siblings are never impartial," he said softly.

"Tell me about yours."

"Only if we operate on an exchange program. My stories are primarily sad ones, so I'll need something cheery from you in exchange."

Sheyla nodded, guessing he could feel her agreement. "That's fair."

"I'll start with Leander then. He was the next oldest, nearly as strong as Tycho, and the one who presented the greatest threat."

"To succession?"

"I suppose, but also to Tycho's obsessive need for adulation. If one person out of a hundred wasn't gazing at him, he always knew. Whether it was devotion or fear, he didn't care. Tycho would win one if not the other. Whereas Leander... people simply loved him. He didn't even have to try. There was... goodness in him. He was always trying to protect us, speaking up, pissing Tycho off on purpose."

She couldn't imagine having an adversarial relationship with her brothers. Though she was the oldest, as soon as

Zaran came into his height, he was always threatening to pummel someone for messing with her. Likewise, the two of them protected Avi and Darvid to the best of their ability, and if somebody hurt one of the Haleks, he had to face all of them.

"How..." It was impossible to complete the question, but Alastor knew.

"Tycho challenged Leander. Blood battles are common to settle grievances or answer a question of strength, but there was an... accident in the arena. Tragic." His voice sounded rusty and thick, and she reacted without thinking.

Not as a doctor, or as a woman, but as she would want to be treated. Sheyla wrapped her arms around him and was shocked by how tightly he held onto her, as if nobody had comforted him before this moment. Stroking his back, she considered all the details he hadn't imparted: how brutal that death must have been, how impossible to deal with grief when murder masqueraded as tragedy.

"Tycho probably didn't let you mourn," she guessed.

"Not for long. He paid lip service and executed the person in charge of maintaining the sparring equipment."

"Fuuuuck." Sheyla drew the word out because it stood in for her unanswered rage, surely only a shadow of his own.

"Quite. I was fifteen at the time and about to die. I thought about challenging Tycho then. I knew I couldn't kill him, but I could've stopped pretending to accept his lies at least."

A cold hand seized at her heart, clenching tight. His illness felt like a mortal enemy, one that she must fight with all the skill at her command. "The serum...?"

"Over time, my body adapts, the medicine loses efficacy, tumors return, and the doctors must adjust the treatment." He pulled back enough to give that heartbreaking smile and brushed the hair from her forehead. "We're in that stage now, more or less, with you trying to find a chemical configuration that works."

"I will. The labs in Hallowell—" She broke off, recalling that she needed to tell a happy story now. From the sounds outside, the camp was stirring, so she should make it quick. "Never mind that. Let's talk about my brother, Avi."

"Which one is he?'

"The youngest. You saw him briefly, but right now, he has long hair... does that help?"

"I remember. Go on."

He didn't let go of her, which was a little distracting even if he wasn't naked. In the past, Sheyla hadn't spent much time curled up with her sex partners. Work always seemed more pressing than conversation or simple contact. Now she wondered if she might've missed out.

"Right. Anyway, about Avi, he learned to shift young. Not just pre-puberty, but he was barely *verbal*. I'm not sure how much you know about the Animari, but that's rare."

"I bet it was challenging."

"You have no idea. Toddlers are bad enough when they can run off as bipeds. Now imagine how much trouble he caused as a kitten."

His laughter rumbled through her since they were so close, and she liked it. More than a little. Instead of medicine, she might take up amusing Alastor full time. A strange sweetness shivered through her, so that her hands curled on his shoulders. An idle wish surfaced—that she wasn't the only one undressed, so she could touch his skin.

"I love this story already."

"He drove us all crazy. But one morning, we woke to find him missing. At first, we thought he was hiding, so we called for him, moved all the furniture. No Avi."

"He wasn't in the house?"

She shook her head. "I was angry at first, and then worried. We all missed school, scouring the hold for him. No luck until nightfall."

"What happened?" he urged.

"We got a report that our little runaway had been stuck in a tree all day. He was fine, just hungry and scared. The next day, we Avi-proofed the house so he couldn't escape."

"It must be… good. To be part of a family like that."

"I like it," Sheyla said. "But I'm starting to think I don't appreciate them enough."

There were disadvantages of course and sad moments that it wasn't the time to share. Her goal was to cheer him up, not make him feel sorry for her.

ALASTOR COULD'VE HAPPILY talked about her family longer; in truth, he would've done almost anything to keep her close. Questions teemed in his head. *What to ask first?* He had a fervent curiosity about everything Sheyla.

The crunch of boots on the snow outside the tent quelled him. Then Dedrick called, "We're moving soon."

"Be right there."

It had been a long, strange night; that was for certain. With no little regret, he detached from the warm tangle of limbs and left Sheyla the covers for privacy. Keeping his back to her, he layered up in winter gear, packed his things, and pulled on his boots. Since she was Animari, she ought to be able to get her clothes on fast. Finally, he got his medicine and downed it in a single swallow. Bitter, as always, but it should keep him alive until they reached Hallowell.

"I made enough to last two weeks," she said. "I'll tweak the formula when I have access to better equipment."

"It will be fine." With that, he slipped out and found Ded waiting, impatiently pacing in the snow, so that his tracks framed the tent entrance. "Any trouble in the night?" Alastor asked.

His injured arm throbbed, but it was tolerable. Transformation would probably open the wound again, so Alastor hoped for a quiet day.

"Nothing much, though I hear the Eldritch didn't sleep well." Ded's white teeth flashed in the predawn light, showing only a hint of his true amusement.

His lips twitched. "That's too bad."

Without further comment, he set to work beside Ded, packing up supplies for the next leg of the journey. Because of the battle, they were a bit behind schedule, and they had to figure out how best to move the RVAC. The platform was unwieldy and would slow them down... as he labored, he sorted possible solutions and only once he settled did he seek out the Noxblade leader, Gavriel. Who was clearly in a mood.

"What?"

Alastor held up a hand in a pacifying gesture. "Have you worked out what to do with the weapon yet?"

Because I have.

"One problem at a time," Gavriel snapped. "We're still working on the comm array and dividing up the rations."

"I think I can help. I'll put my men on the RVAC and detach it. I'll ask for a volunteer to transport it."

The Noxblade paused long enough that it seemed as if he must have a thousand objections. What he eventually said was, "Very well."

"You're welcome," Alastor muttered.

Lack of sleep seemed to have all the Eldritch on edge whereas his troops were cheerful despite the cold. He huddled up with Ded, Rowena, and a few others, briefing them on what needed to happen with the RVAC. The five of them partially dismantled the platform mount, and then Ded transformed to rip it loose.

"You won't be giving that back, will you?"

"*I'll carry it,*" Ded said in base-Gol.

Rowena was already gathering cords to fasten the cannon to Ded's back. "This should help balance the load and make it easier to haul."

"I hope we don't need to use it," Alastor said, only half-joking.

"We will," Rowena answered. "Sooner or later."

Whether they fired it on the way to the rendezvous or in defense of Hallowell, there was no disputing that. Tightness claimed his chest when he thought about the body count. For somebody who had never participated in blood battles or proved his strength in Golgerra, it seemed unspeakably brazen to rise against Tycho. *If not me, who? There's no one.* Alastor touched the spot on his arms where the names of his dead siblings were inked and took strength from that silent promise. Justice could be bought, if only he bolstered himself to pay.

"Are you well, Your Highness?" Rowena took an anxious step toward him, but he waved her away.

Given half a chance, she'd offer to carry him. Since he'd saved her from the execution block, her devotion bordered on unbalanced. He was struggling with similar feelings toward the doctor, likely for the same reasons. Alastor didn't like hearing that his attraction probably stemmed from some deep-seated psychological motive, but it made sense. Too bad his sex drive didn't grasp the nuances, because he still wanted Sheyla.

Want wasn't quite the right word. *Ache* came closer, and the feeling intensified as she stepped out of their tent. That thought alone made him feel possessive, not a distraction he could afford. Alastor had long suspected that he likely wouldn't survive long enough to take a mate, so it was fucking inconvenient for those instincts to manifest now. In his current situation, the match that made the most sense was a political marriage to Princess Thalia, who wouldn't give a damn when he died, and who would, hopefully, honor the alliance after he expired.

He supposed a high-ranking female from Pine Ridge or Burnt Amber could serve as well. In any case, he shouldn't be staring with hungry eyes at his personal physician, who had made it clear that she wasn't interested in even a brief liaison. Before he could let himself wilt at the thought, he swiveled his gaze to Gavriel, who was shouting orders.

"Get the last of those tents packed, we're moving in five!"

Since his was one of those specified, he strode over to help with the stowing, thus avoiding Sheyla. Things felt different since he'd kissed her breathless, left his mark on her throat, and then whispered about his dead brother in the dark. For both their sakes, it would be better to keep his distance.

After that, he didn't have time to contemplate such things. As he'd expected, running in the cold stole his breath and sent fresh sparks of pain with each stride. It seemed like a thousand years before the group paused for food, rest, and water; it would be even longer before they stopped for the night. He'd seen the distance they had to cover.

Though it was just past noon, it felt later since the sky was overcast and the scant sunlight was already filtered through the evergreen canopy. Some of the trees were dead with winter, branches bare, and he leaned up against a quaking aspen, angling his head back to narrow his eyes on a sliver of sky so pale that it looked like an ice field overhead. Someone pressed a mug on him, steam rising from the cup, and he murmured a thank-you before realizing it was Sheyla, not Rowena, who normally hovered.

Thankfully she didn't ask if he was holding up all right or how he felt at all. It was probably written in the half-frozen sweat trickling down his face. "We have *how* many more days of this... Is it too late to back out and wish you well?"

Since she was smiling, Alastor reckoned she was joking, a welcome change from her somber hospital mien. "I won't hold you," he said.

Something flashed in her face, a shadow, perhaps, but her smile stayed. "Well, now I can't even complain. Don't be so serious."

"That's not something I ever pictured you saying to me."

"Life is change," she said, blotting away his sweat with a gloved hand.

"If only all change were good."

Alastor stared across the clearing at the RVAC, now propped beside Ded in the snow. He couldn't help but notice the tension between Eldritch and Golgoth troops. A better leader would probably have found a way to mitigate that by now. Leaning beside him, Sheyla followed his gaze and nudged his shoulder with hers.

"What are you planning to do about that?"

There was no reason to pretend he needed clarification; she had to see the conflict brewing. The Eldritch gave the Golgoth a wide berth, and he heard whispers from his own people. "I'm open to ideas."

She shook her head. "Dealing with people isn't my forte."

"Traveling limits my options. Otherwise, we could have a tournament."

"Actually..." Sheyla paused, seeming as if she wasn't sure she should continue, so Alastor leaned where their shoulders were still touching, a silent *go on*. Her heat permeated all the layers between them, summoning a delicious memory of how she felt against him. Deliberately he stepped a pace to the left, breaking contact.

"From what I've seen in the pride hierarchy, everything starts at the top. The soldiers aren't missing the fact that Gavriel doesn't like you. And vice versa."

"Brilliant, as ever. Then... my next mission is to make peace with the Noxblade."

8.

OF ALL THINGS, Sheyla didn't expect Alastor to invite a handful of Noxblades to his tent for a gaming session, including Zan and Gavriel.

Yet here they were, arrayed in a circle, each guarding their cards like it was a holy mission. She had some in her hand too, but she was tired enough from the day's run that she didn't care about winning. Reluctantly she had to admire the prince's determination because he must be exhausted too, but he'd taken her remark to heart that morning and seemed committed to improving his relationship with the Eldritch.

"Call," Gavriel said.

"I fold." Sheyla gave up and the other Noxblades followed suit.

With a rueful smile, Alastor showed his cards and lost gracefully. Again. Sheyla narrowed her eyes. Even if you were terrible at 18 Jack, the odds were, you'd get a good hand at some point. Such continued bad luck seemed suspicious. She studied him as Gavriel collected his modest winnings; they were betting for paltry coins, nothing exceptional, but the white-haired assassin radiated a quiet gratification. Zan met her gaze with silent amusement, then glanced at the prince, seeming to share her conclusion.

You're doing this on purpose.

Such an obvious tactic, but the atmosphere had eased from angry acquiescence to casual enjoyment. She had been heating some barley wine for the past quarter hour and now it steamed deliciously as she topped off everyone's cups. When Gavriel raised his glass to Alastor, he didn't seem to feel the same animosity. The hot drink had a stronger flavor than Sheyla was used to, brewed in Golgerra, and it tasted earthy and dark, a hint of burnt toffee, both bitter and sweet in the lingering aftertaste. From the Eldritch reactions, she guessed it must be quite alcoholic, too, but her metabolism burned through it too fast for her to notice more than a mild tingle.

"Another game?" Alastor asked.

"I would rather have a candid conversation." Gavriel drained his cup and set it down, high color glazing his sharp cheekbones.

"Please, speak freely," the prince invited.

"Can we count on you?" The bald question startled Sheyla sufficiently that she nearly dropped the thermos.

"That depends on what you're expecting," Alastor said.

"None of your sophistry. I've heard you talk circles around people in Ash Valley, all mockery, and amusement. But sending my men to battle on your orders isn't a game, and the princess stands to lose everything if we ally with you in vain."

"I cannot promise you victory. That would be irresponsible. What I *can* swear is that I will give everything I have to stop my brother." Sheyla had never heard Alastor sound so grave, and he held Gavriel's gaze until the Noxblade nodded.

"That's enough. I'll quell my resentment at being sent away from the princess. She doesn't need me beside her." Those words came out glazed with bitterness, and from the flicker of chagrin on the assassin's face, Sheyla could only conclude that the barley wine had loosened his tongue. "And that's none of your doing, in any event."

"Let's work well together," Alastor said, offering his hand.

From what she could tell, the handshake sealed the peace, and the Noxblades left shortly thereafter. The tent remained warm with their leftover heat, so she didn't need to shift to get comfortable enough to sleep. Outside, the wind buffeted the fabric walls, so they seemed to be shivering. It was hard not to think of everything that could go wrong, how quickly they could be exterminated by Tycho's forces.

We are so few.

Sheyla didn't let herself linger on those fears; there was no point. As she rolled into her blankets, she said, "Good job."

"Are you *praising* my efforts?" He turned off the light but she could still see him, sharply delineated in the darkness.

"You say it like it's never happened."

"It hasn't."

"Me in particular or… anyone?" It was easy to keep him at a distance during the daylight hours, when there were only the cold and discomfort and endless running. Once they took shelter, it was another story entirely.

"I don't know," he admitted. "Before, you said I was brave, but that's not the same."

"I suppose not."

She had the idea that in Golgerra they had made his life entirely about his illness, but she'd asked enough intrusive questions that she hesitated over inflicting harm for the sake of her own curiosity. Still, she was tempted to ask; in the end, she decided that if he wanted her to know more, he would volunteer it. Nearly holding her breath, she waited for his next words.

Which were, "Good night, Sheyla."

His withdrawal left her oddly disappointed. Though she'd told herself that she shouldn't feel anything other than empathy for him, she didn't enjoy his silence or the sense that he would prefer not to confide in her. It took her longer than she expected to fall asleep, though the awakening came sharp and cold, sooner than she would've liked.

Icy air blasted her when the prince slipped out of the tent. She groaned and wished she could take a hot bath as she downed the last of their packed provisions. *From now on, we hunt.* With an Animari patrol that would prove no problem, but the Golgoth seemed better suited for mass carnage than securing food. Likewise, while the Eldritch might be effective silent killers, she wasn't sure about their woodcraft. Worst-case scenario, she could hunt for herself and Alastor. If the others arrived at the rendezvous hungry, it wouldn't end them.

The next two days were harrowing. Sheyla wasn't the fittest of her pride and the constant movement took a toll. They played hide and seek with another of Tycho's patrols and in the evening, she couldn't rest; she prowled the forest in search of prey. That first night, the caribou herds were skittish and she couldn't get close enough to take one down. In the morning, there was no breakfast other than dry crackers and hot barleywine.

Alastor was pale, not as he usually was, but with trembling hands and pronounced bruising in his joints. "I'm fine," he said, trying to wave her away.

"You're not. The serum isn't working properly, and you're not eating enough."

"Nobody is. The cold's taking a toll too, and not only on me. Have you seen—"

"I'm not in charge of them," she snapped.

"There's nothing more we can do out here. Let's just keep moving."

Before the squad departed, she treated two Eldritch for mild frostbite and she bit off a curse that she couldn't help them properly. Vowing to do better, she stripped, shifted, and ran ahead, ignoring the prince's protest and Gavriel's questioning shout. As the sole Animari in this group, she could stalk and scout at the same time. *I have to get some proper food in him.* That thought drove her forward.

The ground froze her paws. Unlike Dominic, the pride master, she wasn't adapted for winter and would rather not hunt in the snow. *At least I have fur, unlike the Eldritch.* Their chilblains and cold-numb hands troubled her. Though she'd signed on as Alastor's personal physician, she couldn't ignore others who were suffering.

Her head cocked, ears swiveling. Sheyla lifted her face to the wind, wishing for camouflage, but her spots stood out warm and stark against the winter wood. Above, tree limbs groaned with the weight of icicles dripping from their branches. Holes perforated the snowy ground from where they'd fallen like frozen spears. Smaller paw prints dotted the white as well; identifying them by scent required nothing more than a sharp intake of breath.

Her tail swished. Nothing big enough nearby to make a substantial meal. Most of the birds had flown for warmer climes. There were only the herds, lean and dwindling in the gloomy months. Overhead, the sky was gray, cut with shivering clouds, and the sun no more than a slice of light that failed to yield warmth.

Yet she smelled something in the air—to the east, the caribou she needed to run down and drag back to the others, and to the west, the coppery stink of blooded Golgoth hung heavy as a threat. She snarled softly, torn between needing to hunt and to acquire intel. It would likely save lives if she could report how many enemies were nearby, but if Alastor collapsed on the trail from a combination of low caloric intake and her insufficient serum configuration—

What would he have me do? After a moment of reflection, she sprang off to the west.

"THIS IS UNWISE," Dedrick said in base-Gol, some hours later.

The doctor had been missing the entirety of that time, but Alastor couldn't show how shaken he was. He pretended he didn't know what his friend was driving at as he sipped from a steaming hot drink. "What is?"

"She kept your mark, sire, and you scan the horizon, not for threats, but for her."

It was impossible to deny. He could've claimed that he did it because he only had a limited number of vials left, and that he'd begin dying in increments when he ran out. Those rationalizations would even be true, but they didn't encompass what he was feeling, like a taloned hand had reached into him and tangled in his intestines. Gavriel had already chewed him out because he didn't know why Sheyla had split from the group or what she was planning.

Finally, he said, "She's necessary. You know that."

They had reached the halfway point in the day's march, pausing briefly for rest and hydration. It wasn't a campsite but the Noxblades still set watches. The tension had improved enough that at least he wasn't worried about infighting anymore. He wished he could change and spell Ded on carrying the RVAC, but he had to ration his energy. Already it seemed like continuing might be more than he could manage. That was nothing new, but the circumstances had seldom been so dire or so demanding.

His bodyguard said nothing more, though his eyes spoke volumes. Rowena interrupted just then, trying to offer her meager rations; Alastor declined, as he didn't miss how delicate she'd become in only a few days. She was shivering nonstop, a discomfort he shared, and it seemed as if he might never be warm again. There was no one he could tell either, as the Exiles looked to him for leadership. With Sheyla, it was permissible to show when he was weak, when he was hurting, and not simply because she was a doctor.

Where the hell has she gone?

"Moving out," Gavriel called.

Possibly he should take a more active role in dictating their movements, but he couldn't muster the vim for a pissing match. Let the Noxblade handle logistics. If they engaged on Alastor's command, that was enough leadership. For all he knew, the troops might fight as long as he was propped up as an alternative to Tycho.

Damn depressing thought.

Since they were only hours away from reaching the

rendezvous coordinates, he focused on getting there. The pain was constant in his joints and his chest kept tightening—to the point that it seemed he wasn't getting enough oxygen as he ran. Sparks popped before his eyes, a distant drumming in his ears that he knew was only the echo of his accelerated heartbeat. Soon, this would escalate into a full-blown attack, and the frosty air exacerbated his condition.

A shout from the lieutenant, Zan, made Gavriel call for a halt. "Report!"

Stopping the forced march gave Alastor a chance to cling to consciousness. He leaned on Ded, glad everyone's attention was focused elsewhere. The soldiers in front parted to reveal a cheetah dragging a bloody carcass toward their group. *She went hunting?* His astonishment nearly distracted him from the waning spasms in his lungs.

As if that wasn't maddening enough, she didn't stop, no matter who stepped into her path. Leaving a blood trail in the snow, she dragged her kill right up to Alastor and dropped it before him. Her whole body shuddered and then there was a naked woman on all fours at his feet. Alastor swooped down on her so fast, his head swam. Without hesitation, he stripped out of his coat and wrapped her in it.

He half-expected her to shove him away, but instead, her icy hands curled into his shirt, holding on for dear life. Through chattering teeth, she tried to speak and he barked an order at everyone within earshot. "Get her a hot drink and something to wear. Now." The last word came out in a roar and Ded almost dropped the RVAC.

Rowena scrambled away, returning in two heartbeats with an armful of clothes and steaming metal cup. He held up the coat to shield Sheyla from the curious looks; apparently naked women weren't common in Eldritch culture either. When Gavriel strode toward them, Alastor strangled the urge to tear his face off.

"Not now. Give us five minutes."

At Alastor's gesture, Ded stepped between them and six more Golgoth soldiers, including Rowena and Graff, formed a protective circle. Sheyla was trembling too hard to get dressed on her own, so Alastor swore as he helped her. *She's so fucking cold.*

"I need a fire built yesterday and someone to field dress that wildebeest."

Gavriel said, "It's not a—"

"Is that what matters right now?" Damn, but he wanted to change and wipe the attitude off the Noxblade's face.

The Eldritch didn't back down. "We don't have time to warm ourselves around a crackling fire. It'll give away our position, too."

"He's right," Sheyla managed. "Get our heater. We should have some energy left and there will be no plume of smoke for the enemy to follow."

She was dressed, but she didn't look good. Hell, none of them did, but he'd never seen her like this, as if she was shards of amber glass that would puff to powder with a touch. It was all but impossible to check the fear that bubbled into his throat, interfering with his breathing.

Ded was already doing as she asked as Rowena put the cup in Sheyla's hands. He left his men circled as a windbreak, the best he could do. She drained the mug and whispered, "Please," for more in a voice so raw that it hurt him to hear it. *What happened to you out there?*

While they located the heater, Alastor followed his snarling instincts and drew her to him, wrapping them both in his voluminous coat. Tucked against his chest, she seemed smaller than usual, as if this experience had already diminished her. That was just his imagination, of course, but it was hard not to feel that he might devour everyone in his path, seeing nothing, permitting nothing but an undifferentiated march to power.

Just like my brother.

The heater kicked in, glowing orange, and she immediately drew back to squat before it. Sheyla gulped down another mug of hot barleywine as she warmed up. On the other side of the clearing, the Eldritch were making short work of the beast she'd brought, butchering and cleaning it with an expertise that suggested they might be skilled hunters. Blood infused the air, and all around him, he watched other Golgoth faces go hungry and avid. Alastor felt the same urge, a twitch in muscles that wanted to burst and swell, hands that wanted to stretch into claws.

"*You must stop.*" Ded's snarl in base-Gol cut into Alastor's aching, violent impulses. At first, Alastor thought he meant the bloodlust, so he was already nodding, shamefaced, when Ded went on. "*You offer a blood mark. She brings food to fill your belly. You will not allow others to gaze upon her. It was bad enough when I only saw flickers of it in you, sire, but she is responding in kind. Even if you want her, you cannot have her. You must look higher—*"

"Enough," he bit out.

Alastor already *knew* this, so why was he so blisteringly angry over hearing Dedrick state the facts? His hand curled into a fist, and he turned away unexpectedly enough that he caught a haunted light in Rowena's silvery eyes. She ducked her head quickly, still sending a pang through him. After all this time, she still thought she wasn't worthy to gaze upon him; they'd fucked her up properly in the undercity... or maybe she was reacting to Ded's warning. At least Sheyla didn't seem to understand the conflict.

Before he could address Rowena's reaction, Sheyla straightened. She no longer looked half-frozen and urgency brightened her gaze. He shouldn't be looking at the curves of her mouth when she spoke or admiring the raven spill of her hair, tumbling from the flaps of her hat. Gavriel tried to push forward to hear whatever news the doctor had delivered at such cost. Though it irked him, Alastor splayed his hands, indicating his guard should give way.

"Sorry, it's been a tough day and I needed to collect myself."

"What did you learn?" Alastor asked, mostly to preempt the Noxblade.

Sheyla took a breath, let it out, and when she answered, her tone was somber. "Over two hundred Golgoth stand between us and the rendezvous. They've laid a trap…and if we don't warn our allies, we're looking at our first massacre."

9.

RELIEVED TO HAVE delivered the message, Sheyla relaxed a little as reactions rumbled through the group. She'd eaten plenty of meat when she brought down the caribou, so she wasn't weak, just weary and half-frozen. Alastor wore a troubled, pensive expression, which meant he was working out the implications. He and the Noxblade seemed to reach the same conclusion at once, though it was the assassin who spoke first.

"We have to change the meeting point," Gavriel said. "Get on the comm."

Alastor held up a hand, forestalling movement. "There's a risk of signal jacking if we make plans on the wireless. Right now, they're searching for us. If they overhear, they'll know exactly where to look."

"That's true enough. Caution is warranted." Gavriel turned to Sheyla. "Anything you can tell us about the enemy camp would be helpful."

Everyone in their immediate vicinity quieted, leveling their gaze on her. She'd only gotten such a reaction from anxious families waiting for her to deliver a diagnosis. Into the sudden silence, she reported on equipment and weaponry, though she hadn't gotten close enough to get a completely accurate count.

"Could you tell who was leading the troops?" Alastor asked.

Sheyla shook her head. "Sorry. I skirted the perimeter and noted as much as I could, but I was in a hurry to get out of there."

Those numbers...

A shiver that had nothing to do with cold rocked through her. Sheyla had never been more terrified than in those moments when she crept toward the encampment, certain that any moment, one of the watchmen would stumble on her and sound the alarm. Because there was no question of her passing for an actual forest dweller, not in this territory, highlighted by the icy backdrop of a winter wasteland. Eamon's condition when he was ransomed from Golgerra told Sheyla everything she needed to know about how she'd be treated as a prisoner of war.

She started when Alastor pulled her against his side; since he was arguing with Gavriel about the risks involved with contacting the other Animari, she suspected it was a reflexive move. For a couple of seconds, she considered elbowing him to get loose, but his body heat felt so good that she couldn't force herself to do it. If she was completely honest, there was comfort in his unconscious support, too.

"Can't we encrypt?" Gavriel was asking.

Alastor sighed. "Of course, but we're using *our* tech. Don't you think Tycho's people can crack it? Hell, since we *stole* it from them, they might even have the key already."

That made perfect sense to Sheyla, though Gavriel seemed irritated that Alastor was only offering problems, not solutions. "Someone has to carry a message," she said.

"Someone quick and quiet, preferably."

Gavriel beckoned a pair of Noxblades, but unease gnawed at the back of her mind. She'd heard whispers of how first contact between the Noxblades and the pride master had gone catastrophically wrong. On the whole, the Animari didn't trust the Eldritch, so she didn't know if sending one of these fey bastards would work.

She vaguely recalled that the Order of St. Casimir was donating war machines, so the meeting might be with Callum from Burnt Amber, but it was unlikely that Raff would be leading the Pine Ridge delegation in sending reinforcements and supplies to Hallowell. Additionally, she had no reason to believe that these assassins knew shit about Animari diplomacy. The problem was, the Golgoth wouldn't fare any better. In fact, the Animari might attack first and ask questions later, just as Dominic had done at the retreat.

Alastor nudged her, jolting her out of her thoughts. "You look like you ate something bad. What's wrong?"

Sheyla raised onto her toes to whisper, "This won't work. The rally point was arranged through channels, and they won't agree to deviate from orders because a random Eldritch said so. They'll question the veracity of the intel and probably wonder if it's coming from the remnant of Talfayen's traitors."

"I can't raise those objections without a plan B. You saw how he reacted to my suggestion that using the comm could be risky."

Dammit. Only one solution that made sense. She was reluctant to speak up because she didn't *want* to do it. The feeling was barely coming back into her fingers and toes, and she was so damn tired. Sighing, Sheyla rested her head against Alastor's shoulder for a moment. Something flashed in his green gaze and then he brushed a gloved hand over her cheek, shaking his head in silent discouragement. Somehow, she knew he was thinking, *You can't.*

I must, she told him silently.

"It appears you have an idea," Gavriel said sharply.

Belatedly she realized there were scores of witnesses to this inappropriate intimacy and pulled away. "I'll go."

"That's absurd," Alastor snapped. "You've only just returned, and you're a physician, not a scout."

"But I'm the only one the Animari will believe."

There was no arguing that. Yet Gavriel didn't seem sold on the notion either. "I'll send Zan with you for protection."

His lieutenant stepped forward; he had unusual eyes, dark as pewter, and burnished coppery hair, unlike most of his compatriots, though otherwise, he was all Eldritch beauty with fine features and a lean build. He executed a neat bow before her.

"I hope we make good time. In Ash Valley, I'm a doctor, not a patrol officer."

Zan smiled. "Everyone knows who you are. You treated my cousin's frostbite."

"Ah. Well…" It would be nice to have company, even a Noxblade she'd hardly knew, but she didn't see how this could serve. "I doubt you'll be able to keep up with me."

"Let me worry about that," he said. "I'll also carry provisions and gear for you, which should make your return trip more comfortable."

As Sheyla nodded and went to unbutton her coat, Alastor grabbed her hands. "You can't actually intend to do this."

"It's not my first choice either but it's the best hope for

saving our allies without compromising our position."

"She's right," Gavriel said. "We'll maintain radio silence until we arrange a new rendezvous."

The prince clenched his jaw on whatever he wanted to say, holding onto her hands until she thought she might have to pull free forcibly. Then he deliberately schooled his features, opened his fingers and stepped back. He beckoned to the pale-haired girl who always seemed to be hovering in proximity.

"Fetch the maps, lovely. We need to plot a new course."

A frisson of annoyance curled through her at the casual endearment. Alastor shouldn't flirt with a girl who already saw him as the moon and stars. She resisted the urge to scold him as Zan leaned in to say, "As soon as they give new coordinates, we should go."

She nodded. Hopefully, the new site would permit them to skirt the huge group of Golgoth. Engaging those forces with their current numbers and supplies would be suicide. Sheyla didn't realize she'd said it aloud until Alastor cut her a sharp look.

"Unless we use the RVAC."

A weighted silence fell. Using an auto cannon in the field meant pure carnage. She suspected the group they'd intercepted had meant to lay siege to Ash Valley. Properly deployed, one such weapon would decimate hundreds of soldiers, even changed Golgoth shock troops. By Alastor's grim expression, he was willing to make that dreadful choice. For the greater good. Judging from the flicker of self-loathing she caught before his lashes swept down, he too thought there should be limits to what sins he'd commit in pursuit of victory.

She wanted to comfort him. The urge swept her from head to toe, and she even took a step toward him like they were magnets with an opposite charge. Zan stayed her with a hand tapping lightly on her shoulder. "What would you like me to pack for you?"

"I've never had valet service before," she said.

His mouth quirked in quiet appreciation of her attempt at humor, considering their overall shitty circumstances. "It's my pleasure."

It took all of five minutes to load Zan's rucksack with useful items, another five for Gavriel and Alastor to decide on a new site to meet up with the Animari. Before Sheyla shifted, the prince leaned close and his whispered "come back to me," gusted so sweet against her ear, that she shivered.

"Ready?" Zan asked.

"As I'll ever be."

"Then let's do this."

WRONG. YOU CANNOT *take her. She is my, my...my what?* Once, the answer would've been doctor, and he could've stopped there. But now, there was only one word for her, one he could never speak aloud.

Mine.

As the Noxblade assigned to protect Sheyla spread his cloak so she could change, Alastor bit back a snarl. He could've happily snapped that bastard's neck for sheltering her, for touching her clothes, plucking them from the snow and tucking them away in his pack. It didn't matter that he was only following orders; that knowledge did nothing to assuage Alastor's wrath. He rumbled deep in his throat and clenched his fist against the burn of the spikes needling down his spine. From the hot trickle of blood, he guessed he wasn't entirely successful. Ded clenched his forearm, he contained himself. Took a deep breath. Another.

"Enough," Ded growled. *"This is bigger than you. And her."*

The other man had acted as his bodyguard and friend for years, but never had he served as the voice of reason. With effort, Alastor turned his back and moved away. Each step felt like he was treading across razor wire and broken glass. A glance over one shoulder showed him the faint spatter of red left from his near lapse of control.

This is best. This is the safe course.

Yet no amount of logic silenced the word *mine* echoing in the back of his mind. Alastor didn't look again until he was sure she'd gone. Instead of thinking about the doctor, he strode toward Gavriel, conscious that everyone was waiting to see what he'd do next. His own people knew of his condition, but it wasn't common knowledge among the Eldritch yet.

"There's no need to push the men," he said. "We can pause for a meal before we move. The new rendezvous will take longer than six hours to reach, even at a hard march, and we have to allow Dr. Halek time to reach the Animari."

"Agreed," Gavriel said. "But the no-fire rule still applies.

Alastor shrugged. "My people will eat the meat raw. Will yours?"

In answer, the Noxblade jerked his head toward the caribou, which was nearly carved down to the bone. His men had such expert knife skills that they were slicing the steaks wafer thin and wolfing them down. Reluctantly amused, Alastor inclined his head, acknowledging that the assassin had scored a point.

"We are not as squeamish as you imagine," Gavriel said, and there was a wealth of darkness in his blood-red gaze.

"That's an unsubtle hint if ever I heard one. Consider me cautioned." With a faint smile, he spun and raised his voice to carry. "Time to feast, you will need your strength!"

From their expressions, the men wanted to shout their support, but they contented themselves with raising an arm skyward, and then, one by one, they dropped to a knee and bowed their heads, pressing a fist against their chests. The silent act of fealty and obedience moved him so fiercely that he had to swipe at his eyes. Alastor blinked once, twice, and then scraped away moisture that froze almost the second it formed.

"Enough," he muttered. "Eat. Eat!"

When he turned, Gavriel was there, like he *always* was. When Alastor moved to step around him, the Noxblade spoke. "I wasn't sure until this moment, but I understand now why they follow you."

"And why is that?"

"Not from fear of your brother. Not out of respect for your good deeds. It is pure love. There's nothing stronger to compel complete compliance."

"I don't care if they obey," Alastor snapped. "I wouldn't stop a single soldier who wanted to go his own way, even now."

"Your men know that. It's part of why they love you." Gavriel paused, not seeming to be aware of the picture he was compressing into the snow. It looked to Alastor as if he was forming the letter T. "Our princess is that way. She cares nothing for hierarchy, only free will."

"I'd venture to guess that you esteem her more than

most," he said.

The Noxblade let out a sigh. "We're all guilty of wanting what we can't have from time to time."

"Why can't you?"

Gavriel only lifted a shoulder and headed for the raw steak. That seemed like both a good idea and an indication that the conversation was over, so Alastor followed. With Ded and Rowena close at hand, he ate his fill. There was next to nothing left when everyone finished, and Alastor suspected some still weren't full. Physical comfort had to wait until they reached the comparative safety of Hallowell, assuming it wasn't already too late.

"How long until we make the new rendezvous?" Alastor asked Rowena after she'd eaten.

"Twelve hours, if we move a little faster than before."

Inwardly, he winced. He was already running on fumes. He gave a curt nod. "Let the Noxblade know, will you?"

She hesitated. "Must I?"

Alastor tipped his head. This was the first time she'd ever quibbled over a request. "Has Gavriel done something to offend you?"

"Not exactly."

"Tell me," he ordered.

"He seems to think I'm..."

"What?"

"A camp follower. It's nothing he's said. Just... an impression I get. Maybe I'm being too sensitive." Her shoulders hunched and once again, she couldn't meet his gaze.

"Unlikely." Considering how broken she was when he pulled her from the block, it was a huge leap forward that she trusted him enough to object. "Never mind."

In the milling confusion of two separate squads, he found Ded sucking the marrow from a rib bone, then he crunched up the shards and downed them with relish. *"You need me?"*

The guard had to be exhausted from holding his changed form for so long, plus battling primal instincts. Alastor asked, "Did something happen between Rowena and Gavriel?"

"He gave her a…look that first morning. After the fight. Seems to think that she was the center of an orgy. She was in my tent, and most of the men were entertained with each other." That was a lot of words in base-Gol, and the conversation drew stares from the Eldritch nearby.

A few narrowed their eyes, like Alastor was plotting against them. He ignored the scrutiny. "Fuck. Regardless, it's not his place to approve or disapprove. I guess the Eldritch tend toward prudery. I'll talk to him."

"I recommend you drop it down the priority list. We have more important issues."

"Noted. I'll put a pin in it. Let's get the men motivated, shall we?"

Gavriel joined them in time to hear that. "Sounds like a plan." When he beckoned, an Eldritch ran toward him. "I need you to check our route. Double back instantly if you spot trouble. We only get one shot at this meetup."

"Understood, sir."

The group rolled out ten minutes after the scout, and by then, Alastor had mustered enough energy that he could pretend he wasn't half-dead already. Pain throbbed through him, so generalized that he couldn't even figure out what was hurting. They had only been running for an hour when the sentry burst from the trees, snow churning beneath his feet.

"They're moving," the man gasped. "Only a few klicks out."

Gavriel swore. "They're on a search and destroy. Either us or the Animari."

"Or both." At this point, it hardly mattered who the Golgoth death squad planned to kill. Sooner or later it would be everyone who refused to swear fealty to Tycho.

"Best analysis?" Gavriel prompted.

The scout took a deep breath. "It's impossible for us to avoid hostile engagement before we rendezvous with the Animari. I picked up some chatter on the comm… they're running vehicular sweeps in a twenty-klick radius with shock troops on standby. They've got two C-TAKs, a whole Rover full of artillery, and—"

"We must clear a path," Ded cut in.

There was no way he could permit those soldiers to carry out their orders. Knowing his brother, this would end in a scorched earth initiative, and the worst part was, there must be multiple units in the field, geared for mass extermination.

Have mercy on my soul, Alastor thought.

Then he made the only decision he could. "I want the best tech we've got, front and center. We need the RVAC targeting system online as soon as possible."

10.

SHEYLA'S EARS FLICKED backwards.

They were finally on the right track. Dark had fallen hours before, and for the first time, she caught a scent of wolf on the wind. Her breath huffed out in relief, as she'd been worried that she wouldn't find the Animari before they reached the original rally point. Zan had been quiet during the run and surprisingly swift. Not once had he needed to ask her to slow down or let him rest, a feat she'd inquire about when they had time to spare.

As the brindle wolf broke from the evergreen tangle, she shifted and said, "The main group can't be far behind. Take me to them."

The wolf growled; she understood enough rudimentary canid to know it was an assent. Switching forms yet again in the cold, after running for what felt like two days straight, sapped the last of her strength. All four of her legs trembled as she sprang after the scout. She went muzzle first into the snow and hissed as she scrambled up before the Eldritch could offer a hand.

There's no time for this.

She found enough reserve energy to catch up with the

wolf. The smell of unchanged wolves and bears lit up the forest, but well before that, she heard the clanking gears of the vehicles transporting the promised war machines. Luckily, they didn't have to run far, less than two klicks before they reached the Animari reinforcements. The scout shifted first and shouted for the company to halt; Sheyla took the opportunity to layer up and keep from developing her own case of frostbite.

The icy wind still bit through her clothes. She didn't recognize any of the wolves by sight or scent, but Callum McRae must be overseeing the delivery of armaments for the Order of St. Casimir. She tucked her gloved hands into her sleeves, wincing at the cold ache that went all the way down to her bones. Professionally she knew she needed to worry when the feeling went entirely, but this still sucked. The soldiers didn't seem happy to be cooling their heels in the cold either, but this was life and death.

Now changed and dressed, the brindle wolf scout turned out to be a rangy man with salt and pepper hair and permanently weathered features. "What the hell is this?" he demanded.

Sheyla shook her head. "Don't waste my time, we don't have a lot of it. If you don't have clearance to authorize a new rendezvous, find me somebody who does. I'll talk to Callum and whoever's in charge of the wolves."

He stared for a long moment and then whirled with a mumbled, "Fucking cats."

"Is there tension among Animari factions?" Zan asked.

Probably she shouldn't answer truthfully, but they were allies, right? "Some is inevitable. Generally, we get on well enough."

She stamped her feet, pacing in a tight circuit, until a

towering figure broke through the lines and strode toward her. He looked like a statue come to life, stone-faced and imposing, wrapped in layers of wool, leather, and bristling fur. She would've recognized the bearded Callum anywhere; it was a relief to find at least one familiar face. A lean, silver-haired woman followed him, wolf by the smell of her.

Callum was terse, as ever, one of the things Sheyla liked best about him. "This is Raff's second, Korin. You have something to say?"

Thus prompted, she spilled the news about the Golgoth combat unit and provided the new rendezvous coordinates. "We can't afford to lose any of these supplies," Sheyla said.

"We *might* be able to take that many Golgoth on the ground, but if—"

"The battle goes south, Hallowell is fucked," Callum finished. "We won't risk it." His long legs ate up the distance as he went to spread the word.

Watching him, Korin sighed and shook her head. "He didn't bother telling me your name since he already knew it."

"I'm Sheyla Halek, resident physician in Ash Valley."

"Korin Bowery." The other woman surveyed her and then asked, "How long has it been since you ate?"

Sheyla shrugged; it was too much effort to count back. Beside her, the Eldritch assassin was subtly tallying men and equipment. That shouldn't worry her since he was a member of Gavriel's team and surely he was well-vetted, but the cries of the wounded from the bombs Talfayen had set off were still fresh in her head.

"Follow me. One of the vehicles has hot food."

She had no thought of protesting. As she took the first

step, the ground rumbled beneath her feet. Zan caught her when she went sideways, eyes locked on the massive orange glow on the horizon. The booms and rumbles kept coming after that first strike, continued for a solid five minutes, while everyone stood in shocked silence. Icy winds carried the smell of burning wood and molten metal, charred earth and—

"They used it," Zan whispered.

Before she could reply, Callum had a hold of her arm, shaking her until her teeth clacked. "*Who* has the RVAC? Someone authorized a strike, I need intel."

Sheyla knocked his hands away so hard that it probably would've broken fingers on anyone else. "You won't get info any quicker by pissing me off."

"Cal," the wolf lieutenant chided.

"Fine. Sorry. Now *speak*."

"I was promised food," she said pointedly.

With a muffled curse, the war priest led the way to a Rover, a cramped space for the four of them, all dented metal and rusted rivets, where she curled up in between piles of supplies. Callum prepared a plate and shoved it at her with the least gracious expression ever. Partly to be an asshole and also because she was starved, Sheyla scarfed her food in silence. The Eldritch was just as hungry, she noted, though he kept a watchful eye on the atmosphere.

"We took the RVAC from Tycho's Golgoth a few days ago," she said at last.

"Our allies deployed it," Korin said darkly.

Callum swore and slammed out of the vehicle. At first, Sheyla didn't process the danger. She was too full, too comfortable, and frankly, she was fucking exhausted. But she caught the whispers of depravity as Korin argued with someone outside.

"We pull the plug right now," someone was saying sharply. "No rendezvous, no supplies. We'll be better off on our own."

"I agree." Sheyla recognized Korin's voice, now tight with rage. "I've said since the beginning, we can't trust the fucking Golgoth. This rebel prince is using us to fuel his war of succession, and he might even be worse than his brother."

Sheyla was on her feet and moving before she thought twice. A shoulder nudge banged the door open, revealing a furious Korin, impassive Callum, and the wolf scout. Six eyes locked onto her, but she didn't flinch.

"*That* is bullshit," she snapped. "Prince Alastor didn't order that strike lightly. He wouldn't have done it for power or…" She hesitated, trying to figure out why he would. And then she knew. "He was protecting us. I was already in the wind when the situation broke and they had no way to update us without compromising their position. He's not like his brother. Hell, he doesn't even want the throne. He's fighting to save people, not slaughter them, I swear."

"You're willing to stake everything on that promise?" Callum met her gaze, grave as a funeral song.

She didn't look away. "I am."

"Let me talk it over with some people. Feel free to wait in the Rover." The war priest wheeled away, and the other two followed him like he had a magnet on his back.

The Eldritch hadn't come out into the cold, but he did scrutinize her when she returned. "Did you settle it?"

"I hope so." She couldn't entertain the opposite prospect, and anxiety was chewing at her now, for the survival of the alliance, how Alastor might be faring without her. She asked the question nearly in self-defense. "How did you keep up with me anyway?"

"You *did* seem surprised." Soft, delicate amusement threaded the words.

"Are you telling me or not?"

"It isn't a secret. Much like the Animari learn to shift around puberty, my people develop a gift. Gavriel can manipulate data streams, for instance."

"You mean like wiping his image from surveillance?" Handy for an assassin, Sheyla had to admit.

"Precisely. I, on the other hand... am fast."

"You make it sound so mundane, but from where I'm sitting, it seems like magic."

"That's our mystique," he said lightly.

She had follow-up questions, no chance to ask them, because Callum burst into the Rover and said, "This decision's all on you, doc. We're rolling out on your word."

THERE ARE NO SURVIVORS.

For hours afterward, Alastor replayed those words until it felt like they must burn their way out of his brain and blaze a trail of fire on the snowy ground. Both Ded and Rowena were watching him with anxious eyes; he didn't look at them. He couldn't. With one order, he'd executed hundreds of his own people. They would be calling him a traitor and a butcher in Golgerra, when the news reached the city.

"The crisis is averted," Gavriel said.

The Noxblade's report on salvage echoed in his ears, oddly distant. He couldn't focus and when he lifted a hand to brush away a lock of hair straggling from his untidy ranking braids, he was surprised to see how much it trembled. Quickly Alastor curled his fingers into a fist and tucked it into his pocket. He wasn't cold anymore; actually, he was hot as hell—to the point that an ice bath sounded heavenly.

Feverish. Should've realized it sooner.

They had reached the rendezvous site an hour before, and Alastor wanted to wait out the Animari arrival—to formally offer greetings to his allies—but his strength might not hold. Ded took two steps toward him and Alastor held up a hand, silently shaking his head. He wouldn't get any rest fretting about the Animari, so there was no point in retiring. If he got worse, he'd prop himself against Ded's shoulder and make it look insouciant.

It was a near thing and he was swaying when the rumble of engines broke the silence, followed swiftly by the halogen lights riding high on the front of the Rovers that led the convoy. The vehicles transporting the war machines were slower, grinding of gears that made them sound scary as hell. Alastor squared his shoulders and joined Gavriel, standing at attention for the arriving dignitaries. He nearly tipped over in bowing to the bear leader whose name escaped him, someone else from the wolves, and the whole time, he was scanning for a certain doctor. A sliver of ice dissolved in his heart when he located her, clambering wearily from a rear vehicle, closely flanked by the Eldritch that Gavriel had sent with her.

Other people's words spilled like a river around him, just a rushing of noise, because she was standing ten meters from him and the snow turned to liquid silver at her feet, drowning her in moonlight. His heart turned over or tried to, so there came a wrenching pain in his chest. He wanted to push past everyone and bring her to him, tuck his face in the curve of her neck, and then maybe he could taste again that glimmer of peace that only came when he was listening to her breathe. He wanted to frame her face in his hands and see if her cheekbones would nestle into his palms, if his fingertips would alight perfectly beside her temples. Then he would whisper a thousand endearments, followed by the simplest of questions.

Are you tired? Have you eaten? To someone else, those prosaic queries might reduce him to yeoman status, hardly befitting a prince. But such tender curiosities were the brick and mortar of a life built together, one memory at a time, and it was a magic that he might never possess.

The moment splintered like some mystic mirror when Gavriel elbowed him. "Say something."

Shit.

He'd lost the thread, no context for what had been spoken or asked. "I'm sure you must be exhausted," he managed. "It is late and all of your questions will keep."

"True enough," the bear muttered. "But it's by Dr. Halek's grace that we're here at all."

He had no idea what that meant, but doubtless Sheyla would supply the details. Suddenly he couldn't wait a second longer, executing an ungainly bow and then he carved a path toward her. She didn't pull away when he took her hand and drew her to the tent they shared. Inside, the warm air felt thick in his aching lungs. It seemed as if it had been years since he'd seen her.

Her gaze was appraising, clinical. "You look terrible."

"I missed you," he said—with the wry, silly smile that simultaneously shared and shaded his true heart. "So much I thought I'd die of it."

"Don't even joke. My reputation's at stake."

"Sorry."

"Let me take your temperature." She moved toward her gear bag and he intercepted her, not with a forceful hold, but with a gossamer wreath of fingertips, more easily broken than a whispered promise.

She stilled.

"It's elevated," he said. "Not high enough to damage my brain. Can we not?"

"What?"

"Be doctor and patient. Just for tonight."

"What do you want instead?" A not-quite-casual question and her head was bowed, eyes fixed on that sole point of contact.

To hold you, he thought.

He said the next best thing, and perhaps she wouldn't think it was strange since she'd heard it before, but he *knew* his tone was aching. "To listen to you breathe."

Alastor remembered telling her that he wished not to be alone but to be with someone who didn't need him. His will had changed since then, a slow shift inexorable as lunar tides. Now he could not imagine anything more splendid than being the first face Sheyla Halek sought. Not even stopping his brother and ending the war.

Those dreams he must keep locked away, wrapped in chains like an old treasure chest.

She surprised him then. "I'm cold."

It wasn't like her to complain, and this had a different tenor, as if she was asking him for permission. He said, "Yes" without quite understanding what he was agreeing to. Sheyla put her fingers over his, and she was chilly, a welcome respite from fever heat.

"I'm prescribing energy exchange therapy," she whispered. "To warm me and cool you. It should help both of us rest better."

Alastor swallowed hard, nearly choking on a groan. His hands were deeply unsteady as he adjusted the heater. She was serene in stripping down whereas he was all eagerness and thumbs. Somehow, he managed to get them wrapped up in the thermal bedding. His breath hitched as she snuggled in; her hands and feet were icy when she tucked them against him. By morning, she'd either incinerate him or his fever would be broken, no middle ground.

At this rate, he might never get to sleep but it would be worth it. Not only could he feel her breath rushing against his shoulder, her scent was all over him, her hair spilling on his skin. Pleasurable chills rolled over him each time she inhaled. He thought she would pass out as soon as she warmed up, but little movements said she was still awake.

"Are you... doing something to me?" she whispered finally.

"Pardon?"

"That pheromone you mentioned before. Is that—"

"No." He couldn't contain the smile; it leached into his voice, too. "There's no bloodlust." *Just normal desire, so if you want me...* Alastor didn't say it aloud, but he did feather a fingertip down her back and she rewarded him with a jerk and a shiver. In truth, he felt too ill and miserable to muster an erection, but he ached for her and it kindled the sweetest glow that she seemed to share his need.

"We have to sleep."

"Please do."

"You're enjoying this," she accused.

"You've no idea how much."

Alastor stopped teasing her then, stroking her back in a soothing way, and soon, she melted into him, breath leveling out. Eventually, he slept too and in the morning, he was neither reduced to ashes nor completely well, though his fever did seem a little lower. He extricated himself from the delicious clutch of her arms and legs, downed his medicine, and headed out to have that postponed discussion with the other Animari. Fortunately, they were content to talk in the Rover. He crammed into the vehicle with the other leaders and did his best to explain while they covered the last leg of the journey to Hallowell in style.

"If that's true," said Callum eventually, "then we owe you our thanks."

"It is," Gavriel confirmed.

"Feel free to speak with our scout personally. Dr. Halek is right. I did not come to that choice easily."

I'm so tired.

Still, he managed a smile for the bear leader and the wolf lieutenant, who didn't seem to hate his guts. The tension eased as the driver called, "I've got Hallowell in sight!"

When the vehicle shuddered to a stop, Alastor choked back a groan. At some point, his fever had spiked again, and his knees felt like water. He took a single step out of the Rover and the world slid sideways.

As it had so often before, darkness claimed him.

11.

"Low blood sugar." Sheyla made the excuse on automatic as the prince's guard caught him before he hit the ground.

"We haven't eaten much in the last day," Gavriel explained, presumably to the other leaders. "Supplies ran out a while back."

She had no interest in how the bear leader or the wolf lieutenant responded. Sheyla leaned in to check Alastor's breathing, ignoring the incipient chaos. *Steady. That's good.* His face was like alabaster with desperate roses blazing high in his cheeks. *He still has that damned fever.* This was no place to examine him properly, however, with tons of soldiers milling around the city limits, surrounded by armaments and war machines.

After taking the prince's pulse, she beckoned to Dedrick. "The hospital is this way. He needs fluids at the very least."

"I'll go with you!" An ethereally beautiful Golgoth female shouldered through the crowd, eyes wide and desperate.

The guard shook his head. "Stay here. Keep the men calm and give orders in my stead. Cooperate with the wolves, bears, and the Eldritch, understood?"

She let out a slow breath and nodded. "As you say."

"Let's go," Sheyla urged.

"Do you need any help? Is it serious?" Probably Zan meant to be helpful, and he had been silent on their short trip together, but she didn't trust him fully yet. Without meaning to, she flicked a look at the Golgoth currently holding Alastor, gauging his reaction.

Silently the soldier implored her to keep Alastor's secret. There was no gain in making his condition common knowledge. "We're fine. Stay with everyone else."

Practically running, she passed beneath the arches that marked the entry to Hallowell. Normally she'd pause to evaluate the changes as it had been years since she left, but she didn't spare a look. *Unless I'm remembering wrong, we're four blocks away.* Muscle memory didn't lead her astray; she had stumbled this path more times than she could count, half-asleep and called back on duty after a ridiculously long shift. She led the way across the quad to St. Casimir, a weathered white stone structure that had all the charm you'd expect in an institution constructed three hundred years ago, by a monastic order. Still, despite the austere exterior, the inside was well-kept and modern, brightly lit and absolutely bustling. A pang went through her when she spotted a few familiar faces, as the old scent of antiseptic washed over her.

"Dr. Halek, isn't it?" A former professor was smiling at her, though his expression dimmed when he processed the situation.

"It is. I need visiting doctor privileges. Can you help me out, Dr. Seagram? It's urgent."

"I'll get the paperwork started. You head to admissions

and see if they can find your friend a room."

"Thank you." She called that over one shoulder, already navigating the labyrinthine crisscross of hallways, easy for visitors to get lost.

A semi-secret shortcut deposited them at admissions, where she sped through registration with the ease of familiarity. The clerk balked when she heard the patient was Golgoth but Sheyla overrode her. "I'm the attending physician. Get me a room and I'll handle the rest. You don't even need to put him on your nursing rotation."

Sighing, the woman said, "Fine. We have space in the cardiology ward. 507, last room on the right."

"Perfect, we're on the way." Curling her fingers at the silent guard, she hurried off.

It was harder than normal to keep fear at bay. She'd known he wasn't well last night, but she'd succumbed to his blandishments, acting like a woman and not a doctor. This afternoon, when he collapsed, it took all her self-control not to react emotionally, too. She'd seen family members melt down in tears, shaking their sick loved ones and calling their names, like that ever did any good. But she'd suppressed the same damn impulse a short while ago.

And I know better.

Dedrick spoke then. "Will he be all right?"

It was a loaded question, full of a tacit request for reassurance. "I'll do my best."

As she'd remembered, the hospital rooms were small but clean, and this one was private. She opened the door for Dedrick, who needed no invitation to deposit Alastor on the bed. He was taking off his boots when she rushed off to get some supplies. She didn't know the cardiac unit well, but a brief Q&A with the floor nurse soon got her squared away.

By the time she got back, Dedrick had him ready for pajamas, which she passed over.

"When you're done, I'll start the IV."

"I'll be quick."

And he was. He was also a capable assistant, handing her supplies before she asked for them with an assurance that made Sheyla suspect he'd done this before. "Hold his arm in case he moves, please."

She needed to bring the fever down, but he'd said that other medications interfered with the serum, diminishing its efficacy. The physician in her called bullshit; there had to be *some* medicine he could take safely for pain and fever. In any event, she wasn't inclined to heed doctors who were now working for Tycho and who would have executed Alastor on command. *Not exactly the best care, that.* In fact, she wouldn't even be surprised if his asshole brother had ordered Alastor's doctor to make him suffer as much as possible. As soon as Sheyla had a more accurate chemical analysis of the original serum, not the stopgap she'd created, she'd cross reference and check for interactions.

"How is he?" Dedrick asked, once she completed her preliminary check.

"This seems to be mild malnutrition, combined with exhaustion and dehydration. I can't confirm anything else until I run some blood tests."

It was best to take the samples while Alastor was out, so she collected them efficiently. Normally a nurse would do a good portion of this, but she'd promised not to impose on hospital staff. That choice didn't stem so much from a desire to be considerate, rather from her need for privacy. She'd probably need to consult with Dr. Seagram at some point because he specialized in oncology, but if possible, she'd keep the prince's secret.

Dedrick indicated the vials in her hands with a tilt of his head. "I'll wait with him if you need to take those to the lab."

"Not your first time, huh?"

"Unfortunately, not."

"I'm glad he has you," she said.

The big Golgoth half-smiled. "It's the other way around."

"Let me guess, he saved you?" Though her tone was light, she wasn't joking.

"Unquestionably," came the firm response.

"Maybe you can tell me about it when I get back." With that, she hurried off to complete the analysis. If she went through channels, it would take a lot longer, so she went down to the practicum resource room, used by residents who needed lab credit. The equipment was top notch, nicer even than the machines at Ash Valley had been ruined in the bombing, so it was a pleasure to get to work.

A few students slid her silent looks but nobody interfered. Once she had his blood work in progress, she opened her bag and withdrew the last of the original serum. The high-end chemical spectrum analysis unit—or CSAU—should be able to pinpoint components and ratios down to a minuscule decimal point, a precision she hadn't possessed in Ash Valley.

His blood analysis processed first, and soon she had data that she alone could interpret. A few of the results concerned her, nothing that indicated a life-threatening shift. Yet. *I have time to stabilize his condition.* That thought served as reassurance, calming nerves she hadn't realized were so ragged. No surprise, she was used to *this* environment, not desperate dashes in the cold carrying life or death tidings.

There was still three-quarters of an hour left on the CSAU, so Sheyla sent Alastor's blood work results to a private data file, put away her tablet, and rotated her shoulders. She stretched a little, rolling her neck until it popped. Maybe it was paranoid, but she wouldn't move five steps from here until she had the results. His life depended on her recreating the treatment from Golgerra precisely. From there, she intended to monitor his response to the medicine and ensure it was the best course. Too many people had left him to suffer, it seemed.

Whatever it takes, I won't fail him. Not ever.

ALASTOR WOKE TO darkness held at bay by a dim golden glow. His gaze homed in on Sheyla, curled up in a chair at his bedside, poring over a steady stream of data. He'd come to in hospitals often enough that he experienced no uncertainty, no panic, or confusion. The only thing he didn't know was how long he'd been out. He could've asked straightaway, but instead, he hoarded these secret moments, savoring the unforeseen pleasure of her unguarded face. With her free hand, she tucked her lovely dark hair behind her ear, mumbling words he only half caught.

"…phospholipid phosphatidylserine… hmm, a nanovesicle that fuses with tumor cells. Apoptosis… that makes sense. So, it's a binary formula… and carnosine…"

By the deep quiet enveloping them, he surmised it must be nighttime. The astonishing comfort of waking to find her close by… he hadn't known anything like it since Caia died, and his sister had certainly never inspired such an emotional tsunami, waves of joy and despair creating an inner storm.

Alastor would've spoken in a moment or two more, but she caught him, brows lofting as she realized he was awake. A sweet shock jolted through him when her eyes met his; they clung and held in a way that he was afraid to interpret. Her relief was unmistakable, though, and it wasn't the clinical appreciation of seeing diagnostic skills prove true.

After a moment, she rose and came to perch on the edge of his bed. He expected a question like "How do you feel" or perhaps an observation on how awful he looked, because she hadn't been shy about such comments. Instead, she extended a trembling hand to touch his cheek, not checking for fever. She grazed his brow, feathered her fingertips down his cheek, little compulsive touches that just about did him in.

"Worried for me, were you?" Somehow, absurdly, he was smiling.

"This has to stop." She tried to sound stern and succeeded only in producing a bittersweet desperation that he understood all too well.

There was no point in arguing about what couldn't be changed. Probably he should ask how she'd managed to dismiss Ded, but that wasn't his primary curiosity. "What were you reading over there?"

"The results of the serum analysis. I put together the missing pieces while you were out and sorted where I went wrong in my first attempt."

Alastor registered the self-recrimination in her tone, and since she hadn't dropped her hand yet, he turned his face into her palm, waiting for the moment when she pulled back and lectured him about boundaries and whatever else came to mind. Instead, her other arm came up and she let him nestle into her while she drew a hand through his hair.

The sensation was... exquisite. He closed his eyes briefly, basking in her attention.

"That *is* good news." He murmured the words because some response was called for, but currently, he didn't care about the serum or her research.

"It was irresponsible to administer a treatment I wasn't sure of." Though he couldn't see her face from this angle, he knew she'd stew over this all night if he left her to it.

"Our options were limited," Alastor said. "And I was willing. Don't forget that part."

"You're trying to cheer me up."

"Is it working?" Without much hope that she'd let it happen, he shifted to pull her fully onto the bed with the arm that wasn't connected to tubing. She curled into his side, permitting the realignment, so it wasn't just her petting his hair, but him holding her as well.

"Somewhat. I keep doing things with you against my better judgment."

"Like this?"

"And this." She brushed her lips over his jaw, a whisper of a kiss.

He exhaled. "You missed a spot."

"Did I?"

Deliberately he lifted his chin and relaxed his mouth, silently daring her. His heart skipped a little when she leaned in, until her face was so close to his, he could smell the plain soap of her skin, and her features blurred. With a frantic leap of desire that faintly embarrassed him with its urgency, he closed his eyes, completing the portrait of a lover waiting to be kissed.

No matter how much Alastor wanted that, he still sat tense, fully prepared for her to muss his hair or crack the moment with a brusque dismissal. Instead, after an excruciating pause, her lips found his, at once hesitant and sure. She stole his breath and then even more when her hand curved against his cheek. His heart rang unsteadily in his ears with each soft brush, each deliciously sweet press and stroke of her tongue. He'd never simply let someone kiss him before, offering himself with such patience, and the reward was a rush of near-delirious heat.

She made a soft sound into his mouth, as if his taste delighted her, and he tumbled into the kiss with everything. He was acutely conscious of how little they were moving elsewhere, bodies not straining, but he wanted to, and so he put that want in each desperate kiss, more, more, more, and then a soft, devouring gasp, when she thrust her tongue deep, and he let her, welcomed, sucked and nuzzled until her breath went fast and rough, just from the repeated glide and stroke of lips and tongues.

Lightheaded, he broke away at last and put his face on her shoulder as he'd wanted to the day before. Her skin smelled like sunlight, tasted of a sweetness like that of a perfect fruit. Alastor brushed his lips there, her collarbone, her throat, and could scarcely breathe when she quivered against him, her heartbeat audible, even though he didn't possess her enhanced senses.

"That was..." Apparently, words failed her.

"A wonderful idea? Endorphins are excellent for pain management."

Sheyla let out a shaky laugh, putting a hand through her gorgeous hair. "If I agree, you'll probably propose sexual healing next. I was thinking more along the lines of extraordinarily unprofessional, terrible for my career—"

"But fantastic for my ego," he cut in with a little grin.

"Why don't we have a quiet affair? Otherwise, the tension will distract us from more important matters."

He nearly fell over when she sighed and said, "Hormones are definitely clouding my judgment, but this isn't the place for it under any circumstances."

"That's not a no."

"Don't push me," she warned.

But if she was in full retreat, she wouldn't still be cuddled up next to him. "Noted. When can I get out of here? There's so much to do and so little time."

"If you're feeling up to it, tomorrow." Unconsciously, her hands were moving in his hair again, clutch, smooth, stroke, as if he'd become her worry beads, an icon she needed to touch, and he was completely fine with it.

"I would never choose to linger in a hospital." A sudden thought occurred to him. "Did *you* undo my braids?" It wasn't a service Ded would volunteer without being asked, as it was a matter of rank and status.

By her expression, she knew there was some significance to the question. "They seemed to be bothering you. Was that... not all right?"

Alastor smiled. "It's fine. You have my permission."

Sheyla didn't know the bonds required for such liberties and he had no intention of informing her that between accepting his blood mark and unspooling his braids, she had essentially declared that she was his mate. Her eyes narrowed. Really, she was too good at reading the layers of his amusement.

"I don't like that look."

"But I adore yours. Let's call it even." On impulse, he kissed the majestic slope of her nose, and she blinked at him like a startled bird.

"Don't," she muttered.

"Adore your face? Kiss your nose? It's too late. That ship has sailed, the port is ablaze, and the enemy is at the gate." He kissed her brow, both her cheeks, her chin, and then her ears. "Prepare to do battle, I shall show no mercy."

A little whimper escaped her and she hung her head, adorably downcast. "Hell."

"What's the matter?' A tinge of worry flickered to life.

"I'm starting to find you endlessly amusing. Endearing, even."

His heart split wide open and possibly grew wings. "My darling Sheyla, that's the best news I've had, possibly ever."

12.

DISCHARGE WASN'T DIFFICULT since Sheyla had essentially commandeered a room and supplies. The supervisor in billing would probably have some sharp words for her, but she didn't care. In following this exiled prince, she was making all kinds of questionable judgments, to the point that soon, her own pride mates might not recognize her anymore. With Dedrick's help, she packed up Alastor's things—not much for royalty. It came home to her then that he'd turned his back on everything familiar and owned only what he carried with him.

Thankfully, his color was better today and the nutritive IV had strengthened him. Proper medicine would help even more, but it would take time to gather the necessary ingredients and find somewhere to manufacture enough serum to last at least a year. There was no telling if Hallowell would even still be standing at the end of that time, but she locked down such thoughts. Her mother always said that you gave life to darkness by believing it; whether or not that was true, it seemed best not to tempt fate.

"You've already been assigned to diplomatic housing?"

Alastor was asking the guard.

"We have. It's like the apartments in Ash Valley. Small, clean, serviceable."

"That will do." He gestured at their rucksacks. "Please drop off our things. I'll be along after I've met with Chancellor Quarles."

"As you wish, sire."

A flicker in Alastor's expression told Sheyla he wished Dedrick would dispense with titles, but she supposed the other man had too much reverence to permit it. "Am I going with you or Dedrick?"

Once she asked, she thought better of it. *Why* would *I go with Alastor?* It wasn't like he required constant care, and she wasn't part of his mission in the official sense. Yet he reached for her without hesitation, with a smile so joyous it hurt a little to witness it.

"With me, of course. You'll be my local guide. None of my people have ever been here before." She suspected he added the last sentence as a consolation for Ded, who dipped a half-bow and hauled their belongings off.

"You salved his pride," she noted.

"He's a good man, but he tends to be overprotective. The moment someone in the city doesn't kowtow properly, he might start something...regrettable."

"Avoidable, certainly. You can rely on me not to pick fights with people who don't fawn over you."

"I can rely on you for anything," he said tenderly.

And that softness pierced her like a titanium arrow, all silver, shining, and abjectly terrifying. She was losing her objectivity where he was concerned, or perhaps lost was the better word, for she couldn't see him as simply her patient any longer. His smiles mattered to her now, and even more his frowns. Sheyla let out of a quiet breath and took the hand he had been offering in silence, so long that it might have been awkward, except that it whispered of extraordinary patience.

I will wait for you, his jade eyes said. *Until you're ready. Forever, if need be.*

His fingers were warm today, ridiculously comforting wrapped around her own. "This way. We need to stop by billing so I can settle your account. Otherwise, they'll dun me mercilessly. The Order of St. Casimir does not work on credit."

"If that's a nudge, I'm quite destitute, you know. Not a single ducat to my name."

"You mean being a doctor pays better than being a prince?" Sheyla feigned surprise.

"Apparently so, though it's possible that I'll become obscenely wealthy if I defeat Tycho and claim our familial assets."

"An obvious deduction," she said.

"So *that's* why you're so good to me. I am adrift in disappointment."

"Your yardstick for measuring such things is broken. I'm adequate at best."

Alastor laughed softly and kissed her hand, before letting go. "Is that so? Then I shall rein in my discontent and await true goodness."

"Are you ready?" she asked.

"Almost. I can't attend a formal meeting with my hair like this."

Nodding, Sheyla perched on the chair as he went to the mirror and used a folding brush and comb set to infuse elegance to his long, tangled locks. Since she rarely did anything with her hair besides wash, comb, and tie it up, it was fascinating to watch him weave and plait. He was wondrously proficient, creating a gorgeous cascade of interlaced strands.

"You asked before if I was the one who took down your braids. Is there some significance to them?"

He nodded with a final check of his reflection. "They reveal my rank. It's impolite in the extreme for anyone to modify them without permission."

Sheyla suspected he was omitting something important, but she didn't press. "Among the Animari we don't have anything like that, though we communicate a good deal of information on an olfactory level."

"Ah, yes, your infamous enhanced senses. Can you hear the way my heart races whenever I'm close to you?"

"Yes," she said, seeing no point in pretending otherwise.

His smile was delightful, even more so the slow bloom of color in his pale cheeks. For the first time, she admired that pallor because it gave her such delicious ammunition. "Are you blushing? This is *such* fun."

"You are so wicked to tease me. My mother warned me about women like you."

"Did she?"

His mouth drooped, the amusement gone like a pale sun in winter, and it left her shivering, that sudden withdrawal. "No. Mostly she murmured of treachery and poison and how I must never, ever trust anyone."

While his mother kept him alive with such talk, it was like he had been reared by sword and scythe; it seemed to her a miracle that there was any laughter in him at all. His truths cut her, down in tender depths no one had touched before. Never had she cared for any single person more than her research. Though she loved her family, she sometimes resented their need for her time and attention. There was always something more to study, a mystery to unlock, but she wasn't pining for a silent lab any longer. A fire had been kindled beneath her neglected imagination, and now she couldn't stop picturing the sorrowful boy he had been.

"Mine was always after me to go outside more, play with others," she said. "She often chased me for a hug, pulling a book out of my hands in exchange for a plate of food."

"How magical." And she registered no sarcasm in those two words; he was all wonder and yearning at the simple description of her childhood.

She stared at his mouth for the longest while.

"If I kiss you now," she whispered. "We won't leave this room for at least a day."

"That's not much of a deterrent. In fact, it's more of an enticement and you ought to be ashamed, trying to seduce me when I'm so steadfast and dutiful. Come along, you siren."

She was equal parts relieved and let down when he claimed her hand again and tugged her out of the room. As promised, they stopped to settle his bill, paid from Sheyla's own account. Waving away his rueful apology, she guided him out of the hospital for her first look at Hallowell in so many years.

It was one of the oldest cities, over a thousand years of building and tearing down. War and fire had left their mark, and one could track the centuries by the architectural styles that grew more modern farther from the city's heart. In the center of town, there were short, narrow buildings of crumbling stone, shoved together so tightly that hardly a shadow could pass, and toward the limits, the towers stood watch like a steel and glass army. Per Sheyla's history lessons, Hallowell had once been a fort, built to defend against long-ago human incursions.

She gave Alastor the brief rundown on the way to the chancellor's office. He seemed interested in everything she had to say, but had questions especially about the trolleys that sped throughout the city. "From what I understand, they banned private conveyances two centuries ago. The city has been much cleaner since."

"Even the chancellor takes the trolley?" he asked.

Sheyla shrugged. "I've never met the woman. We didn't run in the same circles when I was here."

"That means she's been in power for a while. Good to know."

"You'll be able to make your own judgment soon enough. Let's go in."

ALASTOR ADMIRED THE bas relief mosaic on the far wall and the shiny marble floors as the receptionist clicked a path toward the chancellor's office. Hers was at the back of the building on the ground floor and he read placards in passing for Exchequer and Roadwork and Historical Preservation. Their route ended in magnificent mahogany double doors with frosted glass etched in sigils he didn't recognize.

"Wait here please," the woman said primly.

"She's wolf clan," Sheyla said, as soon as the lady stepped into the antechamber.

It might be an insult to leave them cooling their heels in the corridor, but his task was too critical for him to obsess over minor issues—and this was the sort of thing that would set Ded off like a firecracker. "Pine Ridge?"

"Probably. They're the majority, but if she's posted here, she probably doesn't have strong clan ties. Her first loyalty will be to the chancellor. It's also possible that she's from Ice Spire, a rarely seen enclave of wolves in the far north."

Before he could ask more, the receptionist returned and gestured for them to step inside, then she hastened back toward the front desk where they'd found her. The waiting room was all polished dark wood panels and expensive maroon carpets threaded in gold. Fine leather volumes lined the far wall, and there were a couple of upholstered chairs that pretended people were allowed to sit in them. Alastor recognized this sort of décor, everything ordered to impress.

At an immense desk, another watchdog waited, a handsome man who rose with a smooth and empty smile. "I'm told you seek an appointment with the chancellor."

"My business is urgent," Alastor said. "It pertains to the safety of Hallowell. If necessary, I can summon Korin, lieutenant to Raff at Pine Ridge and Callum McRae, the leader of both the Order of St. Casimir and the Burnt Amber bear clan, to corroborate my words."

It was an effort to hold the smile when urgency sang in his blood. For each moment he lost to bureaucracy, Tycho trod closer to achieving his ambitions. The other man's lips formed into a disapproving line. "Name dropping will avail you nothing, Your Highness." He spoke the final word with a little sneer that told Alastor everything he needed to know.

Sheyla folded her arms. "Maybe not, but if you don't get off your ass and tell Chancellor Quarles we're here, you'll have an angry bear lord kicking down your damn door next."

Since that dovetailed with what he knew of McRae, he waited to see what the aide would say, maybe something about security?

The secretary paled. "I'll... be right back."

"That wasn't very diplomatic," he observed.

"We don't have time for that. He wanted to humble you, but the time he wastes on gamesmanship will have a cost in terms of civilian lives."

He saw that she was thinking of those who died in the bombing of Ash Valley, and he wished he could comfort her, but the doors to the chancellor's inner sanctum swung open. Inside her space, it was much more welcoming, small and cluttered with files and papers and open books and half-read petitions. Her furniture was worn too, a rug showing the track where she likely paced and fingerprints on the window that overlooked a private garden, now dead and dry with winter.

With her white hair and rosy cheeks, the chancellor could have been someone's kindly grandmother, if not for the keen light in the brown eyes behind her wire spectacles. She wore a simple gray suit and thick-soled black shoes, sensible down to the silver-tipped walking stick propped beside her desk. She shut the door behind them and indicated the two chairs opposite her desk; they were simple wood, not designed for anyone to occupy long, Alastor decided with a trace of amusement.

"I'm Chancellor Quarles," she said briskly. "I hope you'll accept my apologies for Anton. He tends to be... protective of my time. I suspect he senses I haven't much of it left."

Alastor appreciated her forthright nature, though the

last comment was worrisome. Hallowell could little afford any political upheaval just then; the external danger was dire enough. "I'm sure you've some idea why we've come."

She inclined her head. "My sources bring rumors. I'd like it if you sorted fact from fiction for me. Concisely, mind. I have a meeting in ten minutes."

Thus incentivized, Alastor gave her the nutshell of events, starting with the failed conclave, the breakdown of the Pax Protocols at Ash Valley, followed by the bombing and the deaths of the old bear leader and Lord Talfayen. The chancellor listened with a brow growing more furrowed with each revelation. By the time he finished with, "Therefore, we concluded that his next strategic target will likely be—"

"Hallowell," she completed the sentence, seeming to share that assessment.

"That's why it's vital that we work with the standing militia to shore up defenses. Burnt Amber has brought war machines for defense and there's a squadron of wolves who are planning to stay and fight."

"Don't forget the Eldritch," Sheyla added quietly.

"Correct. Princess Thalia has also assigned a unit of her best fighters to keep Hallowell out of my brother's hands."

"This must be difficult for you," the chancellor observed.

Alastor raised a brow. "What in particular?"

"Denouncing a member of your own family and facing him on the battlefield."

If she understood the dynamics, she wouldn't offer sympathy. Still, it wouldn't hurt to play on it. "Yet I am resolved, Chancellor."

"Then *I* must be as well. Hallowell has always maintained neutrality among clan conflicts, but with the Pax Protocols in tatters and a tyrant on the march, we cannot ask him nicely to desist."

Beside him, Sheyla smothered a laugh, but she didn't speak. Alastor rose, noting by the clock on the far wall that he had used seven of his allotted ten minutes. "Please send word when we can speak more and coordinate our efforts. I'm sure your secretary knows how to find me."

"Indeed." Chancellor Quarles stood and inclined her head, escorting them all the way through the foyer. "I'll bring your request to the ministers personally and hope to deliver news by tomorrow at the latest."

Her aide didn't acknowledge their passing, despite Sheyla's mocking wave. Minor tensions wouldn't matter when the man learned how great the threat was. Most likely he would stop sleeping, between the new workload and impending doom anxiety.

"She was more reasonable than her assistant led me to believe," she said, as they cleared the government annex.

"Well, she doesn't make all the decisions. Let's hope the ministers she mentioned are amenable to a collective defense effort."

"They can't do it on their own," she muttered.

Her half-audible grumbling followed him down the stairs, and outside the ministry complex, Alastor spun in a slow circle, taking in the city's charm. Apart from the trolleys, there were only pedestrians or people on brightly painted bicycles. The smell of roasting meat reached him, likely from the man selling skewers on the corner. He took a step toward the delicious aroma before remembering he didn't have a copper in his pockets.

Lucky for him, Sheyla was already tugging him in the

other direction or he might've come across wistful as a small boy. "We should get settled and make some plans. While you're in meetings, I'll be at the hospital, at least to start. I'll see about activating secure local comms for us."

"Good thinking." For obvious reasons, he hadn't used his phone since leaving Golgerra.

As it turned out, Dedrick already had two units ready, courtesy of an outing with Korin of Pine Ridge. The men had moved in the night before and were ready to get to work but until Alastor made nice with the chancellor and her ministers, he just needed them to stay out of trouble, a request he made crystal clear to Ded.

"Understood," he said. "Shall I show you to your quarters?'

"Please. And make sure the men know not to change in public, unless I've ordered them to do so for city defense." He loathed the necessity of this, how such concealment felt like shame, but it wouldn't do to frighten anyone in Hallowell.

"As you command, sire." Here, Dedrick hesitated, leading them into a nondescript tenement building. "I wasn't certain of how many suites you will require…"

Without even thinking about it, he wrapped an arm about Sheyla and pulled her to him. "One. The good doctor remains with me."

13.

"IT'S VERY BEIGE," Sheyla said, as if she couldn't sense Alastor's tension.

Things had been strange since Dedrick showed them into the small apartment they would be sharing. The guard gave them a brief tour, not that it was necessary, and then excused himself to check on the troops, who were four to a flat and wagering over who got to sleep in the bed. Now she was watching Alastor flit around, ostensibly investigating the amenities, but it was clear his mind wasn't on the rug or the tiny kitchenette.

Her observation startled him out of reverie, resulting in a shaded look. "Isn't it? I had no idea there were so many variations on neutrality."

"If you're up to it, you should shower. They've gifted us some staples as a show of hospitality, so I'll see what I can whip up."

"Not soup," he begged.

She laughed as he went to the washroom. Digging around, she found that she could make noodles in a basic cream sauce, along with slices of grilled meat. It had been long enough since she'd had anything but the barley soup he'd mentioned that Sheyla's mouth watered as she put together the meal. There were also frozen vegetables, which she steamed on top of the pasta.

Half an hour later, when he emerged from the steamy bathroom, she had lunch—or dinner—ready. Alastor paused, towel in hand, staring at the dishes she'd laid out and Sheyla squirmed with surprising discomfort. Try as she might, she couldn't figure out his intensity, and that was more than slightly irksome.

"I'm no cook," she said defensively.

He smiled then. "I wasn't judging your efforts."

"Then what?"

"Shall we eat?" he suggested. "It would be a shame to let it get cold."

Mildly disgruntled, she sat down at the table and served up generous portions. He would need the carbs and protein for the trials to come. "Here."

"You're offering me food again."

"So what?" She crammed a huge bite into her mouth and half-closed her eyes in pleasure at the combination of cream and cheese.

"I shouldn't tell you."

"Are you *trying* to aggravate me?"

"Perish the thought. Do you promise that the truth won't make you angrier?" He wore the impish expression that she distrusted instinctively yet she couldn't let this go. Curiosity might kill this cat if she didn't achieve intellectual satiation.

"I swear."

"As I said before, these are mating rituals," he said softly.

She cocked her head, trying to put the pieces together.

"Are you talking about the blood mark again?"

"That was the start... and I'm trying to ignore all the other implications because I realize you don't know our ways."

"Explain," she demanded. It stung to discover that he was *making allowances* for her ignorance. The fire of embarrassment blazed in her cheeks; she hadn't felt this silly or small since she forgot the poem she was supposed to recite in junior school.

"You hunted for me, a demonstration of your strength and prowess, a silent statement that you can provide for my needs."

"Everyone ate that meat." She was aware it sounded like a protest.

"You delivered it to me," he said gently. "The fact that I chose to share diminishes your gift not at all."

And there was no disputing that. Sheyla nodded. "Is there more?"

"Most certainly. You've shared skinship with me on multiple occasions. While I understand that nudity among the Animari isn't as rare as it is with my people, it's still difficult for me not to consider it meaningful."

The residual heat of her chagrin melted into deeper color, the flush of simmering attraction. She could've said that kisses, like they'd exchanged, weren't exactly common either, but that would probably encourage him. "Understood. Please, go on."

He was eating steadily, not looking at her. "Next, you took down my braids. That is an intensely intimate act, restricted to kinfolk and lovers."

"I suspected there was something to it when you asked this morning," she admitted. "And I had noticed the intricate designs among your men. I'm sorry for overstepping."

Alastor waved her apology away with a vague smile. "Finally, we come full circle. You've laid a table for me, filled my plate and bade me eat. This is the last stage, where we test our compatibility as mates. We call this first-year trial 'nesting' and at the end of that time, if a bond has formed, we would pledge ourselves to one another."

"That's lovely," she said in surprise.

"Did you think we are all destruction and brutality? Nevermind, don't answer. In any event, don't fret over my odd fancies. I'm fully aware that you're not courting me."

Her overheated cheeks now felt hot enough to fry a pair of eggs, and her heart thundered in her ears. The fact that he wouldn't meet her gaze registered as actual pain. Sheyla wet her lips and laid down her cutlery with sudden resolve. "What if I said that I am? I just didn't realize it until now."

Though their rituals weren't set as the Golgoth appeared to be, worry and wanting to care for someone… that was universal. Alastor raised his eyes then, scanned her face as if trying to gauge her expression. His lopsided smile wavered, and she didn't miss how his long fingers clenched on the table's edge.

"I'd first say it's cruel to tease," he managed in an uneven tone.

"If I said that, it would be sincere."

"Then I would praise all gods old and new and welcome you with open arms. I've made no secret of my desire."

She hesitated. Once she said the words, they would become fact, no longer theoretical. Innate fairness compelled her to add a caveat. "I don't think my family would understand… this. I can't promise a full nesting."

Pain and sadness flickered in his jade eyes, along with understanding. "No need to set terms or limits, I'm not free to choose either. Let us consider this a lovely, unexpected interlude. You have my oath that I'll never stop you when you choose to go."

Her heart ached at hearing that. "It seems sad to start when we already know there must come an ending."

"Everything ends, some way or another. The question that we should ask is whether the good memories will someday be more precious than the pain."

Sheyla finished her food in silence, and she could tell Alastor had taken her deferred response as a rejection. Out of respect, he might never mention this again, but she required some deliberation on the matter. Once made, she would never regret the decision, either; such certainty took time, so she let him simmer while she washed the dishes.

If we're doing this, I can't continue as his primary physician. I need to turn my notes over to Dr. Seagram and manufacture medicine instead.

As dark fell and Alastor switched on the lights, she turned, leaning on the kitchen counter, stared at him across the width of it. He wore disappointment like a laurel wreath, his shoulders slightly hunched, though she doubted he was aware of it. Then she reached for his hand and kissed the palm deliberately.

"I've decided," she said.

"Oh?"

"While we're in Hallowell together, I want to be yours. Or more candidly, I'd prefer you to be mine, because I've never been... passive in that regard." It was hard to tell if he took her meaning because he was smiling so brilliantly that she almost went sun-blind.

"We can take turns. Will that do?"

"Probably," she said.

"I've never begun like this before," he said in a wondering tone.

"What do you mean?"

"This feels... weighty because I'm so certain that you've sorted through the ramifications and chosen me."

That seemed obvious. "Yes."

Alastor tipped his head back with a sigh that was nearly a groan. "I thought I'd be suffering the whole time, unable to touch you for fear of losing control. My darling Sheyla, you are such an unanticipated gift."

In the past, she hadn't been susceptible to sweet sentiments. Flattery slid away from her like oiled leather. Yet Alastor's words arrowed to the core of her, and it felt like her entire body might be melting. Back in Ash Valley, he'd teased her about a wartime romance, and it seemed they were destined for precisely that.

So be it.

"If I'm a gift, then unwrap me."

ON THE VERGE of acting on her suggestion, Alastor stilled when Sheyla pulled her shirt over her head. He had seen her beautiful tawny skin before, but never with the surety that he had the right to touch her. It seemed proper to let her set the pace, and besides, he was trembling too much to trust his hands right then. Thankfully she continued that measured unveiling, sexier than if she had been flinging clothes everywhere. Her care assured him that this wasn't a hasty impulse, one that would have her crawling from his bed tomorrow in shame.

"Are you planning to watch me all night?" She stood before him, gloriously naked, and for a few seconds, he was speechless. "If that's your preference, you *can* but I'll admit to a certain level of disappointment."

Alastor shook his head quickly. "I am overcome by your magnificence."

And it was true. Her body was a wonder, strength and muscled curves, thick thighs and generous hips, breasts that he ached to touch and taste. Everything about her filled him with a yearning so strong that he didn't know where to start.

"That doesn't sound like a joke," she said.

"It isn't. I often want, but I rarely achieve my desires, you see."

"Then let me assist with some instruction. Do you mind?" She was smiling now, her expression so open and avid that he couldn't get his breath.

"Not at all."

"Fetch a cushion from the sofa."

Alastor complied at once and when he brought it to her, she rewarded him with a hot, open-mouthed kiss. "Good. That's for you, not me. You'll need it for your knees."

"My…oh."

He understood at once what she was proposing. No one had ever asked him to kneel and offer worship with his mouth. Of course, no one would dare; he was a prince, but excitement built ferociously as he placed the pillow and settled before her. His cock had been hard for half an hour, but now it swelled until he was uncomfortably conscious of how it pressed against his trousers.

Her hand tangled in his hair, tugging his head up. The eye contact sizzled through him as he hovered, a mere breath away from tasting her. "You owe me an orgasm. I've been so frustrated because of you."

"It will be my pleasure," he managed to say.

"Don't go straight for my clit. I want kisses first on my lips, some light nuzzling. When you start feeling how wet I am on your face, then you can suck on it."

At those explicit instructions, he almost came and he hadn't even touched her yet. "I am your willing pupil."

He leaned in at last, fixed on following her orders to the letter. Her lips were full and soft, already glistening a little, and she tasted like heaven, sweet and salt. He pressed delicate kisses against her until she let out a groan and lifted a foot onto the stool nearby, opening herself fully to his mouth. She worked against him in slow undulations, until his face was coated with her juices, and he could only think of getting her off. The insistent throb of his own desire seemed distant compared to the hands tugging at his hair, urging him where she needed friction most.

"Yes, that's good. Feels so..." The words dissolved in a moan when he licked each of her lips in turn and then sucked on them.

Her clit was swollen now, begging for attention. He grazed it with his thumbs and her whole body jerked. He pulled back enough to ask, "Can you come standing up?"

"Don't stop," she ordered with a yank on his hair.

Alastor took that for a yes. When he touched his mouth to her clit, her back arched. He raised his eyes to watch her face, adjusting the speed and pressure in response to how she quivered and her lips parted on sweet little gasping breaths. Without waiting for an invitation, he slid one finger inside her and then two, and she went wild, fucking his face with urgent lunges.

She cursed as she came and her knees buckled. He caught her in a move that was near miraculous because his legs were stiff. Sheyla snuggled into him as he carried her to their very beige bedroom. Aftershocks were still ticking through her, so he cradled her against his chest, thoroughly pleased with himself.

Eventually, she pushed up on one elbow and touched his sticky cheek. "You don't want to wash up?"

"In a bit. I've some hope that I'll become messier yet."

"Ah," she said, smiling. "You *have* been remarkably patient, and it seems utterly unfair that you're still dressed."

"Let me remedy that."

He was reluctant to let go of her even long enough to strip out of his clothes, as if she was a creature of pure light who might vanish if he blinked. He did the job quickly and came back to bed in record time. Her amber eyes gleamed with warm gold as she drank him in. His cock responded to her look with a pulse that doubled as a wave.

"Signaling frantically, I see."

"What can I say, he's a greedy bastard." His voice emerged rasping and thick.

"Is that where you want me to begin?'

Alastor couldn't think, let alone make requests. "Do as you will with me."

A pleased purr escaped her, full of throaty appreciation. "You won't regret giving yourself to me."

She started with a soft, deep kissing, and it felt like she was licking up her own juices, savoring her flavor on his skin. A jolt of pure lust shuddered through him. With anyone else, he would've put her hand on his cock or possibly forced her face down. Alastor wanted to know what Sheyla would do, given complete freedom, so he kissed her back until he was half-mad and breathless. He panted as she nibbled down his throat, over his shoulder to his chest. It seemed as if her lips must leave a white-hot imprint on his skin.

Rolling atop him, she sucked at each of his nipples, then bit into his chest, not hard enough to break the skin, but the sting contrasted deliciously to the soft heat of her mouth. Blearily he realized what the intermittent pressure meant. "You're marking me?"

"It's only fair."

The blood mark. He almost lost control over the idea of Sheyla leaving her stamp on his skin, not that it was her sole claim on his body. Her wet cunt slid against his abdomen, so that his dick rested beneath the ripe curve of her ass. It was too much for him to be still, so he rocked against her, slowly at first, and when she sat up, he understood that she meant to tease.

"I'm not fucking you tonight, so don't hold back."

"You want me to come like this?"

"If you can."

"Not if. When." Gazing up at her lovely face, stroking against her soft ass, it didn't take long until the pleasure spiked to excruciating levels. She made it even hotter by moving with him, studying his face as he had hers. His pleasure became a story she could read, written in each new gasp and moan.

"You're watching me get there," he whispered.

"Yes. It's making me want you again. You're so beautiful like this."

And he could feel the heat in his cheeks, the hardness of his nipples, nothing compared to the diamond-bright need thrumming in his cock. Pressure built in his lower back, tightening his abs. With a groan of pure need, he sat up and pulled her in for a devouring kiss as he spurted against her round ass and he couldn't resist rolling her against him until they were both slick.

Trembling, he leaned his forehead against hers. "See? Messy."

"We should shower. I doubt they provide limitless linens." Her amusement didn't even faze him.

"Give me a moment. my legs won't hold."

"Take five, then." She held him the whole time, arms firm about his back until the shaking stopped.

Alastor had never felt so secure in his life. "That... was amazing."

"It will get better," she said with a remarkable, serene confidence.

"You're so sure?"

"Of course. This was merely to take the edge off. I don't intend to take you tonight because anticipation will only make completion sweeter when the time comes."

14.

BETWEEN THE WITCHING hour and dawn, Sheyla awoke to arms drawing her close. The room had grown chilly and she pulled up the covers around them. After showering, they'd tumbled to bed in an exhaustion so profound that couldn't be mended in one night. The last time she was this tired, she had been on duty at St. Casimir for three days straight.

At some point Alastor had shifted to his side, facing her, and the moonlight streaming through the window illuminated his features. Hardly daring to breathe for fear of waking him, she traced a fingertip down the slope of his nose. As she studied him, his lashes flickered and then his eyes drifted open.

"You're still here," he whispered, kissing her chin.

"Where would I go?"

"I've no idea. Wherever lovely spirits sleep."

"You persist in the charming idea that I'm a figment of your imagination. Does that mean you would've invented someone like me if I didn't exist?"

He paused a moment to consider before replying, "It seems so."

For that bit of improbable sweetness, she framed his face in her hands and kissed him. Her eyes closed of their own accord and his skin just naturally invited her palms to skim onward, down his throat to his shoulders, arms that tightened on her with every touch, until her cheek was against his chest. Unlike the Animari, he had no body hair, sleek and hot beneath her hands. For once, her first thought was that he felt good, not that he might have a fever.

"Tell me about Golgerra," she invited.

"We have an hour before we need to get out of this warm bed. Is that truly how you prefer to spend those moments?"

Sheyla tapped his shoulder in mock reproof. "An hour wouldn't be long enough."

"True. Then... where shall I start?"

"Anywhere." She slid an arm across his hip, content to listen.

"I'll assume you know next to nothing about our capital. Is that fair?"

She nodded. "What little we learn about the Golgoth in school, well..."

"I expect it's that little children ought to be wary. Moving on. Golgerra is built into a mountain, I don't suppose you knew that, either?"

"No, definitely not."

"Ages ago, it was established as a stronghold and became known as virtually unassailable, though the Eldritch and Animari both tried on separate occasions."

"The entire city is underground, then?" That sounded strange, and try as she might, Sheyla couldn't quite picture it.

"There's no sky overhead, but I don't feel... entombed.

Over the last five hundred years, expert engineers and artisans have expanded natural caverns, carving and refining the stone. You can find some true wonders in our Hall of Heroes, our important figures etched in precious minerals and gemstones."

"That sounds beautiful."

His voice softened on a wistful note; he must be wondering if he'd ever see Golgerra again, whether this war would end in death or exile. "It is. High in the vaults, there are crystals embedded to reflect light, so we have a day and night cycle. The hydroponic gardens are gorgeous too, and the smell of drying herbs at harvest time…"

"You make me want to see it with my own eyes," Sheyla admitted. "And that's not something I ever imagined I would say."

"I haven't even mentioned the market at the center of town. It's open all hours, day and night, and since floor space is limited, the stalls rotate by shifts."

"Which means you need to know what time to find your favorite vendor. The way you talked before, it seems like there's an actual palace…?"

"I suppose you could say so. Golgerrans know it as Vega Rising and I… I called it home. It's a massive complex built above the city on a stone piazza with balconies and terraces, hallways that honeycomb outward and lead down into the city. You might think everything is brown or gray, but the stone is exquisite, variegated like your eyes, and when the light reflects off the mezzanine it shines like a star."

"Wow."

He went on, encouraged by her soft exclamation. "It's not all beauty, of course. The poor are consigned to the barrens or forced to stand watch outside in exchange for subsistence rations. And I haven't even touched on the undercity reserved for traitors, dissidents, prisoners. There are families who have been imprisoned for generations, all because they offended some royal a hundred years ago."

"That is—"

"Barbaric." He spoke the word quietly, before *she* could, and she had the sense that it hurt him to do so. "Golgerra is a city of wonder... and horror. I have both in my soul, *shalai*."

"As do we all."

"That is a kinder response than most would offer," he said.

"Let's agree that each of our people have moments that we lament." With a kiss that landed solely on his lower lip, she pulled away. "Little as I like it, we have too much to do and too little time."

"I wish you weren't so wretchedly right all the time," he muttered.

Alastor didn't protest when she got up, though, and soon, they were sharing bathroom space while she cleaned her teeth and he tidied up his braids.

"No shaving," she realized aloud. "I wonder if your people created the ranking braids to—" she cut herself off. "Sorry, was that rude?"

"In anyone else, I'd consider taking offense. To you, I offer latitude because I rather enjoy being the subject of your intellectual speculation."

"I'm not sure quite how to take that."

"As you please."

"Then I'm logging it as a compliment."

This teasing felt strangely natural, something she couldn't have imagined before. As she prepared a quick breakfast, she asked, "What's on your agenda today?"

"Factory, I think. If permissions are handed down from the ministry, I need to have a facility ready to convert to munitions, which means spreading some charm first."

"And here I thought you were too pretty to be this clever."

"I'd rather if you reckoned me both," Alastor said, stealing the toast from her fingers and biting it nearly in half.

With a feigned grumble, she buttered another slice and slathered it with berry compote, then fed it to him with her own fingers. "I will admit that at first, I thought you were an empty vase, but I have come, truly, to admire you. For your quick mind and kind heart."

After she said it, she winced because such things didn't sound right coming from her mouth; colleagues at both Ash Valley and St. Casimir in Hallowell would laugh until they fell over. Something about her prince made it easy to be gentle, though, and she no longer had any desire to quell the impulse.

Together, they finished breakfast, he took his medicine, then they headed out. Dedrick was waiting at the top of the stairs, and his rough features lit with relief when he spotted Alastor.

"I've managed to find a factory owner on the east side of the city who is willing to meet with us." By his exhausted countenance, Sheyla guessed it hadn't been easy.

"Then let's figure out how these trolleys work, shall we?" Alastor led the way, though not without casting several adorably forlorn looks over one shoulder.

While she couldn't encourage him to shirk his duty, nobody had ever pined for her before. It wasn't a disagreeable sensation to walk off knowing he would likely count the hours until he saw her face again. Sheyla had always been mildly baffled by the urge to shackle yourself to the same person for a lifetime, and while she wouldn't go so far as to say she got the concept now, it was looking less like voluntary incarceration all the time.

The day was bright for winter as she strode along the pedestrian walk toward St, Casimir. Impossible not to breathe in the familiar smell of spiced milk tea sold on the corner, poured from steaming kettles. She'd gotten used to a certain homogeny in Ash Valley, but here the air spoke of all types of Animari—wolves, cats, bears, even the reclusive bird clan whispered in the wind. Added to the Eldritch and Golgoth, it was a veritable potpourri for enhanced senses.

When she entered the hospital, she went straight to Dr. Seagram's office. He was just stepping out when she arrived, earning her a curious look.

"Something I can help you with, Dr. Halek?"

"Yes," she said. "I'd consider it a personal favor if you'll take on a VIP patient, so I can revert to clinical research on medication to treat his illness."

TROLLEYS WERE... FUN.

Delightful, even, bright blue with silver letters that named each one. The Maribel went west while the Talleyrand traveled east. Alastor didn't expect any of that, but he loved the sparks flickering from the wires above and the wind whipping through windows that children kept opening, despite the persistent scolding of old women failing to keep them in check. At first, Dedrick tried to operate as a bulwark between him and the 'commoners' but he shook his head.

"Don't call attention to us. Here, I'm nobody of importance."

By his glum reaction, Ded understood the futility of arguing, but he still hated to see Alastor being jostled by people who should be removing their hats in his presence. For his own sake, he wished he had one to keep his ears from icing over. Plus, anonymity felt like a healing balm. It didn't matter if he clung to the handle and wallowed off-balance when the trolley slalomed down the hillside, so that the buildings seemed to rush at them.

His obvious enjoyment attracted a few indulgent smiles and one middle-aged woman even offered a teasing remark. "Your first time in the city, is it?"

"Yes. Is it obvious?"

"Quite. But I like your enthusiasm, it's rare these days."

"Thank you, ma'am. Have you lived here long?" He chatted a bit more, aware that she'd probably scream if she knew she was engaging with a Golgoth brute.

Before they reached the east side of Hallowell, which involved a transfer at the hub station, he had comforted a toddler, amused a baby, and yielded his seat to an old man with a prosthetic leg. His mother had seldom permitted him to go out into the bustle of Golgerra, fearing he'd suffer an attack one way or another, either related to his health or an assassination attempt, courtesy of Tycho, so this outing, though it was necessary, also felt like freedom. He was delighted by Hallowell's openness, albeit when he considered how difficult it would be to defend, its charm faded slightly.

Eventually, they got off the trolley and walked the rest of the way to the sprawling factory that currently produced—

Alastor realized he had no idea. "What do they make here again? I should've reviewed the file on the way over."

"Mechanical parts for the city's automated systems," Ded answered with infinite patience. Really, he should be doing this since he'd spent all night preparing.

"Right." Silently he rehearsed his pitch as they reached what seemed to be a checkpoint.

"State your business," the guard demanded.

"I'm here to see Finneas Furbander. He should be expecting us." He added the last words with a look at Ded, who inclined his head slightly.

"Just a moment." The comm unit crackled, and Alastor noticed that these were different than the phone he'd brought from Golgerra, more of an all-purpose device.

Fascinating. He had the one Ded had given him, but he'd been so interested in the people and the trolley itself that he hadn't done more than switch it on. Presumably, his bodyguard had already sussed out Sheyla's importance to him and added her code to his contacts.

I'll check later.

"Just a moment, he's sending someone to collect you." The window slammed shut with no further small talk. Clearly, they didn't employ this man for his people skills.

Five minutes passed with Alastor marching in circles to keep warm, and if he thought, *I'm a prince, dammit,* once or twice, while exhaling like a smoking chimney, he could probably be forgiven since he didn't actually say it out loud. Dedrick was dangerously enraged by the time the apple-cheeked woman came to collect them. She was all breathless apologies and head bowing as she herded them into a small vehicle.

"I'm Mrs. Christie, the one who picks up after Mr.

Furbander. Just call me Christie if you like. He told me you were at the west gate and clearly you're not, so... very sorry about that."

"No harm done," Alastor said with good cheer, mostly to cover Ded's grunt.

She seemed to notice his curiosity as he studied the instrumental panel, solar-powered like most Rovers, but it was comparatively small and light. *What's this thing made of?*

"You've never seen a Sol before, I take it?" When he shook his head, she went on, "They're not street legal but we're allowed to use them here on private property."

Christie talked a little more about the company, facts that he'd already learned from Ded, but Alastor made interested noises until she parked outside a massive building, green corrugated metal that was both ugly and industrial. Perfect for a factory, he supposed.

"This way. Mr. Furbander only agreed to meet you because he's heard you're a Golgoth prince. He'll probably ask you to sit for a photo with him. He's got a wall of unusual—oh. Well." She trailed off, likely realizing that could be construed as offensive.

His smile tightened. *Yes, I'd love to take a photo with a man who considers me an oddity worth collecting.* Beside him, Dedrick's hand was already curling into a fist.

Alastor touched his arm and whispered, "Breathe."

Briefly, he wished Sheyla was here because she could brief him on what clans these people hailed from, any potential pitfalls. Ded hadn't thought to include that data in his dossier, and he couldn't be blamed for it since he was a warrior, not an aide de camp. The big guard probably wished he could settle this shit by kicking someone's face in—and while challenges were perfectly acceptable at home, here, that would get them locked up.

Aloud he only said, "I'm grateful to your employer for making time to see me."

"Of course," she said, sounding somewhat uncertain.

At last, she led them through a locked door and onto one of the production floors. It was too loud to hear with the rumble of machines, so Alastor didn't try to talk. It was blessedly hot, a respite from the bitter chill, and those working the machines stared at him as his small party went past, their faces dirty and glossed with sweat. He could only imagine how hot and exhausted they must be at the end of the day. Golgerra had facilities like this as well, but it was such hard work that prisoners and criminals were sent to do it, often in chains. Since nobody was fastened to their equipment here, he concluded that their employment must be voluntary.

Conveyor belts, gouts of steam, sorting metal bits with a rake, then letting them fall into a funnel—he couldn't quite decipher what he saw. Christie was shouting something, and he couldn't make it out, but he wheeled away in time to avoid a beeping vehicle laden with crates. All told, it felt like he'd crossed a combat zone when she started up some scaffolding-like metal stairs, all utility, no charm, this place.

Ideal for creating weapons of mass destruction.

The office upstairs overlooked the work floor with glass framing it all around. He couldn't believe how quiet it was when the door shut behind them. He took stock of the office, metal everything, including shelves and desk, with a floor that clanked when he moved across it. As the assistant had mentioned, the back wall was plastered with photos, and he would've liked a better look at them to discover what/who Furbander found fascinating enough to commemorate.

Alastor extended a hand to Mr. Furbander, whose head came to Alastor's shoulder. The factory owner had a shock of red hair laced with white at the temples, a ruddy complexion, and a perpetually skeptical expression. Which didn't bode well for this meeting.

Still, he had to try.

He bowed, because that was a courtesy he would offer any important dignitary, and Furbander burst out laughing. "Princely manners, for sure, but they're wasted on me. There are no royals among the Animari, so don't expect any special treatment."

So, he's Animari. It was a helpful clue, and he tucked it away for later use.

"If you'll excuse me, sir?" Christie cut in.

The man waved her away with an impatient look. "I don't want tea or biscuits, so don't bother me for at least half an hour."

Once she'd gone, Alastor took the seat Furbander indicated, a well-worn leather chair with cracks from cold and improper care. "I'm not looking for royal privilege, sir. I only ask that you hear me out."

15.

WITH A GROAN, Sheyla arched her back. For the last eight hours, she'd been in the lab, analyzing Alastor's medication. She wouldn't screw up a second time. Now she had a limited sample to administer, but hell if she knew where she'd get more of some of those ingredients. *Most likely I'll end up scouring every open market in the city.*

It had taken fifteen minutes of pleading to get Dr. Seagram to accede to her request, unsurprising since he'd never treated a Golgoth before, and she had to offer all her data, along with promising to supervise his residents on rounds for a fortnight, and she'd also be on call for emergencies. Though her workload was now lamentable, at least she wasn't on the regular rotation. Seagram had tried for that, but she held firm.

In the changing room, she stripped and showered, washing away that hospital smell. Regrettable, but she shouldn't wash her hair while it was so cold outside. Though it was dim in the back hallways of St. Casimir, it brightened as she headed toward the public spaces, until there came a clear demarcation between what was meant for staff and what patients and their families enjoyed. Light streamed through the stained glass above the clear panes, iconic scenes from the history that the Order of St. Casimir acknowledged, such as when Oleg the Abundant tamed the first wolfkin and taught them a civilized tongue. Doubtless Pine Ridge understood another version of those events. The next panel boasted of Anwen's Ride, where she carried the Burnt Amber flame to all Numina in every corner of the land, a feat requiring such great endurance that songs persisted to this day.

Her comm unit buzzed, pulling her from vague admiration of the play of light and color, but by the time she dug it out, it had stopped. With a shrug, she turned for the doors, only to spot Alastor waiting just inside the hospital, his cheeks red flagged with cold. In that moment, it was like she saw him for the first time, and it was an onslaught of impressions: raven black braids twined together in an intricate cascade, eyes like ancient gems, and a smile so sincere and sweet that her toes actually curled. Normally, physical beauty was a fact she cataloged, not an appeal that she reacted to in any visceral fashion.

She wasn't the only one looking, either. People paused to admire him just as she had the stained glass, and it could've been anything from his graceful height to his fine features. In the time since they'd parted, he'd acquired a brown coat with a wooly lining and a plaid scarf that added a roguish air when he needed absolutely no adornment.

"Have I rendered you speechless?" he teased.

"A little."

Delighted surprise illuminated him; it was the only word that fit. The resultant smile nearly made a man walk into a wall. "Don't *admit* it. I'll become insufferable."

Certainly, she appreciated attractiveness on an aesthetic

level but she'd never been drawn to anyone like this. Her feet were carrying her toward him before she consciously made that call.

"I think my new goal may be to puff you up as much as possible. Dedrick can have the unenviable duty of deflation."

"He will judge you most ungenerous. Just now you were far too absorbed in something that isn't me," he chided. "Though I will own that those panels are quite pretty."

She had nothing to say about architectural features. As she reached him and he took her hands, she fell into his gaze like a deep, mossy well. "Hi," she said, suddenly breathless.

"We forgot to start there, didn't we? Hi. Hello. I missed you." He punctuated the last five words with fluttering kisses, missing her mouth each time with what had to be maddening intent.

It was beyond her to lie, so she dipped her chin, breaking eye contact. "I would have. If I hadn't been so absorbed in my work."

He laughed. "How is it that no matter what you say, it feels like a hug? Maybe it's because you're diabolically gorgeous and only grow more so by the day."

"Thank you?" Her mother had always taught her to accept compliments politely, even if they seemed extravagant or inaccurate. Plus, there was no denying the way he made her heart leap, comparable only to racing across a sunny plain in cat form.

"Come along. This place has held you hostage long enough." He towed her toward the exit.

Outside, the sun was hidden behind the clouds, a light sprinkle of snow dusting down. Whether it was the weather or her company, the day turned a bit magical as she strolled with Alastor away from St. Casimir. He swung their joined hands so playfully that she almost didn't ask, "So how did your mission go?"

His arm slowed. "Not brilliantly. He wants assurances that he won't suffer revenue loss on the conversion."

"Ah. Too bad your brother doesn't give a shit about the free market. He'll claim all the factories in Hallowell, if he can."

"Precisely. But it was overly optimistic that a businessman would act on my word alone."

"Any news from Chancellor Quarles?"

"Not yet," he said.

"It's the first day. You're doing well." She wasn't great at consolation, but when Alastor squeezed her hand, it seemed like that sufficed.

"There's nothing more to be done tonight," he said with an elegant shrug. "What's happening over there?"

At first, Sheyla couldn't see over the crowd but when the golden orbs lit up one by one overhead, dotting the skyline, she remembered. "This is the Festival of Lights."

"The what?" He lit up with interest, and that made her want to share everything she knew, even when it wasn't her area of expertise.

"It's an old tradition, harking back to Anwen's Ride. Do you know that story?"

Alastor shook his head. "My education wasn't the best, and even if it had been, it's doubtful the tutor would've covered this."

"Why don't we get some spiced tea and frybread? And I'll tell you how it began."

He hesitated. "I feel a bit ashamed of letting you pay for

me again..."

"If I didn't want to, I wouldn't offer, and this is a treat you shouldn't miss."

Whatever he saw in her face seemed to persuade him, so she cut a path toward the busy drink stall first and then waited in a brisk line to get their paper-wrapped pastries, steaming in the cold and liberally dusted with cinnamon and sugar. There were tables nearby, and she chose one near the crackling fire barrel. Across the plaza, children and elders alike were skating on a frozen fountain, executing pratfalls and pirouettes with a joy that reminded Sheyla why she'd loved her time in Hallowell. It wasn't home, of course, nor was her family here, but she'd be damned if she let it fall into Tycho's hands.

"This is inappropriately delicious," Alastor said around a huge mouthful of fry bread. "It makes me want to do indecent things to it."

"I've been supplanted by a fresh edible obsession? How lowering." After she made the quip, she realized it sounded like something he might say.

Shit. His humor's rubbing off on me.

His wide grin said he agreed, and his eyes sparkled a bit. "Never fear, you shall forever remain my favorite edible obsession."

Impossible not to imagine the night before, his perfect mouth between her thighs. She tightened them, conscious of a quiet pulse of longing that cared little for location or timing. He had been so eager, willing to do exactly as she asked—to cover her helpless response to that exquisite memory, Sheyla sipped at her spiced milk tea. *Delicious.* And it went perfectly with the frybread; she focused on chewing, savoring.

"I've stolen your ability to speak again, it seems."

Her voice came out smoky and dark with desire. "If I told you what I'm thinking, you wouldn't be able to walk comfortably."

That startled a sharp breath from him, visible in a puff of white, and now she could hear his heart racing. Good, she liked even footing.

"Ah, well. Damn. Too late on that count anyway. Why don't you distract me with that story you promised?"

SHIFTING IN THE chair offered Alastor no relief.

His cock had spiked the moment she hinted at what must be lusciously lewd thoughts, and now he had to listen to a folk tale to calm down. He drank some tea, outwardly the picture of poise while inside his pants, he could already feel the drizzle of precome. Wanting had never cut into him like a wall of thorns before, both brutal and piercing.

On the plus side, he could stare at her face all day and since she was speaking, it was even a normal thing to do. "Where was I?"

Fuck, he had no idea. Guessing, he offered, "Anwen's Ride?"

"Right. Well, as the story goes, Anwen was a high-ranking abbess in the Burnt Amber clan during those unsettled times. This was before the Pax Protocols were signed."

"So, the Numina were all at war, then."

"Just so. She claimed to have had a powerful vision, urging her to take the light of peace to the four corners of our lands."

"To each of the sovereign territories." Despite his

throbbing erection, he was getting interested in the history lesson.

"More or less, though the borders weren't drawn then as they are now. In any event, she set off alone, bearing limited supplies and a torch she could not allow to go out, no matter the cost, as the spirit had prophesied that failure would signal her doom." She fell quiet, likely gauging his response to her recitation so far.

"Well?" he prompted. "Don't leave me in suspense."

She narrowed her eyes. "I could spend hours on this if I offered all the embellishments. You're getting the abridged edition. After many tribulations, Anwen succeeded in carrying the fire emblem of peace to all Numina. That pilgrimage ultimately resulted in the signing of the Pax Protocols."

"No doom, then?"

"Hardly. Anwen lived to be ninety-four, and she wrote seven different versions of her wondrous journey. Since then, many cities honor her with the Festival of Lights. Each globe represents a soul she saved by ending those turbulent times and ushering in a new era."

His heart dropped like a stone, and suddenly his prick wasn't a problem anymore. His brother was threatening an aeon of peaceful coexistence; that was the antithesis of arousing. Alastor forced a smile but his cheeks felt like stone beneath a chisel.

"Thank you for telling me." He finished his food and drink in quiet, and the wind cut through him in icy bursts, little joy to be had in simple pleasures any longer.

Alastor should have known she'd sense his changed mood, for she'd always been able to read him, even before she came to him as a lover. As they walked to the row house, she said, "Do you plan to tell me what's troubling you or must I coax it out of you?"

He didn't want to answer, but he didn't wish to shut her out either. Weighing the balance took until they reached the suite; inside it was warm and he stripped out of his layers mechanically. Dedrick would have snatched the coat from his hands, so it was a welcome novelty to be permitted to choose whether to toss it over the back of a chair or hang it. He elected for the latter, conscious that she was giving him time to collect his thoughts.

"Tycho," he said quietly. "Will they still be able to have a Festival of Lights after this year? He threatens everything those people hold dear, and I, I—" His voice broke; he couldn't speak the rest.

Am inadequate.

Simply defending Hallowell seemed like a daunting, impossible task, so how could he dream of toppling Tycho from the throne as well? Golgerra was too beautiful for him to want to destroy it, though there were certainly weapons capable of bringing the mountain down on top of them. That would mean the wholesale slaughter of his own people, many of whom hated and feared his brother but couldn't risk their lives in resistance.

Weary and flush with despair, he sank to the carpeted floor in front of the tan sofa and turned his face to the cushions. What he knew of Sheyla suggested that she'd leave him be, neither interfering nor judging this moment of weakness. From somewhere deep came the burn of tears, but they were frozen and wouldn't fall. Then he felt her warmth against his side, a gentle hand on his nape. That touch thawed him just enough, and he leaned into her with a raw shudder, buried his face in the curve of her neck.

He cried because she didn't tell him not to; she didn't whisper of weakness or betrayal. She didn't tell him he had to be strong. Conversely, when he calmed, he felt that perhaps he *could* be, just not all the time. His need for her shifted again, benchmarks that might be forever moving. Before, he'd loved listening to her breathe, and now she gave him the space to do so, a circle of freedom when obligations were tightening on him like a noose.

I can do this as long as she's with me.

"Words may not help right now," she said. "But have these anyway. It's early days yet. Don't think of failure or success. Only do what you can, when you can, step by step."

"Is that how you survived your residency at St. Casimir? I understand it's grueling."

Sheyla nodded. "Sometimes, the only way out is through, but the distance to the finish is so substantial that gazing at the horizon would weaken your resolve."

"That... is precisely what I needed to hear."

"Every job seems more manageable if you break it down."

Alastor rested his head on her shoulder and basked in the pleasure of her palms on his back. She petted him as one might a great cat, understandable, given her nature, and he found it beyond soothing. He relaxed into her arms with a flicker of wonder at her strength. There was no doubt in him that she could carry him off to bed, should she so choose, and the mental image jolted him faintly with renewed craving.

"Your heart's racing again."

"This ability is a trifle unnerving, my darling *shalai*. I can't even entertain a carnal thought in private, it seems."

"I am... intrigued." She tugged on his cascade of plaits

hard enough that it hurt a little, and his cock leapt in reaction, stiffening at the promise of rough play. "That's the second time you've named me thus. Shouldn't you explain what it means?"

"I believe I'll keep this secret a bit longer."

Sheyla bent her head to his and bit down on his earlobe. "Is that so? Well, I have ways of making you talk."

"Continue in that line and you'll certainly make me moan." The sharp nip tingled down his spine, lingering in his ass, thighs, and cock, sweet spots where he wanted her mouth. She'd given him a sex bruise the night before, and the sore spot on his chest throbbed in reaction.

"Do you provoke all your lovers this way?" Though her tone was light, she was watching his face, ready to gauge his answer.

"Hm. Are you asking about those who came before?"

"Have there been many?" That wasn't a denial of interest, he noted.

"A handful. I was always constrained by the awareness that anyone I desired might not dare decline my interest."

"You needn't worry about me in that regard. I came to you slowly, but I am steadfast."

Her words rang like a pledge that she would always want him, and he shivered in delight. "Do you mind if I ask who was most recently in your bed?"

Alastor could tell this wasn't simple curiosity on her part, but he had no reason to hide the truth. "Dedrick."

"Ah."

There were *so* many ways he could take that response, and he hoped it wasn't a bad one; he didn't wish to think less of her. "I enjoy fucking *and* being fucked. Is that a problem?"

"Hardly. I could say the same. The reason I asked is because I've seen the way Rowena watches you, how you're so gentle with her, and I wondered—"

"No," he cut in. "She fancies herself in love with me. It would be cruel to...use that."

"Then I need to ask, I should have before. By being together, are we hurting him?"

It was a considerate question, one that made him like her more, and Alastor was already half out of his mind where she was concerned. "We've never spoken of emotions. I don't even know if he *enjoys* being with me. I'm his prince, he does as I will. Because he serves me, it's..." He gave a helpless shrug.

Sheyla smiled then. "Would you like to find out?"

16.

SHEYLA COULD TELL Alastor believed she was about to call the guard in and suggest a tryst, but he didn't seem at all shocked. Belatedly, she recalled the bloodlust and its implications for his people. The Golgoth probably didn't blink over group engagements; three people might qualify as tame for all she knew. Under optimal circumstances, she might be up for an adventure, but it didn't seem like the right time for such self-indulgent behavior.

"If that's what you want. The invitation might ease his mind, in fact."

Does that mean Dedrick is worried about my relationship with the prince?

"I was joking, though I'm not opposed to the notion. But *he* seems rather disapproving."

"He thinks I'll get caught up in you and forget where my responsibilities lie."

"That's fair," Sheyla decided, after a moment's consideration. "That said, I don't have the energy to manage both of you tonight."

Alastor's brows shot up. "Manage? I'm fascinated as to how you envision such an encounter unfolding."

Before she could respond, his comm buzzed. From his expression, it must be good news, but she wasn't prepared for him to pull her into a jubilant hug. The prince spun her until she was dizzy and then he let her read the text.

The ministry has voted in favor of supporting your defense initiative. Please attend the briefing, 11 am tomorrow.

"That's fantastic," she said. "It should be easier to persuade that factory owner too."

Alastor sighed. "He's the first of many. Fortunately, I don't have to figure everything out tonight."

"This is likely to be our last respite for a while. How would you like to spend it?" Sex was the obvious answer, but Sheyla suspected he might have other desires.

"Why don't we see if we'll both fit in the bath and go from there?"

"You want me to scrub your back?" The request was endearingly simple and sweet.

"Among other things."

The vertical tub design was familiar to Sheyla, as they'd had one in the residence hall where she'd occasionally slept. It had a narrow bench where you could perch to wash yourself and a handheld sprayer. She went into the bathroom to start the hot water and set up properly, switching from shower to soak. Alastor came in behind her, naked, all hugging arms and wistful eyes, so she didn't shoo him out.

"You should show me how to do this. I didn't even know this was a tub."

"There's nothing like this in Golgerra?"

"No, our bath houses are more like yours in Ash Valley, with huge communal hot springs that come up through the stone."

"Yours are natural then. Ours are a matter of cunning design." She beckoned. "We should get in and enjoy the steam. Shut the door behind you."

He did as she asked, and the heat felt exquisite misting on her tired muscles. There wasn't a ton of room between them, but given how Alastor snuggled, he wasn't interested in privacy or personal space. As the water rose, he relaxed against her, head on her chest.

His hair was still in braids, so she didn't touch them. The rest of him, she washed with gentle care, earning an 'mmm' of pleasure. He was excitingly thorough in offering the same service; once she had to swat his hands away.

"Soaking is the best part," he mumbled.

A couple of times, Sheyla almost nodded off, but she jerked awake in time to keep from flooding the bathroom. His eyes were closed, and it seemed as if he might be dozing, so she didn't move.

She thought that until he said, "I've never done this, you know."

"Shared a bath?"

He sighed, a rueful sound that emulated a laugh. "No. Attempted anything of such importance. It was nice in the plaza with you, but now I can't stop thinking that if I fail, it's not only my people who will suffer. That was true before, but I've never seen the other Numina just living their lives…"

"I think I'm offended." Sheyla had already spoken all the comforting words at her disposal, so it was clearly time to pick a fight.

He sat up a bit, angling for a glimpse of her face. "Sorry?"

"You should be. Here we are, completely naked, and

you're obsessing over work."

"That's remarkably rude of me, isn't it?" He reached for her and dusted gentle fingertips over her shoulder, trickling warm water on her skin with a delicacy that made her tingle.

"Without a doubt."

"Then...where are the lines drawn tonight? You said before that you're waiting for a certain level of anticipation."

Sheyla laughed softly. "It's no fun if I tell you. I suggest you discover for yourself, what I'll allow."

She made out his sharp intake of breath, the little shiver that rolled through him. His eyes went smoky as he pulled her in for a kiss, a treat she would never deny either of them. His mouth was magical, soft and delicious, and slightly tentative, as if he wasn't quite sure how much he could have. She answered that unspoken question with hungry thrusts of her tongue, biting down on his lower lip until he shuddered and dug his hands into her arms.

"You like when it hurts a little," she whispered.

His answer came in the form of his hand covering hers, urging it onto his iron-hard cock. She squeezed like he wanted her to, but not for as long as he needed. Just as he started to hump against her curled fingers, she let go and watched his length bob urgently in the hot water.

"You need to come, but it's not happening yet."

With a pull and twist, he hauled her into his lap and she wrapped her legs and arms around him. This position granted her dominance because she could decide how much to move, how much friction she allowed their wet bodies. At first, he didn't seem to notice, with his hands all over her ass, and it felt so good that she forgot about controlling the action for a few moments, just circling her hips in his palms as he cupped and squeezed.

When she moaned and arched her back, he took her breast with his mouth. Sheyla pushed his head away, so her nipple popped out of his mouth with a wet sound. The whimper that escaped him told her everything about his cravings; he liked these power games, being teased and denied a little first. And giving him what he wanted… it was driving her wild. Already her pussy was soft and swollen, her clit pulsing in the hot water, so she couldn't stop swirling her hips. Hopefully, he'd take it for more teasing, not a sign that she was about to lose it and fuck him through the wall.

"I'm willing to do one thing for you tonight. Think carefully, then ask. In words. If you put my hand on your cock again, I'm getting out and you can finish alone."

"You're vicious," he said.

"Good communication is important." Sheyla knew her smile had to be feline, but she was a cat after all. "Is it so hard to choose one pleasure?"

He was breathing hard, trying without subtlety to rub against her, but she flattened a palm between them. Alastor gazed up at her with hungry eyes, and she almost gave in, except he didn't truly want her to. So she kissed each of his eyelids and waited.

"If I can't have you," he finally whispered, "then you have me. I need a good fucking."

Lust nearly overwhelmed her. When he climbed into her lap and lifted his hips, she knew exactly what he wanted. She teased beneath his balls with gentle fingertips and he squirmed in pleasure the second she grazed the puckered skin. A brief tension, then he relaxed against her, his breath coming in eager gusts.

Sheyla took her time, loving, softening, and using the warm water to ease her way. With each jerk and moan, Alastor made it clear that he couldn't get enough and her clit ached, so she shifted to get some pressure on it.

He sensed the move and pushed back against her. "Are you going to finish like this?"

"I might." She whispered that right into his ear as she took him.

"FUCK, THAT'S IT," Alastor moaned.

He lifted his ass and raised his legs to give her a better angle. She was good at this, working him just right. Dimly he felt her moving against him and he wanted to make it good for her, but he was absolutely transfixed by the pleasure spiraling through him. He could no more stop his grunts and moans than he could halt the orgasm building with each stroke of her finger.

His head fell back against her shoulder. She reached for his cock with her other hand and toyed with him until he could feel the slickness. Then she let go, rinsing his sensitive skin. With the water sluicing over him, it was like being fucked *everywhere*. He trembled with need.

"Do it for me," she said against his ear. "Right now. I'm letting you."

His cock swelled, and Alastor came so hard that he probably would've cramped up, if he hadn't been floating in warm water. She held her fingers still until he calmed and then she slid free of his body with a softness he appreciated. His entire body felt boneless and if he could have, he would've given her the world on a platter for diverting him from his worries in such a perfect way. They still prowled at the edge of his mind, but he was too pleasantly exhausted for them to gain ground.

Sheyla was still moving against him, and he rocked with her, hoping it was enough. She shivered and made sounds, bit down on his shoulder. *Feels good. Harder.* The words didn't quite come out. He was still glowing when they stumbled out of the bathroom. Probably they should eat food and get some sleep but all he wanted to do was wrap himself around her. She insisted that he eat... something. He did it to please her and then stumbled to bed. It took longer for her to join him and he was groggy, even then.

"Are you all right?" he asked, half-asleep.

"Why wouldn't I be?"

"I don't know if... if you...well, if you didn't, I should probably apologize and offer compensation later."

She wrapped her arms around him and snuggled against his back. "I did, don't worry. This isn't a matter that requires reparations."

"Good, because I'm fresh out of oomph."

"It's enough to feel you close."

That reassurance was enough to let him fall deep, and he didn't stir until a comm buzzed in the middle of the night, and with a whispered apology, she rolled away. In the morning, guilt overwhelmed him when he roused alone. She'd left him a series of notes on the counter. *I'm on call at St. Casimir. Good luck with your meeting.* There was a case next to it, along with a second memo. *Take this instead of what I made before. The formula should be identical to the original serum.* On the fridge, she'd left a final message:

It's hard to leave you. There's fresh juice in here. I'll miss your face.

Alastor smiled over that, plucked the paper, folded it, and tucked it into his pocket like a talisman. To the best of his recollection, she hadn't mentioned working at the hospital before, but it wasn't like he could pay for her time. He drained the full dose, noting that it tasted the same, too. Bitterness lingering on his tongue, he had breakfast and got ready for the appointment. Dedrick would be accompanying him today, provided the guard agreed not to cause any trouble over minor slights.

As if on cue, a knock sounded; it was a novelty for Alastor to open his own door. In Golgerra, ten levels of staff separated him from visitors, half of whom might try to kill him on Tycho's orders. Dedrick had donned his good suit and wore his hair properly today, disclosing his true rank. Sometimes on patrol, he didn't bother since he'd only had status since he started serving Alastor. Before, he occupied the lowest tier of society, equivalent to foreign captives or prisoners of war. His people had only recently been allowed entry into Golgerra, punishment for some ancient offense. Under his silent scrutiny, Ded was pulling at his jacket.

"You look good," he said.

Ded flashed him a suspicious look, but there was no hidden sting in his words. "If you say so."

"I do. How are the men faring? I should check in on them once we finish today."

"They're bored, if you want the truth. A short rest is welcome, too much and they start worrying about their families. That leads to frayed tempers and—"

"Soon we'll have the constable called on us," Alastor finished.

"Since they understand how vital it is for us to succeed, they're on their best behavior, but I don't know how long it'll last."

"We'll speak to the militia captain after the meeting. The sooner we get the men on the city rotation, the better. We should also meet with Gavriel and Korin, find out what they've accomplished so far."

"You're having lunch with them today. Should I send the address to your comm?"

"No point, unless you have other plans."

"My only goal is to keep you safe," Dedrick said in a monotone.

He'd heard variations on that theme for years, so it didn't surprise him this time. After his conversation with Sheyla, however, guilt niggled at him that he'd never delved any deeper. *This is going to be so awkward.* That surety didn't stop him from wading in.

"I know you're not certain getting tangled up with the Animari doctor is a good idea... for political reasons," he started, then he couldn't figure out where to go from there, so he stalled. "Is there any other reason you have... doubts?"

Dedrick blinked. "I have no idea what you're driving at, sire."

"I mean, do you feel bothered...?" *Fuck. This is a bad idea.*

Finally, he seemed to get the gist. "Are you asking if I'm upset? *Jealous?*"

Alastor mumbled, "Never mind," wishing he hadn't let Sheyla put questions in his head. Typically, sex wasn't an emotional thing among his people; it was more like a good workout—sweaty and enjoyable. Bonds did form over time—and with repeated matings—but he should've trusted that Dedrick saw occasional bed-sport as casual and convenient.

"If you'll grant me leave to be candid?"

"Of course."

"I take pride in serving you and I enjoy when that extends to pleasure. But you are my prince, not my mate."

"Understood." An imp of mischief made him add, "You *may* be invited to play with us at some point, if she desires it. I don't expect you to accede, so please don't look on that as an extension of your service."

That shocked the guard into silence, and Alastor enjoyed the rare sensation of seeing Ded at a loss for words. A hot flush started at his neck and flooded upward, making his scar stand out sharper in contrast. He tugged at his collar. "You've... discussed this possibility with her?"

Briefly, he considered recounting the conversation in context, but they were pressed for time, so he replied with a brisk nod. Alastor was sated so fully that he couldn't muster a spark at the notion, even in theory. Which was good since he needed to focus, and he didn't want Dedrick drifting into sex fantasies at the summit.

"Don't start anything," he reminded the guard.

"Best behavior. No biting." Hard to tell if Ded was joking.

"Shall we go, then?"

It wasn't far to the ministry, and this time, nobody gave him a hard time. The receptionist clearly recognized him and offered a respectful nod as he strode past. Chancellor Quarles didn't make him deal with her secretary, either; she was waiting in front of her office to guide him down the hall to the conference room where the ministers were waiting. To his surprise, Korin of Pine Ridge, McRae of Burnt Amber, and Gavriel of the Eldritch were present as well. The first two greeted him with "Good to see you" and

"Hello" respectively whereas the assassin simply raised his chin.

Which reminded him. Alastor dragged Gavriel into the hall to say, "Back off Rowena. Understand?"

A blank look, then dawning comprehension. "Did she complain about me?"

He knows this is about the night after our first battle.

"That's not her way. And it's not *your* place to judge her. Are we clear?"

After a brief, rancorous pause, Gavriel nodded. "I'll apologize to her."

Satisfied, Alastor led the way back into the conference room. There were eleven new faces and he dedicated himself to memorizing their names and titles. Alastor offered a half-bow and a handshake to each, then took his place at the table. Ded sat behind him with Zan and the assortment of aides who would fetch drinks or important documents on demand.

Chancellor Quarles rapped her walking stick on the table "Now that the niceties are attended, let's get down to business."

17.

SHEYLA WORKED FOR six hours without a break, dealing with one emergency after another. This much effort in exchange for Alastor's care seemed excessive, but she'd already made the deal. Certainly, Dr. Seagram seemed pleased with the exchange, and he hadn't even examined Alastor yet. Who probably wouldn't be delighted that she'd made the swap behind his back.

Exhaustion left her sore but it was a familiar feeling, complete with dry eyes and lips that burned from the beginnings of dehydration. Once she fell into hospital routine, she often forgot that she needed to eat and drink.

"Things have calmed down," she told the ER nurse. "And I'm taking a break. You have my code if I'm needed again."

"Thank you, Dr. Halek."

She wanted to call Alastor and see how things were going. His voice would only distract her, so she chose not to. Instead, she asked for directions to the closest market. It was likely shops had opened and closed in the years she'd been gone. The man at the information desk was happy to explain, even drew her a map with a precision that made

Sheyla wonder, as she was leaving, if his extreme helpfulness was a sign of interest. In the past, she'd rarely picked up on such cues, unless someone came right out and said they wanted to sleep with her. Like Alastor. In fact, she preferred that approach.

Stepping out of St. Casimir into the bitter chill, she tugged up her coat collar. She didn't recognize the woman who pushed away from the wall at first, but when she drew closer, Sheyla placed her as Rowena, the Golgoth guard who loved the prince. Oh, he'd used the word 'fancied' to qualify the attachment but from the intensity currently facing her, this wasn't a woman who doubted her own mind.

"Good afternoon." Courtesy was never a poor choice, even if Rowena intended to challenge her for bed rights. Was that a thing in Golgoth society?

"I was waiting for you." That much was obvious, so Sheyla nodded and paused for the other woman to continue. "It's become clear that you share a special connection with our prince, so I thought… well, I'd like to get to know you better. If you'll allow that."

There was no point in explaining that their 'special connection' had an expiration date. Rather than being combative, Rowena seemed so tentative yet hopeful that even if she'd wanted to be left alone, Sheyla wouldn't have been able to refuse. As it was, she was happy to offer, "I'm off shopping now. Do you want to come?"

She offered a shy smile. "Thank you. There aren't many women in the barracks. This will be a nice change."

Sheyla set off as directed, a walk that carried them away from the plaza and the government buildings into gentrified streets where old tenements had been restored and in some cases connected via demolition of walls. There was no risk of mistaking the market, as it had been a former greenhouse, now with some panels replaced with stained glass. The light was radiant with green and gold, adding everyday magic to running errands. Some of the foliage remained, so when she stepped inside, it smelled lush and fresh, part botanical garden, part marketplace.

"This is lovely," Rowena exclaimed.

Sheyla turned with a smile; she'd been so wrapped up in navigation that she'd forgotten she had company. Her one-track mind made it challenging to maintain a relationship. Previously, she'd only been so absorbed by research problems, yet Alastor had tapped his way to the center of her brain, lodging there with disarming tenacity.

"I've never been here," she said. "It's new, or rather, new to me. This was part of an urban farm when I lived here."

"Did you like it in Hallowell?" Rowena asked. The woman was obviously trying so hard to be friendly that her every question came out a touch awkward.

"I did. Once I completed my residency, I needed to go home, though. My family was waiting."

They still are, she thought.

A pang of guilt ran through her. *I should have called to let them know I've arrived safely.* Even if there were potential security issues with the Ash Valley equipment, there had to be tech experts who could encrypt. Anyway, enemy forces wouldn't learn anything of value tapping her family chat.

"I've never lived in Golgerra properly," Rowena said then. "But I understand well the pull of home. It's why we're all fighting, isn't it?"

"No question." She needed to find the items on her list,

necessary to produce a larger run of Alastor's medicine; the hospital only had enough of certain ingredients for that small test batch. But she couldn't help asking, "Have you met Tycho?"

Rowena shook her head, her mouth tightening. "I've seen him. He would never spare a moment for someone like me."

No idea what that means.

If the other woman wanted her to know, she'd elaborate. Unexpectedly, Rowena smiled. "I understand better now. You're a quiet island, and it makes a person want to fill that silence."

"Excuse me?" What an odd thing to say, on par with Alastor wanting to listen to her breathe.

"I don't even know you, but I think I could tell you things, someday. Maybe when we're friends?" Rowena gave such a hopeful look that Sheyla could only nod.

She had the unnerving sensation that if she continued down this path with Alastor, she might be taking on his people, too, and she hadn't planned for such responsibility. With a resolute shake of her head, Sheyla headed for the herb stalls. She asked in three places before being directed to a stand toward the back of the enclosure. This one was like an apothecary shop, full of glass jars that held interesting dried flora and fauna.

"Word's already gotten out. You're searching for rare and expensive components." The wizened old woman grinned at Sheyla. "Don't tell me you're trying to create the elusive Philosopher's Stone."

That was a joke, she thought, so she offered a polite chuckle. "Something far more precious, actually."

"Then let's have your list. I'll put together what I can.

How much do you want of each?"

"Everything you have and leads on direct purchase, if you're inclined to offer them."

The old woman shook her head. "That would be cutting off my own foot. The middleman needs to eat, too."

"Figured as much, but it doesn't hurt to try." Sheyla angled her head in rueful acknowledgment of the failed gambit.

Once she handed the shopping list over, she realized Rowena was staring at her. "This is... you're making medicine for the prince, yes?"

There didn't seem to be any point in denying it. "It should be as effective as what he had in Golgerra."

To her astonishment, Rowena clutched one of her hands in both of hers and then touched her forehead to the back in a simple obeisance. "Thank you. Dedrick said you would save him, but we've all been so afraid."

She pulled free, trying to be gentle. "Er, yes, that's my job."

He's your lover, not your patient.

Rowena's jubilant expression didn't shift, and it was impassioned enough to make Sheyla uncomfortable. The way Alastor's people adored him told a story, one that made her wonder whether leaving him would be as easy as he'd made it sound.

"Here." The herb seller handed over the package and named a price, steeper than Sheyla had hoped, but with what she'd bought here, she could make six months of serum. "You're only missing one item, and for the right price, I could tell you where to find it."

"You're extorting me for information?" she asked, half angry, half amused.

"We all have to make a living, doctor. If money matters to you more than time, feel free to search."

She ground her teeth. "Fine. How much?"

The sum wasn't unreasonable, but in principle, it didn't set well with her to pay up. *I'm doing this for Alastor.* "If this lead doesn't pan out, I'll be back." She let a touch of the great cat out, fueling the threat in a deep snarl.

The old woman only laughed, as if she was threatened by angry felines every day, so the information must be good. Unfortunately, the merchant didn't keep a stall here; they needed to take the trolley across town. Sheyla was about to invite Rowena along when her comm buzzed.

CODE ORANGE. Immediate assistance required in the ER.

Reality made no sense.

Alastor smelled blood, everywhere, blood. Stinging wound, but it was distant from the roaring in his head. *This, no. It's impossible.* Zan tried to hold him up, but he slid to the floor anyway, smearing red everywhere, the scene on loop in his brain. *Burned in, really.*

There should have been a sign.

There was no sign.

After a productive meeting, he'd gone to lunch with Gavriel, Zan, Callum, Korin, and Dedrick. Someone had booked a private salon, posh, with silver sconces, dark paneling, and velvet drapes. Their party hadn't drawn unusual attention and Gavriel was talking about the upcoming appointment with the captain of the militia. The Eldritch would be attending that while Callum meant to meet with the engineering corps to give them a crash course in Burnt Amber war machines, and Korin had demanded to be taught as well.

All good. Delicious food, spiced tea that reminded him of that afternoon in the plaza with Sheyla. Everyone safe and sound.

Before and after.

"The waiter has a knife!" Zan shouted it. Eight invaders, dressed in black, masked, and they all had weapons. Alastor flung himself sideways. The blade sliced across his shoulder, but Dedrick was there, always there. He grabbed the attacker, breaking his arm with a brutal twist.

Like this, I'm a liability, Alastor had thought. His best move was to change. Dedrick guarded him as he transformed, shredding clothes like the brutes the other Numina called their people in secret. As ever, the shift hurt, torn skin and blood and spikes, and the others were staring, assassins and allies alike.

The memory cut out. He didn't know, he didn't. *The knife. Where did it come from?*

Suddenly it was spinning toward him, and Ded shielded him. Took it in the chest. *Too busy protecting me, he should have shifted.* The aftermath spread in his brain like spilled ink, a scramble of bodies, and he just dropped, cradling the guard against his chest. Zan and Gavriel gave chase, and Korin was calling for help while Callum pounded the last assailant into the floor.

The trip to the hospital was a blur. And now...

Alastor sat on the floor and rocked, his suit in tatters. Zan handed him a lab coat, and as he shrugged into it, red stained the white jacket, Alastor's blood, Dedrick's. Nobody had realized he was injured yet. He lacked the wherewithal to mention it when his friend might be dying.

Zan crouched beside him, a hand on one shoulder. "Can I get you anything?"

He closed his eyes, hoping the Noxblade would go away. Instead, Zan stayed nearby, a silent presence whose comfort he didn't deserve.

"We underestimated them," Callum was saying. "I never expected Tycho would choose the silent path."

"Strategically, it's a smart move," Korin answered. "If he takes his brother out, the internal resistance collapses and he's leading a unified people again."

"Marching to glorious conquest instead of ignominious fratricide." The bear lord sounded weary.

Alastor wobbled, trying to get to his feet. Zan hauled him upright and he shoved the man back. It didn't matter how kind the Eldritch lieutenant seemed; he'd only accept solace from one of his own… or Sheyla. *Where is she?* With a trembling hand, he braced on the wall and left a red print on the pale plaster.

They'd evicted him from the treatment room, but he'd peel off his own skin if they didn't brief him on Ded's condition. He stumbled through the swinging doors in time to spot Sheyla and Rowena rushing in from the opposite side. With all his heart, he wanted her beside him, and she did take one step, but a fellow doctor snagged her arm, drawing her to Dedrick's bedside.

He needs her now. Not me.

Rowena reached his side in an instant. "What happened?"

He couldn't form the words; the scene was too fresh in his head, but also weirdly jumbled. With his chest so tight, it hurt to breathe and the fire from his slashed shoulder seemed to be spreading. He ate the pain as he moved toward Sheyla, already conferring with the other specialists. From here, he could tell Dedrick didn't look good. His color was off, slipping from ashen toward gray, and Alastor had been attached to enough medical machines to interpret his vital signs.

"We've given him at transfusion and performed laser surgery, but he's not better." The doctor handed Sheyla the datapad with all relevant information.

"It sounds like this was an assassination attempt. In that case, there's a good chance the blade was poisoned," Sheyla said, once she finished the review.

Fuck no, Alastor thought, or breathed. He might have even wept.

The medical team scattered, one of them shouting about bloodwork. By the time they figured out what was on the knife, it might be too late to administer an antidote. Plus, Ded's wound went deep, so the venom was already pumping through his body.

No, no, no.

He wheeled and ran for the hallway where Callum and Korin waited, but they weren't who he needed. *Where the fuck is Gavriel?* Alastor couldn't remember if the Noxblade had come with them to the hospital, and his inability to focus made him slam his fist into the wall, until the blaze of pain cut through the fog. His hand was also a mangled wreck, a red smear of clarity.

Zan put a hand on his shoulder, preventing him from taking another swing. "I'll call him for you. Keep it together."

As soon as Alastor heard Gavriel's voice, he grabbed the comm. "Where are you?"

"Still at the detention center. They won't let me speak

to the prisoner yet. Something about fearing for his safety."

For maybe the first time ever, Alastor was on the same page as the Eldritch. "Did you recognize anything about the attackers? Do you know what kind of poison they might've used?"

There were echoing noises, clanging doors and the chatter of passing law enforcement. Each second Gavriel delayed for privacy might cost Ded his life. He paced, waiting for an answer.

Finally, the Noxblade said grimly, "I think they were renegade Eldritch, still loyal to Talfayen. We use a variety of toxins. Give me an hour alone with our prisoner. I'll find out."

"Dedrick may not have long," Alastor said, aware that he was begging.

"I'll do my best. Wait for my call."

When he disconnected, Zan steadied him on one side, and he lacked the strength to fight. A long shudder escaped him as he bowed his head.

"Sounds urgent," Korin noted.

He hadn't even heard the wolf lieutenant approach. Unsurprising, he was a bleeding mess. "It is."

"He'll need permission from the local authorities," she said. "And finesse isn't Gav's specialty. I'll head over, better than cooling my heels here. Plus, I suspect this is outside their usual protocol."

"Hurry," he urged. "And take Zan with you. Maybe he can help with the fact-finding."

With a last look, Korin rushed off with the Noxblade, leaving Alastor with Callum. The war priest clapped a hand on his uninjured shoulder, a touch that was probably meant to be bracing but felt like the weight of death instead.

Alastor slid out of his grasp and went back into the treatment room, where Rowena was standing watch from a discreet corner.

"He'll be all right," she whispered.

He has to be.

This... no.

Tycho had given Dedrick to him as a subtle insult, for who wanted a bodyguard pulled off the mountainside, from a fallen family, who had never set foot in Golgerra before? He didn't care about any of that. All that mattered was having someone on his side, who listened and looked after him, and didn't make him feel like shit for having bad days where breathing was the best he could do. Maybe sensing that he was about to lose it, Rowena drew him out into the hallway again.

She guided him to a row of chairs that were bolted together. Just as well, he felt like flipping them because there was nothing he could do. Rowena was talking but he couldn't sort the sounds into disparate words. The burn in his shoulder got worse, lighting up all his nerves, to the point that it hurt to move his right arm. That didn't seem normal. Leaning close, she said something else, eyes wide, and then hurried off.

He leaned his head against the wall and closed his eyes. Anything else seemed like too much fucking effort. When she got back, she was towing the giant bear lord. Who peered at him and said more things, words burbled underwater. Callum shook him and swore when he spotted the wound, still lazily oozing blood. The skin around it seethed with strange purple streaks. *Poison.* Kind of a relief to realize it. The rest of his strength trickled away like blood down a drain. No more pain.

No more *trying*.

In that moment, Alastor was willing. If there was any justice, any balance on a cosmic scale, the universe would take him in trade. He couldn't worry about the greater good, or what would happen once he was gone.

This is right, he thought. *It should be me. Not Dedrick.*

With that deal on the table, he stopped fighting and let go.

18.

TWO DAYS.
In that time, Sheyla hadn't slept. It had taken Gavriel five hours to break the captive, another for the hospital to locate the antidote. Neither Alastor nor Dedrick had awakened yet; while the prince's injury wasn't as serious as the guard's, his illness might complicate treatment.

Her eyes burned as she gazed at his pale face. She took his hand, as she had countless times before, but he didn't flex his fingers or respond to her touch. The beeping machines logged his vitals, regular enough that she could take some comfort in them.

Rowena had stepped up with admirable fortitude, taking command of the Golgoth soldiers with a certainty that it seemed as if she had been born to lead. The woman knocked on the door a few minutes later, despite the ridiculous hour.

"I've come to report," she said.

"Go ahead." There was no point in reminding Rowena that Alastor couldn't respond, and professional opinions were mixed as to whether an unconscious patient could hear and/or comprehend what was said in his presence. Sheyla leaned toward them recognizing familiar voices more than understanding words, but it wasn't as if her beliefs were provable.

Rowena stood at the foot of the bed at attention. "We've set up checkpoints, sire, and rooted out five Talfayen loyalists. There may be more in hiding, but Korin has her men questioning the populace. If strangers have gone to ground, the wolves will hunt them down.

"Korin has completed flight training in her war machine. The bears have finished installing artillery around the perimeter of Old Town. The Chancellor has specified that will be the final fallback if the war effort goes badly. Local masons are repairing the ancient earthworks from the historic fort and we've cleared two warehouses that will shelter civilians. We've also…"

Sheyla let her attention wander as Rowena went on listing preparations, like the raid siren. It came to her then that Alastor wouldn't thank her for haunting his bedside when there was so much to do. That galvanized her into motion and she cut into Rowena's monologue with a brief, "Please stay with him until I get back."

First, she needed to clear her conscience. It took several calls since Callum wasn't answering his comm, but she eventually tracked down the war priest in Old Town, overseeing instruction in proprietary bear-tech war machines. As she drew closer, even his majestic beard couldn't hide the exhaustion.

"What?" he demanded when she pulled him aside.

"I need to call my family. Once it gets real here, I don't know when or if I'll be able to again."

He scowled. "Just call. What do I care?"

"This is a local comm. I'm not sure what channel to use, as the tech in Ash Valley may be compromised."

"Ah." He seemed to understand her problem then, took her unit and fiddled with it for a few minutes. "This is the best we can do on our end. Don't assume it's secure, which means—"

"Don't report anything about defense, got it. Thank you."

No putting it off any longer. It was past dawn at least, and since her parents were both early risers, they should be making breakfast. Picturing it sent a pang through her as she input their comm codes, after using the secure prefix Callum had provided.

"Who is this?"

Voice-only calls were rare, so no wonder her dad sounded suspicious. "It's me, Pap. How is everyone?"

"Who is this? I have no daughter."

In the background, she heard her parents scuffling and then her mother's voice sounded in her ear, not cranky as her father's was but shaky with relief. "Sheyla! Are you all right, my baby? I can't believe you didn't call us to let us know you arrived safely. Your father's angry, don't worry, he'll get over it."

Since she had been disowned six times, she already knew that. "We're in Hallowell. I'm safe. I can't say more, I'm afraid. How are things there?"

"A little better. We won some breathing room and we're hunting again, so the food's better. We're still rebuilding. Your brothers are asleep. Let me wake them…"

Before she could say not to bother, her dad was talking again. "You know what you must do, yes? Do it straight away and I'll try to remember if I have a daughter or not."

"Come home?" she guessed.

"Damn right. We didn't let you study medicine so you could fight a war."

Conflicting emotions assailed her, so fucking uncomfortable when she preferred not to deal with them. Sheyla swiped her free hand across eyes that weren't dry at all anymore. She leaned her head against the wall and listened to her father's chastisement, which didn't end until Darvid snatched the comm away.

"Zaran is furious. Maybe don't ever come back. He said—"

"I don't need you repeating my words." Her oldest brother got on then, voice thick with sleep. "I'll offer the beating personally. You know how hard it is here? Mum cries herself to sleep and she—"

"Don't tell her that," Mum exclaimed.

More wrestling sounds, and then Avi seemed to emerge victorious, that or they let him win. He was quietest and the gentlest of her brothers, so maybe he wouldn't threaten her. "Be safe, Shey. I won't tell you what to do, but just know that our love goes with you, no matter where you are."

There was a hiss and crackle, and an alarm code played. **723: communication compromised, please check**—then she lost the connection completely. *Shit.* So Talfayen's people—or maybe Tycho's—were monitoring Ash Valley communications. Her father would certainly report it, but that only added to her worries.

If the Golgoth attack again—

Sheyla fought the urge to curl into herself and cry. Ash Valley had barely survived one assault—with multiple doctors working flat out. *Now that I'm gone...*

"I ask myself that all the time," Callum said quietly.

Her head came up, defensive posture. "What?"

"Would it have gone different if I'd been there? But I didn't care to bother with treaty nonsense, too much protocol and etiquette. I'm a bit of a hammer, you ken, so to me, all problems look like nails."

"Is that so?" She really didn't know what she was supposed to say, if anything.

"It is. That's also the least productive question in the world because even if the answer is yes, you still can't do anything about it. Only in the present can we act and bring change."

These were the most words she'd ever heard from Callum, but it was clear he saved his speech for good purpose because she took heart in his message. Sheyla squared her shoulders, and marched out of Old Town with a mission. One trolley ride later, and she was at the ministry, prepared to wait all day if she had to. As it turned out, the chancellor was happy to have her secretary provide a writ of authorization.

Maybe I can't force him to wake up, but I can continue his work.

Shortly before noon, Sheyla presented herself at the factory gate without an appointment. The ministry-stamped documents smoothed her path, and in record time, she took a seat in Finneas Furbander's office.

"I don't know if you've heard," she started.

"About the assassins? Foreign royalty in peril. Yes, my sources informed me."

"Then you won't be surprised by this, either." She slapped the writ on the table between them. "Chancellor Quarles has approved our defense imitative, and you are to cease production of machine parts and convert immediately to weaponry. Burnt Amber is willing to share schematics."

Furbander offered a rueful smile. "That would've been my primary objection." Then he picked up the letter, adjusted his spectacles and then skimmed it. "There's no reason to resist, is there? Whether I like it or not, we'll soon be under siege."

"It's pointless to pretend otherwise," she agreed. "I've made a list of other essentials that we'll need. Since you're well-connected in the industry, would you mind reviewing it and giving me some idea whose facilities are best suited to conversion?"

The factory owner raised a brow. "I thought you were a doctor, not a requisitions officer."

Sheyla studied the various photos on the wall. "Nobody is only ever one thing. You're a husband, a father, a philanthropist, and a businessman, are you not?"

Furbander laughed. "Well-put, well-put indeed. I'll do you one better, Dr. Halek. Not only will I evaluate your list, I'll also contact my associates on the matter. If I know my colleagues half as well as I suspect, they'll take Hallowell over our dead bodies."

THIS TIME, ALASTOR was surprised to wake to wake at all.

He had a vague recollection of making a deal with death, promising his life in exchange for Ded's. Possibly that was a hallucination. More than usual, he felt like shit: sore shoulder, tight chest, bruises where the needles had gone in. The usual tubes and sensors were affixed, a testament to the fact that he'd survived. Again.

"Dedrick?" he rasped.

The woman in the chair stirred. Rowena, not Sheyla.

He shouldn't be disappointed—it would be unkind to display it—yet he was. She brushed back her pale waterfall of hair and he was startled to see how worn she looked. No ranking braids, he noticed; she still saw herself as the lowest of the low.

"Don't you sleep anymore?" he tried to tease.

"With both you and Ded lying down, somebody has to work."

"Is he—"

"Alive, if only just. Between the knife slicing past his heart and the poison in his system, the doctors are impressed at Golgolth durability."

"And the men...?"

"They wanted to come. I said they could best serve you by sticking with their rotations and keeping Hallowell safe."

Relief swelled higher, rivaling physical discomfort. "You did well. What else have I missed?"

Rowena reported on all the progress thus far: the capture of the assassins, what the Eldritch, wolves, and bears were doing. Then she proved how well she knew him by answering his next question before he asked it. "Dr. Halek asked me to stay with you until she got back."

"Where is she?"

"Not sure. Early this morning, she just got up and ran out."

"How intriguing. We have a mystery," he said lightly.

It did sting more than a little not to find her waiting. They were... what? No words readily came to mind, and the only promise he'd made was that he wouldn't cling when she decided to leave him.

She wouldn't, though. Not like this.

Sheyla was a woman of courage, conviction, and principle. If she'd realized she couldn't walk this path farther, she would say it to his face. Odd, people had been leaving for as long as he could remember, and normally, he saw it coming, could brace for it. Today it was a little hard to get his breath, not for the usual reasons.

Rowena read his distress, if not the *why* of it, and she offered him a cup of water. He drank it down.

"Better?" she asked.

"Thank you." Not really an answer. "Can I see Ded?"

She hesitated, but in the end, he got his way. Rowena rounded up a wheelchair and they received permission to visit the critical unit, if not the room. It was harder than he expected to see his oldest friend so still and pale. Still huge but also shrunken. Machines beeped and whirred, monitoring him and keeping him alive; Alastor gave thanks for that technology in a fervor so sincere as to feel religious. He pressed two fingers to glass, wishing he had the words worthy of the devotion he had received, time and again, not because he was a good person, but due to an accident of birth.

"That's not true, you know." He didn't realize he'd spoken aloud until Rowena responded. "Ded loves you, we all do, because you are the only light in Golgerra, the only hope any of us have."

Those words were both comfort and salt, for they added to his burden. Somehow, he caught a smile like a fish struggling on the line and brought it to his face. "Thanks."

"I see how you are. The minute my back is turned, you're off gallivanting about the hospital."

His heart skipped. Sheyla's voice, full of amusement, as she knelt before him, mindful of his various attachments as only a doctor could be. She leaned in so their foreheads touched, then she kissed him, a beautiful hello of a caress, that carried layers of meaning, fear, and sweetness.

"Sorry," he said, when his mouth was free. "I can't be expected to wait for you all day, can I?"

"Not at all. Are you curious where I've been?"

"A little," he allowed.

At some point during the kiss, Rowena had vanished like morning mist. Probably he owed her an apology or a bonus. He wasn't quite ready to leave the critical unit, so Sheyla fetched a chair, arguing with a ward nurse on the way past. There, she perched beside him and summarized her day while they kept Ded company from the other side of the wall.

When she finished, Alastor just stared. "You... you!" It was hard to know what to say or how to say it.

Her smile was a touch cautious. "I have mediocre people skills, but I'm great at delivering ultimatums."

"I can't believe you enlisted Furbander to our cause."

"That's the only reason I left. I wanted to be there when you woke, but then I thought of all the work you couldn't complete and timing is so crucial, so—"

"You finished what we started."

"Is that all right? I know you can do it. But..."

Alastor reached for her hand and tenderly traced the curve of her knuckles, memorizing the feel of her skin. There might come a day soon when such reminiscence would be all that she left him. "My ego doesn't matter. Hallowell does. I must devise a suitable reward."

Her amber eyes met his, the most exquisite heart unveiled in them. It took all his self-control not to reach for her. His blood thundered, *here. Now. This moment. There may not come another.*

"The way you're looking at me right now is enough," she said softly.

"That's not like you. Were you so very afraid?"

She swallowed hard before speaking. "Yes. And I hate you for making me admit it."

"Never fear, *shalai*. I am tenacious and hard to kill, much to my brother's dismay. Do you know, he poisoned me once?"

Her hand tightened on his. "No! Before, you said he didn't bother with you."

"I don't count it as a serious attempt because he didn't try again. Given Tycho's nature, I suspect it was a prank."

"Hilarious," she said grimly.

"It is, a little. He laced my breakfast with grayvine, but I was on new medicine and couldn't keep anything down."

Clever girl, she figured it out right away. "Your illness saved your life."

"Exactly so. Mother replaced my food tasters after that."

"I have never been especially combative, but the more I hear about your brother, the more I want to pull his heart out with my bare hands."

"A scalpel would be faster," Alastor suggested, "and more suited to your talents."

"I should've said claws," she muttered.

Her anger was...soothing. If she was outraged over his wounds, then he didn't need to be, like her wrath had the power to shield him. Despite the chaos unfurling around him, Alastor had rarely felt so peaceful, or so free.

"Thank you."

By her bemused look, she wasn't sure why he'd said that. No matter. He was alive, and so was Dedrick. The outcome of that attack could've been so much worse, and he would never forget the lesson it imparted.

Be on your guard. The enemy is waiting for a chance to strike.

"Do you remember when I mentioned bad doctors?" she asked then.

"In the tent. Of course."

"You just shared another story about your brother, so I should keep my promise. This isn't a particularly happy story, though there is some satisfying comeuppance in the end."

"That will do," Alastor said.

"During my residency, I worked under a doctor who had such a stellar reputation that people believed he could cure any ill. It took months to arrange an appointment with him and if he agreed to take your case, your survival seemed guaranteed."

"But…?" Alastor asked.

"He took too much pleasure in it. Eventually, there were whispers that he took gifts to push certain patients ahead in the line and those who couldn't afford the incentives…"

"They died."

"By the dozen. In the end, he was acting as a god, deciding who deserved to live and die. Our oath is to do our best for all patients equally. When the Ethics committee learned of his shady practices, they stripped his license. Which isn't much of a story, I suppose. At any rate, that disillusionment served as a strong lesson of what *not* to become."

"Thank you for telling me."

Her tone became brisk. "It's been forty-eight hours. Dedrick should be cleared for visitors. Let me check on that."

He waited where he was and only caught flickers of her

dispute. Ten minutes later, she returned wearing a triumphant expression. "Only family is allowed in with critical care patients, but I successfully argued that as his lover, you're the same as family and should be permitted to see him. Furthermore, patients benefit from company and the comfort of a familiar voice."

"You are unstoppable," he acknowledged with a smile that wouldn't quit.

When this woman committed herself to your cause, there were apparently no limits. That instilled in him equal measures of joy and fear. *Don't follow me until the road ends, love. Don't follow wherever I lead.*

"I don't know about that, but I'm pretty slick with hospital regs. You've got fifteen minutes every four hours. Go wild."

It wouldn't be long enough to say everything, but Alastor tried. And when he took Ded's hand, the guard held on with what Sheyla would doubtless call a reflex. Still, it heartened him.

"You're fighting," he said softly. "That's good. I will be too. Remember that, even if it means I can't come as often. Understand that every victory will feel hollow if you're not beside me. You know that, right?"

Squeeze.

Not a sign, just a reflex. Yet Alastor didn't let go of his friend's hand and his heart let in a sliver of hope as he cried.

19.

IN THE WEEK since the attack, Hallowell had changed. The mood was dark, passersby tense and wary, not least because of the new checkpoints and armed patrols. Before, it was a welcoming place, full of citizens who felt safe. Impossible not to realize that Hallowell had become a city on the brink of war.

Two more loyalists had been hauled in, all Eldritch, so far. If any of them had gathered intel on Hallowell's current plans and preparations, Sheyla had to reckon that word had reached Tycho as well. *We're as ready as we can be,* she thought. Not that it helped much.

Sheyla was heading to St. Casimir's practicum lab, finally having acquired the last ingredient to make a larger batch of Alastor's medicine. *Once this is done, I can relax a little.* With brisk steps, she climbed the steps and passed through the lobby, intent on her destination.

"Do you have time now?" Dr. Seagram asked, startling her.

The man moved much too quiet for her to believe he was a bear. There must be cat blood in his family somewhere. Sheyla concealed her startle reflex as she answered him.

"Of course. What do you need?" She wasn't always so polite, even to her colleagues, but Seagram was both her former mentor, one who had never disappointed her, and the doctor now responsible for Alastor's treatment.

"I had a few questions about some bloodwork. It hasn't been easy bringing myself up to speed so quickly, you know. Hard to teach an old bear new tricks." His light eyes twinkled at that terrible joke. Beneath the levity, his intent expression told her that he understood the need for discretion.

They went to his office, talking amicably about unrelated matters. Seagram's space never changed, always like a medical journal had exploded, papers covering every flat surface. His students had been after him to use modern technology but Seagram preferred the crackle of actual documents to the bright shimmer of a data stream.

"Thank you for not asking in the hallway," she said, as he closed the door behind them.

"I have a modicum of common sense. What I'm wondering is..." He dug through his deluge for the results in question until he unearthed Alastor's chart. "Here."

The consultation took twenty minutes and at the end of it, she felt reassured regarding the serum formulation. Nothing in the results indicated a problem; it was just a matter of knowing how to chart Golgoth norms.

"Then it's nothing to be concerned about. One thing I'll note from the scans is that there was some increase in tumor mass, particularly in his kidneys. We'll need to watch that." Her expression must've given something away because he added, "It doesn't require intervention yet. I just thought I'd mention it in case the prince experiences related pain or discomfort."

Which reminded her. "Understood. Could you search for a painkiller that won't interact with his medication? According to the patient, he was told by doctors in Golgerra that it was impossible. That seems unlikely."

"Assholes." That was so unlike her mentor, who was occasionally cranky, but almost never profane, that Sheyla stared. "It sounds like they wanted him to suffer."

"I can't disagree," she said grimly.

With new resolve, Seagram slammed a palm on his desk, rattling his dusty geode collection. "Send me a copy of the formula you're using for his medication. I'll search the database personally and I won't stop cross-referencing until I find something."

Sheyla wasn't normally the cuddly sort but she couldn't resist saying, "Thanks. You know I want to hug you, right?"

"Don't make my mate jealous, he's the vengeful type. Settle for a hearty handshake?" Smiling, Dr. Seagram put out a large, weathered hand.

She shook it and headed to her original destination, the practicum lab. Someone was already using the machine she needed, so she took a number and waited. Not glorious work, but necessary. Two hours crept by, then she finally got to feed her ingredients in, input the formula, and then the fabricator queried: **Preferred delivery format: suspension or tablet.** Maybe she was overthinking it, but she wanted to create a separation between the inadequate treatment he'd received in Golgerra, so she chose the latter. More waiting as the machine got to work. At this point, she'd been at the hospital for six hours.

Her comm buzzed.

Where are you? Alastor's face popped up, the written

words spilling from his mouth. While she didn't fiddle overmuch with personal tech—she preferred lab equipment—Sheyla had to admit this comm code was fun.

St. Casimir. I'll be done soon.

Meet you at Ded's room then?

Sounds good.

Forty minutes later, she had a six-month supply of pills, neatly packaged in foil, altogether more compact and less ominous than the vials. Sheyla tucked the medicine in her bag, cleared her usage history from the fabricator, and then hurried toward the critical care unit.

So far, there had been no change in Ded's condition. There was damage to his internal organs from the poison and the Golgoth didn't heal like the Animari.

Alastor had apparently used his allotted fifteen minutes because he was standing outside the room when she arrived, forehead pressed against the glass. While she didn't know how it felt to lose a friend who was also sometimes a lover, she'd buried a lot of kin after the bombing. Respectfully she waited until he noticed her; she didn't expect him to pull her into a tight embrace. In such a public place, her first instinct was to shove him back, but she quelled it and held onto him instead.

"It's been a long day, love, and I'm badly in need of some vitamin S. I'll be all right in a minute."

Such a cheesy line should make her roll her eyes, but it was so obvious he meant it that she smiled and rubbed his back. "I've never been called a nutritional supplement before."

"Nothing but the best for team Alastor," he whispered into her hair.

She noticed that his braids were a mess, so he probably

wasn't exaggerating about the rough day. "Are you ready to go?"

"I don't want to leave Ded but they won't let me stay overnight anyway, so..." An eloquent shrug.

"It won't help anyone if you burn out. Tell me what you've been up to?" She stepped back, lacing their fingers together in lieu of the hug.

As they headed for the side doors, he said, "In the morning, I patrolled with the wolves and the city militia. They've got a tight rotation with Korin leading a small airborne squad, so we'll know the moment Tycho makes his move."

"And then?" Stepping outside made her shiver and pull up her collar. Thankfully it wasn't far to the flat, as the wind was kicking up sharp and bitter, the sky heavy with snow.

"This afternoon, I toured the factories with Furbander. We've already got a small munitions stockpile. They're allocating resources to militia outposts around the city."

"Sounds like a busy day."

"That's not even all of it. After the factories, I went to Old Town with Callum and received a crash course on war machines. The bears are leaving tomorrow."

Her heart sank a little. "I don't blame them, but it's hard not to fear that we'll need their forces later."

Alastor stopped walking, tipping his head back to stare at the sky. His odd behavior drew a few looks—or that could be his unearthly charm. These days, it hurt Sheyla to gaze on him; he was such an exquisite blend of blasted beauty, thinner than he had been when they first met, feverishly glittering eyes and etched bones. "True. But I can't ask them to give more. They're already worried that they'll need those machines to defend their own demesne."

There was no reply to that, so she held her silence until

they got home, where she made tea. Alastor groaned as he collapsed on the couch. "Good to be home. You know they've assigned Zan to guard me? He's the one who accompanied you before."

"That makes me feel better. He seems like a kind, friendly person."

"Unlike most Eldritch," he whispered.

Sheyla made a face. She didn't like to judge, but Gavriel wasn't about to win any congenial personality contests.

Belatedly, she remembered what was in her bag and dug out the packets with barely suppressed excitement. "Here, I have something for you."

CONFUSED AT FIRST, Alastor accepted the tin sheets without knowing what they were. The bubbles made it clear, once he ran his fingers over them and felt the hard curve of pills inside. Suddenly, he was as sick and miserable as he'd ever been, a knot in his stomach that no medicine could fix.

"Ah," he said lightly. "It seems your work here is done."

"What?" Her disappointment was obvious; she had expected cheerful thanks, no doubt, but he couldn't manage the words.

"You've gotten Dr. Seagram up to speed and produced enough of this..." he flicked a thumb over the sheets, "to last a while. That means you can go home. Didn't you realize?"

"I wasn't thinking of that. I just... aren't you happy, or relieved, or—"

"I should be. But I find the prospect of parting from you... well, it's unexpectedly worse than my fear of a prolonged and painful death."

"That's not funny."

"Nor was it meant to be." He tried for a smile, suspected it was all sharp edges and teeth. "You've been working flat out to get me squared away. Now it's done and there's no reason for you to linger. I'm sure your family wants you to come home."

"They do," she admitted.

By the fresh shadow in her amber eyes, she hadn't considered this aspect at all. Which was faint comfort, better than none. At least she hadn't been working with the goal of getting away from him fresh in her mind. She had a single-minded sort of charm, where she fixated on a problem until she solved it, no mental side jaunts or pondering implications. Well enough, he did that for both of them.

"Then you should go. I don't know which would be safer, if they have a spare vehicle for you to travel in, or if you should—"

She stopped his mouth by setting her finger across it. "Tonight, it's too late to worry. Morning is soon enough."

The pain eased in his chest, enough so he could breathe again. He shouldn't reach for her, he shouldn't, but he did. She settled against his side, her right hand curling into his left, and for a moment he had the mad impression that he could hear her heartbeat echoing his. It was an odd, electric sensation, a current running between them, that tingled the top of his head. He'd never heard of anything like it, so it was probably exhaustion combined with his imagination.

"If you insist. I also need to thank you. This..." He regarded the tin packets on his thigh. "Makes everything feel less dire. Other people get up in the morning, eat a meal, take a pill. Now I'm one of them."

"That's exactly how I hoped you'd feel. I was afraid

you'd think I should've asked you before—"

"You've always known me, almost from the very beginning. Instinctively known things that others didn't believe were true."

"Alastor..."

"Yes, *shalai*?"

"Do you remember when I said that I was waiting for the perfect moment?"

"Of course."

"It's now." Her smile was radiant, a sunbeam, a rainbow, a fusion reaction that went nuclear in his racing heart.

He didn't hesitate, swinging her into his arms and carrying her to the bedroom. Today, his strength was sufficient for that, if only just; it wouldn't always be, and even so, he was trembling, not just from desire, when he dropped her on the bed. Her eyes said she knew and that everything of his was good. It was hard to breathe again, not because of his lungs, because of the emotions scrambling in his chest. A few slow, deep breaths settled him somewhat, good since he didn't want to weep the first—and possibly last—time they came together.

Like a dream, they undressed each other. Every time he saw her, it was like finding treasure: the curve of her shoulder, her muscled thighs, the softness of her skin. She didn't smell like any lover he'd ever been with; she was astringent, herbs and disinfectant, but when her body warmed beneath his hands, his mouth, the scent ripened to an irresistible cocktail that would forever be emblazoned on him.

As pure sex.

Pure love.

She fell back or pulled him down, some delicious blend

of the two, and they kissed forever. His cock was hard, but he felt as if they had all the time in the world, though the opposite was likely true. Her mouth was soft and swollen when he raised his head; Alastor's felt the same. He loved how she was kneading his back, his shoulders, with sharp nails, urging him on like the cat she was.

It was hard to get the question out. "I'm not sure... do you want—"

To take charge. Like she had before.

She smiled. The heat of it drove all but one word from his head. Goddess. He would spend all night worshipping her.

"Tonight, I want to experience you exactly as you wish to give yourself. Is that all right?"

"Perfectly."

Lips, throat, shoulders, breasts, belly—no part of her went untasted. Alastor learned her body as he'd wanted to, since he'd been born, it felt like. He discovered how she responded to nips and nuzzles, where she liked it hard and soft, until she was squirming beneath him, lifting her hips with quick, urgent motions.

"So, you're a tease," she managed eventually.

"I prefer the term 'thorough'."

"You shouldn't be so calm when I feel like this. It's unsettling."

Laughing softly, he pressed a kiss to her inner thigh and then shifted to seal her palm over his racing heart. "Does this feel calm? Or this, perhaps?" He curled her hand around his throbbing cock, slick with the precome that accompanied his patience.

"Not so much."

He moaned when she clenched her fingers around him,

hard enough for it to seem both vicious and superb. "I want you. I wanted to make you come a thousand times, but really, I just want...ah."

Alastor rocked into her hand for a few full, luscious strokes. Any orgasm she gave would be beyond perfection, but from the hungry light in her eyes, she wanted all he had to give.

"You're so beautiful," she whispered.

He felt it with her, if not always. Settling between her strong thighs, he shivered a little. For someone as fierce as Sheyla to give herself to him, he had no words. Her upturned face became his universe, galaxies spinning in her gaze, all the secrets of the world in her smile.

She set a hand on his hip, inviting him, inciting him. In a smooth thrust, he took her, but it was her hands guiding him, her hips that set the pace.

Overload. It was too much, too good. His mind came unhinged, so there were only bursts of impossible pleasure. His cock, as he rocked into her. His chest against hers, her legs locking around him, heels digging into his ass, demanding more.

It was impossible, impossible, but he sensed what she wanted before she asked for it. Yet he was doing it, altering his strokes, so that she responded, clenched on him, gasped and groaned beneath him, and he could *feel* her orgasm building. Alastor stroked her clit before she could ask, then she went wild beneath him.

Her pleasure drove his in a feedback loop, his entire body belonged to her, but she was in his head too. Her heartbeat slammed in time to his, and he took her mouth, half-crazed with the need to taste, to claim, even as pleasure spiked.

He was almost there when she tensed and rolled. They managed to swap positions with his cock still inside her, and then she was holding him down, her back arching as she came. Close, he knew he was close, but her face as she went, the clutch of her cunt, sent him straight over. Alastor held her hips as he stroked a few more times, savoring the feel of his juices mingling with hers. She kissed him feverishly, open-mouthed, and greedy. Spent and boneless, he admired the sweaty dishevelment he'd created, as Sheyla dropped her head on his chest. He'd never felt closer to anyone in his life. They stayed together through the aftershocks, with him stroking her glistening back.

"I'm hungry," Sheyla declared eventually. "That was some top notch fucking."

20.

WHEN ALASTOR LAUGHED, at first Sheyla wasn't sure why that was funny. It was a statement of two facts, not any attempt at humor. Still, his smile was infectious, so she found herself returning it, rolling onto her side to face him.

"This is why I adore you," he said.

"Is it?"

He didn't elaborate, though, on what amused him so much. "I'll see what there is for dinner."

Since she'd done the bulk of the food prep since their arrival, she arched a brow. "You can do that?"

"I'm offended. And relatively certain that there are enough leftovers to make my warming them up pass as a credible meal."

"Then I'll lounge here while you serve me." She offered him a teasing smile and drew the covers up over her hip.

"You're undermining my resolve. We don't actually need to eat, do we?"

Her stomach rumbled in reply, prompting another delighted smile from her tousled prince. Once he'd gone, she pulled the pillow he used to her chest and buried her face in it. This was...

Nothing she'd known before.

There was no question of what she should do, and it was slightly troubling that he'd realized she could return to Ash Valley before it occurred to her. With the Golgoth on the move and her family frightened half to death, she should already be making plans.

We knew it wasn't forever.
I always intended to go.

Yet her throat ached and her eyes burned with a need for tears that she rarely felt. Sheyla didn't cry even when she was sad; she swallowed it and pushed on. Only rage ever drove her to that point, a fact that often confused people who were arguing with her. They never realized that if tears spilled out, she was half a breath from knocking someone through a wall.

Today, it was different, a yearning she couldn't name commingled with the golden glow of Alastor's happiness. Down to the soles of her feet, she could feel it as if he was radiating the emotion beyond any reasonable degree. His feelings spilled over her in a sensory bouquet, palpable as a purr against a lover's skin. Then there came an irresistible tug that propelled her out of bed, like someone had tied silver skeins to her ankles. For a few moments, she resisted, and the impulse became compulsion. Which led directly to him and it didn't ease until her arms went around him and she rested her head against his back.

"I missed you too," he said, and she had no doubt it was true.

"It looks good." In truth, it was the same food, recycled, and she cared only for it as long as it filled her stomach.

I have to leave tomorrow. Right?

That awful certainty resonated until she couldn't think of anything else. She scraped her plate in silence while Alastor regarded her with knowing eyes. On some level, he probably sensed her conflict, the silent struggle between the responsible choice and the selfish one. For the latter, she would stay with him, no regard for clan or family.

The flat was so quiet as they washed up. Odd to work beside a prince with such mundane chores. When the last cup was dried and put away, he set his hands on her shoulders and made her face him.

"Have you decided, *shalai*?"

No. Yes. Sheyla shrugged, unable to articulate her level of conflict. Better to let the issue simmer a little longer and see what truth boiled out.

"Do you ever plan to tell me what that means?"

"That moment is now. Come along, let's trade stories once more." *For the last time,* his sad eyes said, but somehow he was still smiling.

She hated that he could, a little, when her insides felt like a lava lake, endlessly boiling. Even so, following him was easy. His hand wrapped around hers like a promise, and as they settled on the sofa together, he hit the remote to play something soft as a counterpoint to whatever words he had left to give.

"You were saying?" she prompted, past the knot in her throat.

"Shalai is the Golgoth word for a flower that grows in the shade, a pretty purple darling with a heart of gold. I think it's called heart's ease or heart's delight elsewhere."

Almost instantly she identified the flora in question, not from botany but from herbalism and natural medicine courses. Sheyla could easily picture the delicate bloom in the illustrated guide she'd studied. "It's used to treat skin irritations and respiratory ailments," she said.

His expression... how could she ever tire of eliciting that reaction, this precise amalgam of astonishment and delight. "Indeed. And how romantic."

"I wasn't trying to be," she mumbled.

"Trust me, I'm aware. It's also an endearment, as I suspect you've surmised. Reserved for the person with whom you feel most yourself, the most at home."

Oh.

Her breath went, and the tears from before almost got away. Nobody had ever claimed that about her, and she hadn't even known she would like hearing it until this moment. Sheyla blinked two or three times, then a single tear slid down.

"So, I am—"

"My heart's ease, my heart's delight. Yes. You are my lodestar, lady. No matter how long the day is, when I see your face at its end, it gives me the strength to face another and then one more. No matter where, in a flat, hospital, or tent, with you, I am home."

It felt as if he was curling his fingers around her heart, and that if he didn't proceed with care, that she might die. She scrubbed at her eyes furiously, utterly unable to respond.

"I thought you said you wouldn't hold me when I needed to go," she finally managed.

Deliberately he opened his hands but everything was in his eyes, in the words he'd spoken. "I'm not," he said. "Even if you leave in the morning, this truth will stand. You can remember fondly or with bitterness. Or both."

"I don't want to *remember* you." She closed her eyes and

turned her face away, knowing he might misunderstand.

Petal-soft, his lips whispered over her eyelids, not taking her tears, but tasting them. Then he kissed her mouth in a salute strangely formal and chaste. She should have known he would sense how she felt, proven by his next words.

"I wish you could stay too. But I know too well, in this life, we aren't always free to do as we wish. You're needed in Ash Valley and your family wants you safe, away from the front lines." He kissed her forehead then. "You've done enough. Go in good grace."

"Easy for you to say." Steadier now, she leaned into him again and he welcomed her with a warmth that would be impossible to forget. This genuine sweetness... where did it come from? There were glimmers of it in Rowena, but most of the Golgoth soldiers were devoid of it, or it was so well-buried that it would take a mining days to excavate.

"That wasn't the story I meant to tell you, by the way."

She didn't need to say it was a declaration, for they both knew it had been. And it would be cowardly of her to move on without giving him some indication how precious he had become. Neither of them was free to choose—familial expectations on her end and political obligations for him—but it was impossible to stop your heart, once it went. Hers was a bird, circling him.

It's not a mate bond. Not yet.

She'd heard enough of the stories to discern that it was forming. The tug from earlier could be nothing else. So leaving was the best solution on a lot of levels; she tried to suppress the anguish that crashed over her like an angry ocean at the mere prospect. Saying good-bye might make her physically ill.

"Stop thinking about it," he said gently. "As you said

earlier, we have tonight. We'll talk and kiss, love and cuddle, sleep in the same bed, and in the morning, we'll have breakfast together. And then…"

And then sounded endless. Funny how she'd shifted her thoughts after taking him to bed, but if he could bear it, so could she. With effort, Sheyla shut away all thoughts of tomorrow. "Very well. I'm fairly sure you promised me a story."

ALASTOR DREW HER into his arms fully, so that Sheyla rested against his chest. He could feel her heart beating beneath his hands. She smelled of sex and him, dazzling his senses until it was hard to think.

"This isn't a sad story, so you'll be able to spill one of your sorrows later, if you like."

"We'll see. Go on already." A patient audience she was not.

"I was around nine or so, doing well, and my mother approved a rare outing. I went with my siblings…"

"Caia, Efren and Leander?" Touching his forearm, she read the names that were inked into his skin.

"Right. Our eldest brother didn't come, or this wouldn't be a fond memory. We left Golgerra—the only time I can remember being allowed to do so—and went down the mountain to a hot spring, where we bathed and played and had a picnic lunch. There, we picked the shalai the doctors needed for my bronchial treatment, and I was so tired and didn't want to admit it that I fell asleep on Leander's back on the way home."

"It sounds wonderful," she said.

From her expression, she didn't think it was much of a

story. There was no rising action, no climax, no resolution. So he explained, "Until now, during this time with you, that moment was my happiest. I've kept it precious like a jewel in amber and every night, I play it in my head, so I don't forget their faces."

"Alastor—"

"I don't mean to imply there haven't been moments of brightness, of course. When Tycho gave Dedrick to me, when I saved Rowena, when the Exiles pledged themselves to me. But by and large, happiness has been a butterfly I could not catch."

"I hear butterflies are more apt to land on your shoulder if you stand and wait."

Too well Alastor understood that she said such things to cover emotional confusion; she didn't think he wanted tips on catching insects. Still, her comment put a smile on his face.

"I wasn't even waiting, anymore. When I met you. Hope, that was something I'd heard of in stories. You've given me so much that I wanted to share my happiest time with you. Because of you, I now have a treasure trove of beautiful moments to sift through at night when I'm alone, and there really are no words sufficient to—"

"Stop. You're too good at this and I'm melting. Fate knows I'm terrible at this sort of thing, but I have to try."

"What?" Astonished, Alastor tried to shift so he could see her face, but she wouldn't let him.

"You can't keep pouring such sweetness over me without expecting reciprocation." She took his hand, and the heat of her fingers sent a pleasurable chill through him. "First I need to tell you a story, though. For context."

"I'm listening." Her voice was lovely, and if she wanted

to talk, holding her while she did was the best job in the world.

"I've always been...different." Sheyla hesitated over the word before continuing and he squeezed her hand in encouragement. "I established early on that I was always more interested in science than in people. It was to the point that my parents took me in for treatment. I saw six doctors, four seers. I think they were afraid of me being Latent, becoming Aberrant, or worse."

He wasn't sure if he should ask, but he did anyway. "Aberrant?"

"It's someone who can't conform to pride customs. They don't socialize well, they don't care about others, and sometimes they become...cruel. Violent."

"So Tycho is Aberrant. Good to know." It was only a little joke.

Her huff of a laugh and the way her shoulders eased told him it was the right tone. "When I was small, I had a fascination with, well, dead things."

That was a bit strange, not enough to make him react except to say, "Oh?"

"I didn't kill them. My parents *thought* I did, that's why they were so alarmed. But when I found dead animals, I wanted to open them up and see how they worked, thinking that maybe I could fix live ones later. Which is still morbid, I suppose."

He nodded and set his cheek against her hair. "Your parents feared they had a tiny monster on their hands."

"Basically. As I grew, I tried to pretend better, but as my pride mates were eyeing each other, I was only interested in lab work. I'm never attracted to someone by looking at them."

"That explains why you resisted my obvious charms for so long," he joked.

"It is why," she agreed. "I discovered sex late and experimented with it just like I did everything else, with my head in charge and my body following. My first time came about because one of my pack mates told me bluntly that she wanted to fuck. I do better with such obvious cues."

"Which means…"

"I've never *cared* before," she said. "Maybe I'm not a monster like my parents feared but I am… it's probably just as well that you can't have me forever, because I'd probably hurt you in time, or not be able to—"

"I'm guessing there's some perfect median in your eyes?" He cut her off because he couldn't stand to hear the rest.

"What?"

"Relationships should conform to this pattern, a gold standard, and you don't measure up. I'll allow that you're special. For fucking certain, you're like nobody I've ever known, but I will have words with your family, if they've led you to believe you can't make somebody deliriously happy someday."

"Don't provoke my father," she said. "He has bad knees."

"You can't change the subject. There's no right way to partner with someone. What works for one pair won't for another. And I could list so many amazing qualities about you that you'd doze off as if your sterling traits were a bedtime story."

"Pass," she mumbled.

She did lift his hand and seal a kiss against his palm; he wished he could find a way to preserve it. The heat faded by increments as she thought of what to say. He could feel her pensive pause, the way her confusion smoothed to acceptance. Alastor understood that he'd pay a price for this connection; the pain of her departure would be a fresh hell that he walked through for ten thousand days, and maybe even then, it wouldn't cease.

Is the bitter worth the sweet?
For her? Yes. Always.

"Now you understand where I've been, I can tell you where I am. With you, sex is not exercise. I feel things. And you, I want in ways I can hardly explain. I don't have pretty words to give, but Alastor, you matter like my own family. During the day, I think of you, I worry, and I miss you. At night, I want to be with you."

She came up on her knees to face him, her eyes anxious. He curved a hand to her cheek. "What, love?"

"Is that enough? Did I make you understand? I am... not good at this."

"You are perfection," he said honestly. "With this, you've told me that your heart is a lock, I am the key, and I have never felt so fortunate in my entire life. Truly, this is...humbling."

He kissed her; it was inevitable and she wrapped her arms around his neck. For endless moments, he tasted the softness of her lips, the sweetness of her mouth, and it dizzied him to the point that for a wild moment, he thought the rumbling was from his breaking heart, or perhaps that passion could, in fact, make the earth move.

The boom sounded again, distant and terrible.

Sheyla broke away, breathless and...dismayed. Of course, she could identify the sound with her excellent ears. "It's artillery. My turn to tell a story has to wait."

They were already dressed when Zan pounded on the door, shouting, "Your Highness! Doctor Halek! It's begun, the enemy is here!"

"I'm sorry," he said. "It seems as if the choice has been taken from you. It won't be safe to travel now."

Briefly, Alastor wished he was a good enough man to regret that twist of fate.

He wasn't.

21.

OUTSIDE, IT WAS chaos.

When Sheyla followed Zan, she knew intellectually that the battle they'd been preparing for had begun, but it was another thing to smell the cordite and lightning in the air, and feel the ground tremble from the shells raining down. There was an orange glow to the west like multiple fires were raging.

Alastor paused long enough to touch her hand. "Don't engage. Go to St. Casimir if you want to help."

"Sire, we need you at the front. Everyone's waiting for your orders," Zan urged.

"I'm coming."

He let go of her, racing off into the darkness, and Sheyla knew fear on a level so visceral that it was hard to breathe for a few seconds. She got it under control and headed toward the hospital. Impossible not to notice that she was like a salmon swimming upstream—so many people running in the opposite direction.

Finally, she grabbed a militia officer. "Is the hospital still open?"

He shook his head. "Sorry, ma'am. They're evacuating

this entire section of the city. Golgoth are on the march and they'll sweep through here soon."

The newer part of the city had no walls, nothing to check the enemy. Tycho's forces might even raze St. Casimir to weaken the defenders.

We were prepared for this, she told herself.

Still, she ached to think of the ancient building reduced to rubble. Gods and curses, where would they put the sick and injured? What about Dedrick? While healthy civilians could evac quickly, it would be all but impossible to clear out the whole hospital. Some of the life support systems had no long-term mobile equivalent.

She had been about to turn back; instead, she nodded a thank-you at the officer and kept pushing through the crowd, resolute no matter how many times she got shoved or jostled. At one point, she blocked an elbow in the throat, thrown by a man in a complete panic. As she cleared the plaza, the crowd thinned. The path to the hospital was eerily deserted, though she could still hear the low rumbles in the distance.

Four kilometers, give or take. It won't be long.

Inside, only a skeleton crew remained.

All the patients who could leave under their own power had been discharged in a great rush. She'd never seen the place so empty, so still.

"Color me unsurprised to see you, Dr. Halek." Her former mentor managed to startle her yet again.

"This is where I can best lend aid," she said. "With my specialized training, it would be a waste for me to fight."

"But you'd like to."

She let out a sigh. "My skin's itching with the need to change. I want to get out there and—"

"Me too," Dr. Seagram admitted.

"They'd be in trouble if all the doctors died in battle."

"Too true. Sometimes the best measure of courage is forcing yourself to wait when you'd rather go to war."

"Agreed. Is your mate out there?" She didn't usually ask such personal questions, but these were rare circumstances.

"He is, much to my chagrin."

Mine too.

The thought formed before she could stop it. They had made no promises, her family would be appalled, and she was useless to Alastor in terms of political leverage. *This bond must be broken.* Sheyla didn't look forward to that.

For now, though...

"Brief me on the situation here. What patients are left and what's the plan for keeping them safe?"

Dr. Seagram handed her the roster, patients listed in alphabetical order. There were only fifteen, most from the critical care unit. She skimmed the list and was relieved to find Dedrick's name on it.

"You got here just in time, actually. We're about to retreat to the sublevels. The Golgoth army can bring the building down on top of us, but they won't be able to get in. Or hurt anyone."

She stared, wide-eyed. "I thought the bunker was just a myth."

Seagram shook his head. "It was built long ago for use during the human incursion and before the Pax Protocols. I never imagined a day when we'd use it again. The place is stockpiled with dry rations and fresh water, plus we've carried down enough medicine and supplies for us to last a couple of months with the patients we're taking."

"Months."

"They'll either win the war in that time or we'll lose the city."

He wasn't wrong, but that was a grim way to frame the situation. "I understand."

"If you choose to come, it's a one-way trip. We'll be powering down the lift once we reach the bunker to conserve energy and there's no comm signal down there."

That gave her pause. She wouldn't be able to contact her family in the worst-case scenario, no way to update Alastor. Quickly she took out her comm, intending to send brief messages, but there was no signal. She shook the unit and Dr. Seagram touched her shoulder.

"They're already jamming communications to interfere with our ability to coordinate. You don't have to—"

"Dr. Seagram!" A young nurse dashed up, wolf by the smell of her, and she grabbed his arm as an indication of her urgency. "We have a problem. Dr. Manley has run off."

"Not very manly of him," Sheyla said, and then wondered why she was joking at a time like this.

Alastor's influence, damn him.

As Seagram laughed, the nurse turned a puzzled look on her. "Dr. Manley is a woman."

"Never mind that," Seagram said. "It seems our staff is one short, Dr. Halek. Now it's not a choice but necessity, if we're to offer decent care to those depending on us during this crisis."

The decision wasn't difficult. If she wasn't fighting beside Alastor, she wanted to care for his closest friend. He'd told her to head to St. Casimir; hopefully, he'd figure out that she was safe, even if the Golgoth took the upper levels of the hospital.

"Let's go," Sheyla said.

The patients had been transferred already, and half the medical staff had gone down. Sheyla accompanied Dr. Seagram in collecting the last of them, three nurses and another doctor. Then he led the group through the mazelike corridors. He opened a door and unlocked another, leading to a hallway that she hadn't even known existed. By the looks on everyone else's faces, it was new to them as well.

The hallway ended in a lift, dull and ancient steel that looked as if someone had taken a flamethrower to it. It bore various dents and scars, but it radiated an impregnable air.

That proved to be true when Dr. Seagram used three different levels of biometrics to activate it and open the doors. He flashed a cheeky grin as he stepped inside.

"That's your incentive to keep me alive. After I cut the power below, I'll need to do all that again to turn it on again."

The nurse who had brought word about the runaway physician chewed her lip, visibly hesitant. "How will we know when it's safe? You said there are no comms."

An excellent question. Sheyla noticed that they were all waiting for the answer before joining him in the lift.

"There's an old-fashioned signal machine and the other unit is attached to a militia outpost in Old Town. These are antiquated facilities, remember, so I doubt the Golgoth will think to dig up cables that have been in the ground so long and haven't been used in fifty years."

"Then how do you know they're still working?" Nurse Nervous asked.

That was the end of Dr. Seagram's patience. "If you're coming, get in. Otherwise, do as you think best. There are triage teams or you can simply hide and hope for the best."

There's a chance I can get a message to Alastor, if the signal machine is working. And maybe if they take care of the jammers later, he can reassure my family.

In the end, there was no other path for her. Dedrick was down there, waiting. Sheyla stepped into the lift. Slowly, the others followed, one by one, until the nervous girl finally joined them. With a sigh, Seagram activated the elevator, using another cycle of biometric scans. Yellow lights kicked on overhead, sputtering fluorescent.

When the doors closed, it was with a certain grim finality, as if they might never see the sunlit world again.

ALASTOR COULDN'T KEEP up with Zan in this form, so he kept asking the Eldritch to slow down. Mortifying, but necessary, if he wasn't to get lost on the way. Eventually, Zan realized that was the issue and moderated his pace.

"Give me a status report?" He barely had the breath to ask the question. Without Dedrick to shield him from curious eyes, he probably wouldn't be able to hide his condition for much longer. His men knew, of course, but the Eldritch, the wolves, and the city militia didn't.

"They've massed in the south and west. Our scouts think they have sufficient numbers to flank and occupy. They're already attacking in the west using artillery, CTAK, and ground forces."

"Can we hold them?"

Zan slid him a look as he dodged around a terrified family fleeing for their lives. "Hopeful or honest, sire?"

"Honest."

"We have some good defense weaponry, but too little personnel trained and experienced in its use and too much ground to cover. The modern boroughs in Hallowell weren't designed to withstand a siege. It was laid out by architects born and bred in peacetime."

"Thank you."

At least he had some idea of the long odds they faced. *We didn't come this far to give up. A victory here, no matter how hard-won, will send a message to my brother.*

With that familiar tightness in his chest, he ran on, until he couldn't. He put up a palm, asking for a break. Zan didn't question it; Alastor would have told the truth if he had. There was no shame in his illness, and they had come too far, he hoped, for anyone to question his right to lead. Now he believed what Sheyla and the pride matron always had—that he was no figurehead—he was the true center of this resistance to tyranny.

"Good now?" Zan asked, after a few moments.

"Carry on. A bit slower if you can. Your pace creeps up as we go."

Zan smiled, sheepish. "Sorry."

The trolleys were no longer running and the city smelled of smoke. Explosions boomed closer as they went, so he could tell they were approaching the western front. The horizon glowed with the lights of multiple fires; people sobbed as their homes burned but property damage was the least of his concerns.

At last, they reached the outpost where the allied forces were missing a commander in chief. Briefly, Alastor wished Ded or Sheyla was beside him, but these people were waiting for his word, nobody else's.

Mustering all his energy, he vaulted onto a crate, accepting a bullhorn from Zan. Before he took a breath, the collected soldiers quieted. His ability to move people's hearts had never mattered more.

The bullhorn screeched and his voice rang out, booming with a power he hadn't know he possessed. "We will not falter. We will fight to the last man. We will fight until we empty every armory, until our last bullet is spent. Then we will fight on, with teeth and claws and kitchen knives. You have a strength that no invader can ever match, for you are righteous people defending your homes. We will turn the very stone of the streets against them—even the trees and grass may rise up! If we give ground, it will be to lay a trap. No matter the cost, Hallowell stands. We fight. To the last man, woman, and child."

He hadn't known he could *sound* like that, bellowing defiance at a burning sky, and the soldiers echoed it back. In the dark, he could tell some were citizens who had volunteered to fight, men and women among them, and yes, a few that could hardly be judged more than children, clutching their weapons with shaky hands. He made eye contact with those who seemed to want it, silent thanks to wolves who stayed, to the Eldritch standing with Gavriel. A little dizzy, he dropped to the ground and went to join Rowena, fully in command of the Exiles who had followed him from Golgerra.

"The time has come at last for us to take the field," she said.

"Any regrets?"

She smiled. "None. What are your orders?"

"Change and prepare to fight. I need you on the front lines. We must prove to our allies that we are fully committed."

"Understood."

Alastor could have cried as his men transformed, revealing their brute shapes to their allies. He'd worried for nothing, though, because the other soldiers only made room; there were no horrified stares or whispered judgments. He allowed himself that moment of glad grace before hurrying to confer with Korin.

"You've been training most on the war machines the bears left us. Are you confident?" He'd received a brief tutorial, but he wasn't qualified to take the lead, plus ground forces needed him to direct offensive and defensive operations. Once, he'd studied such things for amusement—always in the abstract, as pieces on a board. Never had his stratagems come with such high potential cost.

The wolf lieutenant nodded. "There's nothing like immersion training. Whatever you need, I'll get it done."

"Do you have two more competent cadets?"

She nodded, beckoning to a couple of wolves he didn't know by name. "Ria, Tellan. You're with me."

The male wolf lit up. "War machines?"

"You know it."

Korin turned to him. "What's the op?"

"Aerial assault. Take out of the CTAK if you can but don't sacrifice for it."

"Copy, strafe and run, one heavy hit."

"Be careful. We took one RVAC from them but there may be more."

It was so hard to be sure he was giving the right orders, but there was no time for self-doubt. *Next up, the Eldritch.* Gavriel met him halfway.

"Where do you want us? Sire." The Noxblade gave a mocking smile that didn't seem quite as acerbic as usual.

"Disrupt their forces. Sabotage wherever you can. Destroy weapon stockpiles. Also, see if you can do something about the comm jammers, and if you find an officer unprotected, take him out. That should create chaos in their chain of command."

"Understood. Noxblades, to me."

The assassins fell in behind Gavriel, and as a group, they took ten steps, and then Alastor simply lost track of them. He would never understand how the hell they did that.

Zan didn't follow.

"Did you get culled from the herd?" Alastor asked.

"I've been assigned to guard you, remember? That's my role, until Gavriel orders otherwise."

"It doesn't matter what instructions I give?"

The Eldritch's friendly expression didn't shift. "It would be impolite to answer that."

"Forget it, keep me safe. There's probably nobody better suited to it than an assassin. You'll spot threats nobody else could."

"I will take that as a compliment, sire."

If he had time or breath to waste, he'd ask Zan to call him Alastor, but the militia outpost commander was waiting. Alastor jogged over, stopping the man's attempt to bow.

"Please don't. We're fellow soldiers."

That seemed to be the right approach. The man warmed and said, "You are too gracious. What are our orders?"

"Your squad is on defense, so just back the infantry at range, suppressive fire as you can. This is the first wave, and it will likely get worse before it gets better. You're clear on the plan, should we need to give ground?"

The commander replied, "We blow the outpost along with any armaments we can't carry and retreat to the cathedral first." He listed each fallback site, ending with,

"Our last stand will be in Old Town."

A chill ran through him, as if those words might be prophetic. Alastor shook it off and forced a smile as he studied the sky. Korin and her two cadets went up like rockets, clad in the metal suits that the bears called war machines; they left an ion trail, pale against the night sky as they went to rain death on the would-be conquerors.

Raising the bullhorn, he called, "Does anyone need a word? Once I change, you won't be able to understand my replies."

Nobody raised a hand or called out, so he discarded the device and went over to the Exiles. Rowena hadn't taken flight yet, so her dark wings were furled against her back. In this form, she was lovely, though the Animari and Eldritch might disagree.

"You mean to lead from the front," she asked in base-Gol.

His answer came in the form of quiet disrobing; Sheyla had taught him there was no shame in it, but his men still circled to hide his struggle with transformation. As ever, there was blood and pain—the spikes emerging were like knives in his back but the strength—it surged through him in a golden wave, heady and delicious. Alastor put his head back and roared.

The Exiles called back.

To his surprise, war cries came from the wolves, from the assembled city militia, not base-Gol, but they understood the intent.

Alastor spoke to his whole army then, for they were united. "Come, my brothers and sisters. To war!"

22.

SINCE SHEYLA'S ARRIVAL in the bunker, she hadn't spoken to anyone much, because everyone was organizing the supplies before an emergency cropped up. So far, the patients were stable, coping with the move, but with any critical condition, the status could change in a heartbeat, and patient welfare depended on staff being able to lay hands on necessary medicine and equipment with lightning speed.

Once everything was sorted, she took stock of her surroundings, a thorough inspection that started with the large room close to the lift. It had been originally intended as storage, she thought, but at some point, they'd half-repurposed it as a lounge—with battered couches, tables, and chairs scattered around the space, with all the shelves shoved against the far wall. Like the lights in the elevator, the overhead bulbs glowed an artificial yellow and she could hear them, as if the current was whispering. There was also a smell, musty and close, that she hoped would dissipate in time, if only to be replaced with sweat and pheromones.

Farther down the hall, there were four rooms, two larger than the rest. Those, they had earmarked for the critical ward, setting up life support systems and connecting them to the emergency generator that Dr. Seagram claimed would run for six months, if they were careful. They only had food and water sufficient for two, however, so if they didn't get an all-clear signal from Hallowell's forces before then, the generator would be the least of their worries.

She wouldn't think about that.

The last two rooms included a dormitory and a cavernous wet room with washing and toilet facilities, though they couldn't count on the running water. If there was interference above ground, it would stop, leaving only what they had stored in bottles. That might be a problem for some, but Sheyla could shift and groom herself.

Sometimes it's good to be a cat.

Even if Dr. Seagram hadn't said this was an old installation, she could've guessed by the dingy gray flooring and cracked blue tiles in the lavatory. As for the dorm, it was all bare sheetrock and stacked metal bunks, three tall, four sets. More than enough sleeping space, especially considering that they'd likely be working twelve-hour rotations; there weren't enough staffers to do three shifts.

Lockers against the far wall offered a place to stash personal effects, but Sheyla came out with nothing but the clothes on her back. There should be spare scrubs floating around, one less worry at least. As she concluded her survey, Dr. Seagram called to her from the hallway.

"Now that things are somewhat settled, we're having a brief meeting in the rec room."

"Is that what it's called?" she mumbled.

"If you dig around, you'll find some books and magazines from the turn of the century. Riveting stuff."

"I can hardly wait. I wanted to ask about the signal

ma—"

"The signal machine should be fine. Even if the cables are disrupted, we still have the trolley lines. Our messages should get through. If there's anybody alive to read them."

"You're the cheerful type, aren't you?"

Seagram grinned as they stepped into the rec room. Already assembled, there were three doctors, five nurses, and four aides so adding Sheyla and her mentor to the tally brought the total to fourteen. Not a bad care ratio, but it might get dicey depending on what specialties the group encompassed.

Too late for second thoughts, we have to do our best.

"First let's introduce ourselves since we'll be stuck with each other for a while. Make it quick, mind, so I can go over the first duty roster. I'll start. Most of you know me, but I'm Dr. Eldred Seagram, husband to Franklin, father of two, formerly of Burnt Amber, and Director of Oncology at St. Casimir." He glanced around the lounge. "Everyone clear on how it's done?"

A series of nods, then he pointed at Sheyla. "You start, we move left from there, until everyone's done."

"Dr. Sheyla Halek, research specialty, GP in Ash Valley. Mated to..." *Alastor, the demon prince,* but that wasn't an insult in her mind anymore, more of an endearment. "No one. Three siblings, hate small talk. Next."

To her left, a slender man with fair hair stood, though that hadn't been required. "Nurse Darian Mills, critical care unit, formerly of Ice Spire, Mated to Evelina for six years. I like talking about bees and botany. Next."

Though Sheyla knew she needed to learn all their names, at minimum, she found herself drifting. She pinched her wrist to force sharper attention. In the end, it wasn't easy, but she memorized names and facts like they were medical terms.

Three doctors, besides herself and Seagram. Names: Sherwood of Pine Ridge, Akoni of Burnt Amber, Mitra who had declined to give any information other than medical specialty.

Nurses: Mills of Ice Spire, Harlow, Odell, Laxmi, and Baako. She'd already forgotten where all but one of them were from, but it probably didn't matter.

Aides: Gola, Udek, Chibueze, Enrian.

There was a mix of male and female staff; most were mated. When the last person finished speaking, Dr. Seagram stood. Though he'd requested brevity, the intros still took at least fifteen minutes. It was a minute miracle that no alarms were sounding down the hall.

Quickly, he explained the shifts, divided as Sheyla had predicted. He read the names of the people who would be on duty first and then said, "The rest of you, relax and get some rest. You'll need it."

Since her name hadn't been called, she'd be on second shift. As the others went off to the ward, she stood up, only to be hailed by Nurse Nervous. *Harlow,* she corrected herself mentally.

"Do you think we're safe?" the woman asked.

"More than the people who are fighting." Her tone was curt because it was an asinine question.

"We might not even be able to get a message out. Did you see the apparatus Dr. Seagram mentioned?"

Until this moment, she hadn't even looked but her gaze followed Nurse Harlow's gesture until she spotted the machine in the far corner, near the lift. Perched on a table, it was the oddest piece of "technology" she'd ever seen, with a wooden base and metal knobs attached to a metal wand that sat atop a metal plate and there were the wires he'd mentioned, running from the unit into the wall.

"There's only one way to find out," she said.

She went over to investigate, but there was no usage manual, no hint of how to operate the thing. Dr. Seagram should know, based on what he'd said, but it was a poor idea to have only one person trained on such matters, plus she'd always loved puzzles.

He mentioned old books down here...

Near the hallway, she located the shelves in question, haphazardly stacked with books, files, and periodicals. Most were medical journals, unbelievably outdated, some were fiction, including some rather fascinating vintage pornography. Not what she was looking for, but Sheyla did pause to admire some of the pictures.

"What are you doing?" Nurse Harlow hovered behind her, and she stifled a sigh.

It seemed she'd acquired a shadow.

"Looking for documentation."

The woman seemed puzzled, not Sheyla's problem. On the bottom shelf, underneath a stack of yellow papers, she found what she sought—a usage manual for the wired gizmo, along with a simple cipher system. It tracked logically that the outpost would have access to these same materials, so she sat down on the floor to study.

Unsurprisingly, Nurse Harlow joined her. "Is it helpful?"

We must live together for gods know how long. I cannot snap at her.

"With sufficient review, I'll be able to use the machine and send a test message." She was trying for a nice way of saying, *Shut up and let me focus.*

It didn't work.

The nurse chattered on. "I should have volunteered for the triage team, I think. Being underground unsettles me so much."

"You don't say."

Here, for many people, the urge to comfort would kick in. Sheyla just wanted Nurse Harlow to go away. Somehow, she restrained her impatience. "Is that where the rest of the St. Casimir staff went?"

Eager nodding. "There are med tents set up at all borough outposts."

If things had been less of a mad scramble, maybe she would've chosen the triage team too, but Sheyla wasn't wired for regret. Done was done, and she'd do her utmost to help in the bunker. If he knew, Alastor would probably be glad she was here with Dedrick, at any rate, and sequestered from the fighting.

Offering a longing look at the manual, she tried one last time to distract Nurse Harlow. By offering her the vintage porn. "This is amazing, check it out."

Nurse Harlow took it, and finally, there was blessed silence.

I AM WRATH.

I am vengeance.

No, that was the wrong word. *Justice.* For those who couldn't fight, Alastor led the Exile infantry. Korin and her two flankers provided enough air support for him to maneuver his unit into position, and he raised both arms in salute, hoping she saw it from her eagle-eye view.

He never felt so powerful as when he changed, even if

he was charging straight toward a battalion of his own people. They were coming in hard, echelon formation, and he spotted heavy weapons near the back.

"*Rowena!*" He only needed to call out and point for her to see what he did from her better vantage.

It was a risk to send her in ahead, but he couldn't let them hit the Exiles with that artillery. He slowed and roared a challenge, willing the commander to recognize him. If he did, he'd run straight at Alastor, never mind what the winged Gol might be doing.

It worked.

Following their commander, the whole squadron rushed at Alastor. He guessed there must be a bounty on him, dead or alive. *How many coins for my head on a stick?* That gambit let Rowena swoop in and drop grenades on the back of the line. The weapons and ammo went up in beautiful, fiery explosion that took out at least ten more grunts in pure collateral damage.

Shots rained down from behind, suppressive fire as he'd requested from the city militia. He didn't have time to admire the fireworks, though, because in ten more seconds he was fighting for his life. Dedrick should be here, at his back, but he only had this scrawny Noxblade. Though Alastor had to admit, Zan was both ferocious and quick with his twin blades, which the enemy knew to be wary of, as they were poisoned.

He blocked a strike and another, then went on offense. *We have to hold the line.* Bodies slammed together all around him, the stink of smoke, burning flesh, and blood blending into an intense stench that fired his need to kill everyone who came at him.

Soon, he wasn't thinking at all, no tactics, no strategy,

just teeth and claws and deadly spikes. Corpses piled around him, his kills, Zan's, and still they came on. He knocked three enemies down with a vicious swipe of his tail, and then, it was all butchery: gobbets of bloody meat and entrails yanked through soft spots in armored plating. One by one, he slew them all, until he was simultaneously sick and euphoric at the carnage.

Movement in his periphery, and he spun, narrowly avoiding a strike by the squad commander. Warily Alastor circled; this brute was nearly as big as he was, without the spikes, plating on his chest. By his scars, he'd fought often in the arena.

"You shame our people," the captain growled.

"Don't you respect strength? If so, how can you question my decision to challenge my brother? If you had a chance at the throne, wouldn't you take it?"

Something like respect flickered in the Gol leader's eyes. *"If I was royal-born, I'd challenge and win."*

"Then you understand why I must kill you." Alastor lunged, a fraction too slow to plunge his claws into the other's throat.

A gravelly laugh. *"You'll try."*

"Less talk, more dying." Zan zipped in and slashed, just a slice across the soft skin beneath the Gol's arm.

A bee sting, really.

"You think..." But the leader couldn't get his breath; panting and wheezing, he dropped to his knees.

Alastor finished him swiftly, a mercy, as the poison would take ten more minutes to complete its work. Zan was already engaging more nearby. His prey tended to die from minor wounds, contorted and frothing at the mouth. His body count just kept climbing, and he was so fucking fast that Alastor couldn't keep up.

The initial bloodlust waned as challengers slowed. They'd broken their enemy line, at a cost. Nearly a third of his Exiles lay among the fallen, and more were fighting farther west.

"Fall back!" he ordered.

Rowena repeated the command, calling to the ones who had prowled past the range of his voice. As he'd hoped, the remainders of the enemy squad, now leaderless and frenzied, gave chase. They had the RVAC mounted on a roof nearby and he waited until just the right moment to fire off a flare to the gunner. On that mark, she opened fire, blasting the ground so that an entire wave of Golgoth invaders went up in red smoke, drifted to dust. Even the earth seemed scorched, darker than normal dirt, and the smell—since they'd deployed the RVAC at long range last time, he hadn't breathed in the fresh death.

No one should have this thing, let alone use it. If he took the throne, the first thing he'd do was suggest a voluntary disarmament on all sides.

His surviving soldiers rallied around him, blood-spattered and triumphant. *The west holds.* Now he needed news on how the forces fared to the south. If one side of the phalanx caved in, there would be no stopping the sack and pillage of Hallowell.

His skin felt too small and it was hard to think. Each idea came with too much straining when all he wanted to do was find Sheyla and fuck her through a wall. This wasn't a new impulse, fortunately, but Alastor paused when he realized how specific the urge had become. Before, after the battle in the forest, he would've grabbed Ded or whichever soldier was closest to rut his brains out.

Fuck.

Fuuuuck.

Best not to dwell on it.

"Orders?" Rowena asked.

"We return to the outpost to see how the other units are faring. I'll decide our next move after the status report."

"Fall in," she called to the men.

Borrowed strength from his brute form kept him moving at a brisk clip, but if he kept it up, he might collapse as he had before, unable to hold his shape. *I can't. I'm needed. I have to ration my energy.* Still, he'd left his clothes at the outpost and he didn't care to start wild stories by returning from battle naked and covered in blood. The Animari already nursed enough mistaken lore about his people.

The outpost commander was waiting for a word, but Alastor held up a hand to forestall him. Being unable to communicate easily offered an excellent excuse for him to shift back and dress, doing his best to hide the awkward erection.

At this moment, he could make anyone within a ten-foot radius want to fuck him, and in fact, the outpost commander was starting to look flushed, instinctively moving closer. Alastor took a step back.

"Your report?"

"Yes. Right." The man rubbed his cheek and then put out a hand, dropped it to his side in eager flutters that might have been endearing, if Alastor had been *trying* to seduce him. Eventually, he collected himself enough to say, "I'm sorry, we don't have any information yet. The signal machines are silent."

"They're probably still fighting in the south. Should we move to reinforce them…" It was a rhetorical question more than anything else.

"I'm not sure, sir. I feel…" The commander struggled to find a word that wasn't wildly inappropriate.

"Walk it off. I'll come back later."

To aid in that recovery of composure, Alastor moved away to find Rowena. The Exiles had changed as well, but he could tell by their restless movements and febrile eyes that they wouldn't be able to hold long. Quietly he said, "Find some privacy. Do what you need to. Fast. With each other, no meddling with the locals."

It might seem like an odd move, but he needed all of them sharp and this was the most efficient way to keep anyone from losing control. That was a fucking disaster on deck, if his own soldiers seduced—or gods forbid, ravaged—the people they were supposed to protect.

Rowena added, "You heard him. This is a hit and quit, not the orgy of champions."

Joining them would clear his head, but a lean figure was already headed his way. When the man stepped into the light, Alastor recognized Gavriel, visibly stained with his night's work. Blood dotted his fair features, painted his white hair in streaks of violence.

"Bad news or worse?" the Eldritch asked.

"Surprise me."

"Then I'll let you decide which constitutes which. The south can't hold and St. Casimir Hospital has fallen."

23.

TWELVE HOURS WAS a long shift.

Sheyla had worked for days straight in Ash Valley after the bombing, but prior to that, she'd worked normal hours in the hospital. It had been years since her residency. Unlike the others, she didn't complain. That accomplished nothing and made Dr. Seagram peevish.

She heard him snap at Nurse Harlow, "No, I don't know what's going on in Hallowell. I'm not a seer, and I don't have a magic mirror."

He stomped out of the critical ward, leaving the nurse to approach Sheyla. Again. *If only I had more vintage porn*, she thought.

"He's so mean."

You're so annoying. One of the ways she'd learned to pretend—to fit in better—was not speaking every honest thought.

"Did you change patient Li's IVs?" she asked.

"Of course." The nurse seemed affronted.

"And you've finished all the—"

"Yes. Whatever it is, yes. My list is entirely checked off. Now I'm just counting down the last fifteen minutes of our endless shift."

Sheyla could've pointed out that if the shift was endless, there wouldn't be a finite amount of time remaining, but that would've meant prolonging the conversation. Since she'd finished all her tasks as well, she went over to Dedrick and perched on the edge of the table at his bedside. From experience, she knew people spoke as if their words would be heard, so she tried to imagine what Alastor would say if he was here. She came up blank because he was so much brightness, irreverent and silly and…

Dear.

In the end, she only had her own words to give. "You're healing well. There will be minimal scarring on your heart. It shouldn't impact your physical prowess, provided you recover from the poison."

That was the real threat, not that she'd say so to Dedrick, even in his comatose state. For the first time that she'd seen, his fingers flexed. Hesitantly she reached for his hand; it was warm and scarred, like the rest of him. It seemed to Sheyla that all the marks Alastor's mother had erased, Dedrick bore them on his body in tribute. Probably he'd taken the wounds defending the prince, and she could not be more grateful.

Encouraged, she went on, "Alastor is waiting for you. I don't think he'll ever be the same if you don't pull through, so you know what you should do, right?"

Another flex of his fingers.

"Good. It's all right if you sleep a little longer. There's not much to do down here anyway."

She held his hand until her shift ended and the other crew shuffled in, no more bright-eyed than she felt. The dry ration packs on offer were essential-protein nuggets, the calories and nutrients required to sustain life, but it offered no savor to grind it up with her teeth and wash it down with tepid water. Already she wanted to shift and run, feel crisp wind blowing over her fur. Even the journey from Ash Valley to the rendezvous site that she'd once judged so awful and grueling shone like an inviting memory.

After dinner—or breakfast, she had no idea what time it was—she carried the code manual over to the signal machine. Using the instructions, she fired it up and was delighted to see the unit respond exactly as predicted. Silently, Dr. Seagram crept to her shoulder, but since he smelled a trifle ripe, she didn't startle.

"You've already got it working."

A pointless observation. "Is that all right?"

"Yes. Just don't send any information that would give away our location. I can't fathom why the invaders would come after us when there are higher priority targets, but it seems better to be safe."

"Agreed."

After a moment's thought, she painstakingly input the code for the letters S-H-A-L-A-I. Only Alastor would understand its significance. Random militia officers would have no clue and enemy Golgoth would only know that it was a flower. In the prince's hands, it would become a private message, one that could've come from only one person.

His heart's delight.

"An odd choice for a test," Dr. Seagram said.

Sheyla only shrugged. There was no reason to explain her personal life, so long as it didn't impact her professional performance. After turning off the signal machine, she got a book and chose the most comfortable-looking seat. It was too soon to retire; she would only toss and turn if she tried to burn all her free time in sleep.

This time, the one who interrupted her attempt at reading wasn't Nurse Harlow, at least. A slight male joined her in an adjacent chair, and with some effort, she placed him as Dr. Mitra. He didn't smell like anyone she'd ever encountered before, which was enough to pique her curiosity. It was beyond rude to ask, *Why do you smell so strange?*

He offered a friendly smile. "We haven't spoken much. What are you reading?"

"*The Secret History of Eldritch Queens: A Study in Espionage and Assassination.*"

"Not what I expected."

"Which is?" She wanted to demand the point of this conversation. Social interaction seemed rambling and inefficient, but she surmised that it sprang from a need for contact.

"From what I've seen, you're all business, so I thought you'd be reading a medical journal."

"Those are all fifty years out of date," she pointed out. "Whereas this was already historical nonfiction when it was printed."

"There could be new discoveries in later versions of the text, obviating prior assumptions of historical accuracy."

"True." Finally, she had to ask, "What is it that you want, Dr. Mitra? I can't imagine you came to debunk my choice of reading material."

"Not as such, no. I was just trying to be polite, get to know you before I request a favor."

"No need, just ask." Finally, she could see an end to this.

"I'm quite good friends with a doctor on first shift, and

it would make time go faster for both of us if we were on the same schedule."

"So, you want me to switch."

"If you don't mind. I know you've just come off rotation, but—"

She made a swift decision. *One double shift, and then I'm working opposite Nurse Harlow?* It felt like Dr. Mitra was doing *her* the favor.

"I'll go relieve him right now."

"Really? I can't thank you enough—"

She discarded her book and strode toward the ward. Sheyla found her promised swap partner; they went to Dr. Seagram together. He mumbled a bit, but in the end, he approved the request.

"If this starts a tidal wave of shift trading, I'm holding you two responsible!" he called after them.

Maybe it was a small thing, but the switch cheered her up considerably. The first shift staff was polite but not chatty, just the way she liked it, and work was the best use of hours that otherwise would pass like chilled honey dripping off a spoon.

Gratefully she immersed herself in other people's needs, tended one minor emergency, brought another patient back from the brink of death. Normal. Satisfying. Exhaustion prickled at the back of her eyes, and in that moment of weakness, she let herself wonder.

How is he? Is he hurting? Tired?

Before she could topple into the abyss of bleak curiosity, Nurse Mills grabbed her arm. "Dr. Halek, you have to see this."

His urgency snapped her back to reality, big room, basic equipment, row on row of patients who needed her best.

She went at a run, skidding to a stop at Dedrick's bedside. His vitals were erratic, and just as she feared he was about to go into shock, they stabilized.

His eyes opened. Searching. The unfamiliar surroundings, sounds and smells, and this room was far from inviting, more like a dungeon where medical experiments might be conducted. Panic would set in soon—she'd seen it before. Quickly Sheyla stepped into his field of vision and took his hand, because that was what Alastor would do.

"You did well," she said. "You're safe."

He couldn't speak for the tube in his throat, but his eyes were asking, in abject terror, about the prince, so she added, "Alastor's fine too."

As far as I know.

SHEYLA'S ALIVE.

She must be.

When Alastor first got the news about St. Casimir, his first reaction was pure panic, but once he quelled it, he'd understood it was wrong. Because no matter what had happened at St. Casimir, he didn't feel the empty devastation that would surely follow if his love had departed from the world. *She wouldn't want me to worry.* If she was here, she'd say, *"Do some work if you're wasting your energy on that."*

It was harder to excise his fear for Dedrick, not to imagine his friend buried beneath a ton of fallen rock and dying by millimeters, too weak even to call out. Because of Sheyla, he'd managed to control that terror too.

She's looking out for him. Somehow.

He clung to that truth as a lifeline and focused on the defense of Hallowell. Alastor had no idea how long it had been since he slept. Realistically, he couldn't keep this up. His spirit was willing, and the situation was dire, but his body couldn't keep the pace. Already he was in so much pain that it was hard to function, and he would pay for this overexertion for days.

"You don't look well," Zan said.

He decided to answer honestly. In the last twenty-four hours, the Noxblade had saved his life repeatedly. While he wasn't—and would never be—Dedrick, he'd earned this much of Alastor's confidence.

"The truth is..." Concisely, he explained his condition.

"Understood." If the man had praised him for trying so hard or patted his back, he might've lost his temper since he was already exhausted and irritable. The matter of fact reaction offered no space for it, thankfully.

"Do you want me to see if I can find a Sol to make it easier for you to move around the city? The ground troops can catch up. If you're in the thick of the fighting when it starts, it won't impact morale."

Despite the initial victory in the west, the outlook wasn't good. If they paused to rest, it gave the enemy time to regroup. The invaders had razed St. Casimir along with that whole section of the city, bombarded the east, and were about to overrun the south. There were multiple breaches and the militia was falling back as planned. Their last stand in Old Town might be the final hurrah for freedom.

Belatedly he realized Zan was waiting for an answer. "Yes, please. I'm aware that private vehicles are prohibited on city streets, but I suspect the chancellor can make an exception in wartime."

Zan cocked his head, eyeing the fires blazing in the distance. "I'd be more worried about rubble blocking our path or whether there are streets anymore, myself."

"Gallows humor. I like your style." With an effort, he forced a smile and got to his feet by hauling with both arms, then he braced himself on the cathedral wall.

They had taken a few hours rest here, ostensibly for the men, but Alastor couldn't have continued. It wasn't enough, nothing would be, until he saw an end to this, one way or another.

"I'll be back shortly. We're not too far from the weapons factory. They usually have vehicles on site."

Considering the Eldritch's speed, there was no doubt his jaunt would be swift. As he watched Zan go, Rowena approached.

"Are we moving soon?"

He nodded. "I'll be scouting ahead. I need you to lead the men and keep them strong, no matter what. Can you do it?"

Her level gaze said she understood that the survivors who were sworn to him in Golgerra probably wouldn't see another sunrise. There was no anger in her, only acceptance, and Alastor blinked away weary tears. Everyone who followed him, they were all too devoted and good.

"Don't think that you failed," she said. "Nobody could have done more or better. Tycho committed a lot of his forces, he's counting on capturing these resources, this staging point."

"Thank you." That was all he could manage when he meant so much more. *For staying, for being my friend, for believing in this bittersweet dream.*

By her expression, she understood and she was at peace with whatever came next.

Just then the comm crackled to life. "Some good news

at last," Korin said.

"Bless Gavriel's stealthy heart," Alastor answered. "Channel secure?"

"I wouldn't talk about battle plans on here, but we can check in."

"How do things look at the southern outpost? We're heading out to reinforce."

"Too late." Her grave tone rendered the report even more dire. "There aren't many of us left and those who can move are falling back to Old Town. Checkpoints and barricades are blown to shit, they have an RVAC and..." The comm cut out, but he had the gist.

Alastor swore.

Since Rowena had heard, she went to update the Exiles, and a bit later, Zan zoomed up in a battered Sol; it looked like he'd seen combat in liberating the vehicle. The Eldritch beckoned cheerfully.

"I didn't know how to drive a Sol when I got in this thing, but it's not too much different than a Rover. If we mounted guns on it, this could be a tiny weapon of mass destruction."

It was a throwaway comment, a joke, but Alastor studied the Sol with new eyes. He made a snap decision and barked orders while Zan stared at him in stunned surprise.

"You were kidding. I'm not. Let's get it done."

Another hour wouldn't save the people in the south, but maybe he could clear a path for those trying to make the fallback in Old Town. The Exiles proved to be as deft at jury-rigging artillery as they had been learning masonry in Ash Valley, and soon half the Sol's roof was missing, and he had it rigged out with missiles and a hefty caliber gun. His people were hard to kill in hand to hand, so he'd avoid close combat, as he no longer had the energy left to change.

He got on the comm. "Korin, do you copy?"

"Check."

He remembered her caution—*don't talk battle plans, just in case.* So how to handle this?

First, a fact-finding question, nothing definite. "Can you provide air support?"

"Only two of us left, but Ria and I will have your back. What's the op?"

"Survival," he said. "Farham's Law."

Surely she would be familiar with the adage: **The simplest available course is always best.** Not everyone agreed with Farham, but it was a well-known truism.

A pause. "Understood."

"There are civilians and volunteer militia on the move. I'm on point, clearing the way. My men will guard the rear."

There, that was informative only to Korin. Any enemies who overheard this chatter wouldn't know his location or where he was headed, nothing helpful to extrapolate.

"Copy," Korin replied. "We're inbound."

Taking a breath, Alastor switched off the comm and headed over to his men. "I'm sorry I can't lead you personally from this point. From here on out, treat Rowena's word as mine. Your highest priority is assisting the evac and ensuring the safety of Hallowell's citizens. Guard yourselves well too and get to Old Town safely. It's an old installation, so it's the most defensible point in the city. If we can hold that ground, we can still win."

Each Exile dropped to one knee and pressed their right hands over their hearts. Overwhelmed at their loyalty, Alastor fought to get himself in check and went to them, one by one, briefly resting a hand on their heads. He didn't know if he'd see them again.

"Rise. Fight like warriors, and afterward, celebrate like champions."

The Exiles roared in response, along with a few of the militia who happened to be nearby. Turning, Alastor spotted Zan waiting by the open cathedral doors. Framed in radiant light, for an instant, the Noxblade looked like an unearthly figure, a religious icon instead of a man.

"Are you done inspiring the masses?"

No, not a divine being. Just a joker.

He smiled. "For now. You drive, I'll shoot."

"Do I not get a say in this?"

Alastor shook his head. "I know how to do one, not the other."

There was no further discussion. With Zan at the wheel, Alastor settled into the makeshift gun-pit and activated his weapon of choice with more glee than seemed healthy.

"Target acquired."

24.

For over an hour, Dedrick had been pleading with his eyes for someone to remove his breathing tube, and when Sheyla was satisfied his lungs could cope, she complied. The nurse offered a basin in case it triggered his gag reflex, and he retched but since he hadn't eaten in days, nothing came up. They followed the usual protocols about food and water; it was far too soon to think about weaning him from fluids yet that was Dedrick's first demand.

It nearly always was.

His voice came out hoarse as he strained to sit up and couldn't make his body cooperate. "Unhook me from these infernal machines and tell me what's become of Prince Alastor!"

With a gentle hand, she pressed back on his shoulder; that much was enough to drop him against the mattress. "Calm down. When I have a spare moment, I'll explain. Right now, other patients need my attention."

His gaze followed her, silent and baleful as she checked off tasks from her work list. Sheyla took pride in being the most efficient doctor on any rotation. While others chatted, she rarely took breaks and kept moving, even when she'd rather rest.

Finally, Nurse Mills tapped her shoulder. "I hate to bother you again, but he's getting agitated. Nobody will mind if you spend fifteen minutes talking with him. You're like a damn medicine machine."

That wasn't the first time she'd received such a compliment, if it was supposed to be one. To Sheyla, it never registered that way, always with faint edges of venom and judgment. If she was a machine, tasks would be effortless, and there would be no pain in her shoulders, no tension in her neck, no throb at her temples. Working this way might be her choice, but it wasn't *easy*.

She swallowed the complaint and went to Dedrick because excess agitation wouldn't aid his recovery. There were no chairs for visitors in here, like they had in the good facilities above. When the staff retreated, they'd brought the minimum necessary to treat patients.

"Is it all right if I sit on the side of your bed?"

A flicker of amusement. "Like I could stop you."

It was hard not to see this man differently, now that she knew he had been Alastor's occasional lover. People's features rarely interested her, but she noticed details about him now, like the scar that bisected his dark brow and the burn on his side. Like most of the Golgoth, he was pale, his face was rough, like the side of a mountain—the antithesis of the prince—and he had hair in so many shades of brown that it was almost like a wolf's variegated fur. His latest wound was still bandaged, relatively small in relation to other marks and the overall damage he'd suffered.

Eventually, he cleared his throat. "Shouldn't you be speaking, not staring?"

"I'm sorry. Let me bring you up to speed." As succinctly

as possible, she related an account of recent events. She finished with, "I'm unsure how it's going in Hallowell, but if there's a way to prevail, Alastor will find it. He was safe and whole when we parted."

Dedrick closed his eyes, leaning his head against the headboard. "We're entombed then. No exit unless they send word."

"You're in no shape to fight, so rest and recover," she said sternly.

"May I ask why you're here and not with him?"

"That option wasn't offered," she said. "I think he was protecting me, and I hope it's giving him some peace to know that we're together."

"It sounds as if you're fond of me," he said wonderingly.

Sheyla almost smiled. "Did it? I'm not sure I'd use that word, but I'll admit, Alastor has talked about you so much that I feel I do know you well."

Dedrick plucked at the covers, and it was sweet to see such a warrior reduced to shy silence at the idea he might've received a compliment. Or several. "I hardly know what to say. Good things, I hope?"

"The best. I'm sure this isn't news, but he considers you his closest friend."

"For a long time, I was his *only* friend," Dedrick said.

"Yes, I heard that, too."

"Seems there's nothing he didn't share with you." But he didn't sound aggrieved, only pensive. "I should apologize. When I first noted how drawn he was to you, I discouraged him from…" He winced and she passed him a cup of water to soothe his raw throat.

Probably he shouldn't be talking so much, so soon, but it wouldn't do permanent harm, so she prompted, "From?"

"Pursuing you. I was afraid you'd hurt him. I'm sure you realize, it will benefit him if he can make a marital alliance with one of the Animari clans or even the Eldritch."

"I know," she said softly, ignoring the pang as the reminder pierced her.

Wartime romance, remember?

As if I could forget.

"I'm sorry I did that. It's clear you've made each other happy, and those memories are precious, even if—"

"Dr. Halek!"

An alarm blared, cutting Dedrick off. At the other end of the ward, a patient was coding, so she raced to help. They already had the emergency kit laid out; she took the lead, first with prep meds, then shock treatment and resuscitation efforts. She went for three full minutes before Nurse Mills pulled her away.

"Too long. You have to call it."

Sweaty, shaken, and gasping, she swiped a hand over her face, hoping to hide how shitty she felt. Each time, it echoed like a personal failure. She took a last look at the patient's face, matching to the info from his chart. *Ilan Herovi, age 17. Born and bred in Hallowell, wolf stock, probably emigrated from Pine Ridge.* Like Alastor, he'd suffered from a rare illness, one that was hard to manage and complicated to treat, an illness Animari doctors knew little about.

It could be my prince lying there. He might die in battle instead, faint fucking comfort.

"Call it," Nurse Mills repeated.

In a monotone, she spoke the patient's name and pronounced him dead, though she couldn't be certain of the time. Then the nurse pulled the sheet up, covering the boy's face.

"I need to speak to Dr. Seagram," she said. "I'll be back presently."

They hadn't discussed the protocol of losing a patient. Up above, they would call for an orderly and send the body to the morgue. Down here, there was no such service; they didn't even have a cold room to slow decomposition. As Sheyla skimmed through the available space, no solution seemed ideal.

"I've already heard the news," Seagram said heavily. "I collect you need to know how to proceed?"

"That would be helpful."

"Let's move two sets of bunks into the rec room. We'll use the lockers to partition part of the dorm for... storage."

Though Sheyla didn't say so, nobody was going to lie down in there now. Even if they weren't superstitious about the dead lingering, there were health and hygiene concerns related to sharing space with the dead. Since everyone could shift, there was no reason to worry about beds, really. Sleeping in cat form was fine anywhere. Or maybe at Seagram's age, he needed the comfort of a mattress.

She just nodded and said, "I'll get it done."

Briskly she returned to the ward and gave the orders, concealing how much she wanted to curl up in a corner somewhere. Bitter thoughts filled her head as she finished her shift, whispers of failure and futility.

Dedrick called out to her as she was leaving. "Are you going to bed?"

It had been a full day; she should be ready to pass out, but if she tried to sleep, Sheyla knew from losing prior patients, there would be nothing but terrible dreams.

"You have a better idea?" she asked, without much hope.

"I'm plenty rested and bored. I was hoping you wouldn't mind keeping me company. Maybe read a book?"

"You want me to read to you?"

A shrug. "Only if you want."

Sheyla understood now how this man had kept Alastor alive and capable of hope. His instincts were phenomenal. Even wounded and confined to bed, he was paying attention to *her* mood and found a way to offer a decent distraction.

"I'd like that," she said, smiling.

ALASTOR HAD A job to do.

Clear the path or die trying.

Ahead, the broken city streets were clotted with the Golgoth who had shattered their defenses, now free to loot and pillage. Wheeling the heavy gun, he unleashed a spray of bullets on the brute-Gol squad storming toward them. The ballistic hailstorm tore through even their armored bodies, decimating them in seconds. Their corpses toppled into a twitching pile of tissue, and the survivors scattered.

"Don't stop," he called to Zan, past the howl of the wind. "The Exiles will mop up stragglers, and I only have so much ammo."

The Eldritch called back, "Like I would! I have two modes, fast and faster."

An enormous brute of a Gol stomped into their path, bigger than Alastor when he changed and twice as armored, all plates, horns, and claws. *This must be one of Tycho's Elite.* He unloaded, but the warrior took little damage... until a rocket whistled in from above and reduced him to a flying foot and a spray of blood mist. Alastor glanced up and spotted Korin and her cadet, air support as promised; he raised an arm in a gesture of thanks and she flashed her lights to show acknowledgment.

"We have a problem!" Zan shouted.

"I think we're—oh shit." Alastor locked onto two additional units entering the fray, likely tracking the Sol's movement, at the intersection up ahead, all changed and ready for slaughter, with at least four Elites among them.

"Thoughts? Some of them look like runners, and we can't afford to stall out here."

"We get creative," Alastor called. "Korin, do you copy?"

"Affirmative."

"Are the buildings fully evac-ed here?" In truth, many of them had taken damage, fire, shells, and burn from long-distance RVAC. The one he was eyeing looked like it might collapse on its own, but he couldn't risk this plan if it meant injuring innocents.

"Make it quick," Zan snapped. "We're closing fast."

The Sol raced closer to the knot of Gol invaders, way more than they could handle. Alastor's shoulders tensed.

Korin answered, "There should be no civilians, only looters and shooters."

Alastor released the controls and went for his launcher, unleashing a missile. When Korin saw the side of the building cave in, she likely figured out his plan in a hurry since she launched a swarm of rockets at two load-bearing pylons. It fell like a dying giant, crushing one of the units, and blocking the road, so the Elites couldn't touch them.

With a triumphant cry, Alastor lobbed grenades to the left and right, so they sped by in an inferno of shock and awe. Behind them, more of his brother's soldiers died in the blasts, the rest went down in a hail of shrapnel. Each jolt of the damaged road sent pain slicing through him, and his hands hurt from clenching the artillery. The air was so thick with smoke, rubble dust, and chemicals that it was a miracle he hadn't passed out yet.

"With our numbers, this would've been impossible on foot. Our forces would've been flanked and slaughtered."

Zan nodded, swerving to avoid an Elite that burst from the ashes of a charred structure right nearby. She was immense, charging toward them with intent to flip the Sol. Clearly a veteran, this warrior had only one eye, the other scarred shut, and she roared a challenge in base-Gol, with her gaping mouth, revealing uneven yellow teeth.

"Fuck," Alastor said.

"Less whines, more mines," Zan shot back.

If they weren't about to be rolled, he would've laughed. The Sol was nearly out of juice, and there was no sun in this dark night of the soul, plus this bitch could run. She was about to take them from behind, too close for Korin or Ria to have a shot.

The gun's useless, won't penetrate.

With a growl, Alastor went for the last of his grenades. He pulled the pins off four, let them cook for a few seconds and dropped them onto the road, where they rolled under the target and detonated. Not a clean kill, but with her four limbs crippled, she wouldn't catch them. Once they had some distance, Korin went nuclear and blazed the bitch to dust.

From there, the coast was clear, Old Town in his sights. The Sol was choking, batteries just about dry. His comm popped, hissed, then Korin came across. "You good? There are multiple fires for us to put out."

"Free and clear. Come back when you can," Alastor

said.

"Copy."

All around him, the city burned. His impression of Old Town was heartening, because the old fort walls had been shored up and all the artillery produced by the converted factories had been concentrated here. *For our last stand.* Wall-mounted gunners at the ready, this place was grim and focused. The gates opened slowly, permitting Zan to guide the dying Sol inside. Civilians and Exiles should arrive soon. Hopefully, there would be some breathing room before the next wave.

Weary and half-deafened from the killing spree, he swallowed a groan as he rolled out of the vehicle. Zan touched his shoulder.

"You good, boss?" A clear indication that the Eldritch didn't see him as some asshole royal. Apparently, they'd bonded in those fast, furious moments.

Alastor responded as he would've with Ded—with a friendly nudge and, "Yes. Thanks."

The horizon was lightening, a gray day with hidden pearls. *Dawn now, maybe my last.*

Given how fucked Hallowell had seemed passing through the center of it, Alastor fought the seductive numbness of despair. The damage he'd witnessed, devastating and heartbreaking. Broken streets, bodies burning where they fell. Hallowell was a hellscape, and moreover, a vision of the world his brother would create. Here in the sanctuary of Old Town, the med tent was overwhelmed with the injured, mostly children who couldn't shift. Their dirty faces and disconsolate eyes would haunt him forever.

I didn't do this.

I tried to stop it.

Alastor would give a lot for just five seconds with Sheyla—to hold her and breathe her in. Having her nearby would dispel the lingering specter of colossal failure, that he was about to fuck things up so prodigiously that there could be no recovery for generations. Eventually, he collected himself enough to climb the walls, watching for the rest of his troops.

Gavriel's Eldritch stumbled into Old Town first, worse for the wear, their numbers much reduced. The Hallowell western outpost force arrived next, and it looked like they'd scrapped with some of the survivors, despite his best efforts. Alastor kept watching the pavement as the sun climbed steadily in the sky. No enemies. No allies.

At last, the Exiles rolled in, *much* later than he'd expected. No Rowena. His chest tightened so hard that he saw sparks.

"Where *is* she?" he demanded. "If she fell out there, you should've brought her body, even if it killed half of you to do it." Rage gave his voice power, even though he knew he was talking shit, being wildly unfair.

She deserves so much better. I should have been there.

Graff stepped forward. One of the youngest, he still had seniority with Ded and Rowena out of the picture. He dropped to his knees. "I'm sorry, Your Highness. We're all so sorry."

"No apologies. No excuses. What the *fuck* happened out there?"

"A group of Tycho's Elite jumped us. Rowena... they took her. Cut and ran. Maybe for ransom...?" His voice went up on a hopeful note. "The king knows that you hold her precious."

He closed his eyes to control the absolute fury that rolled over him. Spikes half-shot from his back before he locked his emotions down. "Get out of my sight."

Graff ran.

Not fair.

Don't care.

As if that wasn't enough, his comm vibrated, a new user looking to connect. With an angry gesture, he permitted the link. "Who's this?"

"Finneas Furbander, at your service. With my first and final report." A ferocious noise clamored in the background, nearly drowning the man's voice. "The invaders are everywhere. Swarming. We cannot permit our factories to be taken. Rather than putting weapons into our enemies' hands, we shall take them with us."

"What are you talking about?" Alastor had a terrible feeling, chills rolling in infinite loop.

Furbander went on, "The charges are set. Five factories in all, and we count the sacrifice well worth it. If we time this properly, most of these bastards will die at our hands. It may give you the edge you need."

Suddenly he understood. "There has to be another way, sir."

More noise, like a ram slamming into a metal door.

"Sadly, there is not. I won't say it was a pleasure meeting you, Alastor of Golgerra, but I do thank you for your service. Advise the chancellor that I would like a statue in the plaza. Bronze, I think." Crunch and bang, like a broken door. "Now, good sir, I am out of time. Please tell my wife and children I love them."

An immense boom, and the comm went eerily silent.

25.

AFTER THAT YOUNG patient died, things went sideways. It was slow at first, whispers that ceased when Dr. Seagram entered the room. Normally Sheyla didn't pay attention to gossip, but the words she caught were edged with desperation and malice. Nurse Harlow was usually in the thick of the talk, no reassurance there, for she'd already observed that the woman didn't possess the steadiest personality.

The silence of the signal machine troubled everyone. Nobody had paid much attention when she first sent the test message, but the longer they went without a reply, the harder it became to control the fear of what might be happening in the city above. Earlier, Dedrick had used the word 'entombed' and if they were down here long enough, it might even prove true. Dying in confinement? It would be hell, and in the end, they'd probably go feral and turn on each other when the deepest survival instincts kicked in.

Her stomach churned at the mere contemplation of such a potential outcome. Dedrick called out, rescuing her from the mental image of blood-spattered walls. Sheyla went over to his bed, raising a brow in query.

"You rang?"

"My own personal physician? This is service. I was actually talking to Aide Cabueze."

Who was paying no attention whatsoever. Sheyla smiled. "You have two minutes. What do you need?"

"If you won't unhook me, I was wondering if you had more portable units I could drag around behind me. I won't get stronger lying in bed."

Sheyla shook her head. "What you see is what we have."

They hadn't come down here with plans in place for recovery or the dead, best and worst case scenarios. It seemed clear Dr. Seagram hadn't expected them to hide for this long, more of a precaution than a long-term strategy. Yet Hallowell was silent. Logically, that suggested Alastor was losing. *Perhaps no one is left to answer.*

"Which means I'll be drinking that protein mess again."

"Now that you're stronger, you can chew it if you wish."

Dedrick sighed. "There's nothing that can get me out of this bed faster?"

"For a big, bold warrior, you certainly complain a lot."

In fact, she was already doing it. The fluids he wanted to remove so badly should have him on his feet in half a day. She'd analyzed their cross-compatibility and had deduced that there was no reason he couldn't receive an Animari plasma transfusion. At first, she wasn't certain he could tolerate it, fearing that his system might fight an Animari donor, but she'd tested her theory before he woke up and had found no adverse reactions, so she'd switched his IV as soon as he woke up.

"Your bedside manner is terrible." He was smiling,

though.

"Not the first time I've heard that."

Nurse Mills interrupted the conversation to point out, "There are other patients who need you, doctor, even if they aren't so vocal about it."

The mild rebuke didn't irritate her because it was true. With a nod of apology aimed at both Dedrick and Mills, she went about her work. As she'd predicted, before the end of her shift, Ded was moving around his bed, testing the range of his tubes. She could tell he was chafing to be cut loose and while there was no discharge, per se, it was time to evaluate his condition. Since Dr. Seagram had been studying Golgoth anatomy as well, she called him to consult.

She handed him in the data stream chart, not printed since their supplies were limited. "Everything looks good to me. He'll need to rest and take it easy, but I don't see any reason why we can't let him ramble around the bunker."

Seagram ruminated over the various test results and then checked Dedrick's wound—cleanly sealed, stitches dissolving as intended. "That looks good. Why don't we peek inside?"

"Hold very still," she told Dedrick.

Sheyla fetched the wand and the 3D anatomical map that had so fascinated Alastor what seemed like ages ago appeared over Dedrick. Some of his organs still showed traces of damage, but they were clearing him to stroll between three rooms, not fight a war.

"I see you've used an unusual treatment…" Seagram questioned her about the plasma transfusion and they talked for ten minutes past shift change about the theoretical benefits of cross gene therapy betwixt the Golgoth and Animari.

Until Dedrick cleared his throat. "Excuse me. Still here. Still a person."

"I don't see any reason why you can't get up," Seagram said.

"Congratulations."

Their group was drawing definite attention, most of it laced with disapproval, so she hurried through a facsimile of discharge and brought Dedrick the biggest pair of scrubs she could find.

"You're probably tired of pajamas."

With a surprisingly warm smile, he took the clothes and went to the bathroom to get dressed. *Alastor will be so happy,* she thought, and then uncertainty crashed down.

As she headed for the lounge, she caught the tail of an ominous whisper. "...can't kill him. The biometrics won't work if he's dead."

She stilled in the corridor. Those in the rec room were the first shift staff who had already gone off-duty, which meant the mutiny was pervasive.

"We'll die down here if we don't do something. Just like that Herovi kid." Barely a breath, but Sheyla still caught it.

Dedrick came up behind her and started to speak; she lifted a hand, warning him, but it was too late. The voices stopped. They had Animari ears, too.

What? His eyes asked.

She shaped the word 'mutiny' with her mouth, once, twice, each time slower until cognition sharpened his expression, and then Dedrick tipped his head toward the great room. She nodded.

"There's no point tiptoeing anymore," Dr. Seagram said loudly.

Too focused on eavesdropping, she hadn't heard the old

man. Again. Before she could stop him, Seagram marched into the rec room with a pugnacious expression. "You want to knock my head against the wall, turn the lift on, and flee, do you?" Seagram let out a deafening roar, dropped his clothes, and bristled into a large brown bear.

That escalated quickly.

As others followed, Sheyla mumbled a curse, got naked, and slid into cheetah form. Her growl said, *Over my dead body.* Settling beside Dr. Seagram, she doubted the two of them were enough to get the rest to back down. *It'll probably end in bloodshed. Why are people so fucking foolish and impatient?*

The opposing group suddenly took a step back and when Sheyla spun, she understood. Dedrick had changed too, and these people had probably never seen a brute-Gol before. Unlike Alastor, Ded was quadrupedal in this form, huge and armored, ridged, and awe-imposing. It looked like he could bite somebody in two, one blow, too severe for quick-healing to save anyone. She didn't speak base-Gol, but she could guess he was rumbling a threat, like, *keep at it and I'll fuck you up.*

The would-be mutineers shifted back first. "Let's talk about this. No need to be... impulsive."

Sheyla stretched and luxuriated in being a cat for a few moments, making sure the others understood that she wasn't in the mood to play. *Give me a reason.* She said it by prowling around them, and then she swiped at one for good measure.

Skittish, huh?

It took a few minutes to get dressed, which made the standoff feel slightly ridiculous. Dr. Seagram was clearly still pissed, and she didn't blame him.

"Listen up, you fuckwits. Yes, we may die if we don't hear from the defenders soon, but if you try to take the lift without knowing the situation, you could be stranded in the shaft, and then nobody's getting out. So shut up, do your jobs, and wait. We're here for one reason only—because these patients will die without us. Trust me, I'd rather be working in a triage tent, too. Instead, I get to hole up with you worthless shit biscuits. Any complaints, choke on them and die. That'll leave more protein packs for the rest of us."

"Damn," Dedrick said as Seagram marched out. "Shit biscuits?"

"I know. He's magnificent when he gets going. Once he called me a festering sack of fermented assholes." Sheyla wasn't trying to be funny, but everybody in the lounge heard it, and they couldn't stop laughing.

"We're all gonna die," Nurse Mills said, but he didn't seem troubled.

She frowned at him. "Eventually, everyone does."

When Ded smiled and slung a comforting arm across her shoulder, she leaned in. Faith wasn't something she had a lot of, but the demon prince had never let her down.

He won't start now.

FIVE FACTORIES. FIVE sacrifices.

Hours later, Alastor was still reeling over what Furbander had done. In blowing those facilities, the owners had taken out an incredible chunk of Tycho's force. Smoke was still rising in black columns, a spiraling monument to the power of people defending their homes. There was no price too high; he saw that now.

Alastor wanted to storm out and scour the city for

Rowena.

He couldn't. It was likely she'd been taken as bait, not for ransom, as Graff had suggested so optimistically. When he didn't come for her, Rowena would be returned to Golgerra in hopes they could torture some of his plans out of her. Once she proved useless, Tycho would execute her, as planned before Alastor saved her from the block.

I'm sorry, Row. I'm so sorry.

Much as he wanted to, he couldn't abandon Old Town to search for one soldier. Refugees were still trickling in, straggling militia members who barely made the fallback. Waiting was the worst part. There would likely be one more battle before they broke the invaders entirely.

"Sire? We don't know what to make of this. It's been circulating among the officers and someone finally thought to ask you."

Alastor turned, doing his best to mask his weariness. These men and women were all equally tired, and they'd lost so much, so fast. He accepted a paper with the word S-H-A-L-A-I on it, and his heart almost stopped.

"Where did you get this?"

"It came through the signal machine. We were so surprised, I didn't even know—"

"Show me."

Following the young militiaman, he hurried into what looked like an old telemetry room, full of machines that defied qualification. The one in question sat on a battered desk, attended by a man so venerable he made Chancellor Quarles look like a spring flower.

"Did you want to send a reply?" the clerk asked.

"Please. Just one word: Home."

It was Sheyla; it had to be, for he'd shared that story

with nobody else. Yet he couldn't risk a longer message without confirmation. She had been cautious too, wanting to be sure he was the one who received her communication.

She's alive. She's waiting.

St. Casimir might be a rubble heap, but she'd found a way to survive. *My clever doctor.* His spirit brightened to the point that it hurt. He touched the crumpled note that he kept with him always, such a silly thing.

I'll miss your face.

Miss yours too, love. Be strong. We'll be there soon.

While he reflected, the old man worked the device, then gave a satisfied nod. "It's done."

There were more pressing matters, but he stared and waited, convinced it wouldn't take her long to answer. *Please, Sheyla. I need this. Give me strength, as you always do.*

Seemed like forever, but it was no more than ten minutes when the machine started working again, etching out each letter in response to the signal. "How are you, my prince?"

It's her.

"Reply?" the clerk asked.

"We hold. Location secure."

When he left the building, he realized he hadn't seen Zan for a while. Since the Eldritch had clung like a second skin, that seemed... sinister. In the wake of Rowena's abduction, he went from zero to red alert in about twenty seconds. Alastor deployed multiple men to help him search, until he stumbled across the Noxblade crumpled near the west wall.

More assassins? I'll kill every last Talfayen loyalist myself.

He broke into a stumbling run and tumbled to his knees beside the first Eldritch he'd call his friend. "What happened?"

Oddly he didn't smell blood and in searching, he didn't find a wound, not even a scratch or pinprick that could've delivered some noxious poison. Zan was so fucking pale that Alastor thought he was dead, but as he shook him, the man's eyes fluttered open.

"Let me help you to the med tent."

A faint smile. "No point. There's no cure for this."

"I don't understand. If you're sick, you should've told me." *I told you. I trusted you.* Alastor couldn't get the words out. He'd lost too much, too fast, and he felt like tearing his own skin off.

Zan reached for him with a fair, slim hand. Uncomprehending, he took it, unnerved by how weak the grasp, how thready his pulse. "I don't understand."

"It was... an adventure," Zan whispered. "Worth. It. Finish..."

But it was too late. His body slumped forward into Alastor's arms, and confusion raged through him like a river flooding its banks. For the longest, he just held Zan and swallowed the urge to scream.

When he finally let go and stood, he found Gavriel waiting behind him like a ghost. He didn't even try to avoid the fist that smashed into his jaw; he just took the hit and fell over.

Alastor spat blood. "Tell me what just happened."

"All Eldritch have a gift. Zan's was phenomenal speed, as I'm sure you noted. What you didn't realize is that our gifts come at a cost. There's always an energy exchange. The more we use our gifts, the more energy we expand. Deployed sparingly, we tend to live a long, long time. Otherwise—"

"Fuck. *Fuck.*" Over the past few days, Zan had run constantly, fought like a demon, everywhere at once, defending him.

"You understand. He burned through his entire life in days. For you. I didn't ask him to guard you. He volunteered. And…" Gavriel's jaw clenched. Alastor saw from the Noxblade's balled fist that he wanted to hit him again. "He was my best friend. To this madness, I've lost my blood brother *and* my oath-sworn swordmate. What more will you hell born brutes and beasts take?" The words became a howl and Gavriel sent a blade skimming past his ear.

He didn't flinch, even when it pinged off the wall and rattled by his feet. "I'm sorry. If I'd known—"

"That's why he didn't tell you. 'We need the prince to unite the Gol', that's what Zan said to me. 'Whereas I am expendable'."

"He planned to die?" Alastor asked, incredulous.

"Not as such, but he understood that he might be pushed to it."

How am I supposed to walk beneath the weight of so much sacrifice?

The answer came, clear as if Sheyla had whispered the truth in his ear. It was even her voice he heard, framing the words.

You remember what they've given, but you don't allow that to prevent personal progress. The dead are not clinging to our ankles. Each year when we light candles and speak of their deeds, it is tribute enough for their honor and consolation.

"Please," Alastor said. "Take him. I wish to participate in whatever sacred rites your people cherish, but now isn't the time."

"You and I are finally in agreement," Gavriel muttered,

as if it pained him.

At the Noxblade captain's signal, men came for Zan's body, conveying him to the makeshift mortuary, already filled with Latents, the unlucky, the frail, and the young. Zan joined the number, and as the doors shut, Alastor rubbed his chest. He talked himself silently through the bronchial attack, brought on by the pall in the air and the weight of grief. The tightness doubled him over; Gavriel didn't move to console him. Just as well, he didn't want him to.

Somewhere in the camp, a small child was singing. As he struggled for oxygen, the sweetness of it pierced him like a blade. "Mother, keep me safe and warm. Mother, carry me to your light. Mother, bear me in your arms. Mother, guard me from the night."

It was an ancient, simple hymn yet and as that little girl sang the second verse, more voices joined her, deep and low, light as air. "Father, cradle me to your chest, hold me up as waters rise, and you who guard your family best, take me home so I can rest."

By the final verse, it sounded as if every soul in Old Town was singing with all their hearts, a choir that could reach heaven itself. Alastor was too tired and broken to believe, but he took comfort in the way the citizens of Hallowell reached for each other while the city burned.

The shout came from the walls then. "Sire! The enemy's on the march."

The people sang on.

Alastor nodded. "We've done what we can. Let them come."

26.

SHEYLA WAS HALF-DEAFENED with the cheers, and the entire staff passed around the messages like they were Holy Writ. It held a special resonance when the paper finally reached Dedrick's hands. The big guard stared for a long moment at the scant words and then put his head back, his entire being a study in relief.

Little by little, the small crowd dispersed, until it was just the two of them by the signal machine. Besides Dr. Seagram, she was the only one who knew how to use it anyway.

"Looks like he's coping without us," Sheyla said.

The mood had lightened, now that they knew the defenders were standing strong. Exhaustion crashed over her, too vicious to resist. At this point, she couldn't factor how long it had been since she'd slept. Yielding to the need at last, Sheyla stripped in the lounge, which drew no attention, except from Dedrick. He colored and glanced away.

"I can't get used to that," he muttered.

With a silent shrug, she went cat and sprang to the third bunk in a graceful leap. Up here, it was warm and private. No need for blankets. She dug her claws into the thin mattress, arched and stretched. Since she was used to napping in duty rooms and offices, she had no trouble passing out.

When she woke, it was dark and still. They hadn't dimmed the lights in the lounge before. *Maybe Seagram said we need to conserve energy?* Sensing someone nearby, she raised her head warily, only to spot Dedrick curled at the other end of the bunk. It seemed as if he'd come up to stand guard over her—highly unnecessary if endearing—and ended up dozing off against the wall.

He is *still recovering, after all.*

Lazily, she groomed while watching him sleep, contemplating whether it was possible to nudge him onto his side without waking him. *He'll probably have a stiff neck.* When Sheyla drew near enough to try, he started and slammed his head against the wall.

"Your eyes glow in the dark!"

She opened her mouth on a silent laugh.

If she shifted so they could talk, this encounter would take on a different tone, so she'd stay cheetah a bit longer. In this form, she detected layers in Dedrick's scent, pheromones that told an engaging story. There was a fading trace of fear, but also an enduring warmth. That note brightened as he put out a hand in the dark and then just left it hovering.

She tipped her head.

"Is it all right? If I touch you?"

Like the Golgoth with their braids, the request for such contact construed an intimate overture, but she answered by nudging his palm with her cheek. His hand was gentler than she might have expected as he ran it over her head, barely brushed the tips of her ears.

Tickles.

She bit his fingers, lightly, to discourage that. He was intuitive enough not to reach beyond her shoulders, or she would've really sunk her teeth in. When he rubbed the spot at the base of her head, just so, Sheyla purred to let him know that was perfect. The sound startled him, but she saw clearly in the dark; he was smiling.

"This is... nice," he whispered with a faint note of surprise. "I never thought I'd be this close to an Animari."

Sheyla could've said the same thing. She had the urge to tussle, but she couldn't be sure how he'd react to being tackled by a giant cat. In his current shape, he was large enough to handle her, but his skin wasn't thick, and he needed to take it easy.

Right, no wrestling.

"You look like you're sizing me up." Proof that he was always on alert, reading cues, and making clever judgments.

Trilling an affirmative sound, Sheyla waited to see what he made of it. She got another stroke at the base of her skull. "That's a yes?"

I'm glad I didn't leave you to awaken among strangers, she decided.

The sound of the signal machine stirring drew her gaze and she leapt to the ground and shifted, nearly in the same motion. By the time Dedrick reached the floor, she had her shirt on. She felt him looking, then pointedly not as she pulled her pants up, and stifled a smile. Both he and Alastor were adorable in that respect.

After switching on only the bank of lights near the desk to keep from bothering the people who were still sleeping, she settled to read the latest message. "Enemy inbound. Should be over soon. Status?"

She turned to Dedrick, who had stepped to her shoulder. "What shall I say?"

Together, they worked out a concise yet informative reply and she carefully tapped out the signal. "Bunker. St. Casimir. Safe. Waiting. Inspect site? Advise on aboveground status, pronounce all clear."

That should do it.

"If there's rubble or the lift is compromised, they'll have to dig us out." Sheyla wasn't normally suggestible, but that prospect send a cold shudder through her.

To her surprise, Dedrick wrapped his hand around hers. "We just need to stay calm a little longer."

"It sucks, waiting to be saved." She didn't pull her hand away; the contact was welcome and translated to comfort.

Dedrick grinned. "It would be worse if we were waiting to be slaughtered."

"You... make a compelling case."

Letting go of her, he retrieved a large chair from a nearby grouping and settled beside her. In companionable silence, they waited for Alastor's next reply. This one came faster, and it was more personal.

"Acknowledged. Dispatched Korin to scout. Will advise soon. Miss your face. Dedrick?"

"At last that bastard thinks to ask about me," the guard muttered.

Laughing softly, she nudged his shoulder with hers as she'd seen Alastor do. "Don't blame him, he has a lot on his mind."

That earned her a delighted smile.

"Dedrick safe," she sent back. "Waiting for your word."

Soon, we might be leaving soon.

It was hard to restrain the urge to race around the room

screaming, but that would only aggravate everyone else. They'd been penned up, but she suspected the hardships of the bunker paled against the atrocities of war. *I wish I could've been there.* That thought was half-hearted, however; the rest of her was sick over the destruction she'd witnessed in Ash Valley and Sheyla appreciated that Alastor had sent her to St. Casimir. Where she'd only seen one death, instead of thousands—with Hallowell embattled.

The triage tents must be a nightmare.

"That is…a burdened expression." Dedrick didn't ask what she was thinking.

Perversely, it made her want to tell him. "You saw how it was in Ash Valley. Before and after."

"You're wondering about Hallowell." It was a logical leap, but not an implausible one.

Impressed, Sheyla studied him for a moment before replying. "Alastor truly has been blessed to have spent so much of his life with you."

Dedrick lowered his face, as if she'd said something wrong. "If you want the truth, I had no choice."

"He told me a little, nothing too specific, but since I've heard quite a lot about Tycho, I can imagine—"

"You can't. Not really. And I would prefer not to talk about."

Quite suddenly, the mood was sad and grim, and she felt as if she'd inadvertently stepped on a butterfly. Sheyla had spent much of her life saying the wrong things—to the point that she preferred not talking at all. Yet she had seldom meant an apology more sincerely than the simple, "I'm sorry" she offered just then.

"You should stop caring about my feelings," he said. "If you persist, I'll start liking you."

It was an olive branch, a shaky one, but proffered nonetheless. He'd gotten his demons under control; they weren't hers to wrangle. She pursed her lips, a silly face.

"That would be a shame."

He lifted a hand, but she wasn't to learn what he would've done with it. The machine vibrated to life, and when she had the message in hand, she couldn't suppress a shout of pure jubilation. Ded read it next and he plucked her out of her chair, tossed her three feet up, whirled her until she couldn't see straight, then hugged her so tight, her kidneys might pop. Gasping, she waved the paper like a victory sign.

"What the hell is going on?" Dr. Seagram demanded.

Soon they had everyone on staff in the lounge, all yelling the same question. Even the ones who were supposed to be working.

Sheyla passed over sheet to Dr. Seagram, who read it in a booming voice. "All clear."

PER KORIN'S REPORT, there were no hostiles near St. Casimir.

Half the complex had caved in, but the side where the old clerk claimed the bunker was located hadn't collapsed. Alastor wished he could oversee the rescue effort straightaway, but there were five hundred warriors marching on Old Town, a third of them Elite.

All that's left of the thousands Tycho sent to sack Hallowell. We have artillery enough to obliterate them.

Victory hovered just out of reach, but he was so damned sick of the killing. His illness might be saving him from falling prey to the bloodlust, the way other Gol got lost in it, until death and sex became inextricably entwined. He'd tasted that briefly and managed to stagger away. Since he lacked the stamina to finish the battle in brute form, it also meant that he wasn't lost in a haze that demanded more bones for the charnel house.

Aching from head to toe, Alastor went to the walls to track the enemy's movement. Alone. So many people he wished were beside him in this pivotal moment; reflexively he touched the names of the siblings he'd lost. Rowena should be here. Dedrick. Sheyla. Even Zan. Instead, that damned red-eyed Noxblade climbed the crumbling stone steps and joined him.

Rowena was out there, somewhere. Or maybe she was on her way to Golgerra by now. Between Zan's death and Rowena being taken, he ached as if he'd been shot. The way Rowena had looked that day in the cathedral, full of melancholy acceptance, it was like she'd *known* something terrible was about to happen to her and she was still willing to make that sacrifice.

For me.

"You're begging a sniper to end you," Gavriel said.

I probably deserve it.

He shrugged instead of speaking his bleak thoughts. "They're seventeen hundred meters out. More power to him if he can make the shot."

Gavriel snorted a laugh. "You're bent."

"Often and enthusiastically." He wasn't paying full attention to the exchange, however. Being sardonic and playful was his autopilot. Once he got his mind off Rowena, the situation chewed at him. *Something's strange. They should've struck by now.*

Instead, the battalion maintained a slow, steady pace.

Eventually, they stopped their progress well outside gunnery range. Each side had an RVAC, so it could come down to mutually assured destruction. If Alastor saw them make a move, he'd rain down on them like the god of vengeance and hellfire. As he contemplated a preemptive strike, an Elite commander broke ranks and lifted a flag, pale gray with a white circle.

"Request for parley?" Gavriel said.

He considered. "Huh. I did not see this maneuver coming."

"It's a trap," the Noxblade predicted. "They lure you out, murder you, chop the head off the resistance."

"I *am* opposed to being murdered. On principle."

"Of course." The Eldritch's lips twitched, as if he hated the fact that he found an asshole like Alastor amusing.

It would be the height of stupidity for him to leave the safety of the fort and stroll out to greet this commander. Yet the Elite respected nothing more than strength and courage. Whatever they wanted, he'd finish this his own way, not by complying with outdated traditions.

Besides, that bitch would eviscerate me in a duel.

Which was what Alastor suspected the commander meant to suggest, should he sally forth. *If I reject, I lose face. If I lose, I die.*

No thanks.

"Get the bullhorn," he told Gavriel.

He'd need every iota of charisma he possessed to make this work and while the Noxblade groused about running errands, he sought the right words.

Deep breath. Now or never.

His voice rang out as it had when he addressed the troops at the western outpost. "Warriors of Golgerra, here is what I offer—freedom or death. Following my brother, you *will* perish. Have you not seen how I've rallied even the children against you? I've secured alliances with all clans of the Animari as well as the Eldritch. Wolf-kin spy tech. Bear-clan war machines. You cannot stand against this collective might.

"Don't you wish to be part of something greater? In my Golgerra, there will be rewards for cleverness, wisdom, kindness, and courage. No one shall fight in the arena who does not wish it and your children will no longer be taken as tribute to serve at my family's whim. There will be no more purges of the sick and injured, no more culling of imperfections. When I cast my brother out, I will abolish the penal farms outside the city and the family caste burdens shall be no more. How long must you suffer for shame your grandfathers could not even remember?" He raised a fist in posing the question, and a rumble of reaction sounded from the collected warriors.

"Look around this city. Don't you want more than this for your children? In my Golgerra, anyone will be permitted to travel freely, to learn as they wish. We will no longer be the monsters that outsiders are taught to fear. We can become teachers and sages in addition to warriors and take our rightful place in the world. You have one chance for redemption. I will forgive the harm you've wrought if you kneel, pledge to me, and promise to rebuild what you've broken. It's not too late. Choose freedom. Choose me."

Silence.

"That's your plan?" Gavriel asked, as Alastor lowered the bullhorn.

"Shut up and wait."

He watched the crowd, hardly daring to hope, until a

small figure broke ranks to reach the front. The girl wasn't even old enough to be called a woman. With quick steady steps, she walked all the way to the gates of the fort and dropped to one knee.

Others followed. Slowly, then gathering speed, they came and offered obeisance to a king they'd chosen freely. The Elites were the last to yield, for the caste system and the old ways benefited them most.

They still knelt. Now that they were closer, he didn't need the device to amplify his voice. Now, they sat in the palm of his hands, bending to his will. "Speak the words."

In thunderous unison, the oaths rang out, first in modern usage, next in the old tongue. "We pledge ourselves! *Wa-sei Alastor Rei! Fe toma sui doja.*"

All hail King Alastor. Long may he reign.

"Blood-bond," he called.

This was one custom he'd honor, mostly because it would permit him to test their commitment. As he watched, five hundred warriors sliced their palms. An oath sworn in blood, if broken, would condemn their families for ten generations. Alastor nodded.

"Open the gates," he said. "The war is over. We've won."

Gavriel tried to stay him. "Are you out of your mind? This is a trick!"

He shook his head, declining to argue with someone who didn't understand his culture. When the gates groaned open, he went to his new army and sliced his own arm, just below the names Caia, Efren, and Leander. The significance wasn't lost on the soldiers.

It took a long time to mingle his blood with so many, but as he moved among them, not even one shifted in formation. He shook every hand, locked eyes with each, and received a solemn hand over the heart; he gave each salute back. With the winter sun brightening the pale sky, there was a vital formality to the occasion.

The commander who had lost her chance to challenge, thanks to Alastor's quick tongue, stepped forward after he finished the ceremony. She was half again his height, probably twice his weight. It would've been suicide to duel her.

Her gaze skimmed him up and down. "You're nothing like your brother."

"That should give you hope," he said.

The Elite warrior smiled and slowly raised her right hand to seal it across her heart. "It does. What are your orders, my liege?"

That'll take some getting used to.

"What's your name?" he asked.

She seemed surprised by the question, answered it readily enough. "Chadri, my liege."

"I have but one question, Commander Chadri. What became of the woman your forces took from me?"

From the way her battered features froze, she knew about Rowena. "Gone. Halfway to Golgerra by now, I'll wager."

Though the answer wasn't unexpected, his stomach still sank like a stone. "Divide the battalion into platoons and dispatch half to search and rescue. I want all your medical officers working the triage tents. Everyone else should focus on building emergency shelters to aid those displaced by the conflict."

"You trust us to do this?'

"Shouldn't I? I don't take you for oath breakers."

"Never," she answered firmly. "Soldiers! We have a new mission."

Alastor wasn't a fool, so when he moved off, he asked the surviving Exiles to mix among the new recruits, one to a platoon. At the first sign of problems, his men would warn him.

With a long sigh, he turned to Gavriel and said what he'd wanted to since he first saw Sheyla's message. "Let's go. You're with me."

Gavriel groaned. "Why?"

"To save my friend and win the fair maiden," he said lightly. "Or is it vice versa? At any rate, it's beyond time for my princely reward."

27.

WITH GREAT CEREMONY, Dr. Seagram opened the access panel and proceeded with the three levels of biometrics required to open the doors. There was a tense silence, until they swished open. No alarms, no damage report.

So far, so good.

The lift was still working at least. Sheyla and Dedrick took half of the medical team up in the first trip, along with six patients. Though the elevator was industrial-sized, it was still a tight fit. Normally she'd be ready to claw someone's face off over such enforced contact, but Dedrick's solid weight at her back kept her violent impulses at bay. Returning to the surface seemed to take much longer than it had on the way down.

At last, the box shuddered to a stop and the doors fanned half-open and got stuck. She wasn't close enough to see the problem, but Nurse Mills said, "There's rubble we need to move."

Sheyla maneuvered to the front and slid sideways, wedging her arms and legs against the doors. With all her strength, she shoved; at first, nothing happened. The others crammed in beside her, adding their might, and then the scraping sound of metal against stone said they were winning. A cracking sound, burst of masonry dust and a cascade of smaller bits of broken plaster rained down as the doors splayed wide, sweeping clear the damage that had blocked them.

She tumbled out into what used to be a corridor. It was more of a tunnel now with sloped walls and a fallen ceiling. The floor looked more like tectonic plates in the underworld than the hospital it used to be. Once she had her footing, she helped everyone else out. Getting the patients to safety was going to be like navigating a minefield. While the staff could scramble and crawl, their charges couldn't, and there wasn't nearly enough clearance to permit beds and life-support machines to pass.

Dedrick was already inspecting the damage. He turned to her as if she was in charge. "If we apply pressure here, we can widen the passage without bringing the ceiling down."

"How do you know?" Mills demanded. "We should wait for Dr. Seagram."

The truth was, there wouldn't be room for everyone in this pocket just past the elevator doors. Inside the lift, the patients should be safe from harm. She joined Dedrick at the wall.

"Tell me what to do."

"All hands here. On my mark."

He counted it down and other shoulders joined theirs. Nurse Mills scrambled back into the lift. As with the doors, it took combined Animari and Golgoth might to topple the shattered wall. When it went down, the ceiling rumbled, but apart from another shower of dust, nothing more fell. Now there was a clear path and she could see daylight where one of the exterior walls had collapsed.

Sheyla hauled the first patient out of the lift, checking all his connections. "We don't know how stable the structure is. Let's move."

She and Dedrick led the way, lifting the hospital bed when necessary. The guard stepped through the jagged hole she'd spotted to scout. "It's a bit steep but I can manage."

Over the past few days, she'd come to trust him, so she lifted on her end and with care, they worked the patient free. Pause and repeat. They made a good team, so the rest of the staff clambered to freedom and attended the patients already on the ruined lawn. Dr. Seagram was the last to pass through, only after the fourteenth and final bed landed outside. The building trembled then and Dedrick snatched her so quickly that she let out a surprised squeak.

Not a second too soon.

The walls and ceiling caved, dumping a ton of cement and sheetrock where she had been standing. Sheyla shivered against him as he smoothed her hair with a big hand. "Thanks," she managed to whisper.

"Alastor would never forgive me if anything happened to you."

"That," said a familiar voice. "Is certainly true. And it applies to both of you."

On unsteady legs, she stumbled to the demon prince. Thinner and with fresh lines on his face, he'd brought so many reinforcements, medical personnel, soldiers, equipment, that her entire body slumped in relief. With tender arms, he caught her and put his face in the curve of her neck. She barely noticed when the embrace evolved, and somehow he was holding two of them. Nestled between Alastor and Dedrick, she reveled in the warmth and the reassuring thump of their hearts.

"Thank you, my dear ones. For keeping yourselves safe. It was all that kept me sane, the past few days."

Before either she or Dedrick could reply, the lead Noxblade joined them, but Alastor didn't allow them to pull away. He fixed a gimlet stare on the assassin.

"Your princely reward?" Gavriel asked.

Alastor answered, "You're in charge. If anyone needs me in the next twenty-four hours, tell them to take a number."

Sheyla didn't argue. She desperately wanted a break before considering her next move. The truth of what she needed to do scrambled furiously at the back of her head, but she quieted it like a bird cage covered with a dark cloth. Dedrick and Alastor traded news as the three left the ruins of St. Casimir. He updated them on various battles, the industrial sacrifice, Zan's death, and how the remnants of Tycho's army had sworn to him.

"I am so proud of you," she said.

Dedrick echoed the sentiment. "Me too. But you're making me feel guilty over the nothing I accomplished underground."

"You healed and came back to me," Alastor said. "I'd be a mess if I'd lost you too, friend."

The guard dropped his gaze. "And Rowena?"

"Taken. We'll save her when we liberate Golgerra."

The unspoken *if she's still alive* dimmed the mood, so they walked a bit in silence. Several blocks farther west, toward the ministry complex, their flat building was still standing. It seemed odd to let themselves in and find things relatively unchanged, as if the shape of the world hadn't shifted. No power, the grid was decimated, but there *was* running water.

Sheyla took the first shower and then opened a tin from the cupboard and ate the contents cold. With the tension that had been keeping her alert dispelled, she wanted nothing more than to sleep. To her amusement, she found both Alastor and Dedrick passed out on the bed. They'd managed to bathe but not eat. She could've slept on the couch, but there was no working heater, and they felt like pride mates, so she slid in between them as she would have at home. *Mmm. Crowded but cozy.* Blearily she pulled up the covers and winked out.

She woke to Alastor's lips on her neck and Dedrick's arm across her waist. Since the prince was spooned up behind her, she felt the jut of his hard cock. That didn't necessarily mean that *all* of him was up. Turning her head, she caught the jade shimmer of his eyes. Given what she'd observed about Golgoth modesty, she should've thrown some clothes on before getting in bed. Alastor seemed to think her bare skin existed for no purpose other than his seduction.

Silently, he teased her. With his teeth on her throat, his lips on her shoulder. His clever fingers skimmed the tops of her breasts, over her ribs, and down her belly, until her thighs quivered. Desire was natural after a crisis, and that intellectual awareness didn't diminish her pleasure. There was also a spike of illicit excitement over being caressed with Dedrick nestled against her. If she didn't keep quiet, he would wake and—

"Seems like I might be intruding. Should I go?" His voice was deep and raspy with sleep.

Too late.

Alastor replied before she could. "That's up to you. And

Sheyla."

"You want me to stay?" Dedrick asked.

Her heart pounded with nervous excitement. The time she'd spent with the guard in the bunker piqued her curiosity about him rather than rendering her wary. When she was a cat, his hands had been so gentle; she wondered what it would be like, the three of them together. A frisson of excitement expanded inside her, so her breathing quickened. When she realized what she wanted, she said it aloud.

"I do."

The prince eased against her. Now it seemed he felt he could answer honestly. "Right now, I want both of you, but it's not a demand."

ALASTOR HAD NEVER shared anyone with Dedrick before. In Golgerra, it would've been impossible, as his favor would've marked some poor soul for Tycho's attention, possibly leading to execution or a fate worse than death, life as one of his brother's concubines. He could just about hear Ded considering the offer, but it truly was fine if he demurred. Patiently he waited, teasing Sheyla with luxuriant strokes, working ever closer to her cunt. She squirmed against his cock so deliciously that he almost couldn't stop himself.

Eventually, Ded said, "I wasn't looking forward to leaving a warm bed, stiff and aching."

Alastor laughed softly. "If you do, it's your choice."

"Any boundaries I should know about?" He understood what Ded was asking, if he could touch Sheyla as well.

She's not my property. Part of him ached over that thought because he wished with all his heart that he could claim her as his mate; she'd never consented to permanence. It had taken all his combined eloquence and charm to get her to agree to a brief affair, and now that Hallowell was secure and his health stable, she'd probably go home soon.

Time to soak up enough Sheyla to last me a lifetime.

He kept his tone light. "That's up to the lady. You already know what *I* like."

"I don't think so." She already sounded like sheer sex, her voice airy with desire. "If I don't like something, you'll know. I hope you'll be honest too."

"Promise," Dedrick said.

Perfect. Now that everyone was on the same page, Alastor didn't hesitate. Still stroking toward Sheyla's core, he reached for Ded and kissed him. The scrape of his jaw in contrast to the softness of his mouth was lovely; Alastor knotted his fingers in Ded's hair, slowly rocking against Sheyla's ass. Between them, she was a wicked little fire; he could tell she was exploring Dedrick with her clever hands because of the gasps and groans he drank as they kissed.

Alastor pulled back when she whispered, "Here. Like this," so he could watch Sheyla's pleasure as Ded worked her breasts. He went in for more kisses, first Sheyla and then Ded, back and forth, until his head was swirling with heat. She felt so good against his cock that he could almost come like this, but that seemed like a waste.

Soft and tentative, Ded took Sheyla's mouth, and her pleasure spilled into Alastor. His lips tingled, and he could just about taste his friend's tongue. Yearning reached critical levels as he pictured Sheyla beneath both their hands and mouths. He was about to say, *Ladies first,* when Sheyla sat up, and as if she'd planned it in advance with Dedrick, they shifted as a unit and focused on him. So unexpected, he fell back against the pillows as she took his mouth. Ded went straight for his cock, and his mouth was liquid heat. Sheyla on his chest, biting and licking, sucking, her sharp nails scraping over him. Ded sucked him with gorgeous precision, knowing exactly how much pull and pressure he wanted.

They're trying to make me come first.

He bucked into Ded's mouth, each luscious glide better than the last. Alastor didn't have the will to resist on his own, but he framed Sheyla's face in trembling hands, begging her to see what he wanted. *It shouldn't be all about me. I'm not royalty in this bed.* Her mouth was already glossy and bee-stung from all the kissing, her eyes lambent. Then her gaze swiveled to Ded, who had served his whole damn life, and was doing it still, even if he didn't realize it.

Her lips curved into a feline smile; with full Animari strength, she tackled Ded and pinned him. Only raw physical power could control Ded like that, and he stifled a smile at his friend's surprise. Alastor's cock quivered in the cool air, already so slick with precome that he ached to finish the job, jerk it hard and quick, then spurt all over both of them.

None of that. I'm being good.

Now they had Ded at the heart of the action. Alastor settled on his left and his heart eased when Sheyla curved against his right side. Her bright eyes said she would follow his lead. Where he touched, she did—where he brushed his mouth, she mirrored. Until Ded was taut and quivering, his cock upright and throbbing. Neither of them had touched it. Finally, Dedrick broke, pulled their palms together and humped between them. Alastor showed Sheyla what Dedrick favored; they gave it to him, together. His cock leaked all over Alastor's fingers, so he licked them, and he almost lost his mind when Sheyla did the same.

Shifting closer, he angled his cock and slid it across Ded's. They rarely came this way, but Ded liked it as foreplay. One stroke, two, and then Sheyla cupped her hands around both their shafts, holding them lightly, so that there was a tease with each motion. When she grazed the underside of the head, first his, then Ded's, they both jerked at the startling pleasure.

"Is it good?" he whispered.

Ded stroked his lower lip. "I'm losing my mind. Somebody fuck me. Please."

Alastor smiled. "Ladies first."

Sheyla straddled Ded immediately, and it was beyond sexy to see her pleasure spike as she sank down. Alastor tilted his head to take in the gorgeous picture of her body flowering to take Ded's cock. Beneath her, Ded lunged upward in a couple of convulsive strokes, his hands clutching at the covers, as if he didn't trust himself to be gentle. Alastor nudged closer, so Ded could dig his fingers in, bruise him with every delicious thrust. He raised his head and kissed Alastor roughly as Sheyla rode him, gathering speed. Since she liked it fast and hard, Ded wouldn't be able to hang on long. He felt their orgasms building, echoed in the ferocity of Ded's mouth on his.

In time, Ded couldn't hold the kiss, his breath gusting toward helpless groans. Alastor fell into the urge to taste them. They both jerked over the soft friction he added to their rhythm with lips and tongue. Each time Sheyla raised up, he licked her clit. Her body shook with the need to come, and Ded was pulling her down on him so hard that there might be marks.

Their juices smeared his face. Ded shoved him back, a push forceful enough to topple him since Alastor's knees were water anyway. The bounce angled him so Ded could grab his cock and pull it back to his mouth. *Not selfless enough to stop him.* Pleasure built in simmering hot waves, until he was full on fucking Ded's face, conscious of each groan and grunt. Sheyla came first, and he *felt* it. Her wild tightening set Ded off and Alastor let go at last.

He tumbled back, admiring the sticky mess he'd made of Ded's mouth. As soon as his heart settled, he kissed Sheyla and then licked Dedrick's cock clean.

The guard shoved at his head. "It's too soon, you bastard. You think I'm made of sex?"

"It's after service, not an invite to round two."

"Will there be a round two?" Sheyla asked, from the foot of the bed, where she was dangling, half upside down.

With pudding arms, he pulled her up, so the three of them were spooned into a tangle of satiated limbs. "Maybe," he mumbled. "I hope you're both clear on how precious you are to me."

"I have some idea," Dedrick said, around a massive yawn.

Sheyla rested her head on his shoulder. "Before we started, I wondered how I'd keep track of who should do what to ensure there was an equitable distribution of—"

Ded was laughing too loud for her to finish that sentence. Alastor had rarely seen his friend so relaxed and open. Sheyla had a way about her, once she unlocked her heart and let people in.

"What?" she demanded.

"Of *fucking*?" His friend finally got the question out between chortles.

Alastor laughed too; he couldn't help it, and she was so adorably furious. "I'm glad you didn't attempt to schedule us, love. Some experiences are better lived than directed."

She narrowed her eyes in a look that worried him, slightly, considering he *did* know of her dominant tendencies. "Challenge accepted."

"Feed us first," Ded implored.

Regal as a queen, she left the bed. "Deal. Then we'll see about round two."

28.

SHEYLA'S MOSTLY-FEIGNED MOOD only lasted until she reached the doorway.

It was impossible to stay angry when her entire body was limber and she felt as if she'd run ten klicks—in a good way. She got more food for herself, paused over opening more tins for Ded and Alastor, and decided it wouldn't hurt to spoil them. *I won't be making a habit of this, after all.* She even delivered the plates, pausing to steady one balanced on her forearm.

"Are we good?" Alastor was asking Dedrick.

"Why wouldn't we be?"

Silence, but Sheyla had an odd feeling, one that had to be coming from Alastor. "I just wanted to be sure... since this is most likely the first and last time."

He's thinking about the end, too. Not unexpected but it hurt more than she'd anticipated.

Dedrick answered, "I'll be fine. It's you I'm worried about."

"I'm accustomed," Alastor said, in as bitter a tone as Sheyla had ever heard. "When have I ever done precisely as I wish?"

That answer would probably slice her to ribbons—and besides, she already knew the truth was never—so she bumped the door wide. "Here's the feast I promised. I apologize in advance."

Sheyla propped herself up against the headboard and snuggled beneath the covers, shoulder to shoulder, with Alastor in the center. Since he was the one who'd brought her and Dedrick together, that seemed fitting. When she considered the matter properly, it was more like Dedrick was sharing Alastor with her for a little while, because she had a life waiting, and Alastor had so many fucking obligations that she ached.

Mostly, she had been joking about round two. Since it would be hard to top such spontaneity, it might be a bad idea to challenge such a stellar memory. Questions percolated, but she didn't know if she should ask.

Eventually, she indulged her curiosity. "What will you do now?" she asked Alastor, once they finished eating.

"Rebuild Hallowell. I doubt Tycho will try again, but it wouldn't be right for me to march out without helping to restore order."

Dedrick was nodding. "I agree. If other settlements need reinforcement before you finish here, I can take five platoons or so and handle the defense."

Sheyla realized that just because they'd secured Hallowell, it didn't mean the war was over. It would be fought all over the map, until the last of Tycho's troops retreated, perished, or swore fealty to Alastor. Likely that heralded a lengthy campaign... and her role in it was over. That shouldn't fill her with such melancholy.

"Did Chancellor Quarles survive?" she asked then.

"She went to ground when the bombardment started,

but I saw her at Old Town just before we came to St. Casimir," Alastor answered.

"I'm surprised she hasn't demanded a meeting yet." Such practical talk might seem strange to an outsider when they were still naked and lounging, but her nature didn't lend itself to sweet nothings or a quiet mind.

"Soon, I'm sure." The prince didn't sound eager. "I hope you'll both come to Zan's memorial rites. Gavriel told me they're holding the ceremony tomorrow."

There were a lot of dead to bury, but she had a soft spot for the cheerful, good-humored Eldritch who had escorted her without complaint. Alastor hadn't explained how or why Zan died, and she didn't press. Once they left this bed, the world would reassert its claims on each of them, whether she liked those requirements or not.

"Of course," Dedrick answered.

Sheyla added, "I'll pay my respects too."

Next to Alastor, Dedrick stretched and sighed. "It can't end until we kill him."

No question that he was referring to Tycho, and Alastor nodded, tilting his head against Sheyla's so she could breathe in the spiced sweat of his skin. *Lickable, really.* While visual beauty seldom aroused her, certain scents drove her wild.

"He may recall the remainder of his troops to Golgerra, but no, it will never be finished until he's dead or I am."

An old song came to mind about a fork in the road, and Sheyla nearly hummed a few bars, so strongly did she need distraction from the pain twisting up her insides. "Let's enjoy the respite, shall we?"

A wolfish light kindled in Alastor's green eyes. "We were only waiting for you to say the word, lady."

Dedrick smiled. "I admit, I'm curious what you plan to

do with us."

I have no idea. Let's find out.

Wicked impulse drove her into Alastor's lap, where she settled, knowing he found her ass irresistible, and she reached for Dedrick, pulling him into a kiss. After sex, he smelled different than Alastor, a darker scent, and she tasted that variance as well. Despite his size, his kisses were softer, slower, though that could stem from lack of familiarity. The hands on her breasts belonged to Alastor, so expert that she squirmed against him, eliciting a groan. She couldn't see his cock, but she felt it, swelling from half-hard to a full erection. Curious how their kissing had affected Dedrick, she drew back; he was stiff, but his prick lengthened as she admired it.

"Touching works better," he invited.

This was a new experiment, so she was attentive to his responses in curling her fingers around him. Each press and pull elicited a fresh expression, a flutter of lashes or a soft nip of his lower lip. From Alastor's accelerated breathing and the rock of his hips, he was getting hot watching her learn to work Dedrick's cock. Her nipples were hard, and her pussy felt slick and swollen. It was getting more difficult to consider her next move. Large hands curved over her smaller one and forced her to jerk harder and faster, then Dedrick pulled back.

"I don't want to come yet."

"Taste her," Alastor suggested in a black velvet voice.

Sheyla gasped as he kissed her neck, her shoulders, as Dedrick lowered his head to her breasts. Even here, he was maddeningly gentle, pressing butterfly kisses. His warm lips drove her slow undulations against Alastor's cock. His hands were everywhere, caressing her, stroking Dedrick's back and shoulders, urging them to greater pleasure. Her belly quivered as Dedrick licked lower. She grabbed his head and pushed it down, in no mood to be teased.

"Fuck, yes." The muffled, profane praise came from Alastor as he lifted her, gliding smoothly inside. "Make her come. Let me feel it."

With the prince's cock inside her, she tried to move, but they held her still with tender hands, and Dedrick kept her thighs spread so he could lick and sip at her aching clit. She'd never known anything like those dual sensations, but when she fell into those feelings, they spiraled into sheer need. Liquid heat washed over her, and she circled her hips, to feel Alastor more and to get more friction on her clit. Dedrick teased her a little, so she pulled his hair, and he rewarded her with exactly what she needed as Alastor started to move.

Sheyla came so hard she almost passed out.

After that, it was a straining tangle of urgency. They fucked each other and then her, until she literally couldn't move. She'd never lost track of orgasms before. By the time Alastor came with a grunt, the last to finish, she was slippery with sex and sweat. Cuddling wasn't something she'd done much of, but now she understood the purpose. *It's what happens when you lack the energy for anything else.* In Dedrick's arms, she received soft little kisses from Alastor, but she lacked the energy to respond.

"Thank you," she said finally.

Both Alastor and Dedrick were laughing again. She didn't bother asking why that was funny, though the prince was kind enough to elaborate. "It's delightful when you're so polite after fucking us both into shadows of our former selves."

Put that way, she got it... and she laughed, for once feeling like part of the whole instead of an alien on the fringes, unable to comprehend the local customs. For a bit longer, she relaxed, but a repetitive and annoying sound plucked at her attention. *My comm*, she realized. Scrambling out from between them, she grabbed the first article of clothing she found from the floor and padded out of the bedroom.

Fortuitous because when she picked the unit up, the screen activated to display her mother's furious face.

"Fuck," Sheyla said.

ALASTOR FROZE WHEN she swore, trained to expect the worst.

Instead of an alarm sounding, however, someone began a tirade. "What are you wearing? And your *hair*. I raised you better than this. Your father is going to die, you awful girl. I hope you can live with yourself, killing a perfectly healthy soul in the prime of his life, so you can—"

This must be Sheyla's mother. Impressive, she doesn't even pause to breathe.

He wasn't trying to listen in, but it was impossible not to hear the screeching. His poor doctor hadn't been granted a single opening to respond and her mother ranted on without flagging. Madame Halek would surely hear the bed springs if he shifted, and that would only exacerbate the situation.

"Explain this to me, Sheyla Halek. *Why* did I speak to Dr. Seagram before you? How is that your mentor can let me know you're alive, but you can't be bothered. And just wait—"

"I'm sorry," Sheyla finally cut in.

Alastor dared a glance at Dedrick, whose eyes were watering with the effort not to laugh. That didn't make his own plight any easier, so he buried his face in the pillow and tried not to eavesdrop. No luck.

"Your apologies are meaningless. Come home and prepare to spend the next two days on your knees, begging for forgiveness. Do you think this family is an optional service? Don't you care how hard your father and I worked to send you to school in Hallowell? And for the love of all gods great and small, have you no consideration for your brothers? Darvid won't eat, Zaran fights with everyone and Avi barely sleeps. Nightmares that he won't talk about because he overheard how dire things were in Hallowell. Our boy is afraid you've been burned to bone dust and you can't even—"

"Mum!" Sheyla shouted. "I'm not trying to hurt you or Pap. I'm sorry about the boys, Avi especially, but you don't seem to understand—I went to *war*, not on vacation, and I have a few things to finish here. I'm burying a friend tomorrow."

This didn't seem amusing anymore. Alastor prickled with guilt over keeping her this long, though strictly speaking, the bombing of Hallowell hadn't been his idea. Because Ded could read him like a book, he touched Alastor's shoulder with a rueful expression.

Free to speak, he'd say something like, *it's not your fault.* Alastor couldn't entirely agree.

More ranting from Sheyla's parent, the length and breadth of which he couldn't help but find impressive.

Until Madame Halek snapped, *"Enough* with the demonkin and their issues, Sheyla. If you're not home in two days, I'm sending Zaran to collect you. When you get here, you'll accept the mate your father selected for you, no backtalk, no nonsense."

Tense silence from the other room indicated the end of the call.

"Damn," Dedrick said.

Alastor couldn't disagree. He'd lost the mood to lounge, so he punished himself with a quick cold shower. It wasn't that he regretted a single moment he'd spent with Sheyla, but he did mind being used as a weapon to shame her.

Demonkin.

That was how her family regarded him. Since she'd become as necessary to him as water and air, the sting was inescapable. To her mother and father, it probably wouldn't matter how many times he defended an Animari settlement, how often he showed mercy instead of brutality.

I'll always be a monster in their eyes.

He was shivering when he came out of the bathroom, his fingers clumsy and numb as he dressed. Ded hugged him briefly before taking his turn at washing up. For long moments, Alastor tried to decide what to say to Sheyla, still so quiet in the next room.

She surprised him by coming to the doorway before he made up his mind. "I'm sorry you had to hear that. My mother can be... volatile."

"Mine once threw a doctor off a balcony for pronouncing me incurable," he said lightly. "Hope you're not too overset by a sound scolding."

She lifted a shoulder. "Everyone will calm down once I'm back."

Why did that sound so awful and inevitable? *Steady,* he told himself. He'd promised to take what she offered freely and not hold her when she chose to go.

Keep your word and your dignity.

An imperious knock sounded at the door, likely Gavriel or Korin. Alastor didn't think it had been the full day of peace he'd requested, more like half. He couldn't hide from his responsibilities any longer, though. Little as he liked it, the world was calling.

He opened it to find the two he'd predicted together, glaring at each other with a peculiar tension. "Strange bedfellows. Do come in. We have cold water, natural daylight, and tinned meat. I'm afraid that is the extent of my royal amenities."

Gavriel and Korin spoke at once, talking over one another until he couldn't parse any of it. He was in no mood for games, so he folded his arms and stared, trying for icy incredulity.

"I was here first," Korin said, scowling at the Eldritch.

"Since I like you better than Gavriel, please proceed."

The Noxblade snarled and flung himself into a chair, waiting with poor grace.

"My offer is simple," Korin said. "One of the reasons I stayed to fight with you is because Raff is considering an alliance."

Alastor's brow shot up. He wondered what Sheyla made of this, whether she cared, or if she was already packing up what little she'd brought.

"You're his second. To clarify, are you marrying me or is Raff?"

"Whichever you prefer," she said.

"Perhaps I'd like one of each, a matched wolfkin set. Is that all right too?"

"You're mocking me," Korin decided, seeming unconcerned. "Yet I assure you that we are completely sincere. We're willing to open free trade between Pine Ridge and Golgerra and train your people in our drone technology in return for—"

Alastor held up a hand. His head was a mess, and it was too soon for him to have any mind for political machinations. "One of my small pleasures. While I'm cognizant of the great honor afforded me, I need some time to reflect."

Korin accepted that, bowed and exited, leaving Alastor to angle a look at Gavriel. "Let me guess, you want to marry me as well?"

The Noxblade snarled a laugh achingly devoid of humor. "I don't, but my lady has an offer for you."

In what seemed like another life, Alastor had entertained the idea of pursuing Princess Thalia, but now the prospect made him want to flee to human lands, where he'd probably die of one of their bizarre viruses. Since Gavriel would eviscerate him if he didn't respond appropriately, he displayed only mild reluctance.

"You're not going to call her, are you? I'm not feeling social."

"Then let me relay the terms. Your achievements have impressed our princess. 'To start with so little, defend Hallowell, and end the final battle by turning the enemy without a single shot fired? Remarkable. Together, we could accomplish much.' Her words, not mine." Gavriel's expression said he still thought Alastor was an asshole. "She is open to negotiations that would establish her as consort instead of Golgoth Queen, so long as you permit her to retain her title as Queen of the Eldritch. You would have full rights as consort, no title as king in our lands."

"Two rulers, united in diplomacy and military might,"

he said.

That future sounded lonely. It sounded like hell.

"You'd be a fool to refuse her." That was the most honest thing Gavriel had ever said to Alastor, and for an instant, his heart was his in eyes, bleeding for the fairy queen who would never love him.

"Would I?"

That little nudge was all it took for the normally acerbic Noxblade to extol Princess Thalia's virtues for a quarter of an hour. Alastor was no more interested in the match when Gavriel finished, but he did know quite a lot about the assassin's unrequited love.

Poor bastard.

"Thank you for your candor and your visit. Now, kindly get out."

When the coast was clear, Dedrick stepped out of the bedroom, wearing his, *Well, that was a thing*, expression. "Two favorable offers. Will they expect you to be faithful?"

"Unlikely." Alastor tipped his head in question. "Did she hear?"

"Hard to say. She's in the bathroom right now, but..."

Sod everything, I want to stop. Haven't I earned the right to do as I wish?

The worst part was that he couldn't.

29.

ENDINGS WERE AWFUL.

Before, Sheyla had heard others weep over the failure of a relationship, but she'd never known that pain. *Until now.* Though this didn't count as a failure so much as a terminus. She bore Alastor no ill will, despite her silent hurt. At least there were no concerned glances when the occasional tear trickled down her cheek; that was the suitable response at a memorial service. The ruined cathedral provided the perfect backdrop for the service with the ancient stone walls and the scraps of stained glass clinging to the window frames.

The Eldritch Song of Death was haunting and resonant. She never would've guessed that Gavriel had such a beautiful voice, but he led the Noxblades in the pure harmony as they sang their brother on to the underworld. She found their funeral customs familiar and strange at the same time. Like the Animari, the Eldritch cremated their dead, but instead of saving the ashes in a columbarium, they gave them to the wind with the final cantabile played on a pipe so mournful that it sounded like a woman weeping for her lost love. There were no words spoken for the dead and afterward, each attendant received a blessing in the form of oil on their foreheads. In the final rite, Gavriel blew out a candle that she supposed represented Zan's soul.

The crowd was larger than she'd expected. Sheyla had known that the Eldritch would be here, but there were also Korin's wolves and Alastor's entire army, lining the streets in the most impressive honor guard anyone could wish. Plus, soldiers from the militia who had fought with Zan at the western outpost came to pay respect to the fallen. Later, Chancellor Quarles was holding a candlelight vigil to honor those who had fallen, including the Fearless Five, which was what they were calling the factory owners whose sacrifice made this moment possible.

Though she had arrived with Alastor, there was no getting near him. So many people wanted a word or a moment of his time that Dedrick couldn't hold them back. Alastor wore a frozen expression, a rictus of his charming smile. She took a last look at her demon prince and then faded into the departing crowd.

Sheyla had one stop to make before she left. Nothing in the apartment was worth carrying, and supplies would only slow her down. They might be able to offer her a vehicle, but the roads were uncertain in winter, and it was a bit warmer, faint suggestion that spring was on the way, so she shouldn't have any problem returning to Ash Valley in cat form soon enough to keep her mother from dispatching Zaran.

With her plans set, she'd left her comm at the flat, along with a note she'd placed where Alastor would certainly find it. Maybe that wasn't the best way to say farewell, but Sheyla believed in the benefit of surgical precision. Long kisses, sorrowing eyes, and clinging hands would just make it harder. In all honesty, she couldn't stand to see the rest; it had been hell hiding in the bathroom, unable *not* to hear how many options he had, both of which would benefit his people.

Moving past the immovable rows of Golgoth soldiers, who had been trying to kill them until a couple of days ago, unnerved her a bit. The crowd thinned once she reached the next intersection, and Sheyla set off toward the hospital. As expected, she found Dr. Seagram scolding the work crew at St. Casimir.

"Ho there! None worse for your sequestering, Dr. Halek?"

Smiling faintly, she shook her head. "I came to thank you... and to remind you to follow up with Prince Alastor. He has plenty of medication for the moment, and I'm leaving you all my data in case you need to make more."

"I take it you're leaving, then?"

The question shouldn't feel like a knife to the heart. "I am. Also, please don't forget you promised to search for a viable pain—"

"I found it," Dr. Seagram cut in. "There's no earthly reason why he can't take Salicine. I didn't have a chance to speak with the prince before, well, everything. I'll contact him when everything settles down here a bit."

That's all I can do for him now. I have to go home.

"Thanks for everything, sir." It occurred to her then that she should ask. "Did your mate come through the battle all right?"

The old bear smiled. "Franklin's well, I'm happy to report."

"That's good news. Please stop by if you're ever near Ash Valley."

"Take care of yourself, Dr. Halek, and give my regards to your family."

"I will."

Sheyla headed out on foot, but the fallen stones around the side of St. Casimir offered a convenient place for her to strip and stash her clothes. As a cheetah, she bolted from the city at top speed, reveling in the freedom. In Hallowell, it wasn't unusual to see wolves and great cats frolicking in the park, but she'd always been too busy or too exhausted to play. That pattern had held true for this visit as well.

The woods were silent, a blessing after the city noise. She cocked her head, listening to the alarmed chatter of mundane animals. They spoke of nothing so much as the threat she posed, reassuring that she likely wouldn't meet hostile forces on the way home. Top speed put kilometers behind her quickly, and she savored the rich scent of the trees and the wind.

Odd, though. The farther she got from Alastor, the more it hurt, as if her heart had a hook and a line attached. As she ran, it spooled tighter, until each step felt like she had thorns in her paws, blades in her chest. Once she even wheeled back toward Hallowell to ease the sensation. Snarling, she swiped her claws over the nearest tree.

Why? I need this to be over. We agreed—

The truth hit her like a fallen building. *We're mated.* In the bunker, Sheyla had suspected the bond might be forming, but she hadn't even known for certain that it was possible since he wasn't Animari.

Her first ridiculous reaction was, *My parents will be furious.* She'd have to keep it a secret. Over time—and without contact—mate bonds could be broken. She planned to refuse the person her father had chosen anyway. Her parents were more interested in public opinion than in her personal contentment. Silently, she admitted that had always been true. While her family loved her, they had always wanted to wedge her into place like a square peg in a round hole. She wasn't willing to have her edges filed off anymore.

She hunted, catnapped when necessary, and mostly, she ran. From her memories, from the pain. Sheyla required no map to find her home territory; the closer she came, the more familiar everything smelled. Early on the day her brother would be sent to Hallowell, she broke over a rise to spot Ash Valley in the distance. Not lovely and gleaming pale purity as it had been. Now Ash Valley was battle-scarred with patches visible on the exterior walls.

Yet the fact that the settlement still stood, despite tragedy and treachery warmed her heart. Her happiest moments might have been spent with an exiled prince, but work had offered great solace here. Eventually, it would again. Her chest blazed with an anguish she could only compare to a broken bone. For the Animari, those mended swiftly. For this, there was no treatment but time.

Weary, heartsick, and aching, she circled to the postern doors, as the main gate seemed to be soldered shut. An understandable precaution but she couldn't help but process the message it sent. *Outsiders beware, Ash Valley is closed.*

At the side entrance, Sheyla shifted and input the code, naked and shivering. After she saw her family, a visit to the bath house would be her first move. She raced down the tunnel into the staging room and grabbed some spare clothes and slippers, dressing for warmth rather than modesty. In the winter, they left coats as well, so she added one of those too. Maybe nobody would notice that she was back, but just in case, she pulled up the hood.

I'm not in the mood to talk if I don't have to.

When she reached the front door of her family home, she hesitated a few seconds before inputting the PIN. *I'm ready for this,* she told herself as she stepped inside.

"Hey, everyone. I'm finally home."

THIS FUCKING DAY.

Alastor lost track of Sheyla when Chancellor Quarles dragged him to the ministry, where they had various summits scheduled. He had been listening to the Director of Municipal Development drone for what seemed like a week. It was important, and he *did* care about the relief effort; his involvement in reconstruction efforts would go a long way toward assuring the Animari that he could be trusted to keep his promises—that deals signed with him would be honored, even after he returned to Golgerra. Still, six hours of meetings were five too long.

In the evening, he'd committed to a call with Princess Thalia; the wolves were demanding equal time. Victory had resulted in less freedom rather than more. On the surface, he was coping. Yet the longer he played by the rules, the more they felt like the rope that would strangle him.

"Can't we all agree that children are the priority here?"

Someone clearly disagreed and went on a tangent about trolleys and infrastructure. Alastor let his eyes glaze over and wished himself elsewhere. Eventually, Chancellor Quarles banged her stick on the conference table, signaling the end of the session, and he was free to take a break. Ded was waiting for him in the lobby, sprawled in a comfortable chair. Not for the first time, Alastor envied his friend.

"Hungry?" he asked.

"Do you even need to ask? They're selling skewers in the plaza, and I almost got one an hour ago."

Impossible not to remember that day with Sheyla when he'd first arrived, hot spiced tea and sugared pastries in the snow. Thinking of her, his sternum ached as if he'd been shot, and it hadn't even been that long since he'd seen her.

"I'm glad your loyalty overruled your stomach."

"It was a close call," Ded smirked.

Alastor nudged him with a shoulder and headed for the front doors. Late-afternoon light warmed the pavement, and the snow was melting, running along the gutters in tiny rivers. With so many restaurants in ruins and the power out all over the city, Hallowell was handling the crisis with grace. Kind folks had set up food carts near the fountain, offering hot food for a pittance. Unsurprisingly, the queue snaked around the square.

"They'd likely let you cut in." Ded gestured at the front of the line.

He shook his head. "Let's wait. Even if we're polite, there should be time to eat with Sheyla before tonight's festivities begin."

Service came at a brisk clip, so it didn't take as long as Ded feared for them to reach the counter. The cook greeted him with an expectant look; it was oddly comforting *not* to be recognized. Alastor bought nine skewers, roasted sweet potatoes, and a carafe of creamy soup that smelled delicious.

"Let's go home. I'd like an hour of peace before the circus resumes."

"Good luck with that," Ded mumbled.

"You're enjoying this, aren't you?"

The guard appeared to ponder as they walked. "Not as

such. More, I'm grateful that I'm not burdened with your obligations."

"I can't interest you in swapping lives?"

"Not a chance in hell."

In brooding silence, he walked the rest of the way to the flat. The prospect of an hour with Sheyla should be brightening his mood, but it just kept darkening. Foreboding hung over him like a storm cloud. Now anxious for reasons he couldn't even name, he shoved the food into Dedrick's hands and raced up the stairs.

"Sheyla?"

The flat was still and quiet, no sign of life. Alastor tore through every room, calming a trifle when he spotted her belongings. *It's fine. She's probably working. I'm too tightly wound, that's all.* He clung to that likelihood until he went into the bathroom. There, he found a note stuck to the mirror: *I will always miss your face.* With shaking hands, he plucked the paper and smoothed it between his fingers.

She's gone. It's over.

That realization swept him at the knees and he crumpled, leaning his head against the wash basin. Without her... without *her*, he had no will to continue, no matter what he might achieve. Illness wouldn't end him after all; it would be the loss of Sheyla Halek. Alastor didn't even realize he was crying until the tears dripped off his chin.

I should have said to hell with my promise. I should have begged.

On some level, he suspected it wouldn't matter. Sheyla wouldn't be content with scraps of his time, shadowed by his obligations, and what more could he offer? That was how Ded found him, a few minutes later. He didn't resist when the guard hauled him to his feet.

"You need to eat. As I told you in the beginning, you can't afford—"

"What?" He knocked Ded's hands away, visibly trembling. "To want anything? *Need* anything of my own?"

"Sire."

"Fuck this. Fuck *everything*. I'll die without her." In that moment, it felt true.

Distress had always exacerbated his condition, and he doubled over wheezing. Dedrick scrambled to find the inhalers Sheyla had left, and Alastor almost fainted before he brought the thing to his face. His vision cleared, spots fading.

"You understand what you're giving up?" Ded wore a somber look.

The answer was nothing. No political marriage could bring anything compared to how he felt when he was with her. *With her, I am whole.* He'd always carry the guilt of sacrificing Rowena to save Hallowell; he couldn't lose Sheyla up as well.

Alastor had never been more certain. "I never wanted to rule but if I must, then so help me, I'll do it on my terms. If I'm king, I can do as I wish, sign peace treaties, and they *will* hold. Keep order here, you have the battalion." He bolted to his feet.

More time must've passed than he'd imagined because it was dark when he raced out of the apartment. He passed Korin and Gavriel on the stairs and the Noxblade grabbed his arm.

"Where do you think you're going? What about Princess Thalia?"

Korin elbowed the Eldritch hard enough that he grunted. "Did you forget promising to speak with Raff?"

"Sod both Thalia and Raff," he snapped. "Let them marry each other."

I have to see her. As soon as possible. He ran down two steps before the solution occurred to him. "Korin, did you leave your war machine at the armory?"

"I did, but—"

Alastor was already running. One benefit of being a hero was that the officer on duty didn't question his right to commandeer the unit Korin had used during the city's defense. His training might not be sufficient for combat, but he got the thing in the air and set the navigation for Ash Valley. This was the fastest path to her, end of story.

It got claustrophobic inside because the suit was meant for conflict, not extended air travel, but he ignored the discomfort and kept watching the visor screen update. The trip that had taken days, at top speed, he reduced to hours. Middle of the night now, and it wasn't as bright as it should be in Ash Valley, a sign that they were still recovering, too.

He set down half a klick from the settlement to avoid alarming anyone, then keyed the unit to his biometrics so a prowling kit couldn't take the bear war machine for a test flight. Plodding through slush and mud, he practiced his speech.

If she accepts, her family can't refuse me. We've come too far.

This time, his arrival was much different than before. Many of the Exiles who had come with him to Ash Valley were dead, and now he was a lone petitioner, ringing the gate bell in the dark. It took a little while for someone to answer.

"I don't recognize you," a guard said.

"Prince Alastor Vega of Golgerra. I've come to collect my mate, Sheyla Halek." There, that was firm.

A startled exclamation, quickly cut off. "Come to the postern door right fucking now. We don't open these gates anymore."

That sounded ominous, and when he was dragged inside the hold, he understood the reaction. Alastor recognized this angry cat as one of Sheyla's brothers. *Zaran, I think.*

"Explain yourself."

Calmly he broke the young man's hold. *No fighting. He'll be my kin soon enough.* "I'd rather do that once the whole family is gathered."

"And I'd rather kill you than let you take one step closer to my sister."

"She'll know if you do, and she'll never forgive you."

The Animari sagged, bracing himself against the wall. "You're mated. Is that true?"

There was only one way to convince Zaran, even if Sheyla would hate the revelation. Hell, she'd probably hate that Alastor could feel it, but her sadness was a weight that barely let him breathe. "Your sister… she's weeping. Ask how I know."

Zaran swore. "Come with me, asshole."

30.

SHEYLA HAD NEVER doubted her own eyes before. True, they were red and swollen, but her vision remained unimpaired. Nonetheless, her mother was still standing in the doorway in a nightgown, Alastor and Zaran behind her.

Alastor.

And Zaran.

None of this made any sense. It was three in the morning, and... this must be a dream. Since that was the case, it did no harm to come into the living room. No harm in devouring his face with her eyes and admiring the intricate braids whose significance she was barely beginning to understand.

"I made tea," Mum said.

Sheyla nodded. "The obvious response."

Her parents seemed strangely cowed for a dream like this one. Usually, they shouted just as they did in real life, but now they were stealing glances at Alastor like he was made of shadows and moonlight. When Avi and Darvid crept out of their rooms, things felt a little more real, especially when she noticed Avi's ragged cuticles. That wasn't the sort of thing her subconscious usually showed her.

"I apologize for my poor timing," Alastor was saying. "But I couldn't wait a moment longer to speak with you. I'm aware you have certain expectations of Sheyla, and that I don't fit your criteria. Even knowing this, I'm still asking for your daughter. If you entrust her to me, she will not only become a queen in my lands, I will also treat her as one, for she's the ruler of my heart, and there can be no joy for me without her."

"Sheyla," her father repeated. "Our Sheyla." As if Alastor might've stumbled into the wrong house and asked for someone else's daughter.

Slowly it dawned on her that she was having what appeared to be a formal marriage meeting in Zaran's old shirt. She pinched her inner arm, closed her eyes and waited, but when she opened them, all the players were still in place.

"Sheyla can't be queen of the Golgoth," her mother said. 'She doesn't even like most of her pride mates, let alone—"

"Does no one care what Shey wants?" Avi cut in softly.

It was hard to say if Avi realized he'd spared Alastor's feelings when he prevented Mum from spouting the slur. She mouthed a silent thank-you and her youngest brother smiled. Of them all, she liked him best. His quiet mirrored hers, though it concealed a passion for art, not science. She'd already convinced her parents several times not to drag him off to the seer because he could spend hours staring at clouds moving across the sky.

"I do," Alastor said. "If she rejects me, then your blessing becomes a moot point."

Frowning, her father worried at his knuckles, then

glanced at her. "Is this the life you'd choose?"

"Yes." She said it before she even knew the answer consciously.

Whatever accepting Alastor meant, she would bear it. Once she would've said she didn't have the capacity to bond with anyone. Now that it had happened, she wanted to nurture the connection.

"You'll really be a queen?" Mum asked in a marveling tone.

Alastor inclined his head. "When I take Golgerra. For the time being, we'll remain in Hallowell. There's much to be done."

Darvid poked her. "I'm not calling you Your Majesty. Not ever. Unless... does this mean we're princes now?" His dark eyes sparkled.

"We don't acknowledge royalty," Zaran growled. "Or did you already forget you're Animari?"

"It's as he said," Alastor told Darvid gently. "I could convey a title on you, though, if you like, such as Grand Duke Darvid."

He's already charming them.

"Your Grace, you're already up way past your bedtime. Take Avi and go to sleep." Her father turned to Zaran. "Aren't you supposed to be on watch?"

He swore, but he didn't argue. With a pointed look at Alastor, he stomped out. Her mother had stars in her eyes, so Sheyla could well imagine that she was entertaining the possible bragging rights.

Pap didn't seem nearly so taken with this proposal. "You speak very prettily, but Sheyla isn't like other girls. She's neither given her heart nor seen it broken. If we send her away with you, I'm afraid she'll be lonely, or that you'll tire of her. She's not made for a concubine's life."

"With all due respect, sir, your daughter is no mere girl. She's a remarkable woman. I could not have aided Hallowell without her support, and I do not say that lightly. I would sooner carve out my own heart than set her aside. Why do you think I disregarded all obligations and chased her as soon as she left me?"

"You love me," Sheyla said. "Not just in wartime."

He wasn't simply convincing her parents, she saw. These words were for her too, dispelling any doubts she might have.

"It will be you or no one, *shalai*. If you refuse me, I'll join the Order of St. Casimir, drink myself sick with that enormous bear, and sob nightly over how you broke my heart."

"I think you have to take him," Mum said. "He's too pretty to be a monk."

Her lips twitched. "Stop. Too many people need you for you ever to behave so selfishly."

He offered a faint smile that revealed little. As ever, his eyes did the talking. They said, *You know me well.*

"I'm caught. True, I'm needed by many, but you're the one *I* need."

Since her parents were no longer objecting vigorously, she had only one question more. "Can a Golgoth Queen research rare illnesses? I won't give up my work, and I've already decided that I don't want to continue as a practitioner."

"My Queen can do whatever the hell she likes," he answered with the assurance she'd come to love. "But what prompted the decision?"

In telling him about the boy who died in the bunker,

Sheyla barely noticed when her parents slipped away. Their withdrawal indicated approval, and it was nearly four, so she took Alastor's hand and tugged him toward her bedroom.

"Am I allowed to stay?"

"You're family now. Our home is yours." Such a simple thing, and it was the Animari way; she wasn't prepared for how tears welled up, for how urgently he pulled her into the dark room and pressed her against the door. His mouth came down on hers with a desperate sweetness, and he kissed her as if it was the first time.

"I was prepared to come back," he said between roving kisses. "Again and again. To beg. To camp in the hallway."

She muffled a sound as he found the spot on her neck, dug her nails into his back. "Let's not talk about my parents."

"Agreed."

His entire body was hot and quivering. Maybe it was because she'd actually left him, but she'd never seen him so needy. As he walked her back to the bed, he skimmed his fingers into her panties, stroking with each step they took toward her bed.

"I'm sorry," he whispered. "Before, I said I need you. If you ever leave me again, I'll shave my head."

That's their deepest symbol of mourning.

Touched, Sheyla wrapped her arms around him and kissed him, all melting delight. Alastor's hands roved her back, her hips, cupping her ass to pull her against him. There was nothing of the playful lover about him now. Sheyla loved all of him, all angles, all sides, because he didn't make her feel that she needed to change a single thing. *I am perfection in his eyes.*

"I don't think I can be elegant," he gasped into her neck. "Or patient."

Just as well, she didn't need any of those things. She pulled him on top of her, and he pushed inside as soon as they hit the bed. He panted into her ear, thrusting in strokes so wild that she had to bite him. That only drove him harder, and she wrapped her legs around his hips. He was racing toward the finish, eyes clenched shut. He kept whispering, "Fuck, Sheyla. Fuck. Just... mmm." Sexy little gasp.

He felt good, but the pleasure she swam in wasn't enough to make her come, so she focused on him, watching how he reacted to each minute movement. The way his throat worked, the sweat trickling down his jaw... she licked it and whispered, "I love you."

TOO MUCH.

Her hot breath against his ear, his cock working inside her slick cunt. Alastor pushed deep, held, and came. Long, urgent pulses. He moved just a little through the aftershocks.

It was impossible to deny that he'd just behaved like a pig, but he couldn't stop smiling. "You. Love me."

"Definitely," she said.

"And I adore you, as I'm sure you've gathered."

She tugged at his braids. "Prove it."

Alastor required no prompting, though it did remind him of that first time when she'd ordered him to his knees. His mouth watered as he kissed a path south.

"I'll make it up to you. Since I had one without you, I'll give you two."

"Promises," she breathed.

He could already see that her clit was stiff, but he didn't go straight for it. Now that he'd fucked the fear of losing her out of his system, he could focus on her pleasure. She took the reins almost as soon as he started licking, positioning his head with demanding hands.

"Here. Harder."

Alastor wasn't about to argue; Sheyla fucked his face to a quick, intense clitoral orgasm that left her groaning. At first, he tried to shush her and wondered why she was laughing.

"Animari construction. Good sound proofing. Otherwise, we couldn't live with each other."

"Ah. So, I can make you scream as much as I wish this next time."

She caught his head before he could resume the delicious work. "That's not how I want my second orgasm."

By now he should be used to the way she took charge, but the thrill still went straight to his cock. Since he had to take charge regarding the rest of the world, he fucking loved doing as she wished in private. Controlling his erection was impossible as she rolled over and whispered the filthiest demand in his ear.

"Play with your cock for me. Oil it up. I want to watch your face. But you can't come. If you hold it long enough, I'll let you have my ass." Her voice dropped low, teasing him. "I've seen how you look at it, the way you touch me. You want it there."

Fuck yes, he did. His head felt like it might explode.

"Have you, before?" he asked hoarsely.

"Toys. I liked them. Suspect I'll like this more."

If she wanted a show, he would strive to be entertaining. His knees would hardly hold him. "Where's the oil?"

She got a small bottle from the bedside table and he poured some, warmed it in his palm.

"Get comfortable, love," she said, patting the pillows.

The endearment reacted on him like a tug on his cock, and it was all he could do not to reach for her instead of settling back to wank like she wanted. His entire body flushed beneath the warmth of her gaze; she took in everything, until he wanted to show her more. Eyes on hers, he worked his cock just as he would on his own. He liked it quick and vicious, and he took himself to the edge before stopping. His cock was leaking, and he couldn't control his quivering stomach.

"Again," she whispered.

He could hardly speak. "Give me a moment, love. If I go on, I'll spill all over myself. I can, if that's what you want."

She kissed the sweat off his forehead. "Then take two minutes. Rest."

In these precious moments, it didn't matter what was going on in Hallowell or that he still needed to liberate Golgerra. Sheyla, taking control of him, felt like flying. When his breathing steadied, he jerked his cock for her again. This time it was even harder to stop.

He shuddered and moaned, wordlessly begging her, and she was all fire, all beauty, when she finally came to him. She'd already prepared herself while he worked, and when she rolled over and raised her ass for him, he almost came all over her back.

I'm not a king. I'm a fucking animal.

"Have me," she said.

She was relaxed and ready. The first thrust almost sent him. Shaking, Alastor held on as he pushed deep and reached around her hip to stroke her slick lips, her aching clit. Her need surged through him, nearly eclipsing his own.

She's so excited. Have to make her...

That was all he knew or cared about. With each stroke of his cock, of his fingers, he willed it, losing himself, until his own satisfaction was secondary, elusive. Her orgasm came with a furious clench and scream, Sheyla scrabbling at the covers. She wanted to bite him, he could tell, and he kept moving, until she went again, her body going boneless beneath him.

"Do it," she mumbled.

Alastor hadn't even realized he was waiting for permission but when she said it, he let go, so deep and hard that his lower back ached.

Trembling, he eased out of her and then reached for her, arms and legs clinging in a sticky tangle. He kissed her eyelids, her ears, her lips, her chin. "Don't make me live without you. Don't ever let me come home to an empty flat again."

"I won't," she said sleepily. "You're mine. No going back now."

He'd never been happier. At some point, he must have slept because a tap on the head roused him. Sheyla, freshly showered and dressed. He took his turn in the lavatory without making eye contact with her parents. Soundproofing or no, by the dark look he was getting from her father, the older man had some idea what went on in her bedroom last night.

Dammit. There was no way he was apologizing for something he didn't remotely regret, but still. *Awkward.*

While Sheyla was in the bedroom, packing, he sat down with her father in the living room. "Do you mind if I ask a question?"

"You just asked one," Mr. Halek pointed out.

He could see where Sheyla got some of her literal tendencies. "Another then."

"Go ahead."

"Why did you give us your blessing?"

"I haven't, exactly. But I'm not standing in your way, either."

"Because...?"

"Last night I saw how you look at her. Like she's the only star in the sky."

"She is," Alastor said.

"And I saw how she looks at you."

"Which is...?" He thought he knew, but it'd be good to confirm with her father.

"Like she's been speaking a different language her whole life and she's finally found someone who understands it."

Since Sheyla had said nearly the same thing—in different words—he let the sweetness sink in. "I've never had a higher compliment."

"On the surface, that sounds like nonsense but I want to believe you mean it. Last night, you asked her about her career decision, and she *wanted* to tell you. Really, that's enough for me. I've never seen my girl willing to explain herself to anyone."

She is the lock and I am the key. That was a truth for the two of them alone; they were complementary in ways others would never understand. Nor did they need to.

Sheyla soon came out with her luggage. The future might be uncertain, but if she was walking beside him, Alastor could face anything. There would be fences to mend with the wolves and Eldritch, more damned meetings at the ministry, but he had never felt more like royalty than the moment he decided she must be his queen.

"We'll visit you in Hallowell," her mother said, sniffling.

"Soon," her father added.

"And don't forget to make me a Grand Duke." Darvid offered a bright smile.

Alastor's was startled to receive hugs from everyone except Zaran, who looked as if he'd rather punch his princely face in. "Be good to her," Zaran snapped.

I'm part of a family again. And none—well, hardly any of them—want to kill me. Reflexively, he touched the names on his arm through his sleeve. In time, he might even tell these new brothers about the ones he'd lost.

"She is the greatest gift I'll receive in my lifetime," he said softly. "There's no way I can do anything but cherish her."

"What if I hate being a queen?" Sheyla teased.

He kissed her nose. "Then I'll abdicate and open Golgerra to free elections, if you find the role burdensome. Whatever you want of me, you shall have, my precious, clever love."

Her brothers made gagging noises and her mother pretended to stumble against the wall. "Please take him before I swoon."

Sheyla's father only gave a nod, as if he'd expect no less. "Be happy, both of you."

Alastor locked eyes with Sheyla, who was so lovely that his heart flew to her all over again. Before meeting her, he'd never known that home could be a person instead of a place, but anywhere she was, he would be at peace.

She smiled; he returned it. In unison, they turned to her father and said, "Always."

Author's Note

I'm so thrilled that you read *The Demon Prince* and hope you're eager for more in the Ars Numina world. *The Demon Prince* is the second book in a projected six-book series, as follows:

The Leopard King
The Demon Prince
The Wolf Lord
The Shadow Warrior
The War Priest
The Jaguar Knight

Would you like to know when the next book will be available and/or keep up with exciting news? Visit my website at *www.annaguirre.com/contact* and sign up for my newsletter. If you're interested, follow me on Twitter at *twitter.com/msannaguirre*, or "like" my Facebook fan page at *facebook.com/ann.aguirre* for excerpts, contests, and fun swag.

Reviews are essential for indie writers and they help other readers, so please consider writing one. Your love for my work can move mountains, and I so appreciate your effort.

Finally, as ever, thanks for your time and your support.

Made in the USA
Lexington, KY
04 August 2018